SWIMMING
in
STARLIGHT

SONG OF THE ETERNAL SEA I

SYWEN L. FEUERSTEIN

First Edition October 2025

Alpha Reader Avina Pereira

Editor Rebecca R. Eddy

Cover Design by Nightsky Graphic Book Design

Stella Ehrhardt | @nightskygraphics

ISBN: 979-8-9989404-0-8

Library of Congress Control Number: 2025922698

For the family and friends,
both in life and fiction,
who filled my soul with stories
and my mind with words

CHAPTER 1

The net was nothing special, made from salvaged scraps of rope and cast-off fibers found in corners where none of the proper fishermen would miss them. The boy who made it didn't think he was much special either; in this way, they were something of a matching pair - a boy and his net. Yet, he had mustered all of his determination and taken his collection of cast-off scraps and sea-worn strands, placing them by his knees as he knelt at the feet of one of the oldest of fishermen down in the village. Despite the advent of the net weaving looms in town, the older fishermen still knew how to make and mend their nets properly; like the fishermen's wives, they knew all of the knots, the warp and weft of the pattern, and could feel their way through the weaknesses in the weave long after their sight had escaped them. The fisherman in question took in the tiny scrap of humanity before him and snarled at the boy, his wind-worn skin folding deep and disappearing into a beard that appeared to be encrusted in decades worth of sea salt and the shimmer of discarded scales. The old man was reluctant, obviously finding the idea distasteful, but eventually he relented; the younger men of his trade rarely sat at his feet in search of knowledge, did not care to weave or preserve their nets, and he knew deep down that his traditions were dying. So, in time, he had felt the still soft pads of the boy's fingers and told him in a voice that practically dripped with scorn that he had carpenter's hands, and all of the instruction in the world was probably pointless; yet he taught the boy nonetheless.

Toddy didn't want to be a carpenter like his father, and his father's father, and his father's father's father before him. Living on the coast as he did, the most glamorous job he could conceive of was that of a fisherman: the big burly men who hauled in giant nets full of wriggling fish that sparkled iridescent in the sunlight, who swam like fish, and dove for long minutes at a time to emerge with shells full of delicate meat and occasionally pearls. They sang bawdy songs that made his mama blush and told stories that kept a body up at night, sneaking out windows to steal down to the beach and stare at the sea. With just over a dozen years of life under his belt, Toddy was quite sure that being a fisherman was the answer to all of life's wishes. Even if his fingers struggled to catch the fibers properly and his knots were always a bit loose and lopsided, even if he had not yet learned to swim, he was certain these considerations must be trivial in the face of his absolute determination.

The net was nothing special, not in the grander scheme of things. It was smallish and lopsided, only this was the first one Toddy had made that looked like it might have the ability to *actually* catch a fish. It was a matter of practice, to be sure, but also one of superior materials. Luck had been with him one morning as he scanned the beach on his way into town. Rather than the discarded chunks of fibers or net he normally collected, he found a whole blessed length of unbroken rope. Being eldest of five, his mama often sent him on errands. That morning was much the same, and he had been tasked with retrieving a large bag of flour from the miller's. Perhaps such a task would have felt like a hassle, except that each errand that led him to town provided an opportunity to scan the beach for his precious materials. On this day, in his excitement over the amazing find, he would completely forget the intended trip for flour and run back to his stash of fibers with the length, eager to incorporate it into his most recent attempt at netting. This forgetfulness would earn him six stripes with a switch and send him sprinting down the beach in hopes of arriving before the miller would take no more business for the evening. This was ultimately unimportant; what was important was that he finally had made a net that he could probably use to catch a fish. It was an easy matter to slip his net into the bark pot the following day, sealing his work against the effects of salt water and weather; one of the fishermen off the Celeste, one of the greatest fishing boats at port, caught his eye and quirked a smile as Toddy retrieved his net and raced home, leaving the pungent aroma like a trail in his wake.

The Windle family lived on a moderate plot of land situated within a reasonable, if not convenient, walking distance of the town by road. This was not Toddy's preferred mode of travel, he would argue that the distance by shore was far superior, as the edge of their property lay directly along the water. A winding path ran behind his house and down to the shore, spilling out onto a quiet stretch of beach that was sheltered on the leeward side of a narrow promontory of land. Their particular patch of sand extended out from the dunes onto the water in the form of a small pier, really more of a small dock, no more than fifteen widths of the wooden planks that made up its surface.

Toddy hung his net loosely from the two deepest pilings and wracked his brain for all of its assorted fishing information, his head hanging off the dockside as he stared into the water in search of the small fish and squid that often hid from the sun beneath. So absorbed in thought and observation was he that the sun slipped across the sky and began to descend into its resting place. It was there, in an odd trick of the light, that he momentarily thought he saw another face staring up at him through his own shimmering reflection, but as quickly as it had appeared, it was gone.

"Toddy!" his Mama's voice pierced his reverie in a manner uniquely hers "Tiddley-Winks, get your narrow behind home right this instant!" He cringed at the nickname and rolled over onto his back with a sigh, taking comfort where he could from the solid feel of the dock beneath his shoulders, if only he could figure out a way to get her to give the moniker up.

"Tiddle-y-winks-y," she drew it out this time. Sometimes, Toddy swore his mother's entire mission in life was to be as vexing as possible to the men in her life. By which he, of course, meant himself and his father - though arguably her antics didn't seem to bother Father as much as they should. Perhaps the man had been gifted with a touch of the divine. He pushed to his feet and began to jog homeward up the sand to the dunes. When he saw his Mama, she was standing at the end of the path on the edge of the woods, just before the green spread into the dunes and was overrun by sand. He stuck his tongue out in passing, earning himself a swat with the bonnet she had removed as she stopped to enjoy the sunset.

When the sun rose the following morning, barely before the fingers of red began to grip the edge of the sky, Toddy slid out of his window, snagged two apples and a peach from the basket just inside the kitchen door, and hightailed it through his mama's mullein and lavender to the wild-growth of the path. The long grass tickled his ankles as he wound his way down the trail that loosely bordered his Mama's garden. In the quiet of the early morning, the susurration of the wind rustling through the trees and the approaching rush of waves were his only companions as he climbed the low hill before the dunes. He shivered a little with the last of the night's chill breeze when he hit the open air of the shore. He was picking his way on bare feet along the wooden planks of the dock, knowing from experience where the splinters were more likely to form, when he heard a splash from under the end of the dock. He froze; the splash repeated itself, followed by what sounded like a frustrated sob - *was there a person down there?* he wondered, more concerned with his creation than its captive. A person would completely ruin his net if they didn't know how to get themselves loose properly.

Caught somewhere between frustration, concern, and horror, he stomped his way to the end of the dock; opting to settle on anger, he prepared himself to lay into whatever idiot had been mucking about under *his* dock with *his* net during the night. His anger curled his fingers into fists and drew his tense shoulders towards his ears, but all of his preparation was for naught. Upon looking over the edge of the dock, the tension vacated his body in a rush, leaving him a little bit dizzy, and he froze. He froze because what looked up at him from beneath the wooden planks was like nothing he had ever seen before. It stared up at him with large, limpid eyes, over which a thin membrane snapped shut protectively as a wave washed over its face and then opened again in the morning air. Its skin was tan but thin and translucent; multicolored lights darted underneath it, not unlike the shimmering lines on the comb jellyfish that often washed to shore. When she moved (upon observation, Toddy was becoming quite sure that it was a she), great fan-like fins flared around her. They billowed like sheer white and red patterned fabric and were given structure by long spines. It was, minimally, those wicked looking spines that were caught in his net. He couldn't see much further down her body to assess the damage to his work, not past the dangerous looking fins and not past the veritable cloud of what must pass for her hair but looked like it might be more closely related to the very long, very fine tentacles of a jellyfish.

"Tiddle-y-winks-y?" She spoke very slowly, but quite clearly, effectively answering a question he hadn't even thought to ask yet; namely, how long had she been there? Long enough to hear his mother call him the night before, with a nickname that had just become more embarrassing than he could ever have previously imagined. Here, he was presented with the opportunity of a lifetime, one where he got to meet a completely new sort of creature for the very first time, and already it was tainted by that vexatious woman's sense of humor.

"My name is Toddy, actually." He tried to correct her. "My Mama has a penchant for horrible nicknames." It was a little tough to gauge, but he was pretty sure she looked perplexed.

"Winksy?" the, for lack of a better ready term, he had to suppose it was a mermaid, inquired. A mermaid. He came to the realization with a jolt and almost recoiled; he was speaking to a *mermaid*. He had heard the fishermen talk about mermaids before, horrible stories that clearly portrayed their character as tricky, malicious creatures that lured men to their doom. The sound of the waves lapping against the dock filled the silence left by his realization as he frantically attempted to recover his wits.

"Well, no, not properly. You see, they named me Todrick Windle, which my rather deranged mother decided sounded like Tiddley Winks." His mind raced; the mermaid didn't *look* like the wily sea-vixen they said she would be. He wasn't quite sure what a sea-vixen ought to look like, but when he looked at her face, her features had the same soft roundness as his younger sister, which didn't seem quite right.

"I call you Winken," She said, in a fashion that sounded unfortunately final

"Really, I would prefer Toddy." He replied, then sighed in resignation as she shook her head.

"Winken"

"Is it just the nature of those of the female persuasion to be as vexing as possible?" It was an old conversation, having taken place repeatedly with his mother, and therefore, familiarity made it rather too easy to settle in for a chat - completely disregarding her status as both alien and quite probably dangerous.

"I am stuck in your net, which is most vexing." She spoke as though she were choosing her words with care, which got him to wondering about how she spoke the language to begin with. If no two human countries had managed to come up with the same language, he didn't imagine that an entirely different species would come to the conclusion that this particular configuration of sounds was best, no matter how obvious that conclusion should be. When he inquired, she gently touched a series of shells and coral chunks strung about her neck and replied simply, "magic."

"Magic?" he scoffed. Magic was for children, and, being twelve now, he was quite beyond such things.

"Magic, yes. Not that your talking is so complex, with this I can understand the stories of the great migrating turtles; your human talk is hardly a challenge."

He was not naturally inclined to take this slight against humanity without comment, but the reference to turtles telling stories distracted him quite effectively. He had heard of the great migrating sea turtles; the sailors said they were gentle giants compared to the turtles of the ponds and that they made delicious soup. A part of him wanted to scoff once more at the idea of them telling stories, but considering that he was talking to a real live mermaid, he had to acknowledge that there was a slight possibility that the world had more wonders to offer than he had previously been inclined to believe.

"Sea turtles tell stories?" He tried to control the child-like wonder in his voice and mostly failed.

"Yes, most of The People of the waters tell stories, as I am sure humans do, and of course, The People of the air and land do likewise. The great migrating turtles are often old and long-winded: having hundreds of years to learn, reflect, and retell stories will do that."

"What sort of stories do they tell?" he asked, almost surprised after his prior concerns to now find himself lying on his stomach, toes wiggling between the planks, staring down into the water with interest.

"You know, not to be rude, but I am still caught in your net, and it is not exactly what I would call comfortable. Nor is it inspiring me to tell stories. If you cut me loose, I might be inclined to share some Sea People wisdom with you." She gestured vaguely to the net that held her fixed to the dock.

"If I let you go, you won't just swim away?" He wasn't sure he was ready to risk it; how often did one get the opportunity to talk to a mermaid?

"I won't."

"It's some of my finest work there. Are you sure you can't shake free?" He was loathe to cut through the product of so many hours worth of twisting, weaving, and knotting

"If I could have done so, we would never have met, I would have set myself loose last night and gone my way. You need not worry about me doing that now, I've hardly ever talked to a human before, and never for this long; I'm finding it quite intriguing." Slightly less concerned, he continued to assess the situation from his vantage point above; those spines really did look rather dangerous; her hair looked rather dangerous as well. The truth was, the longer he looked at her, the more concerned he became that he might not exit the water should he decide to enter it, depth and swimming capabilities, of course, notwithstanding.

"Do those bits sting?" he gestured vaguely at her fins.

"Well, they *can*, but if you don't touch the ends of the spines, they're nothing much to worry about. That's how I got caught, you see, your wicked little net caught on one of my spines and the more I tried to wriggle loose the more caught I became, and the next thing I knew I was well and thoroughly stuck." She splashed the water in obvious frustration. The resemblance to his little sister was now strong enough that the twinge of guilt he'd felt grew to become quite bothersome. He eyed the water warily, and his eyes caught again on her, for lack of a better word, hair.

"And what about those tentacle-y bits, your hair, is it? Will they sting me? Because I'm not coming down there to get all stung up and purple or possibly dead." He had once had the misfortune of seeing a fisherman hauled from his boat who had been stung by one of the big sea jellies. The man screamed bloody murder whenever he was jostled, and the whole side of his shoulder and neck was swollen, a horrible purple color with dark veins that stood out as though they, too, wanted to scream, only lacked the capacity. That sight had kept him up for at least three nights in a row with visions of all of the horrific creatures sailors claimed to have seen.

"I could sting you, but I won't." Her response broke him from his reverie, and when he looked at her again, the vision of her as a young girl in trouble conflicted with the anxiety-ridden vision that centered around the threat of her natural defenses.

"But how do I know?" He tried to make the question sound rational and manly, but was quite certain that what came out was a child's question. A question in a tone that asked for a hand to hold or for someone else to make the decision on his behalf. A question of uncertainty about the big world around him, a world that had seen fit to put this new and interesting creature about as close to his doorstep as an aquatic being could manage.

"I swear it." She said it like it meant a great deal. "I, Nimmawni, do swear it on my life and my name; if you enter the water to help me, you will come to no harm; may the Old Man of the Great Abyss swallow me whole do I lie."

Well, that tore it; the oath may be unfamiliar, but he had heard his father give his word before, and the tone was much the same. When someone gave their word, it was serious business and should be treated as such. Because without his word, a man has no worth - that's what his father said. He wasn't sure quite how that applied to girls and even less sure how it applied to mermaids, but he supposed that honor was honor when all was said and done. He scrambled awkwardly over the side of the dock, and - using his own net for a ladder - he descended the feet, that felt rather more like leagues, to the water below. He froze when the first wave broke over his ankle and reminded himself to breathe. He would have to submerge even more of himself to properly assess the problem, a problem he chose to focus as much of his attention on as possible as he eased himself into the cool water. The texture of the spiny fins was softer than he had anticipated; the loose folds obscured his vision as they rippled with the push and pull of the waves, reinforcing the impression of fabric while their pattern of irregular splotches made it hard to interpret what he saw with any clarity. He moved his focus to the net and was almost immediately met with the sensation of swallowing bricks. There was no way around it; between the tangle she had created and his concern about the stinging ends of those spines, he was going to have to cut through his precious net to set her loose. He slid his folding knife from his pocket and began to saw recklessly through the ropes surrounding the snag, hoping the frustrated tears in his eyes would pass for the spray of seawater. One rope, two ropes, eight ropes, ten. He tried not to think about how much work it would take to reattach and reweave the fibers. Every single knot would need to be undone and reworked, every broken strand retwisted and added to for stability. At last, the spines were free, and he could see the point where her tail was trapped. He thought it would be a simple matter to cut one last rope, but in less than a second, the water swallowed him - like great transparent lips closing over his face and cutting him off from the precious air above. He began to kick and thrash, trying desperately to breach the surface but watching as the edges of his vision bled from blue to green. His chest began to burn for air, and it took all of his will not to open his mouth and allow the waiting ocean in. *This is how it ends*, he thought. He supposed there were worse ways to die than saving a mermaid, though he did take a moment to feel betrayed. She had promised he would come out unharmed, and drowning was certainly harmful to one's overall health and wellbeing. He hadn't realized that, in this moment of acceptance and contemplation, he had stopped struggling. Not until he felt a tug at his collar, then an arm slid through his and locked against his underarm, and the next thing he knew, he was being towed upward through the water at an alarming rate. Just before his head broke the surface, his will gave out, he came up spluttering and gasping, coughing up ocean, but savoring the sweet deliciousness of the salty air. The arm shifted slightly, and his vision was obscured by the large, dark eyes of the mermaid.

"Winken, you should have told me that you could not swim." Her voice held an exasperated tone he was all too familiar with, having encountered it often enough with his mother. He wondered if that tone was simply distributed among all creatures of the female persuasion, or perhaps it took time to develop naturally. Having now encountered the same tone in two different species of female, he was forced to consider a rather jarring third option. Perhaps, being the only commonality, it was through direct exposure to *himself* that this tone was acquired. It was largely this thought that rendered him silent as the mermaid continued to address him with growing concern.

"Winken!" she poked his face quite rudely. "Winken, are you in some way damaged? Answer, please." He sighed and wiped his face with his hand, an action which did nothing productive so much as it served to re-wet his face with more sea water.

"Yes," he croaked, "I'm fine," which set him to coughing

again. With a sigh, once again all too familiar in nature, she began to tow him towards shore. He watched the ripples that formed in their wake and did his best to tune out the muttering of the young mermaid who propelled them.

"Winken. Winken, stand up now; those useless little legs of yours should touch bottom now. Why did you not tell me that you could not swim, Winken? I could have been forsworn! The Old Man of the Deep could have reached his gargantuan tentacles out across the ocean, and he could be snacking on me right now, Winken! If I had known, I could have held you up, and your head would have barely entered the water, you ridiculous land creature with your stubby legs and your ridiculous free-wiggling fingers - like tiny little eels that cannot cooperate." She continued in this vein as he let his legs drop and his toes sink into the sand and silt. He had to admit that he felt somewhat foolish. He didn't much want to think on creatures with gargantuan tentacles; he wasn't even sure he could put that size into perspective. A boy in town had caught a squid just last week that he had called gigantic, and it was quite a prize, but it was not much longer than the boy's forearm and certainly not big enough to go about digesting anybody whole. It hadn't even occurred to him that the mermaid *could* hold him up; his little sisters certainly wouldn't have been able to. Of course, he had also been so focused on his sense of honor in the rescue attempt that he hadn't even noticed that the last rope he cut was so closely connected to the one supporting his weight against the piling.

"Do you know I had to wait to grab you! I had to wait so you would stop swinging your ridiculous appendages about in such a senseless manner. You almost stung yourself on my barbs with your ridiculous behavior, and you almost hit me *twice.*" He winced at that. Her critique, while hardly complimentary to the human race as a whole, was probably a fairly accurate description of his behavior, and no matter how much it stung his pride, she had earned the right to tell him so. She had saved his life after all and apparently dodged some blows in the process.

"I almost hit you?" he didn't really want the confirmation, but it came nonetheless

"Twice!"

"I apologize," he grumbled into his shirt as he wiped ineffectively at his face. "I mean to learn to swim, I just haven't quite got around to it yet. I thought the rope would hold so it would make no difference knowing that I couldn't swim." He could feel his cheeks burning and was momentarily distracted by the possibility of imminent spontaneous combustion. Jeremy, the Miller's oldest son, told him that they had found a body burnt quite to the crisp at the lodging house; he said it was spontaneous combustion. Of course, Jeremy also said that flour was explosive, and while Mama's biscuits may not always be good, they had never once burnt the whole house down. When he'd tried to test the theory, Mama had caught him and would not be convinced to listen to reason about the nature of healthy inquiry. She had grabbed him by the ear, read him quite the lecture on wasting flour, then set him to chopping wood until he could no longer see straight.

"Are you sure you're all right, Winken? Your face has taken on a most peculiar color. Does something need to be done about that?" The mermaid stared with an utter lack of comprehension at his surely beet-red cheeks, definitely compounding the situation. No, Jeremy was definitely not on to something with his spontaneous combustion theory; if it could happen, it would certainly have done so by now. He coughed, giving himself time to collect his thoughts and try to redirect the conversation. He had seen the men in town do this to great effect; of course, they had generally not just been breathing seawater. His fake cough set off a whole new wave of actual hacking, which did nothing to soothe the mermaid's concern. When Toddy finally collected himself, he climbed back up onto the dock and lay on his stomach, giving the sun the opportunity to dry at least the one half of his clothes.

"I believe you said something about sea turtle stories; I'm quite interested in hearing about that. Also, what did you say your name was again, Nee-Moony?" The mermaid squinted up at him as though not certain that his behavior was to be trusted, then lay out on her back just beneath the water's surface.

"Nimmawni, Nim-Maw-Nee, that's my name, and I'm much more interested in human stories. I hear things about humans, but I have no clue what stories you tell yourselves."

Toddy wasn't certain what to make of such a statement. Most of the stories he heard were about people's daily lives, and he told her so. After a couple of examples, the Alderman's stolen chickens and the time Jeremy got his shirt stuck on the watermill, he wasn't quite sure how to proceed. He was almost certain that there were other sorts of stories she would find even more interesting, but he couldn't quite fathom what they were. Nimmawni sat with him in silence for a while before deciding to fill it herself.

"I heard that the humans have forgotten the magic of talking to the Land Folk."

"What do you mean, land folk?"

"The People, all of the Land People"

"Well, people speak all sorts of different languages; there's nothing magic about that. I could learn other languages if I wanted to. Most of the fishermen speak at least two or three since they travel up and down the coast." Nimmawni waved her hand dismissively

"No, no, that's still all human people. I mean The People, all of The People. The furred, the four legged, the winged, the rooted, all of the People." At the shocked look on his face, she only nodded sagely as though it was just as she suspected. "The pelican was right, it seems. One never really knows with pelicans."

He found himself wondering what it would be like to talk to a pelican, or to his father's old hunting dog, or the frogs that sometimes scared his little sister; that would be a wonder. But when he found his voice, he found himself instead challenging the thought.

"That sounds crazy, I don't think we've *ever* done such a thing!"

Nimmawni scrunched up her face, wrinkling her nose and exposing sharp teeth before sliding her necklace over her head. Remembering her previous claim that it was magic, his fingers almost itched to touch it. Instead, he listened as she grumbled to herself. Without the necklace on, it was as though her voice was coming from a long way off, and underneath it he could hear sounds as though the wind and the sea could sing with the voices of bells, punctuated with clicks and trills that still, *somehow*, seemed to convey a deep sense of exasperation. She fiddled with the string for a moment before slipping it back over her head and reaching up to where he had let his arms flop over the edge of the dock. He felt something small and rough pass between his fingers with an unfamiliar tingling sensation and almost dropped it before he realized it was a small chunk of red coral.

"Now, what you need to do is focus on one of The People. The ones more similar to you will probably be the easiest, but right now, we will make do with what is close." She reached down along the closest piling and brought back a small crab that clung to a tiny fish it had recently caught and begun eating. Its little articulating legs shifted back and forth indecisively as she whispered to it,

"It's alright, Shell Brother, I won't hurt you. I simply need your help for a moment." She lifted her palm so that Toddy was effectively face to face with the tiny beady eyes of the little brown crab. It waved its decapitated fish in his direction. He was certain he was being warned off even before he thought he heard a voice, barely more than a whisper, that somehow sounded like the rushing of sand in the wind,

"My fish. My fish, not your fish, big critter, my fish. Go away. Far away."

The coral chunk slipped from his fingers in shock, almost striking the crab in its descent. The crab scuttled over Nimmawni's finger webbing, dropping back into the drink, and she snatched up the bead before it could follow.

"Don't lose this! I don't know how to make this, and I won't give you any more of mine!"

"But... but I think I heard it, the crab. I think I heard the crab!"

"Well, of course you heard the crab, silly. That was the whole point of the exercise."

He sat in shock while she swam to the end of the dock and retrieved a length of rope fibers. She strung the coral chunk on the bit of rope and tied it in a loop before handing it back to the boy whose world seemed to have cracked to pieces over a single interaction with a disgruntled crustacean.

Over the following hours, she spoke to a number of animals, and Toddy learned how to listen, how to hear The People. Nimmawni had heard all sorts of interesting things about the Land Folk, telling him bits and pieces of stories between conversations with birds and fish and a local fisherman's dog, for whom her presence so close to shore was very confusing indeed. It seemed to Toddy that the mermaid's magic held them, softly suspended as though in a private shimmering bubble, not quite a part of normal life throughout the day. So it was that, shortly before sunset, Toddy found himself lying on his back with his eyes closed, listening once more to the waves rhythmically splashing against the pilings, when he heard a low singing voice that seemed to reverberate within his very bones.

"That's the Great Mama of the Deep, I hear her always and always." She said it simply as though it were a matter of fact.

"But I can't understand what she's saying."

"Of course not. She doesn't sing all day in the languages of The People; she sings in the language of the Universe. She sings in the language of the Gods." She took one look at his dumbfounded expression and sighed. "I guess now is as good a time as any to tell you that story of the turtles."

CHAPTER 2

It is said that long long ago, in the vast stillness that is now and always; all that has been, all that is, and all that will come to be was dispersed as finely as infinitesimal grains of sand; floating freely, cast adrift among brilliant waves of starlight within the great sea of night. Great Mama of the Deep floated as all and part, rolling great waves about her as she slept. Some say that she sleeps there still, and everything we experience is just her dream.

"But that's not the version I'm telling because it's boring," Nimmawni said sharply. Toddy silently nodded, transfixed.

From the very fabric of her dreaming, she formed within herself the glowing eggs of new life, one that shone so brightly it would put the glory of the sun to shame and the other which shone with depths greater than the deepest ocean in colors beyond comprehension. When at last she woke, she stretched every tendril of her being in the expanse, and within the resulting aurora, she began to mold the universe to her liking. In preparation for her children, she set the stars on their courses and separated the seas, creating the Sea Above and the Sea Below. She drew from herself enormous ribbons of water and wrapped it in giant swaths around the body of a star, directing its light inward and creating the great orb of ocean that makes up the Sea Below. When she descended into the waiting waters, she took on the shape of a giant serpent and reshaped the sea floor; the great trenches that marked her passing delved deep into the star-body, displacing the material of her creation and driving pieces to emerge from the surface as she settled into her cradle of life. The two primordial eggs began to swell within her in anticipation of their birth, and so she coiled herself around their growing bodies to sing and to rest, pouring her energies into them as they grew. It was during one of these times of rest that a tiny star slipped between her open lips and implanted itself in secret beside her eggs. So it was that when the time came for the eggs to hatch, it was three divine beings rather than two that emerged.

From the egg that shone with the brightness of a million stars came the embodiment of The Light, and with its birth came also the very first sunrise, a sunrise that rose from its first resting place within the Sea Below to join with the other heavenly bodies in the Sea Above.

From the egg that shone with all of the colors of the deepest and darkest reaches of the Eternal Sea came the embodiment of The Shadow, and with its birth came the New Moon, at first an invisible embodiment that balanced the vibrancy of the sun; eventually becoming a reflective darkness that waxes and wanes, always returning to the shadows to be reborn. Great Mama of the Deep looked on these two and saw that they would always act in balance with one another and bring stability to the cosmic dance.

From the third and smallest egg was born a small serpent with a multitude of iridescent scales, and the Great Mama of the Deep looked on it and named it Pan'chan. Where its siblings had no distinct shape of their own, Pan'chan was born with one form and attained many others, for it soon became apparent that Pan'chan was a shapeshifter who had chosen a form beloved of its mother in which to be born. The Great Mama of the Deep looked on her smallest child and smiled, for the balance of her children was now complete. Where The Shadow and The Light brought a balance of order, order alone may stagnate; existence requires a bit of mischief and disorder to progress and to grow.

In the wake of divine birthing, the energy of creation rolled across the ocean floor and began to give life to the raw materials of existence. In that place which is before and now and always, Great Mama of the Deep, The Light, The Shadow, and Pan'chan began to playfully mold the primordial clay, breathing new life into the rolling vastness of the Seas, and the energy of creation rolled through her as well, taking root in her womb, and thus her children abounded.

In time, the star-body that had emerged from the Sea Below began to soften and teem with life, slowly becoming what is now called earth. As they proliferated, there were divine beings who called the earth and the skies their homes. All the while, new life continued to be shaped and formed by the hands of a divine multitude. Some life remained so small that one might believe them the unintended results of the energy of creation mingling with the silt of the sea floor, while others, Great Mama of the Deep molded playfully with her children, gifting life to a multitude of shapes and sizes. The divine beings shaped and reshaped their creations, imbuing them with their own breath to become The First People.

The first among The People were all of the sea, and they were loved by all, passing freely between one great Sea and the other, swimming among the waves and the starlight alike. Each being playing a necessary part in a glorious cosmic dance. In their great wisdom, the deities of water, earth, and stone saw a piece of the pattern was incomplete. It was with the purpose of filling this void that they came together and wove a beautiful opalescent egg. It was from this egg that Long Tide and Deep Wave were born, the first of the Great Migrating Shell People, they who were given to move throughout the Seas that they might know and learn from all of its People. And when it came time to lay eggs of their own, it was deemed only right that Long Tide and Deep Wave brought their future offspring to land. Only right that the hatchlings might know earth beneath their fins and the breath of the open skies above. The treacherous journey to the waiting arms of the Sea, would become an integral part of the cosmic dance. The very dance which, from the moment of their hatching, would balance risk against experience, the abundance of creation against the culling which allows its continuation. In the face of predation, few of their young would find their way, dragging themselves forward with the stroke of flippers against shifting sands, back to the open arms of the waiting Seas. For their part in sustaining the cycle, as all beings must, they were gifted with long lives and long memories to gather and tell the stories of The People, that none are truly forgotten.

Toddy lay on the dock, staring down at the creature below in rapt fascination, imagining the words pouring from her lips as though they would spread across the shimmering waves. The story was like nothing he had ever heard in his life, but it rang with a quality so deeply stirring, it was as though the ocean itself was telling him it was true.

"Winken," Nimmawni continued, in a voice barely above a whisper, "do you know what I want more than anything? More than anything, anywhere, ever? I want to swim through the great tides of the Sea Above. I want to bathe myself in starlight and cause ripples in the great auroras. Winken, I want to go swimming in starlight."

CHAPTER 3

It was well after dark by the time Toddy stumbled home. He had taken to the path with the best of intentions, intending a quick return home, but found himself distracted by all of the listening he had never known to do. Two crickets in the grass spoke to each other in language that resonated like absolute poetry, and were it not for the specific content, he was certain that any romantic might wish to take notes. His mama stood in the door when he came in from the garden, she had watched him walk up the path as though in a daze, watched him treat her mullein and lavender far more gently than any of the children, or her husband for that matter, ever did. When he reached the center of her garden, his steps faltered and then stopped as he closed his eyes and swayed among the fireflies. Concerned with his changed behavior, Audry propped the switch she had been tapping against her ankle just inside the door. Child must be ill, maybe a bit of the sunstroke, so she went out to join him in the garden. Wrapping her arms around his shoulders, she felt his cheek, which seemed neither hot nor chilled, though his lips were a bit chapped and his eyes practically shone in the darkness.

"Mama, they sing so sweetly." He whispered, his eyelids beginning to droop.

"Who does, my darling boy?" She felt his knees wobble before they went out from under him completely. She lowered him to the ground and heard him mumble before he slipped his consciousness completely

"Everything. All of The People. The whole world is singing."

She called Hal outside to carry his son to bed, remaining behind to look around her at her garden bathed in starlight. The evening breeze rustled leaves, the night bugs sang and danced as they were wont to do, the sweet smell of night blooming flowers mingled and drifted through the night air with the familiar scent of her medicinal herbs. It looked no different than it had the night before; the same moon sat on the horizon, there was not a cloud in the sky, and yet, she could not shake the feeling that something important had shifted.

Toddy was never quite the same after that day; everyone could agree on that. No one truly believed his story, of course, but no one could deny that there was something different about Todrick Windle. He had always been difficult to keep from the waterside, looking for materials for his nets and listening to old sailors tell their stories. Now, he ran down to the dock four or five times a day, and one was just as likely to find him appearing to listen to the cat from the neighbor's barn as an old man with a yarn to spin. Even at home, he seemed distracted by something just beyond his family's reach. When his mama caught him talking to himself one too many times, taking advantage of the moments when he thought the rest of the family was out of the house, she finally broke down and asked him what it was that he thought he was doing. Unsurprisingly, she was completely unprepared for his response.

"I'm looking, Mama." He replied, not wanting to get into another conversation about the improbability of mermaids.

"Looking for what, *precisely*, Tiddley Winks?" He cringed a little at the nickname, and she smirked with a quiet sort of triumph. They were both well acquainted with his temper, and a little annoyance could go a long way, while a lot would shut him up tighter than a drum.

"Looking for the House Guardian, not that I expect you to believe me or to know what that is." When he looked up, he was startled to see his mama looking at him with her own expression of stunned disbelief and more than a little curiosity.

"Who in this town would be telling you about House Spirits, child?" He stuck out a stubborn lower lip and waited, it wasn't just his temperament that they both knew.

"No one in this town is going to go around telling children about House Spirits, that's for sure. House Spirits are Old knowledge, passed down in the quiet spaces and away from the Temple of the Sun."

"I heard..."

"Heard from who?"

"I *heard* that when the house is built, it is made up of all the spirits of the trees and rocks that were part of its construction. Some of them stay to bless the house, and the strongest of them all becomes the House Guardian, and it watches over everything. I was *told* that if you make friends with the House Guardian, it will look after your family like it's own and that it is a beautiful and miraculous thing. So I am *looking* for the House Guardian."

His mama looked at him with even more suspicion than she had the last time her fruit tarts went missing, then pointed to the post that stood at the crux of the great room and the kitchen, the post where she hung flowers and fresh herbs every few days.

"How do you know?" he asked, joining his mama in being thoroughly puzzled by the entire engagement.

"I don't. When I was a girl, my grandmama hung her fresh herbs there, and when I became a woman, she told me that, so long as I do the same, it would save us some hardship as a family. Can't say whether or not it has worked for sure, but we've never gone entirely without, and for that, I am thankful."

Nimmawni had said we had forgotten the magic of talking to the folk, but it seemed to Toddy that some bit of that knowledge remained, masked in tradition and luck and family secrets. So he thanked his Mama, who still looked at him as though he had grown a second head, and the next time the house was empty, he sat in front of the post, in the corner where the kitchen opened out into the great room. He sat and he listened. He sat, and he listened, and he waited. He sat, and he listened, and he waited whenever the house was empty or still for four days, and on the morning of the fifth day, he heard it. Soft and low, with a voice that sounded like the creaking of old wood in the wind and the house settling at night, like dust whispering across floorboards and the shutters rattling in the breeze. The more he sat with the post, the better he understood it, and by the time he went to his Mama to tell her that it preferred wood sorrel to buttercups, she could see something of the old ways in him. Something her grandmama had once had only a touch of. Toddy had walked out one day, deaf and dumb and trampling her medicinal herbs in his hurry to be someone else, and he had come home with a chunk of coral, a wild story, and an insight into something she had only ever begun to touch.

Over the course of the next year, Toddy's visits to the beach reduced from checking five or more times a day to see if Nimmawni had returned to once or twice a day, standing watch at the end of the dock, staring wistfully out into the ocean and wondering where she could possibly be. The year had not been uneventful, and thankfully, by the time of his thirteenth birthday, he had reached a sort of peace with the magic of the coral. Though he continued to enjoy immersing himself in the wonder of listening, he was less prone to losing himself so easily or unintentionally. Whether it be the whispering of secrets among rabbits in the field or the song that shaped the growing pattern of a spider's web, his engagement was, more often than not, his choice. Listening had progressed to a minimal sort of talking, though that would never be as easy for him. His mama would occasionally ask him to do something like move a house spider, but as much as he could soothe the spiders and relocate them with ease, he obviously could not make himself understood, and the spiders kept spinning webs in his Mama's window box.

The day after Toddy's thirteenth birthday, his father took

him to the workshop and put the tools of a carpenter in his hands. Hands he had tried so hard to turn into fisherman's hands. He was more than a little disappointed when he took to shaping the wood with ease. Hands that had blistered and bled as he fumbled with the coarse rope fibers took to a carpenter's tools with barely a nick, and he felt something deep in his heart fracture just a little, as though a version of himself had died somehow, a potential future that would never come to be. Despite that, it can be difficult to hate where one's talents lie, and his resentment was quickly tempered by the realization that he could hear them; he could hear the trees and how they sang. He could hear them, and his hands could bring out of them the shapes that they wanted to be. Slowly, painfully slowly at first, he began to shape his craft to include this art - it was obvious from the beginning that it was simply a matter of time before his knife would learn to swim through the wood shavings like a flying fish darting in and out of the waters. Perhaps that was the sort of fisherman he was always meant to be.

Two years after the first day that he heard the voice of the Guardian, it spoke to him of its face. Toddy unfolded his pocket knife and began to slowly and lovingly carve the face into the wood of the post. Over the course of the next year he shaped and polished, etching out each detail of a vital looking man, with eyes not unlike his father's, a thick beard, long enough to curl and wrap around carved wood sorrel and twigs of oak, a full lip that looked as though it had both the potential for stern frowns and beneficent smiles, thick hair that wound itself around roses and ivy. Almost three years to the day after he first heard its voice, he polished its face with wax and rosemary oil and felt the house's satisfaction. In the years that followed, it was as though the house filled itself with a warm glow that would brook neither drafts nor unrest within its walls. The family had never been poor, but they no longer needed to count their pennies as closely. They had never been unhappy, but now it was not uncommon to hear them whistling or singing as they worked. The change was not sudden, nor was it extravagant, but the entire Windle family quietly prospered under the watchful eye of the Guardian Spirit.

It was only a couple of years more before he could sometimes be found in the marketplace, a series of wood carvings set out before him on a mat of thick canvas. It was occasionally, on market days, that his father would let him leave the shop early with his wares. The market was not only a gathering place for the townfolk, it often drew people from nearby counties; some to sell their produce and wares, others to restock their larders and socialize with friends and family alike. The center of town bustled with life and raucous conviviality as people shouted out their wares and haggled their prices. At the market on the Sixth Day, musicians played on street corners, and ale would flow all the more freely into the evening. Close to the high holy-days, the market of the Sixth Day would host performing troupes who occupied the square. Toddy's carvings always attracted attention, even framed as they were on a modest cloth at the side of the main thoroughfare. Those pieces he sold brought extra money to the family coffers that was always appreciated, even as Toddy relished the chance to observe and listen to new people with new faces and stories. Every so often, he would be visited by an old medicine woman who traveled from up the coast; when she found herself in possession of something special, she would make her way into the market square and sell him new plants for his mother's garden. At seventeen, he was now his father's height; his chubby legs had grown long and lean, and his bright blue eyes no longer peered out from an unruly mop of brown hair but were startling against his tan, fully revealed by his hair drawn back in a long queue at his back. The young ladies who accompanied their parents to market were often quite impressed by the look of him. The parents who accompanied their young ladies to view his wares were also often quite impressed... with his work. They saw the craftsmanship of his work and knew it for talent, but they saw the content of his work and the dreamer's look in his eye, the marks of stain and wax on his clothes and his crooked smile and could not be certain that he was serious enough or sound enough of mind to make a good husband. These observations entirely escaped the young man in question. Toddy was not ready for love and marriage; when pressed on the topic of women, his gaze would drift unerringly towards the shoreline, his lips affixed in a wistful smile that made his mother throw up her hands in all too familiar exasperation. Then came Mira.

Mira was forever out of place. As a child, she had been handed down into the care of relatives in the horrible wake of a hard winter, after her father and mother took ill and never recovered. Growing up in town, her father was a teacher and her mother a housewife who took in decorative stitching for extra pocket funds. Their life was very different from the lives of her relatives out in the country and by the shore. She was left in the care of her mother's brother, a man of rural charm and mean understanding, and though neither he nor his wife were ill-tempered, neither of them knew quite what to do with an adolescent that had never milked a cow, caught chickens, or mucked out a stable. She could sew, but her stitches leaned more toward embroidery than mending; she could speak three languages with at least rudimentary proficiency, but she couldn't be firm with the donkey when he slipped his pen. Goodness knows she tried, but no matter the effort she put to her tasks, she never could quite fit.

Her aunt and uncle were both pious members in good standing at the Temple of the Sun. While her own parents had visited the temple on occasion, for high holy-days and the like, Mira now attended weekly with her aunt, uncle, and cousins. She and her cousins would pile into the back of the wagon as the sun began to peek over the horizon. In time, the wagon would trundle alongside the conveyance of yet more cousins who made the trip from their nearby farmsteads with their husbands and wives and further extended family. After service, there was generally a great reunion of brothers and sisters and young cousins, the youngest of whom were frequently thrust into Mira's arms as though she knew how to properly hold a baby. On the way home, she often fell asleep to the rocking of the wagon in motion. On those occasions where she found herself too energetic to sleep, she would try, more likely than not in vain, to talk to her family about the content of the service; unfortunately, critical thinking and religion were not a welcome pairing among her kin. It was these moments, among others, that impressed upon her the belief that most of her life was uniquely designed to remind her just how perpetually out of place she was. That was, of course, until one day, not long before her sixteenth birthday, when she accompanied her aunt and uncle to the market at one of the larger fishing villages along the coast. She wore her Sun's-Day best and laced a ribbon through the braids of her hair, preparing herself for the abundance of unfamiliar people who would, no doubt, be in attendance. Being of an age, she knew full well that her aunt and uncle would be looking to marry her off soon enough and figured it was probably in her best interest to be proactive on the subject. Without any effort on her part, she worried she might well find herself suddenly married to her cousin's brother-in-law Matthis. The young man was prone to a daunting number of questionable habits and was unduly proud for a man of such indifferent appearance. Unfortunately, he had made no secret of his interest in her as she approached marriageable age, which was more than a little worrisome. Her parents had been a love match, but that was by no means necessity; in fact, all of her female cousins but for one had had their match arranged on their behalf. In all fairness, her aunt and uncle did the best they could by them. All of her cousins appeared to be content with their lot, and she was fairly certain Aunt Jinny would try to find someone better for her before she'd ever agree to a match with Matthis, but culture was what it was. So, if Mira was going to find herself the love match she desired, she felt she ought to go about doing it as quickly and efficiently as possible.

When Mira first saw Toddy, she thought him affected; when she first met him, she thought him beautiful and interesting but rather too ridiculous to be taken seriously; the second time she met him, she saw his truth; and by the third time they met, she was quite decided on the matter of Todrick Windle.

The first time Toddy saw Mira, he was mesmerized and somewhat confused; the first time they spoke, he was enchanted if a little concerned; the second time they spoke, he found himself rather more in shock than out of it; and the third time, he was absolutely taken by storm by Miss Mira Elton.

CHAPTER 4

Mira arrived at the market in tandem with the dawn. The jingling of the horse's tack and the muted murmur of voices endeavoring not to be heard woke her from where she slept, curled between two of her younger cousins and the stack of meats and cheeses they brought to market, in the bed of the cart. Yawning, she helped her aunt and uncle set up their wares and went in search of a well and a reflective surface to wash her face and check her hair in her reflection. She wanted to be completely ready to greet gentlemen and cads alike and hopefully cut a swathe through the lot of them in search of a love match or, at the very least, a good husband. Not wanting to be seen in her current disheveled state at the central square, she opted to focus her search near the workmen's quarter. While she had never been to this particular town, it did seem that most villages of her experience stationed their heavy laborers all in one place, and that place usually had access to a well or a water pump that might be put to good use. Having judged her thought process sound, she set her course by a telltale wisp of smoke and made for the smithy. Her walk took her down a number of side streets, which eventually opened into a clearing surrounded on three sides by what were evidently an assortment of craftsmen's buildings. Glancing across the way, she was distracted by a tall young man who leaned against a post and beam fence, surrounded by at least two dozen butterflies on and about his person, wearing a simple but sweet smile on his face. Mira had little trouble imagining that the man was quite unwell; after all, who would want that many bugs attached to one's clothes and skin - no matter how pretty their wings appeared in the early morning light. She put the peculiar stranger out of her mind, then waved to get the attention of another young man as he worked the bellows at the smithy, asked politely for the use of their water pump, and got herself ready for the rest of her day. A day which would hopefully not be entirely composed of selling meat and cheese to strangers.

The butterflies had distracted him. Their multicolored wings flashed in the sunlight as they wove patterns through the air, each movement adding emphasis as they communicated their joy at the beautiful day that was unfolding. Toddy felt himself caught up in their exaltations and rested against a convenient fence to better allow himself to become immersed in their tale. They were telling a beautiful story that passed from one teller to the next, each voice adding new details and complexities, leaving him absolutely baffled as to whether they all knew the story before or if they had made it up on the spot in the manner of some sort of improvisational dance. If it was the latter, then it was possible that this morning was the only time that this particular story would ever be told, a story that existed in this moment alone and no other, and hence presented an opportunity beyond measure. Not that the brilliance of that moment presented an acceptable excuse to lay before the small group of carpenters who looked up at his eventual arrival. It was a market day today, and he already had permission to leave early to sell his wares. The extra hours of freedom for his part were not meant for the butterflies, and this time of the morning was time not entirely his own; this time of the morning, his hands belonged to his fellow carpenters. His absence amounted to fewer hours where he might provide his fellow carpenters with an extra pair of hands crucial to the completion of any number of tasks. Entering the large barn dedicated to the shaping and joining of wood was akin to entering another world; the smell of sawdust permeated the air, along with the lingering scent of sap. The light that filtered through the windows illuminated the motes of their trade that danced perpetually midair, as though openly defying gravity. He nodded a silent greeting, attempting to draw as little extra attention as possible. Upon finding his bench, he was so immediately ensconced in his work that he was utterly oblivious to the men around him who grumbled, rolled their eyes, or smirked according to their temperament, having long given up on trying to make Toddy punctual.

When the men broke for midday meal, Toddy perched next to his father, both men chewing in contemplative silence. The older man shoved him towards the door as he picked crumbs from his beard and returned to his workbench. Toddy gathered his things, deftly scooping up a large canvas bundled by the door that opened from the carpenter's workshop into the waiting world outside.

In a few short minutes, he strode down a narrow corridor toward the market square, passing buildings of brick, wood, and clay, his canvas stuffed with carvings of a multitude of shapes and sizes. He moved with a single-minded efficiency, nodding politely to everyone who greeted him along the way; if that group was largely composed of young women of marrying age, the fact was almost completely lost on him. In fact, he didn't register much more than a basic necessity for social niceties until he rounded a corner and saw a mass of auburn hair caught up with braids and a white woven ribbon. He found himself mesmerized by the bounce of a single curling lock that had escaped its careful coif. She turned to face an older woman, and he stopped in his tracks. What she wore wasn't fancy, but it was neat and fitted to her figure. She couldn't have been much above five feet, but she was definitely of an age and breathtakingly stunning with it. She passed over him with her stormy gray eyes, and for the first time of his recollection, he genuinely wished that a young woman would notice him. The thought made his heart beat an unnerving tattoo and gave him a strange feeling in his stomach, a twisting pang that he couldn't quite place. Uncertain what to do with the entire encounter, he continued on to his normal spot at the edge of the square where he gently settled his canvas and began to lay out his display to the work's best advantage.

In the lull of the afternoon, the time between the last stragglers who walked the market during their midday meal and the first of those to finish work for the day, Mira asked her uncle if she could be excused to take a walk and explore the other wares at market. He gave her an absent-minded assent, and she quickly grabbed up her small stash of coins and her basket before he could change his mind or ask one of his sons to accompany her. The market wasn't so big that she risked getting lost, and certainly not so crowded as to risk her safety, so she rationalized her way into an unaccompanied meander about the edges of the market square and its adjoining streets. There were fruit sellers and a woman who sold the most beautifully dyed wool yarn. She noted a wine seller she would need to remember to tell her uncle about. As she wandered, she kept a list of each purveyor of interest in the back of her mind, some for herself and some for her family. Eventually, she came across a young man sitting with his back against a wall; before him lay a multicolored canvas decorated with an assortment of wood carvings of exceeding intricacy, the likes of which she had ever seen before. She had the strange sense that he seemed familiar but couldn't quite place him, not until she looked down by her feet and saw the most delicately carved butterfly she had ever seen in her life.

"Butterflies!" The exclamation seemed to surprise them both, but he seemed game enough to try to carry on some semblance of conversation.

"Yes, lovely creatures."

This was not where her mind had gone, the image of an

affected young man covered in flying critters still fresh in her mind, but the comment was enough to start a conversation. Of course, when she glanced up to address the artist, she found herself momentarily distracted by his bright blue eyes and scrambled for something more to say. At a loss, she masked her silence under the pretense of browsing, allowing herself time to collect her thoughts.

"It seems that you like to carve all sorts of lovely creatures," she ultimately pressed on after a closer look at the multitude of pieces at her feet. Thankfully, she had not been wrong; he did seem to love animals, but more than that, more than any other thing, he genuinely seemed to love to carve mermaids. "But there's something quite strange about these mermaids."

"Oh?" he inquired more with his brow than his word.

"Well, yes. Aren't most mermaids depicted as having a flat tail, not unlike a dolphin?"

He gave her question a moment of what appeared to be serious thought before replying

"I have certainly seen them depicted so, and I cannot speak for all of them, but I do try to be anatomically correct."

She huffed a stifled laugh, anatomically correct indeed.

"And what sort of fin is this then? Some of it appears like an image I once saw depicting something called a lionfish, and the rest could be a shark, but like no shark I have ever seen unless sharks have taken to wearing skirts in years past."

"My lady is most observant," the young man had no way of knowing, but he probably could not have conceived of a better compliment. These days, it seemed that, more often than not, her observations were highly underappreciated.

"I do believe that the fins along the waist and lower back function very similarly to the fish of which you speak, and I have only seen a tail such as this on one other occasion. A few years back, a fishing vessel pulled into the docks, and there was a great outcry along the wharf. One of the young deckhands came and fetched me, as he knew I have an abiding interest in the sea. The fishermen had pulled up one of their largest nets and found one of the strangest sharks any of us ever did see. It had a long sinuous body and tiny needle-like teeth; it had two fins by its gills, but the rest were receded way back towards its tail, every one of them with this loose sort of fringe. It was so alien in appearance that I could not say for sure what it was upon observation, but the captain of the ship swore it was a shark, and who am I to gainsay a man who's been fishing longer than I've been breathing."

Mira tried to imagine such a shark and found the image in her head quite horrific, and she told him so.

"Oh, it wasn't winning any prizes for beauty, that's for sure." He smiled quietly, looking instead at the mermaid depicted before him.

"If it was so horrific, why use its tail for your mermaid? Was it just an intriguing fashion statement?"

"As I said, I do try to be as anatomically correct as possible."

The answer was lacking, and she found that what had been silly and charming the first time was rather more insufferable the second. Did he think her a child, to believe in such nonsense as a depiction of a mermaid being the natural product of observation? Or perhaps her initial assessment had been correct, and there was something about him too strange to be countenanced. Regardless of the answer, she had to admit that her interest was piqued.

"I see. Isn't it also rather more traditional for mermaids to be a bit more... uhm... well-endowed?"

He coughed in an obvious attempt at covering a laugh.

"Well, yes, that is often the case. I couldn't say for sure. Once she's older, she very well may be exactly that. Of course, if you take a closer look at her face and arms..."

Mira pinked a bit around the edges at the realization.

"Oh! Oh, she's a child. What a peculiar thing to carve, but I do suppose that if one posits the existence of mermaids, they would have to have been a child at some point." The young man just smiled. It was a very pleasant smile as smiles go, and he was possibly one of the most handsome men she had ever met. A handsome man with a pleasant smile was a potentially devastating combination, though he offset that by seeming so much of a dreamer as to render the resulting combination utterly ridiculous. She shifted her basket and cast the young man a regretful look before bidding him a good day and turning to wend her way back to her uncle and aunt. She hadn't made it more than ten steps when a hand gently touched her shoulder. She shifted to find her young dreamer standing there, looking down at her with gentle if slightly perplexed eyes as he handed her one of his creations. He closed her fingers around the pair of long tines that formed the base of a hair pin topped with a delicately carved mermaid forming an elegant figure eight.

"I'm Toddy, Todrick Windle, that is. Toddy. If you would like to talk again." His eyes flickered across her closed fingers and then looked at his own hands as though he wasn't quite sure what to do with them now that he found them to be empty. She had to admit he had rather nice hands, the roughness of his callouses accented rather than detracted from the gentleness of his touch and demeanor. He flashed her another charming smile and then returned to his canvas by the wall. Mira admired the pin as she returned to her family and quietly slid the mermaid to nestle among her twisted tresses before it could call too much attention. She stowed her basket and coins, quickly inspected her dress, and turned in anticipation of the next wave of customers, determined not to think about the crystal blue eyes, handsome smiles, or gentle hands of Toddy. No, Todrick Windle. No. *Mister* Windle.

Toddy wasn't certain why he had decided to give the girl the pin. What he did know was that almost every young lady who considered his wares had eyed that particular piece, and each one had ultimately opted not to buy it. There seemed to be a certain *rightness* to it, and that was the most he could say for it. Wood could be rather particular at times, and so perhaps the reason that it had never been sold was that it was somehow waiting for *her*.

He considered the young lady as he strolled down the beach that evening, shoes in hand so he could feel the sand sifting between his toes. His eyes, as always, scanned the shoreline even as he took in the vibrant colors that spilled themselves in ripples across the waves from the distant horizon. He had done it so regularly for so long that he barely registered what he was doing until he saw a bobbing shadow by the end of his dock. His heart caught in his throat as he listened to the chattering of a seabird perched above it on a piling, scolding it for scaring away the fish. Sand flew out behind his heels as he broke into a run, barely hesitating at the water's edge as he waded out until the water was chest deep and the shadow's features began to emerge.

"Nimmawni!" The shadow leaned into the light, and his breath caught in his throat; it was her. It was her, almost exactly as he remembered her. While he had grown and changed as any young man would from the ages of twelve to seventeen, the mermaid barely looked to have aged a day.

"Winken?" Her gaze traveled from his face, no longer carrying the vestiges of baby fat, to the coral still strung on the scrap of rope around his neck, to his eyes, and she smiled. "Winken! It *is* you!" It was a brilliant smile, all rounded cheeks and pointed teeth, and as happy as it made him just to be in her presence, he felt a sadness too. The sorrow of an old and half-formed dream losing its wings. In the absence of a hope he had not dared to entertain, his mind drifted once again to the young lady he'd met that day. The compelling feeling the young stranger had inspired was so similar to an impulse he had long felt but only just begun to understand; these feelings that he had never had the chance to explore were the sort that haunted one's dreams and that faded to an indistinct ache on waking. He did his best to set the thoughts aside. Nimmawni was here, she was here in front of him, something he had sometimes wondered if he would ever experience again. He smiled at her enthusiasm as she circled him, going so far as to lift one of his feet and then the other while inspecting the changes five years had wrought; he felt no need to interfere but instead reached out to satisfy his own curiosity and run his fingertips over the sandy pebbled texture of her tail.

"Where have you been?" he asked, "I've been waiting for you for years."

"Ah, well..." she made herself busy brushing her fine tentacles out of her face "I got in a bit of a tiff with an octopus. He caught me collecting sea urchins in his garden and was so put out that he trapped me away in a giant clam shell, but that's all done with now."

Toddy was not at all sure what to do with this information. Every fantastical thing she had told him about the coral and the Guardian Spirit had turned out to be true, but there was something about the way she made her excuses that seemed strange. Perhaps it was simply that it struck him as more ridiculous than fantastical.

"You were trapped inside a clam shell for five years?"

"Is that how long it has been? Well, I suppose that could be the case; octopuses have horrible tempers."

"That sounds terrible," he murmured, incredulous.

"Oh, it's hardly the worst thing that could have happened. After all, I was born in the heart of a giant oyster, and they are practically cousins," she said in a matter-of-fact tone.

"Wait, what? Is that how mermaids are born?" and just like that, he felt twelve again. His mind racing with strange new information and wondrous ideas, and a million million questions just waiting to be thought of.

"That's what they say. They say that down in the deepest depths of the oceans, where the darkness is so black that it seems to fill itself with great multitudes of hidden colors, allowing most eyes to determine no color at all; down where the blind fish sparkle, huge oysters grow. They grow so big due to their proximity to the star-body, where the silt still tumbles and swirls on the abyssal currents, mixing with the dust of creation. It is said that if you offer one a very special token, a giant oyster will encase it in pearl, much as their smaller cousins will encase a very special grain of sand. As the pearl grows, it slowly becomes a living thing, with form and shape, fins and teeth, and eventually the oyster opens just enough for the infantile Sea-Folk, or mermaid, to slip free." She smiled sweetly, "so, you see, not hard at all."

The cool water swirled around them as the setting sun continued to spill its colors across the rippling waves, yellows and oranges dissipating into reds and purples in the dying light. Toddy contemplated the mermaid's tale and was still skeptical, but having no knowledge of the interactions of the Sea People, he found himself unequal to the task of expressing that disbelief. She had a knack for making the unbelievable sound reasonable, though he had long come to terms with the fact that this was largely because the world as conceptualized by humans was so terribly small by comparison with the world of The People. At the same time, his Mama always told him that two things could be true; he could be a generally well-behaved young man *and* have stolen his Mama's fruit tarts, just as one could be untrustworthy and still do something good. By the same token, the world could be full of miraculous things, and what she said could also be absolute nonsense. Of course, if one did believe that it was this strange incident that kept her away, it was only when she put it in a greater context, as she did, that the experience of being stuck in a clam shell didn't seem like absolute torture. When one was not preoccupied with the formation of fingers and fins, the worst thing about the clam shell seemed to be the inevitable and ongoing boredom. Having answered the question to her own satisfaction, the mermaid in question was staring with a fixed interest at the shore. He followed her gaze, and when he looked up towards the beach, he saw a slender skirted silhouette by the dunes; he shifted, blocking Nimmawni from view. His protective intentions all but ignored, the young mermaid, curious as ever, swam around him to peer up at the figure that now appeared to be approaching the water. She blinked at him and then the stranger and back again.

"Winken, do you know that human?"

"I couldn't say; I can't see her face."

Nimmawni's hands clasped over her precious necklace, and she closed her eyes as though to listen without the distraction of sight. Her face swiveled from right to left, like a bat searching for the indications of every minute sound. When she opened her eyes again, they were dark and dilated, the hint of pleasure touching her lips and cheeks.

"Whether your face knows her face, your heart knows her heart." She touched the tips of her fingers to his chest for emphasis, and his heart beat harder for it, making itself known.

"What makes you say that?"

"You have learned to listen, Winken," she pointed to the

coral around his neck, "but *I* can hear things you can't even *imagine*." He had no words for that, and her only response to his silence was to laugh.

"I have to go, but I'll be back."

"When?" he called as she began to float back out into deeper waters. "Nimmawni, when?"

"Someday!" She waved to him before ducking beneath the waves, and moments later, she reemerged, executing a spectacular flip that rendered her entire silhouette against the burnt orange of the setting sun. When he turned, he saw the young woman from the market who had so occupied his thoughts, jaw hanging slack, neat boots and hem dripping from the efforts of an ambitious wave. She looked at him as he approached the shore, and her mouth snapped shut. She swallowed repeatedly, wet her lips with the pink tip of her tongue - but had thus far remained silent, obviously collecting her thoughts.

"That," she finally said, "was a mermaid."

That was all she said. That was all she said for several minutes; in fact, she said it several times, with several intonations. He could do nothing but respond with assent to the pronouncement, the question, the concern that she might be crazy; before she could even begin to articulate her thoughts, entire conversations played out across five words.

"That was a mermaid."

"Yes."

CHAPTER 5

It was absolute insanity. None of it should have been possible, and yet, here she was. When the market slowed down again for the evening, in the pause before loading up the wagon when most shoppers had gone home but vendors still held out hope for a little extra coin, she was able to slip away for a brief period of time and decided to take the opportunity to enjoy the beach. It was a rare indulgence to walk along the waterside. Growing up, she had lived in town, but twice her parents had taken her to the seashore. On both occasions, she reveled in the wonders to be found where land met ocean for five glorious days. For five glorious days, she was allowed to splash in the water and sit in the sand, basking in the sunlight and savoring the fresh seafood. Now, most of her days were spent on the farm or picnicking in the field near the Temple of the Sun, each endowed with their pleasures to be sure, but nothing quite compared to the sound of the sea and the taste of salted breezes as they passed. As she strolled, she found herself thinking back on those days in the sunlight. The sound of her father's laughter, her mother's hands as they tied her sun hat firmly beneath her chin. Their smiles, so full of love for each other and for her that her chest ached. When she broke from her reverie, she found that she had walked rather further from town than she had planned; she was mid-turn, intending to make her way directly back to her uncle's wagon, when her eye was caught by a flickering in the water. She saw the silhouette of a man's head and shoulders above the waves, surrounded by shapes she couldn't quite piece together. As she approached the water's edge, the shapes moved and came into focus. However, focus did not mean that what she saw was reconcilable; it certainly did not mean acceptable to the rational mind. She saw a little girl, a little girl with big watery eyes, a little girl with hair so light as to be translucent, a little girl whose skin seemed to glow as she looked from Mira to the man and back again. He spoke to the girl, but the breeze stole his words away before Mira could catch them. The girl dipped away, and the man began yelling the word "When." Mira had the distinct impression that she was witnessing something important, but she couldn't wrap her head around what it could possibly be. But then, then came the moment that she was sure that she would remember, and question, for the rest of her life. It... she?... *the mermaid* launched itself from the water in an amazing aerial display, hair flying, arms outstretched, a set of fins fluttering about her waist and a long snake-like tail that fanned beautifully in silhouette. It was a *mermaid*. She had seen *a mermaid*. Long minutes after the silhouette had disappeared, she continued to stare in awe. Even as the man came into focus on his approach, and she registered that it was the wood carver from the market. Eventually, she pulled the pin from her hair, stroking it with a deep sense of wonder, her gaze flicking back and forth from the figure between her fingers to the horizon. That was a mermaid.

"That... was a mermaid."

"Yes."

He stood with her until the sun had almost set, thankfully and inexplicably willing to stand in quiet support as her world view shifted on its axis, and when she was ready, he then walked her back to the village. As they walked, it was as though the wheels in her brain finally began to spin again, and she began to ask him questions. Questions like how and when, and he answered her with a story so simple and yet fantastical that she probably would not have believed it had she not seen for herself what she had seen.

"That's probably why she did it," he laughed, "she has some interesting ideas about humans." On this topic in particular, more than that he wouldn't say.

He walked her all the way to the market square, to within sight of her aunt and uncle who would surely take one look at how closely he stood beside her and believe she was walking out with him. He bowed over her outstretched hand like a proper gentleman, though his face came a touch too close, and she could feel the whisper of his breath across her skin before he gave her a mocking smile.

"Have a good night, Miss...?"

"Mira, Mira Elton."

"Have a very good night, Miss Elton. Please give my respects to your family."

With those parting words, his gaze shifted past her and on to the stars, his charming smile turned wistful and she somehow knew it was no longer for her, but that was alright; it seemed he was privy to something fantastical and it took extremely little effort on her part to believe that she had only begun to scratch the surface. She smiled at his back as he disappeared into the night with a sway to his step, as though he could hear music beyond her scope. She stood there long enough for her aunt to come and join her, carrying her shawl,

"Sweetheart, did you have a nice walk?" The woman draped the soft fabric over her niece's shoulders as she inquired, "Who was that young man?"

"Yes, Aunt Jinny, I had a lovely walk." She straightened her shawl on her shoulders and breathed in the warm scent of the wool. "That is Mister Todrick Windle, Toddy, I met him at the market today. He passes along his respects and hopes you have a lovely night."

"What lovely manners!" The woman eyed her carefully, assessing the state of her young charge. "I didn't get a good look, but he seemed like a handsome young man."

Mira considered her intentions before responding. It seemed that in the course of an afternoon, the boundaries of her world had been blown open in a way she could never have anticipated. The smile that had first seemed so simple, the words that had seemed at first so frivolous and so irksome, every moment that gave her cause to dismiss Todrick Windle now seemed all the more reason to be sure of him and the quiet adventure it seemed a life with him might be. So it was with conviction that she told her aunt Jinny:

"He is quite handsome and very nice. I want him."

Jinny and Martin had not been a love match, but they got on well enough from the beginning; mutual respect with the addition of time and some children certainly did eventually deepen into an abiding sort of affection. The arrangement had worked well for her, and when it came time for her children to marry, she spoke to her neighbors and old family friends and found them each a good match as well. Only one of her daughters had been a love match, and there was something beautiful about that which she couldn't quite place but could respect for what it was. Still, arrangement or love match aside, none could honestly say that Jinny approved of a match without doing her due diligence, and no one in her family was getting married without Jinny's approval. So, when Mira told her she wanted to marry that young man from the market, it mattered not one whit that they didn't share a drop of blood; Mira had been left in her care and would be treated as such. On the way home, she told Martin they would need to come back to this market more often for a time. It was further than their normal market day, but it was also larger, and people came from the surrounding villages. There was no denying that they had done well in sales, and he could justify repeating the experiment, but he wasn't too happy about taxing the horses. That being said, when Jinny told him about Mira's potential beau, he softened a bit. The girl was strange, out of place in the country and on the farm, but he owed it to his sister to see that the girl had as good a life as he could afford her. Still, he couldn't help but wonder:

"Why can't she just marry that Matthis boy?"

Jinny scoffed.

"Matthis is a mean-minded, covetous, spendthrift, still on his mama's apron strings. He won't treat her right, Martin, and he won't make a good life for himself or anyone else."

Martin had learned a long while back that the women folk knew all sorts of things that their menfolk rarely found reason to talk about. Some called it gossip, but he had four grown children with good, happy lives because of Jinny; not many of his acquaintance could say the same. Jinny had a good read on people and a good mind for facts and figures; he knew well that he'd made safer bets on his home and his business because of her insight. He had long been of the opinion that it was a small-minded man who couldn't admit that women were keepers of important information. In light of that, he took no offense to her response to his suggestion, nor to her assessment of the young man he had presented as an option. Instead, he took a long moment to assess his options.

"We can probably manage Third Market once in a fortnight. Will that do?" Jinny squeezed his arm affectionately and laid her head on his shoulder as they swayed with the movement of the cart. The sound of the children's deep breathing, the jingle of the swaying tackle, and the hooves on the dirt road lulled them into a comfortable silence as they made their way home.

It was three long months before Mira saw Toddy again. Three

long months, during which every job that highlighted her ineptitude felt all the more unpleasant, every romantic advance during a Sun's Day picnic that much more untenable, and the moments that made her feel out of place were made all the worse by the knowledge of where she wished to belong. Three long months and six times she was left behind to stew while her aunt and uncle made the lengthy trip to the fishing village for Third Market. When they returned, Mira would try to ask her aunt questions, but it wasn't until they returned from the fourth trip that Jinny responded with anything other than infuriating inquiries about housework and livestock.

"Did you see him?" Mira practically hung over the railing at the top of the stairs

"Yes," Jinny said. Her tone was disinterested, but she smiled into her baking. "He has a nice smile, and his carvings are beautiful. Of course, carvings do not put food on the table."

"I'm sure he does more than just carvings." Mira practically skipped down the final steps, glad that her aunt was finally willing to converse on the subject.

"Yes, he works with his father as a carpenter, but he is a very strange boy. I hear he talks to himself."

"He's creative." Mira leaned against the kitchen door, hoping something about Jinny's demeanor would give something away.

"I hear he stares off into space for hours at a time, watching bees and ants."

"You said you saw his carvings. How else can he make them so detailed but to spend time studying his subjects?"

At that, Jinny only grunted, but she continued to smile as she kneaded her bread dough and set it on the counter to rise. Mira threw up her hands in frustration with the obvious close to the conversation.

After the fifth trip, Aunt Jinny told her that she had had tea with Toddy's mother.

"It's a strange family."

"I'm strange."

"You're not strange, you're from town. No, the mother is a local healer, a medicine woman with roots and leaves, teas and poultices. The locals trust her better than the local physician, but she seldom goes to the temple." As far as Mira was concerned, not going to the temple was far from the worst thing about her potential mother-in-law, but she knew it might be an issue for her family.

"They do keep His image in all of the appropriate places." Jinny continued, "Therefore, I see nothing wrong with the mother keeping some of the old knowledge, so long as she simply uses it to heal some scrapes and sniffles." Judging from her son, Mira suspected that there was more to their adherence to the Old Knowledge than scrapes and sniffles, but she wasn't about to go voicing those suspicions. Not when appearances suggested she was going to get exactly what she wanted out of keeping her mouth shut.

After the sixth trip, she was told they would be going to the shore. They would be leaving on the fifth day of the following week. By the second day, she had packed what amounted to her worldly belongings and was resolute in the absolute certainty that she would not be returning to the farm.

In retrospect, Toddy would say that there were three days that fundamentally changed his life. The first was the day he met Nimmawni, and the greater world and all of its People opened up before him. The second day, he woke up to find his Mama already happily bustling about the house. Given the hour, he gave serious consideration to whether she had finally cracked. It seemed to him that sweeping before sunrise ought to be an indicator that one was fundamentally unwell.

"Good morning, Mama," he kissed her on the cheek and ducked into the kitchen to grab a roll and some butter.

"Good Morning, Tiddley Winks." She rarely called him that anymore, but it still caused the desired wince. "Today is going to be a lovely day, I can already tell." Toddy peered out the window in search of some sign of whatever it was that his mother thought she was seeing.

"What makes you think that?"

"Get comfortable, Toddy, you're not going into the shop today. We're going to have company." She looked him over from top to bottom and rolled her eyes. "Would it kill you to bathe and put on a clean shirt?"

"I didn't know I would be needing to. The men at the shop hardly require that sort of formality."

"Well, now you do. So get to it."

The tone would clearly brook no argument, and the look on her face said she wasn't about to tell him anything more, so he sighed and got himself some water to bathe. He took the time to properly comb and plait his hair, and as his fingers darted and wove the strands, he listened for his dear old friend's voice. The Guardian was pleased but wouldn't say why. The house was pleased, his mother was pleased, he wanted to also be pleased, but the secrecy made him wary. When the knock on the front door finally came, his stomach was in knots. When it opened, it was for a woman who looked vaguely familiar, followed by... Mira. No one was surprised but him.

The house was charming, Mira was determined to be charmed, but she was almost certain that she would have felt it so regardless. The garden was planted with a wide array of aromatic herbs and flowers; butterflies flitted from plant to plant, reminding her vividly of her very first view of Toddy. Sometimes, having a good memory of one's first impression was a rather unfortunate burden. She followed her aunt's neat footsteps up the stone path to the door, noting the obvious nods to the Temple of the Sun and some less obvious deference to something far older. She stepped up to the door intricately carved with leaves and small woodland creatures, probably Windle carpentry work, and felt a moment of nervous energy, which she smothered before it could possibly have the chance to grow. She was a presentable young woman of marrying age, she had approval from both her family and his, they had a good rapport if that one day was anything to go by, and, while the extent of their time together may not have been ideal, people made do with far less every day. Somewhere in between her chest and her brain, she knew it wasn't that simple, but in that very same place, she felt an absolute certainty that whatever it was that she was looking for, she would find it with him. So she straightened her skirts, wiped her boots, checked the tilt of her beautiful mermaid hair pin in the reflective light of the Sun Disc by the door, and nodded to her aunt with a smile. It was time. The door was opened by a lovely older woman with long dark brown hair streaked with gray, caught in a half chignon with sprigs of lavender. She had deep blue eyes and a bright smile that greeted her aunt first in familiarity and then turned to Mira.

"Come in, Dears, do come in. I have water on to boil and a nice snack out on the table."

There was enough light from the windows that her eyes barely took time to adjust as she stepped through the front door. Their great room's appointments were simple but elegant, with hand-carved trim and a lovely dining table set in anticipation of tea for four. Her head swiveled to take in more of the room only to be immediately confronted by a baffled looking Toddy.

"Mira?" He blinked several times and rubbed his eyes as though uncertain she was, in fact, here.

"Good Morning, Toddy." She shot his mother and her aunt a questioning glance, looking for confirmation. Because, surely he had been told she was coming. The two older women exchanged a wicked glance and a smile that all but confirmed, instead, her suspicion that they had done absolutely nothing of the sort. More to the point, it appeared that the situation had been orchestrated with the specific goal of Toddy being dumbfounded for their mutual enjoyment. She shook her head at the two of them in amused disapproval, deciding then and there to do her best to use the situation and Toddy's discomposure to her advantage. She strode further into the house, taking it all in.

"Your home is absolutely charming, Mrs. Windle." A carving in one of the posts caught her eye, but moving to take a closer look meant passing the apparently unwitting object of her affection.

"May I?" she gestured to her destination. He nodded dumbly, brow furrowed in consternation. "Thank you. My, but aren't you handsome!" she addressed the wooden face of the House Guardian. "So kind, but stern as well, did you carve him?" She spun to face Toddy, who was looking at her with a sort of rapt fascination. Fascination was all well and good, but she could not quite determine whether it was the fascination of affection or the fascination one might experience in the presence of an irate viper.

"Yes, I finished him when I was fifteen years of age." He stiffened as she stepped a little closer to him than strictly necessary to gaze up at the House Guardian in admiration.

"Well, he's beautifully executed. Did you also help with this lovely table?"

"Oh, no. My father made the table, it's been there as long as I can remember. I helped fix the chairs a few times, but that's hardly the same." He relaxed a bit as she put some space between them, and even further as he warmed to the topic. With the return to his previously placid demeanor, Mira felt the upper hand slipping away. *That certainly wouldn't do.*

"This looks like a lovely treat, Mrs. Windle. Toddy, would you care to sit next to me?" And she had him off-kilter again.
"I believe it's traditional for me to sit next to my Mama, Miss Elton." His mother smiled up at him as she approached the table with a tray full of mugs.

"That's right, dear. Come sit by me." This, of course, had the effect of seating him directly *across* from Mira. The perfect vantage point for him to see every delicate sip of tea, every smile, and every nibble of apple, bread, or cheese she took. There were, after all, reasons for these social niceties. She watched as Toddy sliced a piece of bread and topped it with a slice of cheese and a slice of apple before offering it to her. She accepted it with a smile and her thanks before taking a small bite. The bread was flavorful and still warm from the oven, the cheese rich and creamy, the apple practically exploding with sweet juices, the entire experience so full of vitality as to render her momentarily speechless. In that instance, she was reminded once more that this was definitely not a normal situation. Truly, the entire house seemed rather more vibrant and full of life than she was accustomed to. She took a moment to wonder whether her nerves were getting to her, ultimately setting the thought aside for future study.

"So, Mira, what is it that brings you here?" he asked, raising his tea to his lips.

"Why, your marriage, dear." He practically choked at his mother's words, spilling tea on his shirt in the process. The two women chortled into their tea cups as he looked over his shirt in disgust, then leveled his mother a look of supreme vexation. The chair scraped loudly against the floorboards as he stood, bowed to the table as though it was an afterthought, and then strode towards the stairs, muttering something about derangement and vexatious women.

"Really, Aunt Jinny! Mrs. Windle!" Mira scolded in a whisper, "You told him absolutely nothing? What on earth have you been doing all of this time?"

"Mira, why don't you just call me Audry? I plan to welcome you to the family and this 'Mrs. Windle' business is bound to get tiresome." Audry didn't bother to lower her voice, so Mira followed suit.

"Audry, then. Why does he know nothing about our purpose here today?"

"Oh, one of my great joys in this life is getting under Toddy's skin. He's a good-natured boy, but sometimes he's so focused and so... placid that one can't help but want to ruffle his feathers." Having already felt a similar urge not even an hour past, it was rather difficult to argue the point.

"You say you want to welcome me to the family, but how is that to happen if he hasn't even been consulted?" Audry waved off the question.

"I know my son. He's never been interested in any of the girls in town, never gave them a second look. Not a one could break his focus from his work for longer than it took to answer a few questions or politely greet one another in passing. So imagine my surprise to find that you not only spoke the day he met you, but he walked with you on the beach, and ever since that day, he's been on edge. Not so as most people would notice, but he always wants to go to the market, always looking at the young women. Not to see who they are, but to see who they *aren't*. My son is quite taken with you, Mira; he just hasn't figured it out yet."

The sound of feminine voices drifted up the stairs to where Toddy straightened his clean shirt. His ears perked up at the sound of Mira's voice raised in a mild sort of alarm, but it wasn't until he heard his mother's reply that he felt the heat building in his cheeks. He could admit to himself that the young woman's pretty face, sweet voice, and wry tone had occupied his daydreams. In his mind, the ghost of her listened, with the same rapt attention she had paid his own story, as he retold the tales of The People to commit them to memory. The feeling was unfamiliar, and he took his time contemplating it, mulling it over. He inspected it like the many facets of a crystalline stone or the iridescent whorls of an abalone shell. Having not come to his own conclusions, he hadn't realized that his interest had been so marked as to be obvious to anyone else. Hardly for the first time, he thought back to that day on the beach. *Whether your face knows her face, your heart knows her heart.* He smiled at his secret, knowing that, no matter how perceptive she might be, his mother could not claim to have discovered his feelings first. It was with this moment of smug satisfaction that he headed down the stairs to rejoin his engagement gathering.

The third was the day that Anders was born.

CHAPTER 6

It was another seven years before Toddy saw Nimmawni again. Anders was running full tilt down the beach, as five year olds were wont to do, when he stopped too quickly and went sprawling into the sand.

"Papa! There's a dead crab." Anders' focus, as usual, was unflappable. Toddy watched as Anders scrambled back up the beach, presumably to where he had seen the crab shell, and let out a frustrated sigh.

"Papa, I broke it." He held up the delicate, sunbaked pieces with a grimace that was just too cute to be taken seriously, though anyone familiar with Anders knew that you had to at least try. Mira was much better at humoring their son's serious nature; Toddy was too prone to smiling with amusement and wonder at the miracle that was his child.

Toddy leaned over Anders' broken prize, doing his best to look severe, when a glint caught his eye. A shimmer in the water by the dock, and as he listened, he caught the edge of a sea bird's familiar nattering on the wind, scolding someone for scaring away the fish. It was as though an echo of the past was being carried into the present on the wind, in a manner he could not believe to be a coincidence. His feet started running before he could think to give them the command, and it was more of an afterthought that made him yell over his shoulder:

"I'll be right back Anders!" as he sprinted and stumbled over the sand and down to the edge of the sea.

"... I understand that you are quite put out, but carrying on about it will not bring the fish back. If anything, it will scare the other fish away." The voice from under the dock sounded so reasonable and so familiar, and there she was, so very much the same. He, now above four and twenty with a child of his own, yet she looked only a little older than the day they had first met.

"Nimmawni!" He waved to her from the shore and watched as she waved her arms enthusiastically in response. "Just wait, I'll be right there!" and he ran back up the beach, to scoop a very startled Anders up in his arms, bouncing him along over his shoulder to the sound of high pitched childish squeals until they reached the near end of the dock where he put the distraught five year old down and allowed him to collect himself.

"Do you remember how Papa told you the story about the day he met a very special friend down by the water?"

The small mop of dark brown hair bobbed in confirmation.

"Well, Papa's friend is at the end of the dock. Would you like to meet her?"

Anders had heard the story of his Papa meeting Nimmawni more times than could be counted. It seemed that Mira had paid very close attention to all of Toddy's stories, finding them far more interesting than the stories she had grown up with, and had begun recounting them to her son as soon as he was grown enough to listen. Of course, on very special nights, Toddy would sit down and retell the story in his own words, complete with the story of the sea turtles and the Great Mama of the Deep. Anders straightened his collar, took a nice deep breath to calm himself, and looked to Toddy for encouragement. Toddy offered his hand to his son, feeling the boy's jitters humming through that point of contact as he was faced with meeting a figure of practically legendary import. They walked down the dock hand in hand, but by the time they made it halfway, Anders had placed himself shyly behind his father's leg while practically pushing him along in anticipation.

"Winken!" The mermaid yelled impatiently, "What could possibly be taking you so long?"

The seabird had stopped scolding her, and Toddy soon saw why, as the end of the dock was littered in crab shells and the bird itself was occupied with cornering what was quite clearly the latest of her offerings. Anders tugged at his fingers,

"She really calls you that! Mama said she called you Winken! And she *really* calls you Winken!" Toddy smiled and rolled his eyes.

"Yes, she *really* calls me Winken."

"Does she really have jellyfish tentacles for hair?"
"Winken? Who are you talking to?" Father and son peered over the edge of the dock, and two great big eyes peered back up at them. Anders ducked back onto the dock, rolling onto his back,

"She really does have jellyfish tentacles for hair."

Toddy's face lit up with a grin.

"Winken, do you have a *little* Winken up there?" Anders made a face at the term "Little Winken," and Toddy laughed while nodding enthusiastically.

"My son, Anders."

"Little Winken! Why are you hiding away up there? Won't you come and see me?" The mermaid spoke sweetly, with a sort of melody to her voice that Toddy had never heard before. To be fair, she had never felt the need to coax him to do much of anything; the one time she had wanted something he had been reluctant to give, guilt had been a powerful and effective motivator. He watched as Anders tried to contain his excitement, rolled back over onto his stomach, and poked his head out over the edge of the dock again.

"Hullo, Little Winken! You look quite a bit like your father did when I first met him."

"Good day, Nimmawni! I like your hair! And I like your stories. Papa tells the very best stories, but I think some of them are yours; some of them are stories he heard from The People, but I think I like your story best of all." The mermaid blinked at the flood of words and then covered a giggle and an absolutely charmed expression, flashing only a hint of sharp teeth.

"You like stories, Little Winken? The People do tell some amazing stories. Why, I heard that you can hear five different versions of exactly the same story depending on which sort of beetle you ask."

Toddy shook his head.

"I learned to listen, I learned to hear, but I never did get them to understand me in return."

Nimmawni looked from father to son and addressed Anders in a dramatically conspiratorial manner:

"I think he's doing it wrong."

Anders giggled. Feeling the need to guide the conversation in a different direction, Toddy asked, "Nimmawni, where have you been all of this time? We walk down to the beach every day, and we haven't seen you these *seven* years."

"Seven years, was it? I don't know about seven years, but I did get caught up in a very long game of strategy with a spirit at a shipwreck. He had died when the ship went down, you see, and there was a game of black and white figures and squares in the captain's cabin. I'm not certain that he actually knew how to play the game, as it seems to me that the rules kept changing, but the process was quite engaging while it lasted."

"You spent seven years playing a board game with a ghost?" Toddy knew he sounded more than a little incredulous, but this story did seem beyond belief.

"Well, it was a little more complicated than that," She said as she floated on her back at the surface. "I went in to explore the wreck, and I found myself a beautiful bit of treasure, and the spirit was there and threatened to follow me around indefinitely, to the ends of the earth if necessary, if I took it. That did not sound at all pleasant. So we made ourselves a wager that the one who won the best two out of three... or was it four out of seven? Games would get to keep the bit of treasure. I couldn't say how long each of the games lasted, but it seems I was there for quite some time."

Toddy found this entire story breathtakingly ridiculous,

while Anders lay beside him physically holding his laughter in with his hands across his mouth.

"So, what happened to the treasure? Can we see it?"

Nimmawni suddenly became very taken with a bit of seaweed that had floated up against her fins.

"Well, unfortunately, that won't be possible." She continued to fidget. "Because, you see, I gave it away."

"You gave it away," Anders repeated in disbelief. Nimmawni squinted up at him in annoyance, then went back to playing with the chunk of seaweed.

"Yes, I gave it away. You see, there was this hermit crab that had gotten rather too large for its shell and found the treasure to be of appropriate size and shape... and it wasn't like I had anything I was going to *do* with it anyway." Toddy pinched the bridge of his nose while Anders' laughter attempted to escape through his.

"You spent seven years playing chess with a ghost for a wager and then gave your prize to a passing hermit crab?"

"It was very *uncomfortable*, Winken."

Toddy was rendered quite speechless, so Anders picked up the slack.

"Was the treasure very shiny?"

"Very."

"Did the hermit crab like how shiny it was?"

"I think so, though one can never be too sure with hermit crabs."

"Won't the shininess make other animals notice it?"

"Quite possibly."

"But then won't they want to eat it?"

"I'm not sure it was thinking about that. But the beauty of being a hermit crab in an appropriately sized shell is you can retreat inside until danger passes, and one would suppose that a shell made of shiny treasure is harder to break into than a shell made of shell."

"Do hermit crabs call themselves hermit crabs?" The abrupt shift in the line of questioning left Nimmawni momentarily flummoxed. Toddy could completely relate; the entire exchange had him completely baffled.

"Well, no," The mermaid answered slowly, "because hermit crabs don't speak human languages." Anders heaved a sigh of exasperation that Toddy was certain he had picked up from his mother.

"No, I mean in their language, what do hermit crabs call hermit crabs?"

"Shell brother... or sister, generally speaking. I don't think I understand the question."

"Well, if I say I am a human, what would a hermit crab call himself?"

"Probably something like one of the Nomadic Shell People." Anders repeated the distinction to himself quietly, and Nimmawni redirected her attention back to Toddy.

"So Winken, you have spent the last however many years learning to listen and hear The People. Have you learned anything of interest?" The question caught him by surprise, but what it addressed was far from an unfamiliar thought. After over a decade, it was hard not to consider the impact of this gift and the impact of forgetting. Toddy had long since come to the realization that humans had forgotten far more than they imagined, and in many ways far more than they now believed they knew. Each of The People had their stories, and through the stories ran common threads, common lessons and messages, common figures, and common truths. Humans had lost something important along the way, and they didn't even recognize how precious that something was. He only wished he could find a way to ask The People the questions that might help him to better understand it. He thought out loud, and his old friend listened, deep in thought.

"To speak to The People, you must speak so as to be heard, so as to be listened to, and so as to be understood. I understand you because I want to, because my focus is on you, and that is how the magic works. You have been taught to speak to be heard by ears already inclined to hear you, with little thought to whether they listen to your words or understand your meaning. Most of The People do not bother with human voices because never in their life has a human properly spoken to them. So other than knowing the location of a potential threat, what is the point in paying attention to human speech?"

"I want to hear The People too!" Anders confided, "I want to hear The People, and I want to talk to the birds." Delighted by the momentary distraction, Nimmawni leveled her gaze at the younger Windle.

"Why do you want to talk to birds, Little Winken?"

"Because then I could get the crows to steal my itchy Sun's-Day shirt when it's out to dry with the washing, and maybe that seabird will come tell us the next time you come to shore." Toddy stifled a laugh. It was no secret how Anders felt about visiting the Temple of the Sun; from the nice clothes to the long service, and even the food Mira's relatives brought to picnic, Anders was not inclined to take pleasure in any of it.

Nimmawni was clearly charmed by his reasoning about the seabird and soon slipped the necklace from around her neck, this time presenting them with a shell of iridescent silver, which was passed from her to Toddy and from Toddy into Anders' tiny fingers. It was less fragile than it looked at a glance, for which Toddy was thankful, knowing it for the gift it was and something with value beyond measure. The mermaid gestured to the five-year-old to focus on the seabird and to use his ears to listen. The seabird, having filled its belly with little crabs, had retreated to its nest atop one of the pilings and appeared to be asleep.

"Wing sister!" Nimmawni yelled. The bird responded with only a perturbed ruffle of her feathers. Anders looked at his shell with skepticism.

"Wing Sister! I have a deal to make with you!"

The bird opened one beady black eye and made a show of yawning, snapping her beak shut with a clacking sound.

"Scaly nuisance, first you scare away the fish, then you bring humans to my nest, now you disturb my sleep time. What could I possibly want to do with you?"

Anders' jaw dropped.

"Look here, you greedy guts with wings, I caught you as many crabs as you could fit down that gullet of yours, and yet here you are complaining when I save you the trouble of a whole afternoon's hunt. Do you want to make a deal or not?"

Anders' mouth was opening and shutting as though he, himself, were a fish out of water. Much like the winding of a spring could cause sudden explosive motion, Toddy could see an explosive response building in his son as his tiny body struggled to contain his excitement and frenetic energy. He grabbed the boy's arm, putting a finger to his lips. Anders pressed his lips together firmly and nodded to his father; he would do his best not to disturb this strange new interaction.

"What do you want?" The bird cocked her head to one side and then the other.

"From time to time, I come to this dock to see these humans." Nimmawni gestured to Toddy and Anders. "I would like you, or your descendants, to let them know if you see me coming." The seabird fluttered her wings in obvious annoyance.

"Alert humans? What is the sense in that? They hear nothing, they understand less. Asking a bird to alert a human is like asking a spider to net a star from the sky."

"Wing Sister," the mermaid softened her tone, "take a closer look at my friends."

The bird hopped down from her nest and strutted across the dock, shifting her head from side to side, focusing on them with one eye and then the other, and blinking at them in turn. Neither Windle knew what the bird was looking for, much less what she found, but when the bird returned to her nest, it was not with continued denial but a grudging willingness to haggle for its services.

"What do you offer?"

"Sea urchin."

The bird clacked her jaws greedily.

"*They* will bring me sea urchin?"

"*I* will bring you sea urchin, and *I* will give it to you when *they arrive."* The bird narrowed her eyes at the mermaid but didn't argue.

"How many?"

"Two."

"Four."

"Three sea urchins, no more."

"Fine." The seabird grumbled, "I will alert your humans. Hopefully, they are not too stupid to understand."

"I'm not stupid!" Anders replied. The bird blinked at him. Anders blinked at the bird.

"Maybe not, but we will see."

Toddy had to admit to a pang of jealousy when the seabird responded to Anders, but greater than jealousy was the sense of pride. In all of his hearing and listening, in all of his watching of both humans and The People, it had become very clear that there was a division so wide as to, at times, feel insurmountable. The Temple of The Sun taught a message of human dominion that resonated with the farmers, who shaped the land to their liking and shaped the lives of The People around them to their own purposes and ideals. Yet, here, this tiny young man listened and heard; he spoke to one of The People and was understood.

"Well!" Nimmawni said with satisfaction. "That is one wish granted, and it would seem that the other is under way." She shot Anders a toothy smile, and he blushed with satisfaction. "The thing about Crows, Little Winken, is that they are tricksy."

"What do you mean, tricksy?"

"The children of Pan'chan are all at least a little tricksy. You know of Pan'chan?"

Anders nodded

"Well, some among The People appealed to Pan'chan most, and he blessed them with his gifts. They are often intelligent problem solvers with a mischievous streak."

"Like foxes?"

"Oh yes, Pan'chan loves foxes."

"Raccoons?"

"Of course."

"What about Spiders?"

"Yes, and of course, Crows." Toddy interrupted. Knowing the nature of his son, this exercise could easily progress to Anders listing every animal he had ever heard of, beginning with the ones who made the most sense and then continuing on just to be absolutely sure he hadn't missed any. "So, how does one deal with tricksy children of Pan'chan?"

"It is the nature of the children of Pan'chan to be driven by their hungers, from the hunger for food to the hunger for knowledge." Nimmawni winked one of her big, dark eyes and smiled.

CHAPTER 7

The next morning, Mira woke and found that she had somehow managed to lose track of both her husband and her son. When she found them, it was several yards from the house where her handsome figure of a man dug a hole between two of her mother-in-law's wheels of medicinal herbs. Her son knelt nearby with a slab of wood that almost equaled him in size, which he was hammering with his small mallet, doing his best to connect it to a rough post that would stand about as tall as her husband. They had been out until late in the evening, and Mira had fallen asleep as she waited, her swollen feet propped up by the fire, her hand lovingly smoothing over her rounded belly. She barely woke when her sweet Toddy had scooped her up and carried her with ease to their room; she felt him kiss her forehead and then gently kiss her belly before pulling their heavy blankets up to tuck her in. She heard him shush Anders and then the sound of Toddy's quiet footfalls followed by the dragging thumps of the child being led to his bed. Heard her wonderful, if tired and completely unaware of his volume, child say,

"But I need to tell Mama!" and that wonderful man whom

she wished to shower with kisses, if only she had the energy, tell him that he would have time to tell her in the morning. Yes, there would be time in the morning, and she would be more than happy to listen, she thought as she floated off to sleep.

Of course, it was morning *now*, and as much as she and her growing little bundle appreciated the extra time to sleep, she was not fond of having to search the house for her previously enthusiastic offspring. The view outside was charming, though she did wonder what Audry would have to say about the state of her herb garden.

"What's all this then?"

Anders dropped his mallet and scrambled towards her at a run. She braced for impact but needn't have bothered. He slowed when he was about an arm's length away so he could give her a gentle hug, cradling her belly with a sort of awe that he had developed after the first time his growing sibling had kicked him in the head.

"Good Morning, Mama!" he rubbed her belly affectionately and addressed it directly. "Good Morning, Bunny." No one was quite sure how he had come to that particular moniker, but it didn't seem to be going anywhere, and it was too adorable for anyone to be inclined to debate.

"Good Morning, Sweetness. What are you and Papa up to?"

"We have a project!" Anders, having suddenly remembered his task, went in search of his discarded mallet.

"So I see, but what *is* it?"

Toddy straightened, leaning his shovel against the edge of the hole, as she approached and bent to give her a sweaty kiss.

"We had a visitor yesterday, down at the dock." He smiled. Mira's heart skipped, and her breath caught in her throat for just a moment. The mermaid, the mermaid she had only seen for a second that one day seven years ago, the mermaid who had changed her life. The mermaid, without whom she would never have taken Toddy seriously, without whom she wouldn't have her loving family, without whom she wouldn't have her beautiful son and another baby on the way. She had come back. The moment of shock turned almost as quickly to a flash of anger accompanied by frustrated tears. She struck her spouse across the shoulder.

"Todrick Windle! She came back, and you didn't come get me! I didn't get to thank her, and who knows when any of us will see her again!" Toddy was quite taken aback for a moment by the sudden outburst but then swooped in to give her a sweaty, grimy hug that was both wonderful and, unfortunately, sticky. She wiped at her face as she continued to weep, now almost as annoyed with the emotional extremes of pregnancy as she had been with the inconsiderate lack of action on the part of her spouse. She tapped at him fondly on the back while making as little additional contact as she could manage.

"Darling, I appreciate the affection, but you need to bathe." His chest shook against her cheek as he laughed. When he released her, the breeze cooled the grimy sweat on her cheek, and she had to resist the urge to use her apron to wipe her face. Rolling her eyes at his antics, she returned to the original point,

"And just *how* does a mermaid have to do with a giant post in the backyard?"

"I'm going to make friends with a Crow!" Her son said

excitedly, he pointed to a shimmering shell that hung from a bit of leather around his neck. Her eyes shifted from the shell to her husband's coral necklace, to his face, asking a silent question. He smiled and nodded, then nodded to their son, who had suddenly become very distracted by the interaction of two bees dancing among the blossoms near his feet.

"I think I'm going to need a lot more information," Mira informed her husband. She was happy for her son, happy that he was happy, and happy that her son would get to experience some of the wonders her husband had always done his level best to share. Mira loved all of the stories, the stories he brought home after listening to cats and butterflies and the snake that they all pretended didn't live by the well in the yard, but she also knew that it set him apart. She knew well that the subject of Toddy's strange, inexplicable behavior was often remarked on in town. His ideas were often outlandish, and she knew that it was normal for people to ostracize what they did not understand. Her protective instincts squirmed in her gut, working at odds with her heart and her head and making her wish that there existed a better set of options. Still, life was what it was, and she knew that her husband would not have traded that necklace for anything in the world.

She watched as Toddy showed Anders how to add supports to the large platform they were assembling, as well as when he snuck in a few hard strikes with his own hammer to make sure it was securely connected to the post. Then father and son righted their rough hewn creation, and Toddy held it steady in the hole while Anders filled the space around the base with rocks and dirt, packing it as densely as he could. Toddy circled behind his little helper, stomping the loose dirt into place. Once the structure was erect, it stood at about Toddy's eye level and, aside from the fact that it vaguely had something to do with crows and blocking perfectly good sunlight, she couldn't fathom what it was for.

"Did you talk to your mother about this?"

A question that was suspiciously overlooked in favor of an excited desire for nuts, seeds, and fish guts. Her tiny young man ran past her into the house and returned with a bowl of scraps and some of her good nuts foraged from the woods. Her husband smiled, with the sort of exaggerated innocence that didn't bode well for anyone, before scooping Anders up onto his shoulder with a whooping cry so the child could upend the bowl on top of their creation.

"Now we need to give them space, Mama. Space and shiny things. They like shiny things. Do we have any shiny things that we can give them?"

Later in the day, Mira sat with Toddy in the kitchen as she cut vegetables for supper, watching Anders sitting quietly just outside the door, and he told her what had happened. Not just what had happened, but how he felt about what had happened. She laughed at his frustration with the mermaid's strange excuses for her absence; she wondered at how little seven years had aged her; she smiled at how Anders, her reserved Anders who would barely talk to family members he had known for years, had taken to her almost immediately.

She listened, the sound of her knife slicing through onions, potatoes, and carrots and meeting the cutting board below was the only accompaniment as Toddy told her a story.

"Long ago and now and always, Pan'chan thought to play a trick on his older siblings, and after much consideration, he decided he would rearrange the stars in the sky in honor of one of his little sisters. What she loved most of all was to lay on the earth among the Rooted People and stare up at the Sea Above. He thought to himself about the best form he could use to take to the skies and make changes unobserved. He cast about in consideration of all of the gods' creations, and he saw a small black bird, sharp of beak and claw, and thought it would do quite nicely. Quick as one could think, Pan'chan shed his scales and took to feathers, with body a bit larger, beak a bit longer and sharper, eyes a bit clearer, and claws many times sharper; changes none would notice at a glance as he soared through the darkness of night. He dove headlong into the Sea Above and caught up in claws and beak several of the great stars, for what his older siblings loved above all else was order, and nothing could be more orderly than the stars of the night sky. He picked his stars, some with great thought and some with little care for the fates to which they were woven, though it was well known among all of The People that all that exists in the Sea Above is tied to the Sea Below. Noting that something was amiss, Pan'chan's siblings searched for a cause. When The Shadow and The Light turned their eyes to the corner of the sky where their brother had played his game, they saw the swirling mass of starlight he had created and voiced their shock.

The Light tried to rub away the smudges of stardust, but all he did was make them brighter and more colorful. The Shadow tried to pull the stars back into their predetermined paths but only managed to further change the nature of those stars' fates. They cried out so harshly that they caught the eye of their Mother, and when she saw what the antics of her children had wrought, she laughed and laughed and laughed. For in their distracted rush to rectify their brother's actions, The Shadow and The Light had pulled the star-body into orbit around the sun and brought about the first change of the seasons. It was then that the waiting seeds of Rooted People, which had rarely before seen the sun, began to flourish. The most abundant growth surrounded Pan'chan's little sister and filled her with such joy that The Great Mama of the Deep set the new constellation in the heavens and gifted it to her, proclaiming her a deity of fertility and growth.

When Pan'chan returned to the earth, his wings glittered blue black with the dust of stars. The Wing Mother of the black birds saw him from the tree where she perched and was quite taken with his shiny feathers and sharp beak. On the night that the stars changed place, the Wing Mother, Little Darkness, mated with Pan'chan in the form of a majestic bird cloaked in darkness. Soon after, she bore a nest full of eggs that shimmered with divinity. When the fledglings were hatched, they were so different from one another that the Wing Mother cried out in alarm. One was large and quiet, and when it spoke, it was thoughtful and intelligent; His offspring would become the great solitary ravens. One was not quite so large and far more talkative, its eyes sparkled with the spirit of their father, and it loved the company of its siblings; its offspring would become the flocks of crows that gather to learn and make mischief. Another was given starlit white feathers among the black, with a curious nature and an unsurpassed love of all that shimmered and shined; and its offspring would become the magpies. The egg that hatched next was long of beak and as social as its eldest sibling was reserved, and its offspring would become rooks. The final fledgling would grow to have a chest of white and wing feathers that, while dark as its siblings, played with the light in such a fashion as to appear as blue as the midday sky; its children would become the raucous Jays. Little Darkness preened and doted on them all, immersing them in a mother's love and seeing in them the best of her beloved Pan'chan. So it is that to this day, the black birds know themselves to be children of Pan'chan and the little mother who watches over them all."

Mira listened with a smile. She had always loved her husband's way with words, loved the stories he shared that inevitably seemed so much more vibrant and alive than the stories and myths of her childhood. Each and every tale seemed to open the world before her a little bit more, and she remembered that she had chosen to tell her children those stories so that they could see that vast expanse of world for themselves. For all of her protective instincts, it was this inclination that would already set them apart, and having made such a decision already, who was she to interfere with Anders being given such a gift?

"So, this is why he wants to make friends with a Crow?"

"Well," Toddy rubbed the back of his neck self consciously as though trying to decide what to say next. "The answer to that would appear to be threefold."

"Alright, I'm listening," She tried to prepare herself. Though she was uncertain whether for shock, amusement, disgust, or frustration.

"Part the first," Toddy illustrated by raising a single finger, "he wants to make friends with a crow because he wants to not only hear and listen but to talk and be understood. With those goals in mind, it seems like he focused on finding a clever friend to try to talk to."

Mira nodded; it made sense and sounded very much like the sort of thought process Anders might employ.

"Part the second, at some point during our conversation, he asked Nimmawni about fairies. He said, 'My grandma told me that there used to be fairies,' and she said, 'used to be? Tell me, Little Winken, do you think that just because humans haven't seen something for a while, it no longer exists?' Of course, this was right after hearing a conversation with a foul-tempered seabird, so Anders was up for believing just about anything. Apparently, the Fair Folk are often also favorites of Pan'chan, and Pan'chan's children are often seen in similar places, if not outright in congress with one another. So I believe our son is also hoping that, if he is patient enough, he will get to see a fairy."

Mira was quite intrigued by the implications that fairies had ever been, and possibly could still be, real. Much like the first part of Toddy's explanation, it very much sounded like Anders. She braced herself, having not been taken aback by the first two reasons, she could only assume that the real issue was the one that remained.

"Part the third," Toddy grinned, "Anders has become so completely opposed to his Sun's-Day best that he is hoping to employ the assistance of crows and fairies to either steal them or keep them so perpetually in the mud that they can never be made available for their intended use." At that, anger and amusement warred in her chest.

"Anders..." She grumbled in exasperation. "That child..." She tried to hold on to her anger, and she was indeed angry. Intending to damage his good clothes was definitely a reason for frustration, if not anger. But the ingenuity, the thought process, and if there was any animal likely to disrupt the washing, he had certainly chosen the one. So it was not long before a rumble started in her chest, and warring emotions brought tears to her eyes, even as the chuckle was released and joined by her husband's quiet laugh. It wouldn't do to be caught; that would be tacit approval, but goodness, it was amusing.

Over the next week, Anders' parents watched as he approached the task of making his new friends with a single-minded resolve. His grandma had thrown up her hands in exasperation when she saw the new addition to her garden. Nonetheless, it became a habit that each day, with his father's assistance for height purposes, he brought scraps out to the platform. Each day, whenever he wasn't asked to do something, he was out in the garden, a short distance from the crow platform, looking intently at the branches of the surrounding trees and practicing listening to the bugs and the mice and the little birds. Where

Toddy had drifted and found himself caught up in the role of spectator, Anders took a more methodical approach and came home consistently with a tale on his lips and observations to share. Of course, when the first shadowy figure swooped low and landed on the platform, Anders was so excited that he shrieked and sent the crow rocketing back into the nearby tree, but what more could one expect from a young man of only five years? Anders spent the next ten minutes trying his very best to convince the crow that, despite the volume of his enthusiasm, he was not a threat. He tried to tell the crow all about his new platform and plans, but the crow would not listen. When this didn't work, he tried to bribe the crow, but it would not budge. The crow showed momentary interest in the shimmering shell around Anders' neck as the boy held it forward to tell the crow all about his experience with the mermaid, complete with proof, until Anders realized that it might look like he was offering a shiny thing to a crow and tucked it away beneath his shirt. Eventually, he stomped back into the kitchen, absolutely inconsolable. He lay his head on his arms at the table, his tiny body wracking with sobs of disappointment. Mira bustled over as quickly as she could in her advanced condition, gently laying her hand between his shoulders as she lowered herself with care into the chair beside his.

"He! He... He won't... he won't talk to ME-E-E!" the little boy sobbed. "He won't even L-L-Li-LISTEN!"
"Oh, Sweetness, it may just take some practice. You've only talked to a bird once before."

He lifted his head, thick mucus dripping from his nose and lip, eyes red and swollen. The sound of him trying to breathe through his nose was rough and moist, and before he could reply, Mira situated a handkerchief over his dripping nose so he could blow and remedy the problem.

"But, that time, it just worked! Mama, I told the seabird I wasn't stupid, and the bird understood. Maybe I AM Stupid! Maybe I'm too stupid to talk to crows." And the tears poured down his face anew. Mira wished that she could talk to crows herself so she could give that particular one a talking to. Still, it was unlikely to make her feel any better to talk at a creature to whom her opinions made absolutely no difference. She looked out the window and saw that the crow had returned to the platform and was happily munching on the scraps her sweet boy had set out for it. Stupid, ungrateful bird.

"Sweetness, you are not stupid! You have been so smart and so patient, but maybe you need to be a little *more* patient. Maybe you just need to keep trying."

The boy wiped his wet face across the sleeve of his shirt, leaving behind long streaks of tears and slime, then proceeded to launch into a protracted explanation of all of his actions, thoughts, and reactions throughout his interaction with the crow. Despite her very best intentions, Mira's mind began to wander, and she noticed a sort of niggling sensation in the back of her mind. The bothersome feeling bloomed into a thought, and the thought turned into a question, a question which abruptly interrupted her son's impassioned ramble.

"Anders, is this how you spoke to the crow?"

The question caught him by surprise, and he stopped and blinked at her for a moment in confusion.

"When you spoke to the crow, sweetness, did you tell it a

whole lot of things, or did you say just a few important things?"

"*Everything* I said was important, Mama!" from which Mira gathered that the answer was probably closer to her first suggestion than to the second.

"Anders, please. Think back to what you said and how you said it. Were there a lot of words or only a few words?"

Anders kicked his legs under the table as he thought, his face twisted up in concentration.

"There may have been a lot of words, Mama, but I had a lot to say."

"I understand that, but it was also the very first time you're speaking."

Anders blushed a bit at that, recognizing his breach of human decorum.

"What I wonder is, do you remember what Nimmawni told Papa about speaking to The People?" Anders shook his head.

"If I remember correctly, she said that most of The People don't pay attention to humans speaking because they've never had reason to. Kind of like when you go to the family picnic and the other kids are busy, do you always listen to what the adults are talking about?" Mira was quite certain of the answer, as more than once she had found herself battling frustration while repeating words that had been lost to childish inattentiveness. He shook his head but looked thoughtful.

"Now, let us think about this. When you spoke to the seabird, what were you thinking?"

"That I'm not stupid, and she should know that. Because I'm not."

Mira thought back to what Toddy had told her: *To speak to*

The People, you must speak so as to be heard, so as to be listened to, and so as to be understood. One had to admit that a lot of the time when a five year old spoke it was to hear themselves talk, and that in such moments there was the expectation that they would be paid attention for no other reason than that they were talking. *You have been taught to speak to be heard by ears already inclined to hear you, with little thought as to whether they listen to your words or understand your meaning.*

"It seems to me that you cared a whole lot more whether you were heard, listened to, and understood when you spoke to the seabird, and you very much wanted to hear yourself tell a story when you spoke to the crow. Maybe one day a crow will care to listen to your stories, that's what we do with our friends and loved ones, but first things come first. When we meet a new friend, it is with civil introductions and polite conversation, and it seems to me that this is not so very different. Make your introductions. Listen, and speak to be listened to and understood."

The little boy sniffled and stared out the window. There were now three crows on the platform, and one lifted its head, perhaps to stand guard over the others, looking toward the window.

"Do you really think that might work?"

"I do, my love. I think with thoughtful intentions and a little mermaid magic, it will all turn out fine."

"Alright, Mama, I'll try." He slipped from the chair and quietly walked to the door to the garden. The subdued boy approached slowly and stopped as soon as the birds started ruffling their feathers at his proximity.

"Greetings, Wing Friends," Anders spoke quietly but wanting so very much to be heard. The crows kept eating, unfazed.

"Greetings, Wing Friends!" he spoke a little louder, and one of the crows flicked its tail as though irritated.

"Greetings! Wing Friends!" He tried one more time, with more force and volume, enough so that one of the crows lifted its head and stared at him as though uncertain about what it was looking at.

"Human fledgling, did you speak to us?"

It was all Anders could do not to shriek with joy.

CHAPTER 8

Over the course of days and years, Anders continued to learn to hear and to listen, he learned to speak so as to be heard; he learned to communicate with the intention of being understood. When he spoke to adults, they always commented that he was so mature for his age and, when they thought they would not be heard, that the child was quite strange - not unlike his father. He got to know the local family of crows, their ins and outs, their wants and needs, and found many of their favorite treats to bring to their platform. They, in return, got to know him and watched the daily patterns of his family, providing insight and amusement with their commentary.

When new flocks arrived, Anders was one of the first to notice, long before the farmers who guarded their crops, long before those who saw only doom and dark portents in their presence. He saw them in the sky, and he saw them quarrel with his friends over their spoils and his gifts. After one such altercation, he spoke to the young about the newcomers, their input was hardly helpful and certainly not informative - they thought that the flurry of clashing in the sky and more claws available for the mischief was great amusement indeed, and saw no reason to delve into why they suddenly had more "cousins." It was their mother who landed on the edge of the platform after several days of avian chaos and called for his attention.

"Fledgling." She greeted him.

"Breakbeak!" Anders cried out with excitement. The older crow was not so enthusiastic about approaching where humans walked and carried out their daily chores. "What brings you?" The austere older crow turned her head to stare at him with one deep black eye.

"Fledgling, a ravenous storm is coming. Go and tell the human mother that you must prepare and that we have come to feed."

Anders, all the wiser for ten years of age and a good half of his life influenced by The People, knew when he was being told something of import and when he was being dismissed. He nodded his head in deference to the matriarch and, in only half a moment, ran in search of his mother, barreling through the kitchen door and almost tripping over his little sister.

"Mama!"

"Mama!" Bunny yelled for her, too. To help or to distract was anyone's guess.

"Mama! Breakbeak told me something important!"

"Which one is Breakbeak love? You know I have no knack for telling your wing-friends apart." Mira turned from the pot where the base for preserves bubbled away.

"The matriarch, Mama."

"Oh, well, that's lovely dear," Mira said dismissively, checking Bella over for bruises from her encounter with her brother.

"No, Mama, that's the point. It is not lovely. Breakbeak told me to run and talk to you to tell you that we need to be prepared because... because she says a ravenous storm will be coming."

Mira looked up, puzzled. There was something about the phrase that felt like she ought to remember it.

"A ravenous storm? A Ravenous Storm..."

"Yes Mama, she said that more Crow People would come to feed."

"Well, that is strange, dear. How could a crow feed on a..." and just like that, he could practically see the information begin to fall into place on his mother's face,

"Locusts. Locusts are coming. Go run and tell your father, Sweetness. Just what Breakbeak said, nothing more, and make sure you aren't overheard."

Anders nodded and, leaving his Mama in the kitchen looking a little bit lost, ran from the house to the edge of town; three crows tracked his motion and flew overhead behind him, coming to rest on the tree outside the carpenters' workshop. The run was not terribly far, it was one that he had made so many times on so many days. All of the times he enthusiastically followed his Papa to work, in hopes of a chance to help out in the small ways that Papa and the other carpenters allowed. He had made the run with ease more times than he could count, but on this day, the sense of urgency tightened his chest and made him breathe heavily with exertion. He tried to catch his breath at the door, but the moment he entered the shop, Toddy was on high alert, concerned that something horrible might have happened.

Anders waved his father out of the shop and then went to squat under the tree where his friends had perched, doing his very best to catch his breath and compose his thoughts.

The conversation that followed was much the same as the one with his mother, both uncertain why their day was being interrupted by a message from a crow. Both quickly certain of an impending destructive force. Both at a loss for how to proceed. Though his father could also hear the comments of Anders' companions, who chimed in with their own opinions on the matter. The swarm would not come today or tomorrow, but the crows were certain it would arrive. How does one warn one's friends and loved ones, one's neighbors and customers, of a thing that should rise unexpected from the wild and the wind? How does one prepare oneself for a storm that strips everything in its path with a million tiny mouths?

Mira took her cues from the crows. Over the next few days, she allowed the chickens to run loose, chasing them as far as the neighbor's yard - citing a broken coop door, childish pranks, and any other excuse she could think of for them being so far afield. Each time she ran across another human being, she made a point of mentioning a large bug, the likes of which she'd never seen before, that she had found the chicken making a meal of. She kept an eye to the clouds, watching for her son's friends, and more than once spotted a larger crow with a crooked and chipped beak staring right back at her from the trees. As she quietly tried to raise awareness of the coming swarm, she found herself thinking back to stories about the great cloud that fed on all it passed, sometimes called the ravenous, hungry, or voracious storm. It seemed that sometimes the swarm flew to a place as though driven by a wind all their own, and sometimes the storm rose from the very earth.

"My darling," she caught Anders' attention one such morning, "would you ask Breakbeak a question for me?"

The boy wiped the remnants of breakfast from his lips with his sleeve. Mira winced and had to fight the impulse to comment on the action, not wishing to sidetrack the conversation.

"I can try, Mama. Breakbeak doesn't always like to come down from the trees."

Having been witness to the rambunctious behavior of the absolute surplus of crows that seemed to have congregated near their house in recent days, Mira could hardly blame her.

"You do your best, Anders; I'm sure she will hear you out."

Anders worried at his fingernail, another habit she curbed the impulse to correct, but nodded.

"I want you to ask her if the ravenous storm will be coming like the wind or rising from the earth."

The moment she finished speaking, her son was gone like a flash, barely sparing a moment to nod his acceptance, leaving his used dishes behind on the table.

It was a few hours later when Anders returned, hands cupped before him with a spooked look on his face as he spoke quietly, "Just stay a little bit longer, please. I'm supposed to show you to my Mama. Thank you so much for not biting me. When I'm done, you can go and go far, far away from my house and my chickens."

"What do you have there, my darling?" Mira bent low to look at the contents of the boy's outstretched hands, but all she saw was a black and yellow blur as whatever it was launched itself from Anders' hands and disappeared. The boy cried out in dismay at the loss of his prize.

"What was it, my love?" Mira asked again, trying to bring Anders back to the matter at hand.

"It was a baby locust." She drew back in alarm.

"Breakbeak says that there were too many baby locusts and they drive each other mad. You can tell when they've gone mad because their whole bodies change color! They're bright and weird, and they want to eat everything..." he was interrupted by a thumping noise at the kitchen window. When they turned, they found the matriarch crow perched on the sill with a squirming insect caught in her misshapen beak. She tossed the large black grasshopper with yellow streaks onto the slate floor of the kitchen, where it landed on its back and wiggled its legs in the air, then she clacked her beak in what appeared to be amusement. Mira did her best to hide her distaste as she nodded her head. "Ah, yes, thank you. I see..."

To her surprise, the crow nodded back, then turned her head to level her dark gaze first on them and then the insect, which had twisted the lower half of its body enough to lever itself back onto its feet, now standing still as though taking stock of its surroundings.

"They sound weird, Mama, like they don't think quite right, and it's hard to understand what it's saying. Like when Papa mutters to himself while he's working."

Mira grabbed a canning jar from the counter and dropped it

over the stunned insect; perhaps if she had one in her possession, it would convince her neighbors that there was an issue. It seemed that she and the crow, Breakbeak, were in agreement. Once the insect was secured, the bird shuffled her feet around to face the yard, cawed over her shoulder at the humans, and launched herself into the air.

"So, Mama, the answer to your question is that the storm will rise. But it doesn't rise from the ground, not really; it rises because there are too many babies, and they all go mad, and when they're not babies anymore, they have wings. Isn't that weird, Mama?"

The storm did not rise. As soon as her canning was done, Mira took the jar and its captive from neighbor to neighbor, explaining that, being from the city, she had never seen such a creature before in her life - but she had seen a number of them eating her mother-in-law's herbs. The response was universally one of immediate revulsion; it was obvious that some knew the misery that their presence foretold. It became common to see chickens running loose around town. The townsfolk did not attempt to scare the crows and other birds away but, rather, cheered when they saw wriggling insect bodies snared in avian claws. Every one of The People who could be was enlisted to cull the masses of nymphs. Horses, donkeys, dogs, and cats, even the snake they pretended didn't live by the water pump was spied with a locust nymph snared in its jaws. The human population, not to be outdone, killed the insects on sight. The tavern even offered free ale to those who brought bags full of locusts to their door. The first sign of the threat had been the abundance of crows, and when the threat finally passed, the first sign was the crows' departure. The clashing in the sky came to an end, the beasts of burden returned to their feeding troughs, and the chickens returned to their pens. Everyone settled back into their normal lives, and in a matter of months, the entire incident seemed to have been forgotten. The Windles, of course, knew exactly what had come to pass, and their local crows were richly rewarded with all of their favorite foods on their platform for quite some time to come.

CHAPTER 9

Anders would not see the mermaid again until he was twenty years of age. He carried on with the family business more out of necessity than any particular love for it. The wood did not speak to him as it did for Toddy, though he could hear its living song and took comfort in the presence of the Guardian of the House as they all did, he and Bella and their two younger sisters. Every morning, he still brought food for the crows, though he had not once spied a fairy on any of their sleek feathered backs. He listened to the stories of The People and recounted them happily to his sisters and parents. Occasionally, he thought he saw a touch of envy cross their faces as he spoke, but mostly they were happy to be no stranger among their community than any person who came from this household; strange, mostly by association. The sort of abnormal that could be hidden, for the most part, as they made their weekly visits to the Temple of the Sun, a foray that had become increasingly more focused on looking forward with an eye for marriage prospects. With this in mind, the appearance of normalcy was truly considered a virtue. His Mama had somehow managed to cultivate every bit of that virtue, even while still embracing and loving every moment of storytelling and showing every bit of respect for The People, who were constants in her life; the result of closeness with such a uniquely gifted pair of men. Anders, for his part, earned a reputation rather different from his father's. Where Toddy was thought of as a dreamer and an artist, quick to smile and rather more full of nonsense than the neighbors knew what to do with, Anders was serious, known to listen with great consideration and come to his conclusions with a deliberation that some found admirable and others found frustrating - particularly as his opinion was just as likely to favor the local foxes as it was the local farmer. It was that disparity between his reason and what his fellows found reasonable that gave the town folk pause. Both men had the tendency to absent themselves from the company of others, but where some had despaired at Toddy's strange behavior, they at least saw his charm and his artistry and understood what Mira saw in the man who would become her doting husband. Anders was more taciturn in nature, so despite cutting quite a fine figure with his deep blue eyes and the dark brown hair that he had allowed to grow much like his father's, there was some question about the village as to whether he would ever find himself a wife.

Having a fourteen-year-old sister was, undoubtedly, a trial on Anders' patience. Too young to attend local social gatherings, thank all that was good and sacred, but still quite as social as she could manage. Therefore, where there was one fourteen-year-old sister, there were often two or three young ladies between the ages of twelve and fifteen, and the inane chattering was incessant. Vera, being ten, was more likely to be found helping Grandmama in the herb garden than gossiping about ribbons, thank goodness. Thea was still his Mama's shadow, being eight, though tall for it. No, Bella was definitely the most difficult person in his life at present - something unlikely to change as she was getting closer to all of those social gatherings and responsibilities that occupied her mind, apparently to the exclusion of all else. BrightClaw, Breakbeak's grandchild, so named for the single white claw on his left foot that winked in the sunlight, had commented only that morning on Bella's diminished hold on sense. Anders had laughed quietly, thinking he had kept it successfully to himself, but with the knack of little sisters, Bella somehow just knew she was being made the object of derision. Knew and tattled to Mama, who leveled a glare at both her grown son and his feathered friend. A feathered friend who immediately abandoned him to fend for himself, launching into a nearby tree with a cackle of his own at the dire circumstances of his friend.

Crows.

The call came during one of these casual social gatherings, as he was, once again, subjected to the prattling of adolescent girls on the subject of hats and John; who was either the farmer's son who wrangled the pigs going to market, or the baker's son who carried the large bags of flour from the miller's. He could no longer be sure. Both being named John, and both having been deemed worthy of collective swooning at one point or another. It was a call he had been waiting for for fifteen years. He missed it at first, his mind wandering as he did his best to be present for his Mama and her guest while remaining equally invested in ignoring the girlish gaggle, effectively failing at both. He did not note the call of the seabird until it landed, indignantly and full of self importance, on the open window sill. This immediately achieved what no one had done for the better part of an hour: catching Anders' attention.

"Stupid Human, I have called. You have not answered. I will not be denied my rewards because of your laziness."

The girls shrieked at the seabird, clutching their latest embroideries to their chests protectively, all except Bella, who yelled at Anders,

"Get it out!" obviously not putting the pieces together as to what the intrusion might mean. His mother, however, was not so slow to make the connection.

"Anders, go take good care of the bird," she nodded in the seabird's direction, attempting to walk the line between socially appropriate dismay, excitement, and respect. Mostly, Anders felt, it looked like she was having some sort of palsy, but he wasn't going to complain. "Vera!" she called into the yard, "Vera! Please go run and tell your Papa I need to speak to him, most urgently." Anders saw his little sister nod and then hie off down the road, just a touch faster than normal, but hardly at a pace that could be considered a run, in the direction of town.

Anders held his hand out to the bird, who had stopped squawking just as soon as it was clear that it had made a suitably impressive entrance. The bird waddled forward and stepped gingerly onto his arm, grumbling about the stupidity of humans, and rode that way until Anders was a little over half the distance to the beach. The bird launched itself skyward, the force sent a shudder through his arm, and Anders heard it boasting of its success as it sped to the waterfront and circled the small dock where Anders' father had long ago introduced him to the mermaid. By the time he caught up, the bird had torn into two of the sea urchins and was eying the third as it attempted to scuttle to the edge of the dock. Anders checked around the pilings, looking for big dark eyes that would stare at him from the shadows, but there was no smiling face looking back up at him.

"Nimmawni?" he yelled out across the water, hearing only the lapping of waves on wood in response. The urchins were proof that she had been there, the terms of the deal made right in that spot fifteen years ago with what was probably this bird's great-grandmother.

"Nimmawni!" He yelled again and thought he saw a flicker in the water, perhaps two yards out. He ripped his shoes from his feet and his shirt over his head and dove into the cool salt water below. He was not the strongest swimmer, but Toddy had made sure that all of his children did learn the rudimentaries of how to swim, so he chased what he thought he saw out away from the shore until he was thoroughly out of breath. When he saw no reason to swim further, he turned over onto his back with a yell of frustration. He floated there, wondering what to do next, cradled in the rocking of the gentle sea. Anders spluttered as an unexpected wave washed over his face, marking the end of his rest, and when he lifted his head to tread water, he saw a familiar face bobbing above the surface with a quizzical expression on her face.

"Winken? Could that be you?"

"I believe that the last time we spoke, you called me Little Winken."

"Ah, well, that makes sense. Winken could not swim."

Anders nodded and smiled, then began to slowly paddle in the direction of the shore,

"I certainly don't do it as well as you."

"This, too, makes sense. You lack fins and are poorly designed for the sea."

Anders nodded at this as well, it being a fair assessment.

"You've been gone for fifteen cycles this time. My father and I have missed you greatly."

"Why, Winken!" she exclaimed, seemingly ignoring the content of the statement entirely, "You have learned to speak quite well, though you have rather a lot of bird to your affect; though I suppose that makes sense as you were very taken with the idea of speaking to birds. Don't talk much to the rest of The People, do you?" Anders blushed first at the compliment and soon thereafter at the light being shined on his potential shortcomings.

"It's a lot more difficult than talking to the crows."

"Regardless, you are easier to understand than Old Winken, which is quite nice." Anders couldn't help but wonder what his Papa would think about being referred to as Old Winken.

"But where have you been these fifteen years?" asked Anders. His Papa had once told him that he was almost certain that her accountings for her whereabouts while she was gone were absolute nonsense, but Anders couldn't help the question as it slipped from his lips.

"Fifteen years, you say?" She swam beside him, only appearing a little older than his childhood memory. Had he not known better, he would have estimated her age to be somewhere between his sisters Bella and Vera, certainly not the more than 27 years since she had first met his father.

"Well, I couldn't say one way or another if it was that long, but I did get rather lost for a bit."

"Lost how? Where?"

"Have you ever heard of the Sunken City?" Anders scoffed; the Sunken City was a nonsense story told by sailors. Surely, there was nothing to it.

"The Sunken City? Of course, I've heard of it. The great city that they say was swallowed up by the sea."

"Well, I suppose you could say that." They reached the end of the dock and the small but sturdy ladder that his Papa had installed when he was learning how to swim. Anders pulled himself up the ladder, feeling the moisture dripping from his hair and his completely drenched trousers weighing him down as he exited the water.

"What does that mean, Nimmawni?"

"What the city was makes very little difference; what it is now is a ruin of what it once was and a ghost of what it could have been. Beneath the Sunken City, there is a great maze of catacombs and natural chambers eaten away by time and tide. Some go so deep that they attract the light hunters of the abyss." Anders was intrigued despite himself, and so far, none of it sounded too ridiculous - assuming one accepted the existence of the Sunken City.

"So, I went to explore a bit among the ruins when I saw a

giant school of lantern fish who promised to show me something so amazing and unique that surely I had never seen the like before. This was an enticing proposition, so I followed them down into one of the old cavegates. Only, after I was well and thoroughly turned around down there, the school started splitting off in all sorts of different directions, and I couldn't follow them all at once, now could I? Eventually, I found my way out of the catacombs, but it took me quite a while, and I ate quite a few lantern fish to get there. Too many lantern fish does not agree with the gut."

Momentarily putting aside the rest of the story,

"You ate the lantern fish?"

"Intimidation tactics." She smiled ferociously, baring far more of her sharp teeth than he had previously seen. Anders shook his head in disbelief; he was pretty sure Papa was right about her explanations for her absence, but given that he, himself, had never explored beneath the waves, he could not claim certainty in his skepticism. In point of fact, with the exception of visiting with his Mama's extended family, Anders had barely ventured beyond the villages and woodlands near his home. Where others of his acquaintance seemed quite content to let their world remain small and filled with the assumption of sameness, it was the nature of wearing Nimmawni's necklace that made him aware of just how far from the truth those perceptions could prove to be; and none of those friends had been to the places Nimmawni could have been. So what was it that made him so inclined to question her veracity? He momentarily considered that, perhaps, her youthful appearance was impacting his judgment. It was hard to imagine that a girl, mermaid or otherwise, who looked no older than his sisters, would find herself in such a position. He tried to imagine Bella wandering through dark catacombs and forgotten caves; ultimately, Bunny probably wouldn't have followed the school of fish to begin with. The baker's son? Possibly. But not a bunch of fish or floating lights. Rather than dwell on this, he opted to indulge his curiosity, or perhaps he simply wished to hear more of her stories.

"Can you tell me about the Sunken City?"

"It's not much to look at in the here and now. What do you want to know? Even better, what do you know already?"

"Only the bits and pieces that the sailors and fishermen tell. Every so often, someone claims to have seen it, to have swum away from their boats in pursuit of a gleam beneath the water, a shimmering that shines like gold. They dive down in search of treasure and find themselves above buildings with spires that shine like the sun, but none have breath enough to reach it. When they return to the surface, it is often so far from their ship that they're practically sick from salt and sun by the time they are hauled from the water. No one actually believes them."

Nimmawni leaned a petite elbow on one of the ladder rungs as though lost in uneasy thought. "It is not impossible."

"But it's unlikely?"

"I don't know, Winken, I have not heard of humans at the Sunken City. Of course, the city is spoken of very little; it is a place where many stories ended and much knowledge was lost."

It was obvious that the mermaid found the loss distressing; perhaps there was something in particular that had brought her there. However, when he asked her directly, it was no surprise that the conversation pivoted. Rather than an answer to his question, she responded by launching into a story. Though his curiosity continued to urge him to inquire further, it was not enough to keep him from laying out in the sun to enjoy the pictures she painted with her words.

CHAPTER 10

Once, in a time and a place beyond remembering, there was a great mountain that emerged from the Sea Below and bathed in the air and sunlight. The four winds brought to it the seeds of the Rooted Earth People, and great trees grew, and where the trees grew, so flocked birds, and where the birds flew, so followed humans in search of port. Just as the humans have lost knowledge, so too have most of The People. Too many have died before passing on their stories, and, as a result, too much magic has been lost. In the time of the mountain-island, the Sea-Folk who you would call mer-people could still walk on land when they so chose.

Anders gasped, looking over what he could see of the mermaid from head to tail. She glared up at him. Apparently, this was a sore topic. He snapped his mouth shut.

Those who chose to take to land often did so on the mountain because it was isolated, and when the water called them back, they were never far from the shore. So it was that when human sailors found the island, it was already claimed by the Sea-Folk.

Sailors are a hearty and resilient lot, and as they travel the world from port to port, they are not unaccustomed to the unfamiliar. The Sea-Folk brought them to the springs of fresh water and did not deny them the fruit of the tree. The sailors shared with them their stories and their songs, and soon the two Folk had come to an accord. Over many cycles, the mountain-island thrived, the two Folk working together to build a town which grew into a magnificent city adorned with beautiful spires dedicated to the many deities of both tribes. The Sea-Folk brought up their building materials, dug from the base of the mountain, burrowing beneath the city to create the catacombs that allowed them to travel the path below. The paths led to the many cavegates scattered around the city, providing access from below, and the intricate pathways of their tunnels provided homes and hiding places for many of the other Sea People. The first humans to live on the mountain were happy to live from land and sea, harvesting the Rooted People in accordance with the seasons and returning their seed to the soil, fishing the seas as the Sea-Folk do, though often with line and net rather than tooth and spear. The humans of the original accord lived in concert with the mountain and its inhabitants, and for that, the city thrived. They shared ideas and ideals and created beauty and technologies beyond either tribe's imagination; this is the power of stories shared.

Of course, all it takes is one open mouth to spread a story beyond its scope. Eventually, the existence of the island was made known to others, the description of its shining spires drawing the attention of those who saw the world with eyes tinged by greed. More ships arrived, but these ships brought with them discordant views. They covered over the cavegates, declaring it a human city; they brought The People who knew little of their stories, raised as livestock and bred for food, which required great numbers of the Rooted People to be felled to create fields with shallow roots that could not maintain the soil; and they engaged in senseless expansion in the ongoing search for valuable resources.

All things exist and maintain one another in equilibrium; it is with imbalance that things topple and fall. The original catacombs were burrowed with respect for the mountain, for its structure and stability, honoring the patterns and songs of the star-body from which it grew.

When ideas are no longer shared and heard, actions are often taken at cross purposes. Without understanding of the wending pathways, without the assistance of the Sea-Folk to pull from the wide base below, the humans began digging for resources in their own way. Perhaps if it had been one or the other, or a harmonious and intentional combination of the two, their work would have proceeded without issue, but this was not to be. When one day, as it sometimes does, the star-body shifted in its sleep, the mountain shook, causing many of the compromised tunnels to fail and collapse. Many Sea-Folk were trapped in the rubble, and there were not enough ships for the humans to escape as the mountain crumbled into the waiting Sea. The People of the mountain-island were cast adrift, some to the open skies in search of new roost, but many to waters they were ill adapted for, and without their stories to draw knowledge from, many did not survive. The survivors were cast adrift, and when they found the shore, they spoke of an alien place, unheard of and hard to imagine. In the wake of the great disaster, it was ultimately no longer identifiable to those who searched from above, as it lay beneath the shifting surface of the all-consuming sea. The stories of the Sea-Folk were turned sour by the coming of conquering ships and reinforced by the quake, believed to be the mountain's displeasure, and so Sea-Folk believed it a cursed place, and none would pass there for hundreds of cycles to come.

Anders lay for long minutes on the dock, staring up at the evening sky. The story of the Sunken City replayed itself in his head, each time bringing to mind new questions. At first, he spoke his questions aloud, giving vent to his curiosity. Unfortunately, his questions had only seemed to make her progressively more withdrawn until he began to feel the urge to apologize for dwelling on the topic. Even so, he asked her one final question as she began to distance herself from the dock,

"Nimmawni, if the memories of the place bring such sadness and discomfort, why did you go there?"

The mermaid had smiled, a sad smile that never reached her big, luminous eyes.

"I am searching for a lost story, Winken, and where better to find it than a lost city?"

Before he could respond, her head dropped beneath the

surface, and with an awkward backward wave, she was gone. Anders was still lying there deep in thought when the dock began to shake with heavy footsteps. His Papa collapsed on the dock beside him, breathing heavily from exertion.

"She left a little while ago." Anders barely moved, even as his Papa swore a blue streak that would probably earn him a smack from Grandmama if she heard him.

"I was at the miller's helping to fix the wheel, Vera ran all over town before she found me." Anders quirked an eyebrow at his father, who chuckled, both fully aware of his younger sister's aversion to exercise. "Fine, but she was running by the time she found me. She was actually quite distraught." Anders nodded his acceptance, and Toddy scrubbed at his face with an open palm in frustration.

"But she is alright?" Toddy asked, no longer thinking of Vera.

"She's well, ten fingers, all of her fins and scales. She called you Old Winken." Toddy nodded and then grimaced at his son's smirk. Making the clear choice to ignore the shift in moniker, he asked,

"Did she say where she was this time?"

"The Sunken City, lost in the catacombs."

"The Sunken..." Toddy groaned. "That is just too far-fetched."

Anders stretched and turned his head to look at his father,

"No, I don't think that it is..." his tone mild and contemplative, Anders waited for his father to get himself settled. Laying side by side with Toddy, Anders finally began to speak and, for the second time that evening, the story whispered across the waves; resonating from the stillness of the little dock that lay on the leeward beach of a countryside shaped by humans, and was heard and listened to by ears that wished for greater understanding.

CHAPTER 11

It was not uncommon for ships to travel up and down the coast; some would stop at the port for the sailors to buy supplies and drink in the tavern. The town had grown in wealth and population in Anders' lifetime alone, the edges of the town proper expanding as it became a more desirable place to put down roots and benefit from the profits of the port and the market square. Where his father had boasted of the ability to learn three languages from the fishermen at the dock, most of the words he might have learned would probably have made his mother blush. As the town expanded, Anders now heard those languages, and at least a few more, spoken by traders and sailors as he moved through the marketplace to run errands for his Mama and Grandmama. The pidgin dialect that had spread among sailors shipping up and down the coast, taking on new deck hands along the way, had begun to migrate into the market square to better facilitate business. Living, as they did, a short way from town, Anders watched and listened, noting the liveliness of the square and how, the further one walked, the less people mixed, and once one left town altogether, it was almost like passing from a bubble of exchange and growth into a sea of relative uniformity.

Anders ruminated on this with his old friend BrightClaw, who was a keen observer of the humans in his territory.

"The arrival of the Sea Travelers is a good thing," BrightClaw told him decisively. "The stories of my flock are not always the stories of another; if we share the story, it can grow, and new stories can be learned. If the hunter kills my flock, then my stories will live on in the flock of another, so my flock will never truly die."

No, it was not uncommon at all for ships to travel up and down the coast. What was uncommon was for whole families to step off of the foreign ships with the intention of staying. Anders heard the whispered gossip as he strolled through town, his face and hands still moist from a quick washing at the water pump, while much of the rest of his skin and clothes remained encrusted in sawdust and sweat. There was a large vessel at port, and a large number of crates had been offloaded along with a family who had taken up temporary residence at the tavern, with the clear intention of staying in town.

Anders could admit to a degree of curiosity. The area had not become so populated that a new addition from another land was without intrigue, so he adjusted his trajectory to meander further towards the dock. It gave him the chance to walk home along the shore, he rationalized, and that was always a pleasure.

The ship was no longer at the dock when Anders arrived, but he could see it at anchor a distance out from shore, twin masts swaying with the rocking of the waves. The bowsprit, a familiar buxom shape, diving forward from the hull as though it would split the waves for the ship's passing. He shook his head at the representation as he stood indecisively, to the tavern for a drink and possibly indulge his curiosity? A walk down the dock for a closer look at the ship that had drawn so many eyes? Or the solitary walk along the beach that would remind him that he had not seen a hint of his own mermaid friend in two long years? He was broken from his train of thought by a stream of incomprehensible syllables in what was possibly the most angrily musical voice he had ever heard in his life and the familiar response of the cackling of crows.

Moving was possibly the worst thing in the world. It was exciting, and to be sure, Baba was definitely focusing on the excitement part; but packing up all of one's earthly belongings to get in a boat and venture to a place where no one spoke your language was not Denila's idea of excitement. Thankfully, her stomach did not disagree with the boat as much as her brother's; by the third day afloat, he had sworn to never again set foot on a seafaring vessel. Ultimately, she too was hardly in good spirits when they finally reached their destination. They unloaded into a small port town where Baba's trading partner sold tea. Indeed, they would be moving from their small town to another small town, all because Baba thought he could set up a permanent business. The people had all stared at them when they came off the boat, stared at her, and continued to do so throughout the day. She lost count of how many times she checked her reflection in glass or water, searching for the cause of their continued attentions. She settled her scarf over her head and shoulders, protecting against the growing chill in the air as she ran outside in search of a satchel her brother had misplaced. It was most likely up in their rooms somewhere, but after weeks of close proximity with her family and an abundance of unwashed strangers, any small excuse for a moment to herself was a chance she would not hesitate to take. It would have been enjoyable, too, if it were not for the sudden gust of wind that ripped her scarf from her shoulders and the crow who felt the need to assist it in carrying the fabric away.

"Ay! Ay! Bring that back!" she yelled. She probably looked like a crazy person. The crow had retreated with her scarf to perch on an aging statue of a person spearing a giant fish. She probably looked like she was yelling at inanimate objects now, more reason for people to stare.

"Ay! You dumb bird! Drop it!"

The bird cawed and clacked its beak in her direction. No, maybe not her direction, three more crows on the roof behind her seemed to respond. She let out a huff of annoyance. This was not what she needed right now.

"Ay! Give me back my scarf!" She was about ready to go looking for something to throw to scare the rascal away when she saw, out of the corner of her eye, a man approaching from the direction of the dock. She was both too annoyed and too tired to care that her hair was uncovered; most of the women she had seen near the docks left it bare and tied back anyway. Not that the traditions of another should have any bearing on her own. She was more concerned that she not make a poor first impression with the people of this town where she would apparently be living, for a while anyway, and yelling at statues was not the best first impression. As the man approached, she became even more agitated because he just had to be a handsome stranger as well, didn't he? A head taller than her with a smattering of freckles across his nose and cheeks, he wore his rich brown hair pulled back from his face and dark blue eyes, so different from her own duskier features. She searched her brain for words in the pidgin language she had done her best to pick up along the way.

"The.. Bird.. Has taking my clothes!" she blurted out in frustration, looking from the man to the crow and back again. The man's lips curled in what she supposed you could call a small smile, and, to her utter surprise, he addressed not her but the bird. She listened to his words, trying to pick out anything familiar, confusion knitting her brow as the crow not only seemed to listen to the man but fluttered its feathers, cawed, and clacked its beak as though it were responding in truth. The man said a few more words, and the crow huffed and launched itself from the statue. Denila cried out in dismay, thinking that her scarf was to be well and truly lost, before watching the crow release its claws, allowing the fabric to flutter down before being snatched from the air by a pair of large, calloused hands.

"Your scarf," the warm, low voice said, this time in pidgin as well. She took the fabric, watching it slither from between his fingers before looking up at his deep blue eyes.

"What in the Heavens are you?" she asked, too confused to bother with translations. The man shrugged, once again wearing the small smile that lurked around the edges of his mouth. She stood there as he bowed his head respectfully, as he wished her a good night, as he turned, and as he walked off towards the beach. She stood in the street and felt she was a little more scared of this place where they had found themselves, and yet somehow a little more hopeful as well. A crow cawed from the roof of the tavern, catching her attention and breaking whatever spell that man had cast. She quickly draped her scarf over her head and shoulders, wrapping it a little more tightly to secure it around her neck, stuck her tongue out at the crows that were gathered on the rooftop, and hurried back into the tavern. With barely a moment of hesitation, she bustled away from the cool evening breezes and into the heat and humidity of too many bodies, too many open flames, and not enough windows.

Anders smiled to himself as he walked along the shore, stopping only momentarily to remove his shoes and socks so he could walk barefoot by the water's edge and feel the cool waves lap between his toes. He stared out across the water intently, but he was hardly surprised when he felt the sudden flapping of wings by his head or the weight and pressure of claws as BrightClaw landed on his shoulder.

"You are causing trouble, my old friend," he commented with an amused sigh.

"I was feeling playful, and the winds had already had their fun." Brightclaw plucked at Anders' braid with his beak.

"That may well be, but I don't think the young lady will thank you for it."

"I like her."

"Oh?"

"Yes, she did not shriek like the other *young ladies*; she yelled at me like the baker's wife when I play with her washing. She was not scared or thinking of omens. She stuck her tongue out at Short Tail after you left."

Anders stifled a laugh, but the crow squawked at him in annoyance nonetheless as Anders' shoulders shook with mirth at the crow's description. It was practically a glowing recommendation from his dear friend, and he found himself replaying the scene in his mind. It seemed likely that the woman was part of the family that had moved to town; it was not often that they saw women on the passing ships due to some peculiar bit of superstition that prevailed among sailors. He was hardly a man prone to rash decisions or emotionally charged responses, so it was over the length of the stroll home and the following day that he slowly found himself resolving to get to know more about the young woman who sassed crows.

Countless times during the next several days, Anders found his mind drifting back to his encounter with the young woman staying at the tavern. He thought about the musical tone of her voice and the way she tried to hide her smile when he returned her scarf. While Anders went to work with his Papa, assisted his

Mama and Grandmama, and tried to keep his sanity around his sisters, BrightClaw was up to his own business. Whenever Denila left the tavern, she found herself in the company of crows, some who made mischief, stealing her laundry and knocking over small containers, and some who brought gifts of flowers and shiny objects. The crows rarely got close, but it was clear that she was the object of whatever game they were playing, and she didn't know whether to be charmed or supremely annoyed. She had seen the towns folk's mixed reactions to the dark feathered tricksters, and there was only one person in town who she had seen charm the birds. While she was thankful for his help with retrieving her scarf, whatever warm feelings she might harbor hardly extended to being bothered by birds on a daily basis. When her patience had finally come to an end, she set out to figure out who the man was. The task was made more difficult by issues of communication and an aversion to involving her Baba or brother, but made significantly easier by the common nature of small towns and the man in question being notably strange, even among unfamiliar people. Eventually, she found a pidgin-speaking farmer who she asked about a "strange tall man, with brown hair and little face spots." She found herself acting out his serious face and upright posture, and before she could even finish her practiced statement, the farmer began to laugh.

"Anders."

"Anders? You know this?"

"There are four very strange men in this town; one is an old, mad sailor." The farmer slumped his shoulders and dropped his head to the side, acting out being drunk.

"One is a beggar who thinks he is not himself," he acted out a squat character raising his arms to the sky.

"One is Anders, and the other is his father, Toddy." Acting out Anders, the farmer stood upright and still, and for his father, he slouched a bit with a big smile.

"You look for Anders."

"Many thanks! Where?" The man pointed his chin toward the edge of town.

"Wood Shop."

She thanked him again and turned to go.

"Miss! You seem like a nice girl," The man spoke in a combination of pidgin and his own language, obviously the topic moved outside his grasp of the vocabulary, "Anders may be an attractive man, but he is very strange, and his family is strange also. A nice girl like you should find a good solid man, not that crazy family."

Body language said more than the words conveyed in their combination of quasi-familiar and completely foreign tongues. She nodded and thanked him again, backing in the direction he'd directed. Little did the farmer know that she was going there with a smattering of accusations, a pocket full of questions, and no certainty that she would understand any of his responses.

The way to the tradesmen's quarter was quite clear, easily located by the trail of smoke from the smithy drifting up to the clouds. When the street opened up to a large clearing, Denila paused and scanned its border from right to left. The smithy and a couple of other rough-hewn buildings filled the air with smoke and noise. Across from where she stood was a town well, a sturdy-looking log pole fence, and a gnarled old tree. To the left, at the furthest point from the heat and fires of the forge, providing ample distance between the controlled fires and an abundance of wood, stood a large barn house. It was to this structure that she followed the smell of sawdust, along with the sounds of saws and scraping, and the voices of men raised in conversation. It seemed that she was definitely in the right place. Denila peered around the jamb of the open shop door and saw five men of various ages at work, an adolescent retrieving tools from an impressive display along the far wall, and a young man washing his hands and face in a bucket of water in the corner. An older man with a gentle smile turned almost immediately and caught her spying. Not yet ready to be noticed and struck with a sudden sense of discomfort, she adjusted her scarf about her head and shoulders in an attempt to distract from the reddening of her cheeks. It was her annoyance that had brought her this far, carried her feet on a series of sharply irritated footsteps. Of course, now she faced an actual person, one who was not responsible for her current state, and she worried her emotions might not carry her through to her goal.

"Anders, please?" she asked the man, who looked momentarily perplexed before his smile crept even wider, and he turned to point her in the direction of the furthest workbench, where the man himself sat running a planing tool over a post.

"Anders!" Toddy had long mastered the ability to pitch his voice to carry over the noise, across the length of the large room without having to yell.

"Yeah, Papa?" he responded without looking up, not wanting to disrupt the smoothness of the grain.

"You have a rather charming visitor." Anders' head shot up at that. He never had visitors at the shop, charming or otherwise, unless you counted Vera acting as a runner for his mother or grandmother. The time was long passed that his sister, too shy to brave the wood shop, had waited uncomfortably by the door for the attention of her father or brother; now she was just as likely to tap him on the shoulder or put herself in arguably dangerous proximity to tools in motion to get his attention. He ran his finger over the surface of the wood, satisfied with the smoothness he'd coaxed from the beam, before glancing toward the door and freezing. The young woman who had occupied so much of his mind of late stood with an air of uncertainty at the shop door. He nodded to his father absentmindedly, confusion furrowing his brow, and wended his way to the shop door.

"Good day, miss?"

"*Salouto*." She nodded her head in the direction of the courtyard. His father tried to control his smile, something he had never excelled at, and Anders rolled his eyes at the incorrigible man before following the retreating back of the woman outside. He noted that she, once again, wore the scarf over her hair and that he could see easily over the top of her head to where a small group of crows found their perch in a nearby tree. He slowed, watching the sway of her hips as she walked and the way she seemed to be holding tension in her body as she dug about in her beautifully embroidered pocket. He was contemplating how much his Mama would probably appreciate the handiwork when she spun on him, taking him by surprise, holding out a handful of tiny trinkets and small flowers.

"You do this?" she asked, glaring at him with a look so similar to the one she had leveled at BrightClaw that he found himself rather more amused than threatened.

"Do what?"

She stomped her foot at him in frustration, holding the handful of small objects even closer to his face. He stared at her, completely without comprehension. She sighed, and it was an extremely expressive sound, managing to convey extreme annoyance with the situation, frustration with herself, and disappointment with him all in one breath. It shouldn't have been impressive, but it was. The woman began to speak in a combination of her lyrical tongue and pidgin, which only allowed Anders to understand about one in five words. Unlike the evening in town, she was speaking quickly and without thought to being understood. What Anders did understand was that this was venting, and while he was sure she found it important, it was largely incomprehensible. Luckily for them both, her hands and face were quite expressive as she punctuated in pantomime her verbal explanation. When she finally paused for a breath, he tried to translate back to her in his more fluent pidgin, supplemented with his own language. All the while he fought the impulse to look over his shoulder and see if Papa was witnessing this encounter, certain that the man would be shaking with repressed laughter.

"The crows, birds, have been following you?" She responded with a single, sharp nod, and he continued.

"They have bothered you and your things?" Another nod.

"And they brought you these things as gifts?" she nodded emphatically, this time raising her hand full of crow treasure again. The tree erupted in cawing and clacking beaks as the crows added their two cents, unsurprisingly backing up her story. The young woman jumped, apparently previously unaware of their presence, and gestured toward them as though it were proof of his involvement.

"You think I made them do these things?"

She nodded emphatically.

Anders shook his head, wishing that his friends would try to make his life easier rather than adding to the confusion.

"No, they like you." Her eyes widened in disbelief, even as he found himself wondering if he would believe himself either, were he in her position.

"They like me." Did this man think she was an idiot? Did he think that she would believe that the crows had decided to bother her on their own after seeing him talking to them?

"You talk to birds, you make birds do thing."

She watched him take a deep breath as though trying to gather his thoughts.

"I talk to birds. Crows. Crows are my friends. I don't make them do anything."

This man was so horribly frustrating. Crows for friends? He had probably fed them and trained them in the manner of pigeons and falcons. This was not friendship, this was either profound loneliness or madness, sometimes the two were not so far removed. If that was what he meant by friends, then she really should have listened to the farmer and left this Anders person alone. He did not seem lonely, and while she had come to no verdict on madness, he was certainly not some far gone character yelling in the streets. There was always a third and very likely option; that she had misunderstood. Choosing to believe the latter, she grabbed at her scarf, knocking it off of her hair in the process, and shook it in his direction. It was the very same scarf that he had coaxed from one of those trained crows. The scarf was all the proof she needed that he could tell them what to do. He stared at her with an infuriatingly blank expression, and if he had nothing to say to her, then she certainly wasn't going to stand around to listen. With a noise of disgust, she turned and sped out of the courtyard, making sure she was out of sight before she stopped to take a calming breath and fix her scarf.

Anders stood and watched the woman leave, caught somewhere between annoyance and bemusement. It was apparent that she didn't believe anything he said, and he couldn't entirely blame her, but the disbelief chaffed, and the accusation was irritating. That being said, he didn't think he had ever found a woman so charming, particularly while evidently finding so much fault with him. Once the woman was out of sight, he turned to address the crows in the tree.

"You all seem quite proud of yourselves." He shook his head to show his obvious disappointment. "Please find BrightClaw for me when you get the chance."

Returning to the wood shop, he was greeted by the teasing voices of all of the older, married men he worked with. Men who very clearly challenged the idea that age and experience yielded maturity. His Papa, probably the least mature among them, had shamelessly been spying on the encounter, and his eyes positively twinkled with mirth.

"Whatever it is you have to say, I don't want to hear it," Anders grumbled, the bemused expression on his father's face inciting the same foul temper in him it had for as long as he could remember. In classic Todrick Windle style, the man practically giggled in response.

"Mira will be thrilled."

"What's that?"

"It looks as though someone has rumpled your feathers, my son. It's not often someone manages to do that."

Anders sighed and attempted to rub the tension from between his brows. This was directly thwarted by the continuation of Toddy's assessment of the situation.

"Your mother will be thrilled, she's certainly ready to welcome a daughter-in-law to the family."

Anders scoffed, not bothering to grace his father's nonsense with a response, and attempted to put as much distance between himself and the man as possible. While he might be set on keeping the encounter to himself, it seemed he was alone in that decision. The older men's laughter rang through the wood shop as Toddy relayed a dramatic rendition of the interaction as viewed and interpreted from afar. The sound followed Anders back to his workbench, where he did his best to ignore their amusement and focus on the task at hand.

When Anders left work that evening, a shadow swooped from the rooftop and landed on his shoulder.

"You have been causing trouble, my friend," he gently stroked the feathers on BrightClaw's head.

"Trouble with the lady?" the crow nudged the side of his face.

"Yes, she thinks I sent you to bother her." The crow cackled his mirth at the thought.

"I like her, she's amusing."

"I gathered," Anders responded, patently unamused.

"You like her too." The bird was too observant by half. Of course, if *he* knew that, there was also a decent chance that his too observant mother and possibly even one of his sisters had noticed his distraction. Now Papa was going to go home and tell Mama about the *woman*. He still didn't know her name, a fact that was starting to bother him, and once Mama found out about her, he would never hear the end of it.

"That may be so, but making her angry doesn't help."

"It brought her to talk to you. That helps." The bird shrugged, obviously content with his part in the events of the day.

"She doesn't believe we are friends."

"Then show her." BrightClaw, tired of riding on his shoulder, launched himself into the air and flapped off to find his roost.

The next morning, as Denila walked to the storefront where her Baba and brother were preparing to open up shop, a crow swept past her, almost close enough to brush her cheek with its wingtip. Her eyes tracked it to where it landed by the town dock, and there she saw Anders. She rolled her eyes and did her best to ignore him as she continued on her way, catching glimpses of the pair out of the corner of her eye. If she didn't know any better, she would believe that the man and the crow were engaged in conversation; he didn't offer the bird anything, didn't cover its head or hold it. It was peculiar, but it was no matter; she had never seen him by the dock in the morning before. He was definitely trying to prove something, and that couldn't be trusted.

A crow brought her a flower when she left the shop to take a meal. Later that day, she saw him again, sitting by the fountain in the market square. A crow landed beside him and pecked at his fingers. She thought she saw a shadow of a smile on his face, it wasn't the worst thing she had seen all day. Over the next few weeks, she saw Anders again and again, and she saw no evidence that the man was training the birds; they just seemed, for lack of a better word, friendly. At no point did he approach her or try to make a point, a fact that was starting to bother her a little bit. If he cared enough to let her see this strange interaction, why didn't he care enough to make sure she understood or to clarify his intentions? Part of her wondered if she had simply pricked at his pride, not the most attractive of possibilities. However, having seen his interactions with the rest of the town, it was clear that while he cared for people, he didn't care very much about what they thought of him - which would make her an exception. She found that she liked the thought more than she would have believed a few short weeks ago.

One evening, after a day of minding the shop as it slowly came together and another delivery of small white flowers from the man's feathered *friends*, she spotted him sitting on the edge of the dock and couldn't take the silence any longer.

"What are you doing here?"

"Sitting, enjoying the sunset."

"No. What are you doing *here*?"

"There is a path just there. If I walk down the beach, I will find another path that takes me home. It is also a convenient place to watch the sunset."

She rolled her eyes, the man was being intentionally obtuse.

"You were not here before we talk. Now you are here again and again and again."

"Ah, I see."

"You and your... friends?"

He smiled at her, a proper smile this time, and her breath caught in her throat. It was an inconveniently nice smile, one that he deliberately kept under wraps.

"You believe me now."

"You care if I believe?" She arched an eyebrow at him in response.

"I find I do."

"Why?"

"Because I find myself quite interested in you, Miss Denila Aydin." She smiled; hearing her name rolling off his tongue was lovely. She saw her brother walking towards the tavern, having hung up his work belt for the day. With a little more work, they would be moving in above the shop. Happily, it would seem, they would be ready for that to happen shortly. No more tavern food, no more drunk and sweaty tavern goers, no more hanging her laundry outside her window to be easy game for the crows. She shot the crow nearby a suspicious look.

"They like me?"

"Yes, my friends approve of my interest."

It wasn't what she had been trying to ask, but she found herself satisfied with the answer nonetheless. The conversation was certainly not under her control and had already given her more to think about rather than putting her previous thoughts to rest. Nodding a quick goodbye before he could say anything else of note, she hurried to join her brother, leaving the man on the dock without a backwards glance. She heard the crows cackling and got the distinct impression that they were laughing at her obvious retreat.

CHAPTER 12

The door opened, ringing the small bell above the entrance, and a pair of women walked into the shop. Denila had seen one of the women about the town on market days, she looked to be in her forties with auburn hair, streaked with gray and white, and intense dark gray eyes; she supported an older, white haired woman who Denila had never before seen in town. Both women had the marks of smiles and good humor carved deeply into their faces, a sign that made both Denila and her brother Balian immediately more relaxed.

"This is the one?" The older woman asked the younger, in a voice that was almost certainly meant to be a whisper.

"I believe so; Toddy said so." The younger woman responded with a quiet smile that seemed vaguely familiar.

The older woman made a rude noise, an obvious commentary on the aforementioned person's powers of observation.

"Good day to you both!" Balian greeted them, very proud of his growing grasp of the local language.

"How may we be of service?"

They exchanged a look.

"My name is Mrs. Mira Windle, and this is my mother-in-law, Mrs. Audry Windle. We meant to stop by as a courtesy but also to see the extent of your wares."

The siblings blinked in confusion, and Denila momentarily felt that the name ought to mean something before their Baba burst through from the storage room, momentarily overwhelming them all with an excited garble of pidgin and the local language.

"The Mistresses Windle! I have heard of your good works, thank you for coming to my humble shop. These are my children, Denila and Balian, and I am Mister Duman Aydin, purveyor of teas and imported goods." He gestured widely to the store, which was not so grand as he made it sound, being that it was not one of the grand palaces of the southern deserts and still very much under construction.

"Denila, Balian, these lovely ladies are the local medicine women. Herbalists! We carry many medicinal teas, I am sure, though we are focused more on bringing the soothing flavors of our home up the coast. If there is anything we can import on your behalf, we would be happy to be of service."

The women seemed surprised by his exuberance but eventually relaxed into a state that seemed to be more composed of amusement than anything else. A sentiment that was probably for the best.

"We would love to be introduced to any plants we find unfamiliar to the region, it is always a good thing to expand one's knowledge." The younger woman, Mira, was all graciousness.

"My Toddy used to bring me plants from a medicine woman who brought them from abroad. Some of them grew beautifully in our garden, and some," she shook her hand from side to side, eventually letting it flop lifelessly. While Denila had a little trouble following the conversation, she did comprehend the gist.

While she found the overall interaction quite diverting, she could hardly ignore that the women kept casting covert glances in her direction, which was beginning to make her a bit uncomfortable.

"This is a lovely shop you have, Mister Aydin. Are you doing all of the work yourself?" Mistress Audry gestured to the shelving that had been going up little by little and the empty area of the shop that would one day have a table and chairs.

"Sadly, yes. Balian and myself have been devoting all of the time and effort that we can, we are new to town and just getting ourselves established."

The women exchanged another look

"Oh, my husband is a carpenter. I'm sure he would be happy to help you get set up. After all, a multitude of hands will ease the load of work."

"That is very kind of you, mistress, but I feel I must ask what I might do for you in return." Her Baba certainly did not like to feel himself in debt, regardless of how good-natured the source.

"We would like to be good neighbors to a family who it seems may be so closely related to our own." Denila saw Audry suppress a smirk at her daughter-in-law's phrasing and found herself suddenly more suspicious of the entire interaction. Before anyone could ask for clarity, the woman continued,

"Additionally, we might do some work in trade. Your products in our remedies, our remedies on your counter, this might be good business for both of us."

This offer helped to ease her suspicions, but Denila couldn't help but feel that there was something else going on here.

"Mira, love, go talk to Toddy and get some help for these lovely people." Audry shoved her daughter-in-law toward the door and found herself a crate to make herself comfortable before proceeding to engage Baba in a conversation on herbalism and plants for trade.

When Mira returned, it was with a smile and the news that the menfolk would be arriving shortly. Denila thought little of this, having seen several men at the wood shop. She momentarily wondered if Anders would be one of the "menfolk" but quickly redirected her thoughts to organizing containers and shelving materials. When the bell rang again, she was in the storage room. She heard the low voices of two soft-spoken men and the excitable tones of her father describing his vision for the shop. He paused, and a calm, soothing voice that sent chills up her spine asked him a question. She found herself drifting towards the main area of the shop. It was not long before it seemed that she was close enough to be seen, a fact made apparent when Mrs. Mira Windle called her in to greet her husband, the carpenter with the kind smile, and Anders. Her Son.

Toddy still remembered the day that his Mama and Mira's Aunt Jinny conspired to spring his engagement on him. The day he realized he was very much in love, the day that he found out that Mira loved him, was one of the strangest and most important days of his life. His son, serious young man that he was, had shown some of the same signs of distraction his Mama had pointed out about himself at the time, and when the young woman showed up to his shop, it had all become clear. He had never believed that Anders was going to find some proper, reserved little woman who would mirror or encourage his upright and serious demeanor. Just like Mira balanced and complemented his peculiarities, Anders would need someone who could do the same for him. When the woman so easily rumpled Anders' proverbial feathers, and it resulted in quiet fascination rather than ill will, he was almost certain that Mira would agree with his assessment. Returning home that night, he had felt like a child with a secret that wanted to be spoken, and it took significant self-control to wait until he and Mira had retired to their room for the night to reveal his thoughts on the subject. His sweet Mira was skeptical - but kind about it - and certainly piqued with curiosity. Unsurprisingly, it was only a matter of days before his wife and his mother decided that they wanted to go meet the young lady and form their own opinions. Overhearing their plans, Toddy looked back on that day with his mother and Mira and found that he wished very much to play a part in this potential ambush. Understanding, as always, Mira had patted him on the shoulder and told him that if they could figure out a way to make it happen, both he and Anders would find their way to the shop.

He was well aware that he did not excel at keeping confidences, as a result, he was quite sure that he spent the entire day being noticeably amused by his own state of anticipation. He could only hope that, since he was often amused by one thing or another, his behavior would not be so marked that anyone would know the difference.

When Mira finally arrived at the shop he folded her in a prolonged embrace; in part because, after twenty-three years, she was still as beautiful to him as the day they were married; in part to hide the smile that he could no longer keep from his face, as he relished the thought of being included in an event that would no doubt ruffle their son's feathers and hopefully result in bringing him great joy.

He tapped Anders on the shoulder and told him that his Mama had a job for them to do. They collected some measuring tools, a roll of paper, and some writing utensils. On the way over, Anders asked some questions about the job, but with the exception of putting together some furniture, the rest of the details were essentially unknown. Having clarified the dearth of information, Anders was characteristically quiet, smiling indulgently at the crows that passed overhead. Toddy, listening in on their commentary, had been amused to find that they had been leaving flowers for the girl in question for days; he mentally clapped himself on the shoulder in congratulations. Their involvement was clearly another vote in the young woman's favor.

When they approached the store, he felt his son's steps slowing. He hazarded a glance over his shoulder to see Anders flash him a suspicious look. Toddy restrained his smile just long enough to shrug and turn back toward the door. Upon entering, it appeared that the young woman in question was not in residence, which took a bit of the wind out of his sails. Instead, he was faced with an exuberant man of about his own age, tan of skin, dark of hair, and wild with his gesticulations. It was clear that he intended for his shop to be his palace, and it was very difficult for Toddy to resist the draw of the man's inspired enthusiasm.

"Denila, dear, is that you back there?" He heard his darling wife sing out, "Come join us, perhaps you have some ideas for the shop."

In a matter of moments, there she was, the lady of the hour. Toddy repositioned himself strategically so that he could continue his conversation with Mister Aydin while keeping an eye on both the woman and his son, finding Anders characteristically unreadable. His eyes kept darting to the young lady, her eyes kept darting to Anders. Both suppressed looks of irritation with their parents as the conversation carried on around them. The woman's father once again circled around to express the need to repay their kindness. How could he possibly respond to their offering of help in readying the store for business? It was at this point that Mira opted to enlist Mister Aydin in their scheme, directing a pointed look from her son to his daughter. Mister Aydin followed the movement, seeming momentarily concerned, his eyes flicking back and forth between their standoffish children. It wasn't long before he caught one of the many furtive glances the two young people cast each other's way. With dawning understanding, a huge smile spread across his face, and suddenly, they were no longer arguing about repayment. Now they were planning for all of the time that would be needed in the shop to make it just as grand as he envisioned inasmuch as the limited space allowed. His very own palace, brought from his homeland to theirs. Toddy smirked as he caught Denila rolling her eyes at the extravagance before she grabbed her father's arm and started scolding him in their own, fast-paced language.

Over the following weeks, just as their parents had conspired, Denila and Anders were thrown together repeatedly by the work necessary to open the shop. To be sure, both families were so much in one another's company that the day that Toddy arrived with a finishing touch, the edge of the counter top lovingly engraved with the images of many of the herbs on offer in the Aydin's tea shop - a project that he had worked on in secret for weeks, Duman and Toddy embraced like brothers with tears in their eyes and matching smiles on their faces.

When Anders and Denila married, it came as no surprise; though their courtship was hardly conventional, being made up of thousands of glances, touches, and smiles over furniture and finishings in various stages of construction. Their vows were exchanged, as was proper, at the Temple of the Sun before Denila moved her worldly possessions into the strange house down the coast. A house that held the Sun God's image in all of the proper places but seemed to bow far more heavily to something that most of the villagers could no longer name.

When Denila unpacked her bags, she brought out a small shrine, the likes of which no one in the house had ever seen, its doors engraved roughly with the phases of the moon, flowing water, and fertile earth. It held within it a simple statue of the Moon Goddess, as worshiped quietly by the women of her country. Wife to the Sun God and mother of man; the couple repeated the vows in her presence, with her father and brother quietly in attendance and the warm acceptance of her new family who listened with curiosity to the stories of her childhood, and would not ask her to give up the worship of her Goddess.

CHAPTER 13

A pair of fine shoes sat at the beginning of the dock, just beyond where the sand and wind might swallow them whole on a gusty day. They were placed there side by side, neatly aligned perpendicular to the boards that made up the surface of the aging structure. A pair of stockings peeked coyly from the top of the right shoe and waved with the passing breeze. At the end of the dock, a young girl sat in her Sun's-day best, sans shoes and stockings, with her feet dangling freely off the edge. The light colored dress had certainly seen better days, and the girl picked absentmindedly at the threading as she quietly sat, taking comfort from the sounds of the waves lapping against the wood structure and the birds crying off in the distance. A seabird eventually landed near her but, upon inspection, and seeing that she was not going to be bothersome, he left her alone while he settled into his nest to preen. He was used to her quiet visits, this was one of Melody's favorite places to sit and escape from the rest of the world. This place was private but also so very full, bearing the echoes of her family's stories. It was a good place to sit when one was frustrated as well; the dock was respected in her family, even her rambunctious little brothers calmed down at the dock. She wasn't supposed to be here today; she was supposed to be at the Temple with the rest of her family, but there had been a *disturbance*. Being the center of the disturbance, Baba had opted to bring her home early. She sighed heavily, wishing that her Mami hadn't looked so disappointed when Baba swept her out the door. Disappointment was somehow far worse than a lecture or a swift smack to the head or behind; at least then, it felt like she was worth the effort of trying to correct the behavior.

Spray from a stronger wave sprinkled her toes, shocking her out of her thoughts. The wind must be picking up; she would probably have to go in soon if that was the case. Her shawl was back at home. The spray caught her foot again, this time followed by a feeling that made her shriek in alarm, upsetting the nearby seabird: the feeling of cool, wet fingers closing on her big toe. Melody kicked out and scrambled to her feet, prepared to bolt to the shore until she heard the sound of a girl's delighted laughter emanating from beneath the planks at her feet. It took her a moment, but in a rush of excitement, she realized who it must be. The excitement wanted to be paired with happiness; unfortunately, her bad mood refused to be entirely dismissed just because she might get to meet a mermaid.

"That was not funny!" she stomped hard on the dock. The stomping felt good, so she did it two or three more times for good measure before peeking over the edge of the dock to see if she was right.

"Greetings, Little Winken!"

"Oh my! Uhmm... Good day." She waved shyly before

approaching the now unhappy seabird.

"Wing-brother, would you please go get my Baba for me?"

The bird eyeballed the little girl, then peered down into the water at the mermaid,

"I know the old pact, scaly tail, I expect the reward." The mermaid nodded and waved dismissively to the grumpy old bird, who strutted to the end of the dock before taking to the air in a flurry of feathers.

"I don't think he needs more to eat," Melody observed

"Ah, but a deal is a deal, Little Winken."

Melody nodded, and the two sat in silence for a moment. Perhaps it was meant to be a companionable silence; she couldn't speak for the intentions of the mermaid, but for her part, she certainly didn't know what to say.

"You seemed upset, Little Winken."

"Well, yes. I am a bit upset. I am a bit upset and a bit frustrated, and there's not much at all to be done about it. So I came to sit here."

"I'm so glad you did!" The mermaid seemed genuinely enthusiastic about her company, grumpy though it may be.

"If you hadn't, I would have had to argue with that greedy guts to get him to find you and Winken, and he probably would have yelled a lot, like his grandam and hers before her. Noisy and ill-tempered, the lot of them. Which reminds me..." Nimmawni slipped back beneath the waves, and for a moment, Melody panicked, concerned that the mermaid would leave before they got the chance to talk and before Baba could make it to the shore. The hands that emerged from the water held three spiky urchins, which she struggled a little with getting onto the dock.

"Just make sure they don't go too far, will you?"

Melody nodded and let out a sigh of relief.

"So, Little Winken, it seems that we have a little time before Winken arrives. Why don't you tell me what bothered you so?"

Melody took a deep breath and collected her thoughts, gathering her long hair that was brown like her Baba's and curly like her Mami's. She twisted it behind her head and over her shoulder. It would be easy to let the words run away with themselves out of her mouth, but she felt the importance of presenting herself properly to the mermaid weighing on her chest. How does one address something that feels so big? Something that feels so wrong, but so many people seem to feel is right?

"Do you know about the Temple of the Sun?" She asked quietly.

The mermaid nodded.

"I have heard of it. The birds like to perch on the fancy buildings and look at all of the shiny decorations. They say those places are dedicated to something similar to The Light, but not so."

Melody stared at her hands as she twisted her fingers together - just to feel like she had something to do with them.

"Baba says that the Temple of the Sun is dedicated to a Sun God who is an idea several times removed from The Light, like the Light was his Great-Great-Great-Great-Grandad but as an idea instead of for real."

The Seabird landed heavily beside her and snapped up the

first of the sea urchins, greedily tearing at it with beak and claw. Baba must be on his way, and he was probably still disappointed, too. She sighed heavily.

"We go to the Temple of the Sun every Sun's-Day to spend time with family. I don't mind some of the family, but before family time, we go to the temple for the ceremony and ritual. They tell stories, and I don't think anyone who has ever lived with Grandad or Baba could say that stories are unimportant."

Melody felt the dock begin to shake with heavy footfalls as her Baba approached.

"But the stories are *wrong*. They feel wrong to my insides, and I know some of them because The People tell them, but when The People tell them it's different."

Anders sat down quietly next to his daughter, listening with his characteristic quiet patience.

"They stuck together The Shadow and Pan'chan and took away what is healing, comforting, and generous; they made a villain, an 'adversary' for the Sun God. Instead of learning-stories and always-stories, they made those stories about bad endings and made his stories work against the Sun God. I couldn't just listen anymore, so I said something. I said something, and then everyone got mad and said mean things, and Mami looked so disappointed in me. I just... I don't understand..."

She wiped at her face and realized that her eyes had begun to leak down her cheeks some time during her explanation; the last thing she wanted to do was cry. Anders rubbed her back quietly, a silent support that neither scolded nor pushed. He was just there, like the ground beneath her feet or a sturdy oak tree, with the feeling that everything was eventually going to be okay.

Nimmawni leaned against the ladder on the end of the dock, contemplating the small girl and her father.

"I heard that most of the gods you humans worship stole their powers and their stories from The People's Gods, Gods who you all used to walk with as well."

Anders scoffed, not in disbelief but as if to express his annoyance with a group of imagined human ancestors and their willingness to twist the knowledge of The People.

"It would not surprise me in the least, dear friend. Many of the stories follow old familiar patterns for those of us who've grown up with The People's stories, but they have been shifted and changed and, more often than not, are viewed in retrospect. The stories are told as though long gone and, while dedicated to their remembrance, no longer the concerns of the present."

"That's what I said. They aren't *always* stories, Baba."

Anders snaked his arm around her and gave her a one armed hug, pressing his lips to the top of her head.

"I know, Darling Girl, but sometimes it is better to not call attention to one's differences."

She reached out to reverently touch the silver shell at his neck. Her other hand resting at the base of her own throat where her Grandad's coral rested, where it had rested since being restrung for her only a year before

"I don't understand not wanting to know. I listen to the stories of the bees and the deer, and the Rooted People in Gran's garden sing the most beautiful songs. All of them are alive, all of them are to be shared, all of them are now and before and *always.*"

Anders shook his head and looked to Nimmawni with pleading eyes.

"Your Grandad gave you his coral Little Winken." It was not a question, it was a simple statement of fact. The girl showed her the coral, now strung on a pretty cord with two wooden beads that her grandad had whittled just for her.

"Does your Grandad still hear The People?" It was asked like a question she already knew the answer to.

"Not so much, he says he hears them but it is from far away and he has to listen harder and through the sound of their voices as he remembers them as a child." Nimmawni nodded as though the answer made perfect sense.

"Do his siblings hear The People?"

"No, not at all. They were raised to respect The People, Gran says Grandma Audry would have it no other way, but they never heard The People."

"Do Winken's siblings hear The People?" Melody paused at this, giving it a moment of thought. This moment of consideration made the expression on her face so much the mirror of her father's that the mermaid cracked a smile.

"That's difficult to say. Sometimes I think Aunt Vera can; she has a way with the Rooted People, but she says Grandma Audry just taught her really well. Aunt Thea moved to a farm, and she takes care of the most beautiful horses and hounds, the healthiest and happiest you ever saw, but she never told me she could hear them. Aunt Bunny... Aunt Bella is difficult. None of them ever wore the necklaces, though."

Anders found himself lost in thought, he had noticed that his sisters each seemed to have a knack and a way about them, a hint of something older and more connected. As they were growing up, they were all so concerned with looking normal that he found it difficult to discern anything more.

"We are our stories Little Winken, our history and our understanding, our belief and our interactions with the world around us; these are shaped, informed, and passed on through our stories. When we learn of something new and amazing, we tell our story, and it becomes part of the collective memory that molds us into something new. Our stories tell us what is possible, and with every new door that is opened, the possible expands. When I met your Grandad, he *knew* without a doubt that I was impossible, that talking to 'Animals' was impossible. He almost lost your necklace before he could wear it around his neck, he was so very shocked by the impossibilities that were suddenly laid bare before him as possible."

It was a little difficult for Melody, or Anders for that matter, to imagine Toddy being anything other than the dreamer that accepted so readily the gift of understanding that had been given to him.

"If you think about it, it was rather brave of Old Winken to grab on to that piece of magic and let it change his world. Of course, he didn't just change his world, did he? He changed the world his family lived in, and then he changed the world that his babies lived in, and they all changed the world for you, Little Winken, because you have grown up with that many more stories of The People, and that much more possibility. Of course, your world is different from the humans who have only human stories to shape their reality. You are more a human of The People than I have met since I was a little guppy of a thing. Being of The People, you see the expanse of the world they live in: being human, you also have the advantage of knowing the stories of humans. So, maybe in being of one and knowing of the other, you have the great opportunity to speak and be heard by both?"

The girl shifted uncomfortably at that.

"Mami says I'm not allowed to talk to temple goers about their stories anymore."

Anders hid a laugh in his daughter's hair; knowing his fiery-tempered wife, it was more of a statement made in the heat of the moment rather than an actual rule. These were things to talk about later.

"Perhaps," he offered, "it would be better to wait until you understand better how to approach the subject? How to be heard by humans is not always the same as how to be heard by the bees."

Melody considered this, allowing that talking to her uncle and Aba was not always so easy as talking to Grandad and Aunt Vera. She sighed once again,

"This could be complicated."

"Many worthwhile things are." The mermaid smiled wider, showing the points of her teeth.

The three stayed in what was now a comfortable silence for a few minutes more before Anders turned to Nimmawni and asked her, as always suspicious of the potential response, where she had been for the last eleven years.

"I don't think it has been eleven cycles, Winken; that seems far too long." She looked at him with wide, far too innocent, eyes.

"My dear friend," Anders patiently replied, "it has been long enough for me to find and marry my wife - and for us to have a beautiful eight-year-old girl with two energetic little brothers."

"Oh, well, I suppose you would know then." The mermaid said so dismissively that Melody giggled at the response.

"I was searching for a Giant Ray, but not just any Giant Ray, the oldest of the Giant Winged Filter Feeding People to still travel the seas. You'd think she'd be easier to find, as big as she is, but rays are rather cagey on a good day, and they just keep on moving. I suppose I must have lost track of time."

"Did you find her?"

"Oh yes, eventually. I spoke to a young ray, who also didn't wish to tell me anything worthwhile. We spoke in riddles for days and days, long enough that I was forced to curl up and ride on his back so I could nap, until I finally had enough clues. She was circling a small island that was home to great swimming lizards that grow to the length of a human, playing among the sea vents. Even knowing where she was, she was not the easiest to find. As with many skills, I think she got good at being invisible with age."

Anders sighed, curious in spite of himself.

"Why did you need to see this particular giant manta ray?"

The mermaid blinked at him, clearly not understanding why he would ask such a question.

"Winken! The oldest manta ray in the whole of the Sea

Below! Can you imagine the stories?"

"Did she tell you a whole lot of stories?" Melody asked, clearly excited about the prospect.

"Like I said, rays are difficult on a good day."

"So, no stories at all?"

"I didn't say that. I tried talking to her but got very little response, and then I hid among the sea vents myself when I saw some younger rays join her. It is the task of our elders to pass on our stories to the young, and I listened as they danced and she transferred a portion of her great wealth of knowledge. We all tell our stories to the young; that is how we keep them from being forgotten."

Anders nodded his understanding, and Melody, thinking of her Baba and Mami and Grandad, and Gran, nodded enthusiastically as well.

"After one story, I tried to ask her some questions, but it seems that even she did not know the answers." Nimmawni paused in thought. "I do believe that that was the most straightforward answer I've ever gotten from a ray."

"What story did she tell?"

"How the All came to be, quite similar to the story told by the Great Migrating Sea Turtles. I believe that you will find that to be the case with many of The People. That being said, she told it beautifully."

The story that followed was familiar in nature, though the specifics led not to the birth of Long Tide and Deep Wave but rather the original rays, formed from the clay of creation by the hands of the gods whose purviews were the currents and the shifting sands. The three spoke for hours, and Melody found herself quite taken with the idea that, by combining very different things, something new and wonderful would be brought into the world; not unlike the stories of the sea turtles and rays.

CHAPTER 14

Over the course of the next few days, Melody was abnormally quiet. She was not sulking or angry, but she kept to herself and appeared to be deep in thought. She walked down by the waterfront, she disappeared into the woods, she wandered across the open fields, and she listened intently to all of The People she could. Not once did she speak unless spoken to.

Her mother, feeling guilty for her outburst at the temple, watched her eldest child with worry written plainly across her features. In the moments where she was tempted to confront the child about her odd behavior, Anders wrapped his arms around her shoulders and calmed her with his quiet presence. He had told her the very day of its occurrence about the meeting with Nimmawni, and though Denila had not seen the mermaid herself, she had heard all of the stories, and she had seen the mermaid's importance to her family. On the day of her wedding, her mother-in-law had passed on to her the beautiful hair pin that Denila's father-in-law had crafted in the likeness of the child of the sea. As she watched Melody pace the garden wall, she remembered the story of her husband building the crow's platform, breathed deeply, and wondered how Mira must have felt waking up to her world having shifted around her.

"It was strange and a little overwhelming," Mira said as she slipped her arm through Denila's with an understanding smile. "But I knew I was marrying into a strange family when I decided to set my cap for Toddy. I could hardly complain of further abnormalities when that very oddity was what brought me so much joy." Mira ran her fingers over the journal she had been writing in, writing the story of Melody meeting the mermaid. Denila couldn't help but smile at that; it was not long after she had become pregnant that Mira had shown her the collection of papers and journals that she kept, each one filled with the stories of The People that fell from the tongues of her husband and son. When Toddy had decided it was time to pass his necklace to Denila's beautiful girl, her stories had begun to fill the pages as well. Despite being located in a highly accessible place of honor, it seemed that Denila and Mira were the only ones to read from these precious volumes; it was as though the words were written and engraved deeply into the hearts and minds of all of the Windles who grew up in their presence. Some nights, when she could not sleep, Denila would slip quietly from Anders' loving embrace; she would light a candle and read the stories of her family, immersing herself in the world they inhabited before finally returning to her welcoming bed and the open arms of sleep.

It was on the fourth day that Melody walked into the kitchen and asked her Gran and Mami about the use of the far corner of the garden.

"May I plant something there? I think it will be beautiful."

Mira nodded and smiled, and Denila, uncertain, followed suit. They were rewarded with a giant smile and exuberant hugs before the tiny whirlwind of a girl disappeared to the shed in search of a trowel. They watched in wonder as the girl set to digging a hole deep enough to fit her arm to the elbow. She fished about in her pocket and revealed thirteen iridescent jingle shells, three seeds of different size and shape, a small bottle, and a folding knife. Seeing the knife, Denila found herself whispering an old prayer to the moon as she ventured out into the garden to offer assistance.

"No, Mami, I think I have it figured out." Melody smiled happily as she filled each of the shells with soil at the bottom of the hole in a rough spiral. She used the folding knife with care, scoring each of the seeds and placing them in the center shell as though they might merge into one. She unstopped the small bottle and poured its contents over the seeds before carefully layering the soil into the hole. As would happen on several occasions during her life, Denila was struck by the feeling that she had just witnessed something of reality-shifting import, and the fleeting thought crossed her mind that perhaps her prayer had been heard, and the Moon Goddess would smile on this moment.

Melody washed the soil from her hands with a deep sense of satisfaction, picking the dirt from beneath her nails and scrubbing with a bristle brush. She had stayed up all night after meeting Nimmawni. At first, she just lay in bed doing her best to make sense of the entire encounter, eventually sneaking out into Gran's garden to consult the fireflies. In the end, it had taken some time to tease out what she needed. Thirteen moons, seeds of the flower, the grain, and the tree, and the waters of the in-between time. She had scoured the shore for shells that looked like the full moon; found the seed of a creeping vine that bloomed with beautiful white flowers in the early summer; collected the seed of an old willow tree, hidden away in the forest; scavenged for oat seed at a local farmer's barn; and then stole away from the house in the early hours to collect the dew drops from as many broad leafed plants as she could find. Only time would tell if she had figured out the correct combination; eventually, they would see whether she had managed to plant a Moon Tree. Content with her work, Melody ran back to her Mami and Gran to give them both hugs and make a request for biscuits. Unraveling the puzzle had been hard work, and her stomach was making the cost of those efforts known.

Over days and months, Melody took care of her little corner of the garden, watering the soil and singing made up songs to the seeds. She swore that the fireflies liked her corner of the garden best, gravitating there in ever larger numbers; no one else was quite so certain until the plant broke through the final layer of earth. The tiny sprout emerged under the light of the full moon; its single leaf seemed to catch the moonlight, and the fireflies unmistakably danced around its glow.

The tiny plant thrived under Melody's care, always seeming

to flourish further under the light of the full moon. One leaf became three; the sprout became a seedling with long, thin leaves, not unlike the leaves of the oat, and thickening dark skin; the seedling grew into a sapling, branching and arching in preparation for its future cascade of leaves. No one had ever seen a tree quite like it. Mira commented more than once in hushed tones that she wished that Audry could have seen it. When the first flower bud emerged a full two years after the seeds were sown, they were all the more perplexed. A family of gardeners, medicine workers, and purveyors of exotic herbs and teas, and not a one could identify the developing flower. Under the following full moon, the garden seemed to explode with fireflies, and the air was full of music that lay just beyond the audible range, a song which all of the Windle family could feel down to their bones. As the moon glided across the heavens, it seemed to get caught in the tree's immature branches. Even as it continued along its course, that heavenly orb left an echo of its soft glow behind among the tree's hanging leaves, where it remained to reveal that the bud had opened. There, nestled among the oat leaves and willow branches, was a burst of white petals accompanied by an eruption of glorious song.

"It's a Moon Tree," Melody said with wonder. She had hoped and believed, but seeing it was something altogether different. She danced around the garden among the fireflies, and even though only she and her Baba, and maybe her Grandad too, could clearly hear the tree singing, she found herself dancing with her Mami and Gran and brothers as well.

In the morning, the beautiful flower had already begun to

wilt. Melody sat beside the Moon Tree, pressing her face to its bark as she sang to it the same loving songs that she always did, and the tree whispered to her a secret. With the tree's permission, she clipped the flower from its branch and brought it into the kitchen where Mami was heating water for tea. Melody grabbed a cup and poured the hot water over the single bloom, releasing a soothing aroma as she wandered through the house in search of her Grandad. She found him whittling in the front yard, his aging hands curled around knife and tree branch, leaning his elbows against his knees to relieve his aching back. She knew the swelling pained his hands as well as his knees, twisting his fingers and bowing his legs, but he loved the work too much to stop.

"Grandad," the ten-year-old offered the cup to the man who had given her what was possibly the greatest gift ever, "The Moon Tree says this will help you."

For all of the time passed and the aging of his body, Toddy was still fundamentally Toddy, and he had never lost his sense of wonder for the world around him and his family that continued to grow. He still had the same dreamer's smile that had once made his wife doubt his sanity, even if it was now tempered by pain. When he lifted his head from his work, he gave that very smile to his granddaughter as he set aside his tools to gently take the cup of tea. He lowered his nose over the edge of the cup, inhaling the sweet floral aroma. He sipped in silence for a moment or two before leaning in to kiss his granddaughter on her freckled cheek.

"Your Root friend is magnificent, little bird."

As he continued sipping the tea, some of the tension released from his shoulders. The deep lines on his face that traced the expression of his pain began to smooth, and he breathed a deep sigh of contentment.

The two sat, enjoying the warmth of the sunlight, and that is exactly where Gran found them some time later. She took one look at the relaxed expression on her husband's face, and her breath caught in her throat. She dropped to her knees before the pair to stare up into her husband's loving eyes, for once not laced with his perpetual wince of discomfort.

"How did you do this?" she grabbed Melody's hand with such ferocity that the knuckles of her fingers momentarily ground together.

"It was the Moon Tree Gran, my Root friend said to give Grandad an infusion of moon flower. Willow to ease the pain, Oat to soothe the nerves, Clematis to warm the blood and something special, extra, that only the Moon Tree can provide." She counted off the components of her Root friend's seed on her fingers, information that she had never before revealed. For a moment, the tears streaming down her Gran's face had made her worry, but when she saw how her grandparents smiled at each other, she felt as though she might overflow with happiness.

The next full moon, the tree once again seemed to catch the moon in its branches, this time producing two glowing flowers. In anticipation of their blooming, Aunt Vera was in attendance.

Having heard of the Moon Tree's wondrous properties, she wished to see it for herself, and it was that night that the question of whether she heard the Rooted People was finally answered. When the moon reached its apex and the opening of its flowers amplified the tree's magnificent song, Aunt Vera tilted back her head with tears streaming down her face in unadulterated joy. When asked what she regularly heard of the Rooted People, she admitted it was only a little bit and, still wiping tears from her face, that the experience of this tree was so much more than anything she had heard before. The following lunar cycle, it was three blossoms, and then four, and so on, as though the tree collected each additional moon to adorn its branches. The morning after each moon, they collected the wilting flowers, drying them with care to make Toddy's tea.

The tree thrived, and Melody grew along with it, singing it sweet, impromptu songs, reading under its branches, and learning stories of the Rooted People and the Tiny People who called them home. In the spring of the eighth year after it was planted, the Moon Tree whispered to her again. She grabbed her basket and her folding knife and carefully peeled small strips of bark from the tree's young branches, imitating the patterns of the deer in spring as Gran had shown her to do. Too much or too deep could damage her dear friend, but the tree had offered its healing once again, and she was determined to show her gratitude for its gift. She brought her basket to her Gran and Mami, who were preparing the white willow bark they had foraged in much the same way. It took them a moment to realize what it was before her Gran took Melody into her arms with tears in her eyes.

"Tell your Root Friend I said thank you."

Over the years, the toll of a full life and many years of hard labor had become more apparent and harder for Toddy to carry. His joints stiffened and swelled until he could barely walk and was consigned to his bed. No longer an active man, his heart began to flutter painfully, and it was only a matter of time before it was apparent that Toddy just needed help to manage the pain until he passed away, returning to the cycle, as we all must. The sweet bark of the Moon Tree, steeped to perfection, not only eased his discomfort but allowed him the luxury of uninterrupted sleep for the first time in months. When he woke, he thought and spoke more clearly. Though he was still easily prone to exhaustion, Mira valued every moment she got to spend with her husband, basking in the love and familiar smiles of her blue-eyed dreamer.

CHAPTER 15

The house was fairly quiet. Grandad was asleep, which was how he spent most of his time these days. Gran lay beside him in bed with an old, well-loved book and a stack of journals on the table beside her within easy reach so she could read him stories when he woke. Baba was in the shop teaching the boys how to not be absolute agents of chaos, and Mami had gone to market, leaving Melody, thankfully, alone. She had almost been pulled along for another trip to the town square under the pretense of lending a hand with Mami's shopping, though her true intentions were doubtlessly centered on the off chance that some handsome young man might catch Melody's eye. Unfortunately, she had long come to the conclusion that all of the attractive boys who frequented the market were prigs and scoundrels, and being of marrying age was unlikely to improve on that. Luckily for her, Mami was a believer in love matches; unluckily for her, Mami had met her own love match by *chance encounter* and saw no reason why a similar chance encounter would not do the same for her children. This supposition, therefore, required making herself available for chance encounters. Hoping to avoid further conversations on the topic when her Mami returned, Melody decided to make herself absent and take herself for a walk down to the beach. Defying convention, she left her shoes and stockings at home, unlikely to run into strangers along the path used primarily by her family. Even the beach south of town was less likely to put her in the path of anyone who would take issue with the impropriety. While sea bathing had become more popular in recent years, all of the brightly colored changing tents and umbrellas had been erected to the north side of the town. She caught the glint of a jingle shell out of the corner of her eye and bent to retrieve it. The ground around the base of the Moon Tree was littered with the shimmering disc-like shells, and she had every intention of continuing to add to the collection.

She walked halfway to town, absorbed in the feel of sand between her toes and collecting the shimmering jingle shells in her pocket. White, yellow, pink, and orange, they gently shifted against one another as she moved, earning their name and bringing the hint of a smile to her lips. As soon as she realized how far she had walked, and not wanting to chance an encounter with anyone who might occupy the beach closer to town, she turned and set her sights on a new destination.

Enjoying the soothing sound of the waves, Melody settled herself on the end of the dock. Much as she had on many occasions before, she found herself waiting, once again wondering if her feet would be splashed by an unseen friend. She lay back, staring up at the clouds passing overhead, comforted by the familiar feeling of weather-worn wood beneath her. As was often the case, in this place that felt safe and somehow separate from the rest of the world, her mind drifted back homeward. With only the sound of the wind and the waves for company, she found herself having the very conversation she was avoiding with an imaginary mother in her head. Perhaps the lending library had spoiled her; as they grew, Gran made sure that all of the children could read and write. Some took to their letters more than others, but Melody had thrown herself into the written word and the worlds that they built. It was hardly surprising that she could lose herself in a fictional romance and, by extension, that she wished she could meet one of those dashing men that leaped from the minds of their authors into their imaginary worlds. Unfortunately, it seemed to her that such fine specimens were relegated to the page and therefore the sole possession of the lending library in town. It was true that there was often some bit of bother that the lead characters must overcome in the name of an enduring love, but those trials were often caused by the actions and interference of the very prigs and scoundrels who seemed to be far more heavily represented in real life.

"Ugh!" she grumbled to herself.

"What has you so frustrated, Winken?" the familiar voice inquired from under the dock. Melody was startled; her breath momentarily left her body, and her heart beat a vigorous tattoo. Doing her best not to show her surprise, she answered the question in as bland a tone as she could manage, though it came out as more of a groan:

"All of the best men are fictional."

"What do you need this man for?" She could almost picture

the quizzical look on her friend's face.

"Romance and the like." The reasoning felt obvious, though in that moment, she was struck by how little any of her family genuinely knew about the life of a mermaid.

"Why does it need to be a man?" Of the variety of questions Melody might have anticipated, this was not one of them. Her immediate thoughts were all to do with propriety, and that anything else was simply not done; but it had been many years now that she wore her Grandad's necklace, and she knew that such answers meant nothing among The People. The People were much more sensible about loving as one was wont. Though even as she settled on that thought, another one bubbled to the surface: the image of two elderly ladies who lived on the other side of the town. The spinster companions had lived together for many years, and while it was spoken of as a matter of convenience, there was no denying their mutual affection or the subtle intimacy of the touches they exchanged even in the public eye. Melody felt a conflicting longing in that moment, but only for a moment, because another truth still remained:

"Because I want to have children."

"What's so important about children?" Melody rolled her eyes and took a deep, calming breath.

"So you'll have someone to talk to when you come around here in a few decades with your fresh-faced self, when I'm old and wrinkled or already gone."

"Ah." That thought certainly seemed to give the mermaid pause. "Where does one meet a man?"

"According to Mami, anywhere and everywhere except at

home. One must *go* places and *do* things to meet a man, though the where and the what don't seem to be all that particular." After a moment of silence, Nimmawni responded with an unfortunately valid point.

"Well, it doesn't seem to me that this is the best place to meet a man either, Winken. Here, there is only you and me, the seabird isn't even here at this time." Melody rolled over to look over the edge of the dock, found the smiling face of the mermaid looking back at her from the water, and stuck out her tongue.

"And where have you been, pray tell?" Melody asked, deciding to change the subject

"For the most part, I was searching for a pink dolphin."

"There are pink dolphins!" Dolphins seemed like magical creatures in their own right; the sailors spoke of them as a portent of good luck, and on occasion, they heard about dolphins off the coast. One miraculous evening, her Baba said one had come close to the shore. He ran into the water, hoping to swim by its side, but it left before he even got the chance to try to speak to it.

"There used to be more of them, apparently. I had never met one before. You see, I ran across a pod of dolphins, and we got to talking. They mentioned the pink dolphin, which made me curious. How could it not? There are only so many among The People that the Great Mama of the Deep and her children chose to make pink, and if they were not created in this fashion, then how in creation *does* a dolphin become *pink*?"

Melody nodded her encouragement and then cushioned her chin on her crossed hands.

"It took some effort to find the pink dolphin as it does not live out in the open sea; I had to find the great river they live in. It is a very long way from here, across a vast expanse of sea. The river itself is the widest I have ever seen from one shore to the other. The current does not allow the salt of the sea to enter the river, and so the water tastes of rain and earth and is dark with silt."

"You did this all to ask why they are pink?"

"Well, they're also rumored to remember how to make themselves human-shaped and walk on land, but yes, mostly curiosity about the pink coloring."

"They can walk on land? Among humans?"

The mermaid shrugged,

"So the stories say, though I saw no evidence of it. Of course, lack of evidence is not proof that it is not true. Mostly, they just seemed very aggressive, which *is* in keeping with those stories. Did you know there are birds who do it by eating little Shelled People?"

"I'm pretty sure that is not how birds walk on land."

"No! They turn pink, bright pink, they get it from the shrimp."

"That sounds a little fantastical, but reality is more than a little fantastical, I suppose."

The two young women smiled at each other, and Melody was struck, as her father must have been and his father before her, by how young she looked. At eight years old, Melody had felt that Nimmawni had appeared so much older, wiser, and more experienced, and to be sure, all of this was, and remained, true. Yet, at seventeen, her annoying little brothers appeared older than the woman-child who had met with her grandfather before he reached adolescence. Brown human eyes examined large dark eyes, comparing tan skin sprinkled with her Baba's freckles to light brown skin so translucent as to be see-through, exposing a rainbow of tiny lights that flickered within. As she compared and contrasted their appearance, she was struck by the truth of her previous facetiousness: Nimmawni could return to this dock long after her bones had returned to the earth, and she could only hope that some Winken would be here to keep her company. She found herself lonely on the mermaid's behalf, which should have been ridiculous; nobody knew what Nimmawni did when she disappeared for years at a time. It was absolutely possible that she might have a giant family and friends among all sorts of People to keep her company. Yet, in spite of her rationalizations, Melody found that when she looked into her friend's eyes, she felt a confirmation of her concerns. She is captured by an octopus *alone*, she is exploring a shipwreck *alone*, she is lost in the Sunken City *alone*, and she searches for pink dolphins *alone*. All of her excuses for her absences were solitary. While Nimmawni was out there among the waves all by herself, the family that waited for her on the shore held hands, hugged, shared bread and stories, loved each other, and supported one another. The disparity filled her with a profound sadness. As much as her Mami might drive her mad, and her little brothers may fill her with boundless frustration, she could not imagine a life without their warmth. Melody was certain that this realization would haunt her for years to come, most particularly for however long it took for the mermaid to return again.

"Did they tell you how they supposedly do it? The pink dolphins?"

"Oh, I think they just beat each other up far too often and somehow wind up pink."

Melody tried not to roll her eyes and failed.

"No, I mean, did they tell you how they walk on land?"

"Not at all, but they didn't deny it. Of course, it is in their interest for the Humans and The People to believe it, so who is to say? Perhaps, like many of us, they used to know the magics, but their stories have been lost."

Both girls sighed and then laughed at their synchronicity.

"Who's to say it would even have worked for a mermaid, right? If it's the way for a dolphin to do it."

The mermaid gave it some thought, her tentacled hair shifting around her with the waves that flowed, rebounded, and circulated the dock.

"It could be so, but the dolphins say that they were integral to the creation of the mermaid, so it may not be so distant as you'd think. And, of course, sometimes magic is just magic. I hold a necklace strung with the magic of the ocean floor, I am Sea-Folk; I have given you pieces of my necklace; you are a human; does my 'mermaid magic' not work for you?"

"Well, of course, we know the answer to that." The question didn't even warrant much thought on Melody's part, she was the third Windle to prove it. It was another piece of information that did a far better job of catching her attention.

"What do Dolphins have to do with the creation of mermaids? I thought you said you came from a giant shell in the deep sea!"

Nimmawni floated peacefully on her back beneath the dock, a placid smile on her face.

"Who's to say?"

Melody gawped at the mermaid for a moment in silence. "Well, I would think that by now you would know how you came to be!"

"How I was born? How I came to be? Or how mermaids came to be? Because those are three different questions, Winken, with a minimum of three different answers."

Reluctantly, Melody nodded. While it felt as though it were a little over complicated, the statement certainly seemed like it was *potentially* correct.

"Well, then, would you mind sharing with me how the dolphins believe you are connected?"

Nimmawni, always enthusiastic about stories, lay back in the water and closed her eyes, her lips shaping just a shadow of a smile as she began to recount the tale.

CHAPTER 16

A long, long time ago, or so the dolphins say, The People of the land were living through a time of great sadness. Amu'ya, the goddess of the rain, had fallen out with her sister, Cercha of the rolling hills, and the one had moved her clouds far from the other's grasses. The tall grass, where many of the small People made their homes, wilted and dried, becoming dangerously susceptible to the spreading lick of the passing flame. When the grain of the field would not grow, The People of the skies cried out to their goddess for their lack of seeds. It was because of their growing despair that she blessed them with the urge to migrate, planting the compass to safe haven within their very bodies, so they would always know their place in space and time. The larger People could no longer find their prey in the tall grasses and wailed and gnashed their teeth in hunger, praying to both the sky goddess and her sister to end their quarrel and allow them food and sweet, clear water.

By this time, the Human People had already learned to want more than they needed and stash away what excess they could. The Human People were so focused on preparing for lack that when the lack came, they were able to stall its effects, but when it finally impacted them, they panicked. The great lack carried on and on, and they had neither the food nor the water they needed to survive, so The People, all of The People, began to fade away and die.

A human mother and father had a small child, not yet walking or running on its own little feet. Without proper sustenance, the child sickened and paled; it weakened and was listless. The parents knew that if they did nothing, the child would die slowly and in gnawing pain. The father bundled up the baby, the mother carried a torch to see the way, careful not to set the tall grasses ablaze. They traveled to the coast and climbed onto a fishing raft. The father rowed the boat out into the open water, far enough that they could barely see the shore. So it was that, with a kiss on its tiny forehead and a prayer for its passing, they cast the child into the sea. By the light of the torch, they returned to shore, their tears mixing with the swirling waters that marked the grave of their beloved child.

The baby's tiny body was weak, even if it had known how to swim, it would never have had a chance, and as the fabric of its blanket grew heavily laden with sea water, the baby began to drop quickly, the blanket fluttering around its body like the wings of the great eagle ray. It just so happened that a pod of dolphins saw the baby enter the water, saw it drop like a stone, and it was the instinct of one loving mother that sent her to dive down to greet it, breathing bubbles into its tiny face and sustaining its breath as it cried. One by one, the dolphins followed her example, surfacing and diving over and over again to supply the baby with air as it wailed its horrible sadness. The sounds of its cries reverberated through the water, and the little fish of the shallows knew its strident chord just as surely as did the great squid of the deep. It was there, in the deepest of trenches, that a song so old that it was always and always resounded with all of the power of the shifting tides. In the shallower waters, it was a song so perpetually present that it was almost beyond hearing, as omnipresent as the shift and sway of the sands of the ocean floor; but in the depths of the abyss, it was an undeniable force. When the cry penetrated the darkest corners of the sea below, it mixed and mingled with the song, and the song made space for its plaintive tone. The cries reached the singer, the Great Mama of the Deep, and they spoke to her of a need unfilled; they spoke to her with the memory of all of her children as they were in the moments of greatest need, before their emergence into godhood. The song dipped and swayed; the song changed and rose; the song became targeted, transporting the sands of creation upward and into the frail body of the tiny child.

The sands of creation are a powerful thing, changing and evolving all that they touch. The child's legs no longer kicked out in opposite directions, its thighs fusing and bones melting and reforming, emulating the form of its dolphin saviors. The child's fingers grew webbing to better scoop the water and channel its power. The child's eyes grew wide and clear, no longer pinched tight in fear, as its lungs reformed to utilize water with brand new gills. The child breathed its first breath without air and reached out chubby hands to its new dolphin mother. She darted playfully through the water, beginning to play the same games that taught the children of her womb the speed and strength of their fins, and in response, the child giggled, a sound that had never before been heard so far beneath the surface of the waves. The laughter followed in the wake of the cry, and somewhere deep in the deepest crevice of the star-body, The Great Mama of the Deep smiled at her newest creation.

The dolphins taught the child to swim and to hunt, how to leap through the air, and when to hide. They taught the child how to listen and hear, how to speak to The People of the sea. The child grew slowly into its power and grace, traveling with its pod between one sea and the other, before it set off on its own, seeking its role in the Eternal Sea of its creator.

Melody sat back, her mind filled with the image of a child. A child that was loved in a time without resources, a time when there was no way to keep love alive. She looked around at all that she had access to, thought about all that she had, about her family and their garden, about the town and the farms around it, about the clean water from the wells of the deep earth, the fresh fruits foraged from the forest. They may not be rich, they may not have a grand mansion or servants or their own horses, but she was surrounded by abundance. She had not been lying about wanting children, and she knew that a child of her body would one day sit on this dock and wait for a mermaid to tell them amazing stories.

Melody lay there long after Nimmawni had disappeared into the waves, off to wherever it was that she went during the long stretches of her absence. She lay there until Baba came to check on her and tell her that it was dinner time. She lay there as he lowered himself onto the dock to rest beside her and stare up at the stars, then grabbed hold of her hand and gave it a quick kiss. He always knew when she needed a moment to herself to think, and if anyone understood what it meant to have a story tilt your world, it was Baba.

"Sleep on it sweetheart, but first eat dinner before your Mami whacks you with her ladle."

A startled laugh passed her lips, and she began to slowly push herself to her feet. Laughter or no, the threat of her Mami's ladle was effective, just as its use was a definite possibility.

CHAPTER 17

Under the hot summer sun, the market continued to grow and thrive. The big market days drew greater numbers of both buyers and sellers, and the occasional visiting performer, who added to the enjoyment and spectacle of the day. As the influence of the Temple of the Sun continued to grow, Sixth Market grew with it. Often referred to now as the Great Market, the people partook of its excesses with raucous enjoyment and followed it closely with the solemnity and pious gatherings of the Sun's-Day. Boisterous men sat outside the tavern with ale and wine flowing freely, hardly needing an excuse to indulge but happily using any that presented itself. Women dressed to attract attention as they wandered the market under the watchful eyes of their parents and relations. Children ran through the streets with wooden wheels and sticks, wicker balls, and candied fruit, stopping to watch performers ply their trade.

Melody strolled through the market square with her Mami and her brothers, Jay and Adem, a basket over her arm and one of Mami's beautifully embroidered scarves tied over her hair.

They wended their way to Uncle Balian's shop, baskets laden with remedies for him to sell from the edge of the market. Many people would stop there to sit and drink tea during the market day, a welcome break for those less interested in what the tavern had to offer. Adem would stay with their cousin Leo to help run the shop, while Melody and Jay assisted Mami in the chaos of the crowded marketplace. The market, which was once confined to the center of town where her Grandad and Gran had met, now extended down to the dock and spread onto side streets; if it continued to grow, some day it might reach as far as the workmen's quarter. The big market days were great days for socialization, events where humans from so many towns gathered and mixed together, exchanging news and ideas, greeting family, and establishing new connections. The crows glided overhead, taking note of the best places to find food when the market broke down in the evening, and Melody could not help but smile at their commentary on the human crowds below. Mami, like many mothers, also saw this as an opportunity for her daughter to meet young men of an appropriate age, and was prone to pointing them out with very little attempt at subtlety. Regardless, Melody felt she knew what she was looking for and how unlikely she was to encounter it. Assuming she ever came across a man who did not find her and her family too strange to be bothered with, chances were that she would be expected to join his household, as was common. Aunt Bunny had done it, as had Aunt Vera and Aunt Thea, and though they came and visited, and their children grew up with The People's stories, they were removed from the magic of the household, they were far from the sea, and that was not the life she envisioned for herself.

The back of the cart was far from the most comfortable of places to rest, but having been up before dawn to set up their stall, Aaron was not about to complain. He layered burlap sacks beneath his aching body in an attempt to create more padding, hoping to get some rest before being surrounded by the crush of humanity. All too soon, he was roused as Marcus stood over him, searching for the best vantage point to drop a melon on his stomach; one could say it was a clear sign that it was time for him to get up and be productive. As he removed himself from his makeshift sleeping pallet, every muscle in his body seemed to voice their protest. Rolling his shoulders and twisting to stretch his back, he clapped Marcus roughly on the back with a smile as he approached the stand, readying himself to be helpful and friendly. They were far from the only farm selling fruits and vegetables, it was their quality and variety that set them apart. Come for the figs and melons and buy your apples in the process; that was the idea anyway.

Whatever else you might say about Marcus' father, Aaron's "adopted" father (and there was a lot to be said), he had been a good businessman. He was a good businessman when he decided to plant with variety; he was a good businessman when he took in an unwanted child for a monthly stipend; he was a good businessman when he decided to keep the child instead of paying for additional labor; he was a good businessman when he decided to buy the neighbor's land and expand his crops; and

Aaron supposed one could say he was a good businessman when he refused to pay a medicine worker to come treat him in the days before he died. It was a marked improvement for everyone involved when the farm passed to Marcus, who had somehow managed to be raised by his parents while absorbing almost none of their character and values. His near-brother treated him like a brother in truth, where Marcus' parents barely treated him as a fellow human. So, it was only natural that one of Marcus' first orders of business had been to give his near-brother wages and a proper room. In the absence of his father, both young men breathed more easily, their employees worked with renewed enthusiasm under their improved treatment, and the farm prospered further under the influence of the brothers' charm and good nature.

Lost in consideration of all of these improvements, Aaron examined the scars that remained across his knuckles as he rearranged the melons, shifting them to optimize balance.

"I'll take that one, if you don't mind." A sweet voice broke his reverie, drawing his attention to the tidy skirts of a cheerful yellow dress with a wide belt and three-quarter sleeves, skin like gold with an adorable sprinkling of freckles across her nose and cheeks. Deep brown eyes and a small quirk of a smile under a white and blue scarf that tied her hair out of her face. The image was charming. He handed her the melon.

"Can I help you with anything else, miss?"

She pursed her lips in thought, eyes scanning the available produce, before she selected a small variety of fruits for her basket. She smiled at him as she withdrew the appropriate coin from the petite purse that swung from her chatelaine, and he found himself wishing for a reason for her to stay. Marcus elbowed him, clearing his throat.

"Aaron, will you introduce me to this lovely young lady?" Aaron groaned internally at his brother's ham-handed maneuver but was grudgingly thankful for the excuse to inquire after the young lady.

"Ah, yes, Marcus Hansen, this lovely lady is..." he trailed off, waiting for her to supply the rest. She smirked at them both, completely aware of the game they were playing.

"Miss Melody Windle." She replied, extending her gloved hand to Marcus as was proper. Melody, what a fitting name for a charming lady, particularly for one with such a sweet voice. Though manners dictated it would hardly be proper to say as much.

"Miss Melody Windle, allow me to introduce my near-brother, Marcus Hansen."

"But Sir," she pointed out, bringing her fingertips to her rosy lips, as though suddenly struck by a concerning thought: "who, pray tell, are you?" Marcus burst out laughing while Aaron stood, momentarily dumbstruck, as Miss Melody Windle smirked at him over the apples and figs. It was Marcus who recovered most quickly and took it upon himself to continue the game in kind,

"Miss Melody Windle, this young man impaired of both words and manners is my near-brother Aaron. Aaron," he clapped his brother on the shoulder, "allow me to introduce the lovely Miss Melody Windle." She extended a gloved hand once again, her eyes dancing with unvoiced laughter,

"Charmed, I'm sure."

Was he blushing? He was pretty sure he was blushing.

As much as she was loath to admit it, maybe Mami was onto something with all of her talk about chance encounters. The gentleman at the fruit stand had certainly been unexpected. Judging from their limited interaction, he appeared to be neither a prig nor a scoundrel, though one often could not tell with such limited exposure. Instead, there was something about the way he looked at her that reminded her of her Grandad, which was far from a horrible comparison. Grandad had loved Gran with a great depth of emotion for most of his life, from the time that they met right up until he had finally passed away in his sleep not one year past. He had looked at her like she was the most lovely thing he had ever encountered for forty-two years, longer than some people managed to stay alive. She glanced at Aaron as she offered her hand, momentarily meeting his hazel eyes before taking in his short black hair, skin the color of tea with an abundance of milk, and the scar that ran from the side of his lower lip to the tip of his chin; it should have detracted from his features, but all it did was call inappropriate attention to the fullness of his lips. She saw the blush that touched his cheeks at the banter she shared with his near-brother and smiled; he didn't have the demeanor of a dreamer, but there was definitely something familiar that she found herself wishing she could explore. She wondered what Toddy would have said if he were here, remembering the story of Aunt Thea meeting her husband; it seemed that most of her family knew quickly when they found their perfect partner, even if they were sometimes a little slow to admit it. Aunt Thea liked to be very deliberate about things and was struck by how strong and how rapidly her feelings came to be. Grandad had suggested that perhaps Thea's heart knew her future husband's heart even if their faces were less familiar, echoing the insight Nimmawni once shared with him. Melody found herself glancing over her shoulder as she walked away from the stall, wondering if Grandad would say the same now. As it was, she was already forming a number of excuses to pass the stall again throughout the day.

The sway of Miss Melody Windle's skirts as she walked away held his attention far longer than it should. He caught the look she gave him over her shoulder, hopefully, it was directed at him; if she was looking at Marcus, he might just have to consider himself heartbroken. When she passed the stand later in the day, he found himself strangely aware of her every move, even as she haggled with Marcus over the price of the supposedly forgotten asparagus. Over the course of the day, it happened three times that the young lady appeared to stand by their cart. By the third time, he had convinced himself that not only was it intentional, but there was a decent chance that she was just as interested in him as he found himself in her.

An idea began to form, and, impulsive though it might be, Aaron talked it over with Marcus that evening before coming to a decision. After Sixth Market came the Sun's Day; the townsfolk and many of the remaining market goers funneled into the Temple of the Sun for the weekly gathering. Aaron watched with avid interest, seeking out even a glimpse of those freckled cheeks. For just a moment, he saw what he thought might be her figure slipping through the crowd; it was nice to think so, but it did nothing to change his plans. Aaron had no intention of tracking Miss Melody Windle down in a crowded temple. Instead, he gathered together his small savings, assisted in loading the cart, and when his brother clambered into his seat to return to the farm, Aaron headed in the opposite direction in search of the tavern by the docks. Marcus would return to the Sixth Market in a month's time. In the meantime, Aaron would look for work in town and hopefully find excuses to spend some time with the lovely Miss Melody Windle. He felt a deep pull to give himself every opportunity to get to know her better, but this was not his only reason to strike out on his own; the situation would also give him the chance to spread his wings and experience life outside of the farm. He might go back one day, he might go back when his near-brother returned in a month. In the meantime, it would be nice to experience something new, even if that something new didn't involve a certain young woman that looked like sunshine with little white gloves.

The tavern's matron took to Aaron on sight, he was young, and strong, and willing to work; just the sort of young man she could put to good use when the tavern was busy of an evening. She looked over his arms, hardened from years of working the land, in an appraising fashion. She handed him a platter and began to load it with tankards of ale, each one filled to the very brim. With a grunt of approval, she gestured to a table full of men in the far corner and watched as he maneuvered the crowd with a minimal amount of sloshing. He served the men with an awkward smile, applying the principles of selling apples at market as best he could to the task that lay before him. When he returned, the formidable woman snatched away the platter and chucked a wet rag in his direction. Aaron plucked it neatly from the air before being pointed in the direction of a newly vacated table. Two or three completed tasks later, the woman finally smiled on his return.

"You know your letters, boy?" she asked, taking him by surprise.

"Do you know how to read and write?" she asked again, a little more slowly.

"No, Missis," he felt a pang of shame at his reply, his so-called parents had never seen the need to teach him any skills unrelated to manual labor. "I do know sums." He added, hoping it would make up for his shortcomings.

"Sums are good, I can work with numbers. Can you memorize prices?"

"Yes, Missis."

"Very good, we'll be taking the cost of a room from your wages unless you wish to sleep in the barn with the livestock. Jemmi has a cot up in the loft there. We can throw some more fixin's up there if you like; he won't mind the company. Still, if you'll be needing another blanket, you'll be buying it yourself, understood?"

"Yes, Missis. The loft will do me just fine, Missis."

"Well, good. We'll be needing you in the evenings, Sixth Market, and after temple on the Sun's Day when the crowd calls for it. We'll feed you twice daily from the common pot; anything more comes from your wages. Broken crockery comes directly from your wages. Sun God forbid you should need the attentions of a healer, we'll send word to the Mistresses Windle or that crackpot physician on your behalf, but their services will be coming out of your pay as well."

His ears perked up at the mention of the Mistresses Windle, he set that piece of information to his memory as he continued to nod his assent to his new boss.

"If you have need of more coin, they always need extra hands on the dock to load and unload the ships. You know proper knots?"

He shook his head; he knew his fair share of knots from the farm, but there was no telling if those would be considered proper knots in a shipping port.

"Well, no matter. Don't need to know the knots to lift crates. You just set yourself to standing on the stones come morning, and I'm sure someone will put you to work."

At the end of the evening, when the tavern doors were bolted shut and the fire had burned low, the matron handed over a bundle of worn sheets and a blanket that had seen better days.

"It's not much, but it's warm and soft."

"My thanks, Missis," he muttered sleepily, claiming his bedding with a sigh of relief as the day came to an end. His body might well be fit for physical labor, but he was accustomed to the company of farmhands, folk spread across acres of land unless they congregated for a task that required many hands. That night, he had been surrounded by bodies and the tangy stench of spilled ale. With the exception of his short break, where he filled a bowl from the common pot and tucked himself away in a corner to dig into a blissfully aromatic stew, he had been maneuvering through those masses, filling tankards, delivering and clearing away dishes and cutlery, wiping down tables and otherwise responding to the endless cries of "You, Boy!"

"You, Boy, fetch us another round of ale!"

"You, Boy, what is owed?"

"You, Boy, another from the pot!"

He was pretty sure he'd be hearing the demand in his sleep. Still, his muscles ached in the pleasing way that spoke of a productive day, and he knew his purse would be a little bit heavier for it. He climbed up into the hay loft and barely had time to spread sheets beneath him before he descended into the waiting arms of sleep, the vision of a certain feminine smile following him into dreamland.

It seemed mere minutes before he was woken by the stomping of nearby feet. It seemed that Jemmi did, in fact, mind sharing the loft, if the glowering look he leveled at Aaron as he descended the ladder was anything to go by. The sun was barely peeking over the horizon; Aaron estimated it had only been a handful of hours since he'd laid his head to rest. It was no wonder that Jemmi was out of sorts. He took a few moments to contemplate closing his eyes in pursuit of further rest but remembered the matron's comment about standing on the stones, whatever that meant, and decided it was time to explore his options. He rolled from his tangled mess of bedding and took a moment to fold them, picking prickly straws of hay from the weave as he went. He tucked the bundle out of the way before descending into the stable and quickly washing his face in a rain barrel, no doubt intended for watering horses. Proceeding out onto the morning streets, Aaron was struck once again by how far from the farm he was. The morning light spilled in hues of pinks and oranges over the rooftops of a multitude of buildings; he could peep a straight shot from the open yard by the docks to the center of town from where he stood. Facing east, the spires of the temple cast long shadows across the square. As the building itself shimmered and refracted light in honor of the God, the shadows appeared to point directly to the harbor and out to sea. He slapped his cap over his dark, unkempt hair, spun on his heel, and headed, as directed, toward the docks.

While he had seen very few people venturing outside to begin their day in the direction of the square, the area on the dock was already populated with a variety of folk in obvious preparation for the ships that had anchored in the night to approach the wharf. A number of men congregated on the large stones that composed the sea wall, casting light on the matron's term. Aaron joined their ranks, doing his best to remain inconspicuous, and watched for a sign that he ought to be doing something. The men in question milled about, some quite chipper and talkative for all that it was just past dawn, while others communicated in grunts or stood in relative silence. Several chewed on the ends of their cheroot or smoked heavily from wooden pipes, sending off wisps of tobacco-scented smoke to mingle with the sea air. It was only a matter of time before he was noticed by an older gentleman who spoke gruffly, his dense facial hair framing the cigar he didn't bother to remove from between his lips.

"You're new." A statement of fact, to which Aaron nodded.

"You ever work the docks before?"

"No, Sir."

"The name is Riggs, boy. Or Mister Riggs, if you prefer, though you'll find no one has much time for manners once the boats make port." Riggs gave him an assessing look. "You look strong enough. Name?"

"Aaron, Mister Riggs." Aaron opted to lean on the side of propriety while he could.

"You got your wits about you? Can you take orders and work with others without complaint? We've got no time for whinging." Riggs was gruff and straightforward but not unkind. After years of living with his adoptive father, Aaron certainly knew the difference. Aaron's answers were short and appeared acceptable as Riggs grunted his satisfaction and blew an impressive cloud of smoke over his shoulder, taking in the sight of the first ship making its approach. Several men with staffs ending in large hooks lined the end of the dock, awaiting the dock lines that soon flew through the air. The choreographed dance of dockhands and deckhands in concert secured the vessel in astonishing time, and it wasn't long until Riggs grabbed his shoulder to push him towards the dock.

"I thought you said you had your wits about you. Git to the pier, young'un."

It seemed that Riggs had appointed himself Aaron's unofficial mentor; wherever Aaron was, the heavily bearded man was in easy shouting distance, guiding, assessing, and issuing orders. They were of a height, which eased the task of balancing weight between them, and Riggs soon found that Aaron was more useful than he had initially supposed. These skills would be put to the test when loading his first northbound cargo vessel; the destination made it all the more important to adequately secure its contents, as the northern waters were rough and unpredictable. Riggs inquired after Aaron's skills with a knot, and Aaron explained that, while he had a farmhand's knowledge of knots, he was uncertain whether those same knots applied. Riggs had him demonstrate his skills with a discarded length of line, identifying among them a square knot, a sheet bend, and a bowline knot. He clapped Aaron on the back with a pleased sort of surprise,

"We'll make an admirable docker or stevedore of you yet, young'un."

Aaron glowed a bit at the praise.

At about midday, Aaron spied a familiar figure ascending the stairs from the beach to the dockyard. The crown of her head was covered with a colorful scarf; a few brown curls had escaped and fluttered charmingly in the breeze as she carried a satchel to the far side of the main road, just across from the tavern.

"Hey, Riggs!" he yelled. In a matter of moments, the man appeared at his side, just as he had all morning.

"Do we get a break?"

Riggs nodded his assent. "You looking for a midday meal?"

It was as good a reason as any, so Aaron nodded in response.

"We can take a bit. Though if you're too long about it, that poor bastard over there will take it out of your pay." He gestured to the man he had given his name to at the end of the dock.

"Understood."

"We can sup at the tavern. Not far at all."

"Good, I have something I need to do, but I'll join you shortly."

Riggs nodded, produced a new cheroot from a slim box in his coat pocket, and stuck it firmly between his teeth before taking him to sign out with the harbor master's clerk. The older man set off with a purpose toward the tavern, as Aaron ventured more slowly in the opposite direction. His eyes scanned the buildings and storefronts in search of a plausible destination, finally settling on a shop with a teacup and a number or spices painted on the shingle. The Matron had mentioned something about the Mistresses Windle being medicine women, so teas and herbs seemed a likely place to start looking.

When the door swung open, a bell rang, and four heads, still mirthful from their newly interrupted conversation, turned in his direction. A gentleman with dark hair and kind eyes stood behind the counter with an adolescent boy. A second young man stood on a ladder restocking shelves. The familial resemblance was undeniable, both between them and the pair of brown eyes over freckled cheeks that turned in his direction.

"Good day!" the man said with an unfamiliar accent. "How may I be of service?"

The object of his immediate attention quirked a delicately curved eyebrow at him, as though completely unsurprised with his presence and wondering how he planned to handle his current situation. The hint of a dimple in her cheek belied her amusement, which did nothing to improve his grasp on his faculties. He reluctantly turned his attention to the counter, where Miss Windle's satchel was laid out with luncheon for four and her... father? Uncle? Continued to smile in his direction, though it was now touched with a hint of curiosity.

"I suppose I was wondering just the same." Aaron scrambled for an answer. "Are your teas medicinal or simply for one's enjoyment?"

The man somehow managed to smile wider, while Miss Windle's expression took on the appearance of sudden interest.

"Why, both, young man. We carry teas and spices from many lands, and our close relation to the local medicine women has given us both a greater understanding of our wares and access to some of their simpler remedies." With a quick smirk at the young lady, the purveyor of teas continued. "What appears to be the problem?"

"I'm new to town and have just taken employment both at the tavern and as a dockworker. Do you, perhaps, have something that might help an aching body? Or to restore one's energy?"

"Many traditional teas can improve energy. In fact, even the simplest of breakfast teas may provide the body with a sense of renewed vigor."

Miss Windle leaned on the counter, watching the exchange in a manner that seemed to be weighing both men equally. The man behind the counter shook his head at her and then indulgently waved his hand in her direction as though encouraging her to speak.

"Amo, you know how Mami and Gran feel about the black teas. They will do in a pinch, but they do not reinvigorate the body so much as they force alertness. If you add the ginseng root, perhaps holy basil, or rose root from the north, those would energize the spirit, particularly should they be taken daily. Do you intend to take tea daily?" Her attention settled on Aaron just long enough for an uncertain nod. "And, of course, willow bark will do for the body pains."

"Yega, we can sit all day debating the finer points of tea. While your Mami and Gran may find black teas lacking, they can and do agree that the green teas of the far east have benefit. Additionally, some of the black teas so popular to the north have long contained bergamot, which your Gran assures me is tonic for both joint pain and mental alertness."

It was clear that the two were falling into a familiar rhythm and that they enjoyed arguing, though whether it was in general or confined to the subject of teas was anyone's guess. The young man stocking the shelf, having come to the conclusion that his services were necessary, approached Aaron with a sack full of chipped wood that smelled strongly of roses.

"Do you like the smell? Gran says that if you enjoy a smell

and you feel the urge to eat it, that's a fair indicator that it's what your body needs." Aaron certainly enjoyed the dusky rose smell and said as much, though he wasn't sure he wanted to eat it. He was presented with another container full of leaves that were far less pleasant and another with roots that seemed a little questionable.

"Amo," the young man interrupted the ongoing argument, "pass me some black tea with bergamot." This time, the smell that filled his nostrils had him salivating, and he nodded emphatically.

"Adem, are you mixing the rose root with the black tea?" The young lady asked, re-engaging with the task at hand.

"And the willow bark."

The girl clicked her tongue at him impatiently.

"This will not do." She snatched away the ingredients, glaring at the boy who appeared to be her brother. "The roots and the leaves brew differently. You, Mister... Aaron," she fumbled, obviously realizing that she had not been given his last name. She held out two bags,

"In boiling water, you brew a spoonful from this bag," she shook the one to his left. "Cover the brewing cup, it will be more effective. After ten minutes, you add a spoonful from this bag," she shook the bag to his right. "In five minutes more, you may drink it however you wish, with milk, honey, sugar, lemon, it matters not." He nodded, gathering up the two bags, and paid the bill. He took his leave and pushed through the door, wondering whether his actions had worked in his favor, when he heard the sound of feet following behind him.

"So, young sir, did you truly venture into a tea shop to

sample their wares?" Her voice stopped him in his tracks. He turned to face Miss Melody Windle, who wore blue today, with a green pinafore edged with embroidered daisies and buttercups. The loose strands that remained free around her face caught in the breeze coming off the ocean.

"I may have had other motivations. Still, the tea is a welcome benefit, assuming it works." Her brow quirked as though she might be mildly irritated by his doubt.

"Oh, it will work."

"We'll see." He smiled, taking her hand in his to bow over it like some sort of courtly gentleman. "I'm off to the tavern; hopefully, I can acquire some hot water for myself and give it a try."

Miss Melody Windle met his comments with a quiet confidence that lingered around the edges of her smile as she spoke,

"You wish to try it right now? It might be for the best that I accompany you to make sure you can properly follow instructions."

While the thought of sitting down at a table with both Riggs and Miss Windle gave him a case of nerves, he was hardly inclined to say no to her offer, mocking though it may be.

CHAPTER 18

The courtship of Melody Windle was hardly common, though one might suppose that it should be expected by this point. Riggs became Aaron's unlikely accomplice in both life and love. The older dockhand had taken to the younger man with a gruff sort of affection, helping him to learn the ropes of working the pier. When the two men worked together, it was largely without incident; predictably, this was a quality much appreciated by the merchant sailors whose greatest priority was to deliver their wares in one piece. In the evenings, Riggs would eventually make his way to the tavern, some hours after Aaron dismissed himself at the clerk and pocketed a day's worth of wages. The man sat in a corner of the tavern with an easy view of the rest of the floor. He would order and nurse a single pint for the rest of the evening, sometimes conversing with Aaron when he had the chance, but mostly keeping to himself.

It was after the third time that Riggs witnessed Aaron's interactions with Miss Windle that the man began to comment on the situation. It became quite clear that Riggs had a surprising romantic streak and was full of ideas that he felt he was too old and too set in his ways to implement himself. So the two spoke, and Aaron found ways to bump into Miss Windle, to bring her small tokens of his affection, and, on the rare occasion that she visited the tavern while he was working, plying her with sweets the matron would then shamelessly subtract from his pay. Melody, for her part, made herself easy to be found. She visited the tea shop more than was strictly necessary, walked more frequently into town along the shore, and even stopped for food in the tavern, a place she had rarely stepped foot in before Aaron's arrival. When it became clear that he was genuinely fond of his blend of tea, she brought him more unbidden, with a shy smile and a metal infuser to improve his enjoyment of the experience.

Marcus returned a few short weeks later, arriving the day before Sixth Market, prepared to track down his near-brother and learn of his current situation. When he entered the tavern, it was early enough that the bulk of their normal patrons had not yet arrived. He was instead directed to find "young Aaron" down on the pier. A short walk found him surrounded by men who hurried to and fro with bags and huge crates, and among them stood Aaron, laden with heavy bags and laughing with an older man who chuckled around a cheroot through an impressive beard.

"Aaron!" he waved to catch his brother's attention. When Aaron finally saw him, he sprinted forward as though unaware that his body was weighed down with cargo, and damn near bowled Marcus over with his enthusiasm.

"Marcus! I want you to meet my friend Riggs," he turned, calling for his older companion, who appeared at his shoulder as though by magic.

"Riggs, meet my near-brother Marcus. Just give me a mo' boys, got to put these things down before I sign out." At that, Aaron disappeared back into the crowd of sailors, merchants, and dockhands that swarmed the pier. Marcus extended his hand in greeting to the older man, who looked at him with suspicion and chewed on his cheroot before finally pulling his hand from his pocket for a firm handshake.

"Heard quite a bit about you and your'n," The man said, with an air of disapproval.

"Ah, I hope you won't hold my parents against me."

"No, I suppose that wouldn't do." Still, the man eyed him as though assessing his worth.

"Are you comin' to try'n take Young Aaron back to the farm life?"

"I'm coming to see how my brother fares and what it is that he wishes to do. He has had far too few opportunities to make choices in his life, I certainly wouldn't deprive him of them now."

The old man nodded quietly, then clapped him on the back in an obvious gesture of approval. Marcus felt oddly pleased with the action, a sensation that was only reinforced when Aaron reappeared and beamed at the two men.

"I'm signing out Riggs; it's time for me to check in with the matron." The man waved at Aaron dismissively, caught Marcus' eye with a nod, then swaggered back towards the most recent ship that had made port.

Marcus waited again as Aaron finished his dealings with a pinched-faced man of indeterminate age, who balanced a giant volume against a stack of crates. The two walked the short distance back to the tavern, where Aaron guided him to a table in the corner before disappearing into the kitchen in search of his boss. Marcus was at a loss, having had no chance to speak to his brother at all.

The tavern began to fill with patrons, all yelling over the din for the attentions of the matron and her three servers. Aaron did his best to check in with Marcus where he could, but the farmer could see that there would be limited opportunities until the crowd began to thin. A few hours later, Riggs slipped into the chair across from him with an expression that, Marcus supposed, could pass for a smile. In a matter of moments, a pint seemed to miraculously appear before him, and the two sipped in relative silence.

"Good evening, Mister Riggs," Marcus heard the light, feminine voice from over his shoulder, only moments before a delicate hand tapped his arm. "Sir, do you mind if I join you?" When he looked over his shoulder, he found the young woman from the market, waiting for a response to her query.

"Of course! Please, do join us." He glanced across at the previously blank face of Mister Riggs, who now shot the young lady a look of genuine affection.

"How goes the day, Miss Windle?" the older man inquired. "Nothing too grizzly or gruesome, I hope."

The young woman chuckled, flashing him a good-natured smile.

"Now, Mister Riggs, lies do not become us. You may hope, for my part, that nothing of the sort occurs, but we both know that those are the stories you like best."

Seeing Marcus' expression of confusion, Riggs leaned across the table in a conspiratorial fashion,

"Miss Windle here, and her mother and grandmother, are medicine women. Doing the great work of keeping the townsfolk well, often saving them from the woes brought on by their own stupidity."

Marcus wasn't sure what to do with that information.

"I have certainly never met a female physician before, Miss Windle." To his embarrassment and a degree of relief, the young lady laughed at his statement, and it was a charming laugh indeed.

"Not at all, Mister Hansen. You surely haven't met a female physician now, either. I was raised with the knowledge of medicinal herbal remedies, and these are the tools with which we ply our trade, much as it pains the local physician."

His two table companions laughed, and Marcus found himself laughing along with them. The three spoke for three sides of a square table, leaving the final seat open for the odd moment when Aaron could be spared and allowing ease of access to the servers who darted around the tables with a will. Marcus and Miss Windle both partook of the common pot, Marcus with a pint of ale and Miss Windle with a glass of wine, all the while Mister Riggs slowly nursed his ale and made light conversation. When their supper dishes were cleared, Aaron appeared and presented the young lady with a berry covered confection before asking his brother if he would like anything more with his dinner.

Once he had moved on, Miss Windle finally asked what

brought him to town a day early for the busiest market. However, when he explained his presence, he was not met with the same mild acceptance expressed by Mister Riggs. Miss Windle seemed genuinely concerned. Marcus continued to speak, hoping to ease whatever was causing her discomfort, but he only seemed to manage to exacerbate the problem. It was not long before Miss Melody Windle was in such a state of distress that she rose from the table in search of Aaron. Finding him in the middle of the tavern, she grabbed him by the arm and towed him out the door and onto the sidewalk, raising no few eyebrows and undoubtedly beginning any number of rumors. Marcus rose slowly, doing his level best not to attract further attention, but hoping to gain the door before whatever distress he had caused could negatively impact his brother.

Now that they were outside, Melody wasn't sure what she had intended to say. She wasn't sure she had ever known what she had intended to say, but whatever words she might have had flew from her mind the moment she was alone with Aaron. Aaron, the boy who looked at her as though she hung the moon, whose teasing affection drove her mad, whose sweetness made her melt a bit on the inside. The dumbstruck look on his face did nothing to ease her agitation and, in some ways, reminded her all the more of her Grandad. It was a comparison that continued to make her wish that he could be there to smile like a child and weigh in on her potential romance. Only now, there was the potential that the object of those feelings might be leaving. He might be going back to the farm with his brother, who she could not bring herself to dislike, as he was a lovely man in his own right. She twisted the fabric of her skirt in her fingers and stared toward the pier as she tried to wrangle her thoughts.

Marcus had let her know of the possibility, as though he was looking forward to Aaron's return and missed his brother dearly. In an effort to make the whole of the situation understood, Marcus began to babble, speaking freely of their childhood, the attitude of his parents, and, as a result, how Aaron had been treated. The entire situation was made up of pieces in turn so overwhelming and so cruel that she simply couldn't help herself as she sprinted through the tavern, pulling Aaron in tow.

"Miss Windle, are you quite alright? Is there something I can bring you? Or perhaps I can alert your mother or your uncle to your distress?" Aaron spoke, reminding her of his presence, which she was responsible for, and his kindness.

"Are you going back to the farm?" she asked abruptly.

"I suppose that I could if I wished. I am sure that is the question that Marcus is here to answer. Why do you ask?" This was hardly the answer she was looking for, and barely an answer at all.

"Marcus certainly seems to think you would prefer to return."

"I haven't come to a decision." Aware that she was being emotional and nonsensical, but apparently unable to pull back, she pivoted instead.

"I thought you were taken with me." He paused, as though taken aback by the direct nature of the statement, or perhaps shocked that she had believed it to be so at all. The moment before he spoke felt interminable and filled with doubt.

"I am." His tone was cautious, perhaps uncertain of her motive for making such a blunt assertion.

"I even thought that, perhaps, you might even love me." She continued to stare out at the water, not wanting him to see the raw expression on her face. It wasn't until the gentle touch of rough fingers guided her chin to turn that she dared to look in his direction.

"I believe I do, Miss Windle." He spoke gently, like a farmer trying to stop a feisty mare from bolting; the comparison did little to ease her concerns. The formal manner of his address, however, irked her. She stepped back, putting some small distance between them before responding.

"Really? You're addressing me so formally, persisting in calling me Miss Windle *now*? And if that is so, then why would you consider leaving? And *if* that is so, then why have you not said so?"

"I am not certain I *am* considering leaving; I do believe I am saying so right now; and it is only right that I call you Miss Windle, unless you would prefer that I call you *My* Miss Windle?" a comment that undoubtably deserved the unladylike snort it incited; ripped, as it almost certainly was, directly from the pages of the romantic fictions she devoured.

"I do not think it unreasonable that one might drop one's formal address while confessing their love. However, if we are to proceed in such a fashion, I resent that I cannot return the formality, *Young Aaron*." Her comment was met with exasperation as the man began to turn away.

"Is that all you have to say on the topic? I do, after all, have a job I ought to get back to." He made as if to walk back into the tavern, but her next words froze him in his tracks.

"Do you wish to marry me, Aaron?" He turned to face her, wide-eyed with shock.

"I... Miss Windle.... Melody, was that a proposal?"

"No." His shoulders slumped as though weighed down by a surprising degree of disappointment. "After all, is it not *you* who should be asking *me*?"

It was at this point that it was made clear to them that they were not so alone as they had believed. Marcus' deep chuckle split the night air, the concerns which had led him to follow the couple from the building completely laid to rest.

"It seems to me that congratulations are in order!" Denila took a deep breath as she surveyed the table. "To me!"

Melody dropped her face into her waiting hands, shielding her eyes from view. She had been ready for embarrassment as soon as her Mami opened her mouth, and it had certainly come to pass. Making a scene over Melody finding her potential husband was absolutely in keeping with Mami's behavior to date. Melody had known that it would be a topic of conversation, yet somehow, this was worse than expected.

"Did I or did I not say that if you made yourself available for chance encounters, your chance encounter would appear? And did I or did I not ask you repeatedly to make a habit of accompanying me to the market? And did I or did I not have to drag you along the very day that you first met your sweet Aaron? And I was right, yes?"

Her Mami's victorious crowing began on the day that she knew for certain that Melody had found her beau and ended the day after their wedding.

Aaron did not ask for her hand the night of their conversation outside the tavern, he did not do it the next day, nor within the following week. Almost two weeks to the day after that conversation, Aaron opted not to stand on the stones as he had done most every day since his arrival. Instead, he cleaned himself up and approached the workmen's quarter with hat in hand. He stood outside waiting to speak with Mister Anders Windle, to address his concerns and ask for his blessing. He stood beneath the branches of a gnarled old tree whose branches were soon inhabited by several raucous crows. He was tempted to shoo them away but decided he was happy to have the company.

Around midday, a shadow fell across Aaron where he crouched at the base of the tree. The crows chattered away for long moments as he tried to make some sense of the backlit figure. A hand reached down, and he took it, levering himself back up onto his feet where he stared into the face of a somber but kind-looking man with long brown hair and deep blue eyes. He stood about a hands-width taller than Aaron and bore a definite resemblance to Melody. This must be Anders Windle.

"I believe you're the young man all the fuss is about."

Anders spoke in a warm, even tone, and Aaron had the sense that Anders was completely prepared for whatever he had to say. The crows chattered in the tree, and the older man's lips tilted with the barest hint of a smile, shaking his head the way a parent might when their child was being overly rambunctious. Ignoring this, Aaron decided to press on and began the speech he had spent the morning preparing.

"Mister Windle, sir, my name is Aaron."

"I know."

"I've come about your daughter, Miss Melody Windle."

"She is the only daughter I have, Aaron." Anders said in a mild tone.

"Yes. Indeed." Aaron fell silent, Mister Windle's responses having interrupted his planned approach to the conversation.

"Was there something in particular you had to say, Aaron?"

Anders Windle took a few steps away to seat himself on top of a wooden fence.

"Yes, Sir. I find that I am very fond of your daughter." Anders lifted a very expressive eyebrow. It was suddenly obvious from whom Melody had inherited it, causing Aaron to blush, "I'm in love with your daughter." This was met with a nod, as though the statement were exactly as suspected.

"I would very much like to marry her, but..." at the pause, Anders Windle's eyebrow crept even higher and was followed by the other to form an expression of surprised concern.

"But?" Under the weight of Anders' gaze, Aaron completely discarded pleasantries, instead offering more candor than intended in his reply.

"But I find it difficult to see myself as worthy. I have no home of my own, I don't even have a name to offer her, and I find myself lacking in other ways as well. I was not given access to a proper education, and between two jobs, I have little time or access to better myself. I love your daughter, sir, but how can I say I deserve her?"

Having poured out his confession, Aaron felt empty, as though his words had wiped out his hope in the process.

"Would you, if you could?" Anders asked quietly.

"Would I what?" Aaron, still in a state of distress, replied.

"Would you better yourself if you could?"

"Yes, absolutely." His answer was immediate, and the older man nodded again, satisfied with his response. Aaron was amazed by how calmly expressive the man managed to be. Anders leaned back for a moment, as though collecting his thoughts, as the crows erupted into another chorus.

"You've been in town for how long, Aaron? Less than two months? How often do you work?" Aaron had been prepared for some form of interrogation, so what immediately followed came as no surprise.

"Every day, Sir," he nodded.

"And do you make a good wage?"

"Decent, Sir."

"Do you spend it all on drink or frivolities?"

"No, Sir, I save most everything I can." At that, Anders narrowed his eyes, and Aaron felt his heart drop to his stomach.

"You buy my Melody sweet cakes, let us stick with the facts of the matter."

"She enjoys them, Sir. They make her smile." It had never occurred to Aaron that such a thing might be considered frivolity.

Anders waved the comment away, but it seemed that a smile

was creeping like a ghost across his face. The hint of a smile was enough for his heart to begin to lift and cautiously find its way back to its appropriate position.

"If you make a decent wage and aren't prone to reckless spending, it is just a matter of time before you would have yourself a home. So, it seems to me that you are belittling yourself for not existing in a place for longer than you have."

Aaron gave the older man's assessment some thought. It made a certain sort of sense, though it did relatively little to improve upon what he currently had to recommend him.

"Additionally, you are open to learning, which many of the so-called learned are not. You have a work ethic and are neither a spendthrift nor so parsimonious as to not wish to bring joy to those you care for." Anders stared at Aaron as he mulled over this generous appraisal of his attributes, as though weighing his response.

"Sir, does this mean that you approve?" and just like that, the man's face became unreadable.

"I am inclined to approve where Melody's affections lie, and I see nothing to take issue with thus far."

"Not many would be so open to welcoming a nameless child into their family." Aaron tripped over the words as he gave voice to the deeply seated ache. After a moment of consideration, Anders stood, wiped his hands off on his trousers dismissively, and began to walk back to the workshop. At a loss, Aaron could do little but watch him go. Almost like an afterthought, Anders glanced over his shoulder and looked the younger man directly in the eye.

"I happen to know that Melody loves both her name and her

home. It may be unconventional, and you will find that our entire family is unconventional - but it seems to me that, if this is the correct course for you both, there is no reason that what is hers might not become yours."

It was not a long engagement, as engagements go, though it was far too long for Melody's liking. The very day that Aaron was given Anders' approval, he took a portion of his savings and bought a simple silver band engraved with a delicate pattern of rolling waves. Three days later, he went down on one knee, asking *her* as was proper, and she gave her answer with great enthusiasm. From that point on, Melody existed in a state of anticipation. Some women of her age wanted nothing more than to be engaged, feeling that it conferred a sort of importance upon them and earned them the respect of their peers. Melody cared little for that sort of social climbing; what she wanted was what Gran and Grandad had had, what her Mami and Baba still had, and that was all part of marriage. It was Aaron who felt the need to take things slow. Still far too aware of his social standing and perceived shortcomings, he felt the need to make more of himself before joining his new family. Had he been allowed by his future bride, the engagement might have lasted years, so much did he wish to prove himself worthy. However, Melody's patience would only extend so far. It was a full six months from the day that they met in the market until the day that Melody and Aaron were married. Just as her parents had, they said their vows once in the Temple of the Sun and once more before her Mami's shrine in their family home. On that same day, Aaron moved his small collection of belongings into her room and took on the last name Windle.

CHAPTER 19

It was a year that would be remembered for quite some time, when the cold wind blew along the coast bearing illness on its breezes, like a skeletal rider foretelling great sorrow. Some coughed and sniffled, others were bedridden with horrible fevers, the most extreme of which woke frequently from phantasmagoric visions in absolute horror. The Mistresses Windle, now Denila and Melody, were called from bedside to bedside, treating the ill without bias; often treating townsfolk who were barely polite to them in passing and who regularly spoke unkindly behind their backs. The women were run ragged, called from their home at all times of the day and night, and yet it seemed that the Windle house was to be one of the few to go unscathed, right up until Anders fell ill. When the illness struck, it moved quickly, his breathing ragged, his state feverish, and finally it was his heart that gave out. Denila was utterly bereft; she sat by his bedside for three days after his passing and would neither leave nor shut her eyes to sleep unless someone was sitting beside him. When Melody's aunts arrived with their children, they were pulled into the vigil for their brother, holding hands as they wept for his passing. When they put Anders in the ground beside his mother and father, the aunts wept openly but quietly as their sister-in-law and her brother keened and wailed; their sorrow filled the air and floated across the water with the evening breeze.

As the day progressed, the family little by little returned to the house, staring into their teacups and doing their best not to tax Denila and her children. They helped clean the kitchen and tidied the former sick room, but despite all of their best efforts, it was only a matter of time before Melody found herself overwhelmed by the presence of the bereaved. She gave Aaron a brief hug, grabbed her daughter's hand with one hand and her son's hand with the other, and walked down to the beach. The three sat in the sand, enveloped in their sorrow. Benjamin, at ten, was too young to remember when his Great Grandmother Mira passed. She had lived long enough to see her first great-grandchild but not long enough for him to remember seeing her. Still, they were a family of stories and storytellers. Mira's journals lined a shelf with every story she had heard and written down in anticipation of the generations to come. She had started by writing down stories told by bees and foxes, by owls and turtles. She wrote down the story of every encounter her family had with Nimmawni, but as she aged, she began to write down the more mundane stories, the stories of her children and her children's children, and, through the lens of her writing, you couldn't help but get to know Mira. When Denila began to add to the journals, she made sure to carry on both traditions, and, in the process, she wrote down stories about Mira herself. So it was that, while Benjamin could not remember his Great

Grandmother Mira and, at seven, Mimsy had never met her at all, both knew of her life and they knew of her death. Death was not an untouched topic in their family, but death from illness was unfamiliar, and Anders had been so very alive and vital so recently that it was hard to wrap one's head around, much less one's heart.

"Why did the man from the Temple say that Grampa was gone?" Mimsy had so very many questions. Giving her Mami a break was part of why Melody had grabbed the children on the way out.

"Because that is what the temple teaches, Sweetness."

"But that is not how we tell our stories."

"No, no it isn't."

"So, why do they tell their stories so differently?" Mimsy asked in earnest, her voice sweet and innocent and completely without reproof.

"Death is difficult for people to think about, Sweetness, and sometimes the other stories feel more helpful to some people."

Melody was not about to address her personal issues with the Temple's stories or a belief in an oppositional duality that left no room for so many of the intricacies of life. Not with a seven-year-old, and certainly not in the wake of her grandfather's death.

"Why would it make people feel better to say that Grampa is gone? I think it's better that he has returned to the all and he can see me every day, even if I think that he would be sad about Ama's being so very, very sad."

"I think people like to have a person either here, where they can see them, or somewhere else, where they can believe they will be happy regardless of what is happening here. Like when Aunt Thea goes home to her house, we know that she is generally happy even though we can't see her. It is not so simple when we believe that their spirit is around us and a part of all things, while their body returns to the great cycle."

"As we all must," The little girl said, quoting almost every one of The People's stories that made reference to death.

"As we all must." Melody agreed.

Benjamin remained quiet. He had been quiet for days, barely speaking to anyone and generally being angry at the world. Mimsy's acceptance of their Grampa's death seemed to grate on him. At the end of their exchange, he shot to his feet with a stone in hand and ran down to the water's edge to hurl it into the sea before finally, *finally* allowing himself to cry. Finally allowing himself to be held in his mother's arms. Finally, he hugged his little sister as she wiped at his face, as well as her own, with the fabric of her skirts.

They stood together at the water's edge, holding each other close, as the waves seemed to draw their sadness little by little out to sea with every passing wave.

As they held each other, their feet damp and cold from the edges of the waves that reached out to find their skin, they heard a cry out across the water. They heard a voice that, at first, sounded like the cry of a sea bird. As it drew closer, it became clearer, eventually revealing itself to be a young woman's voice, filled with concern,

"Winken!"

The three instinctively turned toward the dock.

"Winken!"

The voice was approaching along the shoreline.

"Nimmawni?"

Melody saw the mermaid's head bobbing among the waves and gestured toward the dock. The children ran to the end of the structure, excited in spite of themselves. Benjamin clutching the shimmering shell that hung around his neck, and had done since he was eight.

"Winken! What is happening? I heard a sound like so many hearts breaking and a wailing like a soul that would never be happy again. I followed the sound out of curiosity and concern but found it came from up there on the shore."

"I think you heard Ama," Benjamin commented, his feelings on wailing over the dead clear in his tone of voice; Mimsy giggled beside him.

"Nimmawni, my Baba, Anders, he's dead."

The mermaid blinked at them, her eyes full of sorrow.

"He has returned to the cycle, as we all must. This does not keep us from sadness as you return his body to the deep..." she paused "to the earth?"

"Yes," Melody smiled gently, her lip wobbling once again, "To the earth. We are especially saddened because he was not old; we feel he should have had more time, but an illness stole him from our family."

The mermaid shook her head in sorrow.

"I am most grieved to hear that he was taken with discord."

"Discord?" Benjamin asked.

"Yes," Nimmawni explained, "The Sea-Folk, and many of The People, believe that when one becomes inexplicably unwell, it is due to a discordant graft."

Benjamin's response was swift, once again choosing to channel his grief into anger:

"Grampa wasn't like an apple tree; there's not a graft that fell off, he got sick, and then he couldn't breathe, and then his heart stopped, and now he's gone."

Nimmawni shuddered, momentarily taken aback by the fervor of the young man's temper. She looked from him to his sister to his mother, then back to the seething bundle of rage.

"Little Winken, I can understand that losing someone you love may be very distressing. May I tell you what I was told of 'illnesses'?"

The boy did not respond, his chin tucked to his chest as he sulked. Melody nodded, Mimsy agreed, and Nimmawni looked to the young man again, obviously hoping that he would show some sign of recognition before she took a deep breath and began to speak.

"When the gods molded their children from the clay of creation, they were rough in nature and more primitive versions of what they would become. It is nature that we look at that which we create and see pieces of ourselves, and so it was only natural that the gods would look at their creations and wish to imbue them with greater pieces of themselves. From this urge, the grafts were created, tiny pieces of the divine that could pass from one being to another, changing their children and their children's children to be better reflections of the divine. Even so, it is true that all actions have impact. The unforeseen impact of the beneficent graft was its necessary balance. The beneficent graft would naturally make its recipients more capable, more apt to survive and to thrive, an occurrence which would be disruptive to the balance. Such advancement might cause a People to breed and grow rampant, decimating The People upon whom they feed. It was to correct this disruption that the discordant grafts came into being. Where the beneficent grafts merged with their hosts to make them better, smarter, stronger, the discordant grafts attacked their hosts and weakened them, sometimes even killing them in the process. The one is the unfortunate cost of the other, and it is always *someone's* beloved that pays that price."

"But why?" the boy asked, "why did it have to be *my* Grampa? My Grampa was so good and patient and kind."

"And what of someone else's Grampa, Little Winken? Or of their child, or sister, or brother? Would they not have someone who would also mourn their body's return to the cycle? Would it be easier for those who do not believe in the importance of the cycle, who do not believe that the spirit lingers on? These are difficult questions, and they have no simple answers. No answers that explain why the strand of one life is cut shorter than that of another, but we can choose to celebrate the beauty of that life and honor that which was honored by our loved one. Even more than that, we can honor those parts which connect us to those we love. I can tell already, Little Winken, that you carry much of your Grampa's spirit."

The boy scrubbed his feet against the wood of the dock as though trying to pull apart the fibers of the plank with his toes. He chewed on his lip and played with the necklace that hung around his neck, obviously not wishing to be comforted by the mermaid's words. He remained silent as Melody and Nimmawni spoke, as Mimsy badgered the mermaid with her incessant questions, as the sun began to set. When it finally came time for Nimmawni to leave, she splashed his toes with sea water to draw his attention. The two stared deeply into one another's eyes until her sad smile was reflected in his face. At that, she slipped beneath the surface and was gone.

CHAPTER 20

It only took about sixty-six years, but Toddy's dream finally came true. A son of the Windle family finally became a fisherman. After a time, once he had grown tall and strong enough to be of use, Benjamin joined his Dad on the docks, helping to load and unload the boats that moved along the coast. He spoke with the fishermen when they came to shore and, little by little, began to spend more time aboard the ships, eventually joining the ranks of the fishermen who left before the sun rose and returned with nets full of squirming cargo. The seventeen-year-old loved the feel of the wind and the spray from the waves on his face, the sway of the deck under his feet. The fishing itself was rather more incidental, a way to spend time on the water and put money in his pocket at the same time. He had his great-grandmother's gray eyes and his grandfather's serious demeanor, his father's smile, and his mother's temper. He spent so much time in the sun that his tan skin darkened to a golden brown, and his natural freckles proliferated across his nose and cheeks. He was made up of those who came before him, using his hands, descended from carpenters, to haul lines and collect nets, living out Toddy's childhood dreams.

On the day that Nimmawni returned, the seabird followed him out to the fishing boat as it cast off for the day, squawking and screeching about Sea-Folk and sea urchins - though it focused far more on the latter than the former. Flustered, Benjamin did the only thing he could think to do and launched himself into the water, swimming as quickly as he could from the harbor, his shipmates yelling obscenities behind him.

Rather than swimming to shore, he made his way directly to the dock. It was not a short distance, but he had swam the length from jetty to dock on more than one occasion. Over halfway there, Nimmawni found him. Her hair brushed across his arm, giving him a fright. It took him a moment to find the source, but once he did, excitement beat in his chest almost as strongly as the fear that had set his heart to racing.

"It has been seven years, Nimmawni. Where have you been?"

The mermaid scanned him from head to toe - as though examining his swimming form. Apparently content that he would not drown as they conversed, she responded,

"I went in search of the great dragon that encircles the star-body."

"The great what? Nimmawni, how is it that you are only now telling me that dragons are real? Giant, fire-breathing dragons? The sort that kidnapped maidens and were killed by knights in shining armor? How have none of us heard of this before?" Nimmawni continued to swim beside him, though her expression seemed suspicious of his sudden enthusiasm.

"Well, I don't know about kidnapping or armor, and I

suppose some of them might breathe fire, but dragons are most certainly real. I found it down in the deepest depths of the ocean, but then I had to find its head, which is harder than you would think, as it stretches all the way around the Star-body and is constantly in motion."

Benjamin had trouble conceptualizing what he was being told; it was all too grand in scale to be countenanced, and yet there were many things beyond human understanding that they, his family, had come to embrace.

"The dragon encircles the entire star-body? That would be quite a distance to travel, and I can see how its head might be remarkably difficult to find. Why were you looking for it?"

The mermaid chose to ignore the first half of his thought, addressing his question instead.

"I wanted to ask it some questions, and ask it I did, though it spoke so very slowly that it was hard to interpret the words."

"What did the dragon have to say?"

"Mostly that he did not have the answers I seek, that it is old knowledge and, being old, he remembers the how of things deep in his bones rather than with his head. That, should he try to do as I wish to do myself, he probably could do it unhindered, but it is no longer his place. His place is with the star-body, as it has been for time beyond remembering, in the greatest depths and the deepest of shadows."

When they arrived at the dock, Benjamin climbed the old ladder and sat on the platform edge. Her eyes widened, and she hid her cheeks beneath the water's surface as he removed his shirt. He had to admit a degree of amusement as the mermaid, now appearing to be about the same age as a fourteen year old

Mimsy, exhibited about the same response as any adolescent girl to the sight of a fit young man without his shirt. Despite her appearance, it was somewhat flattering to receive such attentions from a being that must be over a hundred years old. He squeezed out the excess moisture from his shirt, smirking as he caught her eyes flicking across his muscles as they flexed, and laid the garment out to dry.

"It seems so strange at times, the things you go looking for. Those that live in darkness are so often vilified by the Temple of the Sun, surely *they* would frown on any beast living at such depths, never mind a dragon." The mermaid eyed him suspiciously, less than impressed with his thought process.

"Winken, really, you have grown up with the stories of The Shadow and The Light; of all humans, *you* should know that living in darkness has nothing to do with virtue." Her gaze cut straight through him, shearing away the protective layers of thought and behavior that allowed him to fit in among his fellow sailors and amongst the folk in town.

"I know," he sighed, "it's just difficult at times. The Temple of the Sun has split all things in two, equating Light with goodness, order, reason, and life, in opposition to Darkness paired with evil, chaos, and death. This is what I speak to every day, what I am inundated by as I walk through town. Despite which, I must say, there are many cases where I find there is a clear lack of introspection concerning which side of the divide some temple goers would find themselves on, should their beliefs prove truth."

The mermaid smirked up at him and swept the tendrils of her hair over her shoulder before responding.

"I told Old Winken once that, being a human steeped in the stories of The People and understanding the stories of humans, perhaps allows you to speak with clarity to both. It seems to me that this only is the case if there are humans prepared to listen, and if you yourself can see that balance with clarity." She leaned against the ladder as she continued. "It is true that the predator waits and stalks in shadow, but she stalks so she may feed herself and her children. Even as the predator lurks, the mouse makes its home in the safety of shadows. The bear hibernates in shadows to wait out the long cold and make better use of its energy. You were born of shadows, held safely in the darkened seas of the womb of your mother, and when you first saw light, it was so vast that you cried out in wonder and fear. Each night, you sleep in the comforting arms of The Shadow and its night. Light feeds us, but Shadow nourishes us also. It is when they are no longer in balance that we experience unnecessary pain. Too much sunlight will burn the skin, too much darkness starves the body. We are, all of us, creatures of Shadow and Light."

Benjamin sat in silence, contemplating her words. When he continued to say nothing, she grabbed one of Benjamin's feet. The feel of the cool water seemed to wake him with a jolt, and she smiled up at him, showing only the tiniest hint of sharp teeth.

"The Shadow and The Light have helped to shape our world and have filled it with creations of their own, not a one of which is wholly good or wholly bad. Grumpy, bad-tempered, arrogant, suspicious, or even judgmental, quite possibly; but such things can be said for many of The People."

"Creations of their own?"

"Of course, all of the Gods have their hand in creation."

The subject of creation, having long been a matter of study for philosophers and religious figures alike, was a subject that Nimmawni spoke of with a sense of absolute assurance. Every one of Benjamin's questions that followed was met with straightforward answers, citing stories that spanned the traditions of many of The People. In time, having recognized his distraction, Benjamin brought the conversation back to the topic at hand.

"So, did The Shadow have its hand in the creation of dragons?"

"Of course, and so did The Light, and so did the Great Mama of the Deep"

CHAPTER 21

When the Great Mama of the Deep first set about molding the forms of The People, some say she started with the smallest among us. Some say she started with the tiniest of plants that floated across the surface of the beautiful green blue of the Sea Below, dining on sunlight and providing the cycle with its immense power. Some say she started with the tunneling worms that built their homes in the darkest silt of the Star-body. But truly, before the tiniest of creatures, before the light eaters and the builders of shadows, before all the rest of her creations, she made dragons. Huge dragons that lived in caves at the bottom of the oceans, that launched themselves from the sea floor and soared through the waiting skies above, that made homes in the mountains of the exposed star-body, and the caverns where the star's fire bubbled to the surface; those dragons passed with ease between the Sea Above and the Sea Below. She made dragons, dragons with huge bodies and scales like great pebbles in all manner of colors. Some with scales the color of fire, others the deepest and darkest of nights, some with the golden glow of sunlight, others the great green blue of the sea itself.

Her beautiful children made their homes in the many corners of the world that The Great Mama of the Deep had created. The dragons aged slowly and grew into their vastness. They hid away from the watching eyes of The People and the Gods alike, sometimes for so long that they were completely forgotten.

When The People began to populate the land, they looked upon the once-forgotten dragons who had made it their home, and many were scared. The children of Pan'chan were an exception, but then, they usually are. The children of Pan'chan, often having more intelligence and less sense than the rest of The People, took the presence of dragons as an amusing challenge. One child of Pan'chan stole the scales from a dragon's toe and created for itself an impenetrable shell. Another stole the shape of a dragon's eye so it could see longer and clearer than The People of its lineage who had come before. Pan'chan's children aside, the majority of The People had the good sense to leave the dragons in peace. The dragons who chose to remain in the water hid themselves in the great trenches or along the sea floor. However, it is a universal truth that all things must be subject to the time and the tide, and all things exist as part of the cycle. The great rosy opalescent dragon, who made its home and nest in the valley from which the sun first rose, was so long in one place that its bones began to harden and fuse to the sea floor. Its body immobile, its flesh and scales broke apart and drifted away on the currents; from those pieces, the first seahorses emerged. The first children of dragons, the seahorses spread far and wide, leaving behind a dense skeleton of coral to be populated by The People. It is possible that some of the Dragons of the deepest abyss remain, still hidden in the deepest of shadows, far beyond the peering eyes of all but the most adventurous traveler. Or perhaps they may have returned to the Sea Above.

It was the greatest of all of the dragons, adapted so well to the deep seas that he appeared as a giant sea serpent who grew to such lengths that he was able to encircle the whole of the great star-body submerged in the Sea Below. He stared up from the depths and felt the call of the stars above him, singing their patterns along their determined dance in the Sea Above, and the serpent dragon began to dance with them, his dance moving in concert with the movement of the Sea Above. It was his deep and abiding love of the moon that caused the tides to form and shift, and it was with this dance that there came the very idea of time. They say that, should he ever stop on his course, time too would cease.

Out in the great open spaces of the Sea Below, there danced another of the mighty dragons, this one was beloved of all of the fish of the rolling seas. It sang in all of their languages and told their stories in each of them. So much did it love its smaller companions that, when it felt so very full beyond measure with the stories of The People, it did not forsake its purpose but rather split, casting from itself with its dying breath new children, children who were not all of one People but pieces of many. Some had the tails of the sun catching ocean fish, others of the great sharks of the deep, others the long flicking tail of the serpent and eel. Each one an amalgamation of all of the stories of The People merged together. Each one manifested with the arms of humans, a new People who had only just begun to tell their own stories and sing the ancient songs.

When the final breath of the dragon had fully escaped, casting its new children into the sea, its body shimmered and shattered into a million pieces of ocean debris. Its children collected all that they could find and used their human arms and hands and fingers to drape themselves in this final magic, a magic that allowed them to hear and listen, to speak and be understood, communing with all of The People as the dragon had done. To fill themselves with stories and cast their echoes out on the waves and the winds.

Benjamin looked down in awe at the shell that he rubbed between his fingertips. He had always known it possessed its own strange magic; his parents had known it, and his grandparents as well. They experienced its power every day when they heard the Winged People overhead, or The People of the woods who sometimes visited their garden. Every time they heard the Rooted People sing, they felt the proof of the gift they had been given. Yet, at no point had they known what it was that they carried strung about their necks. The remains of a dragon, an idea so fantastic as to be beyond reckoning, a dragon so in love with the stories of The People that even in its dying breath it ensured that the story would always live on. He thought of the books that lined the shelves in his home, translating the words of The People to the written human word, and saw that they carried on the dragon's purpose. Perhaps this, too, was just another bit of the dragon's magic.

"You know," Benjamin said after a moment of thought, "It

occurs to me that if you found the dragon that encircles the star-body, then all you really needed to have done to find it was stay still. If it's just going round and round, nose to tail, never stopping... then, if you stay near it, eventually the head would end up wherever it is that you are."

She stared at him, open-mouthed, as though completely stunned - whether with him for thinking of it or herself for not doing so herself was unclear.

She had said, "If you don't believe me, make spaces for The Shadow and The Light, and I just bet their wee folk come to visit you and make amazing things happen." It seemed to Benjamin, as he pondered how to make such spaces, that strange and rewarding projects seemed to be an intergenerational theme. He ran his fingers gently over the face of the guardian of the house before wandering into the yard to consult first the crows and then the Moon Tree. His house was full of shadowed areas, and light streamed in through the windows all day, but this did not appear to be what was necessary. As he sat in the shade of his mother's dear friend, he watched a marching line of ants as they carried small chunks of the Moon Tree's leaves to the entrance of their hill. Their cargo cast irregular shadows that bobbed along the soil, and he was struck with a moment of inspiration. Unlike the twisting forms he now observed, the shadows in his home were all made up of predictable shapes cast in afterthought, based on the form and function of the house itself. There were no shadows for shadows' sake. It was with this in mind that Benjamin began to collect all manner of oddly shaped materials. Sticks, broken shells, split wood that curved around knots and whorls, and discarded materials from the fishing boats; when he had a good quantity and variety, he began to assemble them into small sculptures. Each piece was designed with very little attention to how they looked and great focus on how they disrupted the light and cast shadows against shelves and walls. The largest sat upon a fence post not far from the hand pump, where the shadow shifted and changed shape constantly throughout the course of the sun's progression through the sky. As Benjamin made spaces for The Shadow's children, he was stumped by how to create something similar for The Light; right up until Mimsy came home carrying a satchel of broken glass.

"It seems to me that you keep on making places where shadows can play Benji. Then you stare at the windows and the sunlight in the trees, and you mutter to yourself about light. Well, light plays as it moves through glass, does it not?"

As with many brilliant ideas, it was so simple it made him feel dense. Kissing his sister on the forehead, he gathered up her thoughtful gift. The house, so long inhabited by carpenters, was hardly without tools. He gathered up a chisel, a bow drill, and a plank of wood before setting up shop near the farthest area of the fence. Opening the satchel, he saw a wealth of multicolored glass. Mimsy had chosen to leave out the ambers and black glasses that would impede the light, instead providing him with aquas and blues, clears, greens, and purples; even some textured shards of milk glass, too opaque for light to penetrate but reflecting and refracting it admirably. Multicolored mobiles of glass began to appear around the house, by windows and doorways, even adorning the posts and lintel that housed the golden disc dedicated to the Sun God's visage. His project was far from complete the first time he saw the shadows shift by themselves. Tiny angles protruded from his creation, and he got the feeling that he was being watched with curiosity. The shadow blinked at him, though he could not properly describe how he knew, then withdrew.

Several days later when Benjamin returned, sweaty and salt encrusted, he found Melody and Mimsy wandering around the kitchen with glass lamps, examining both light and shadow. In any other home, the behavior might have appeared quite mad, but Benjamin simply dropped his things by the door and joined them.

"What is it that we are searching for, Ladies?"

"The Sparkle," Mimsy told him and Melody nodded vigorously.

"You are looking for a sparkle?"

"Not just any sparkle, *the* sparkle. Mama saw it while she was making dinner this evening. The sunlight hit the shifting glass and a sparkling light flew off."

"And it giggled," Melody added.

Mimsy nodded, though neither woman turned to look in his direction. They continued to roam about the room, searching corners and checking the walls for every glow of refracted light.

"It definitely giggled. I saw it later in the day myself." Mimsy commented absently.

"It chittered and zipped around the glass, like it was having the time of its life."

A giggling, like the chiming of tiny bells, rang through the room. It was quiet, but it carried, and all three Windles paused in their tracks. They carried on in this fashion until the stars were bright in the sky, with very little result.

In the months to follow, the instances of dancing lights and moving shadows became more and more frequent, some becoming more clear as individual beings. The little sparkle that danced and played in the refracted light, whose favorite room was the kitchen, liked to float on the rising steam from stove top cooking and freshly baked bread. The tiny shadow, with angular limbs that watched humans with an insatiable curiosity, but did not speak - though Benjamin found that the quality of her darkness was expressive nonetheless. Creatures shaped like flashing butterflies, winking in and out of existence with every beat of their wings, circled the Sun God's disc. In the shadow of Benjamin's largest sculpture, a squat old shadow creature made his home, leaving the impression of a giant, ill-tempered toad that spoke in strange poetry and was prone to scratching those who tried his patience. Others came and went; some spoke, others sang or danced, each one found these spaces dedicated to their kind both glorious and strange. Some even came simply to see the novelty of *new humans* who were once more connected to The People. It was one such visitor who knocked on their door in the dead of night, its heavy hand shaking the door in its frame and waking the whole family with its volume. When Aaron opened the door, he was met by a shadow large enough and deep enough that it seemed that even the brightest stars had disappeared. When the visitor shifted where it stood and the stars winked around its frame, Aaron gasped. Acknowledging that the situation was out of his purview, he called for his wife and Benjamin, both of whom had been busily clothing themselves and were already at the top of the stairs. It was clear that the visitor was too large to enter the house, so he bowed to the Windles before motioning for them to join him outside. He sat, in the manner of a storyteller, so they would not strain their necks to look at him, and began to speak. His speech was not something they heard with their ears, instead, they felt it vibrating through their bones.

Greetings

"Greetings, brother who dwells among shadows." It seemed like an appropriate form of address. The shadow nodded, which was promising. "What brings you to our home?"

I have come, in the manner of my children and kin, to greet the New Humans who dwell among The People. To see the sanctuary you have built, away from the blind progression of human interest.

"I had not thought of our home as a sanctuary, though we welcome those who come to us without ill will." Benjamin looked at his house with new eyes, doing his best to see it as The People might. The plants that grew under the loving attention of his mother and sister, the hiding places they all pretended not to notice, where The People thrived, the feeding platform for the crows, and all of the places created especially for the light and shadows to play.

"What do you mean, New Humans?"

You and yours exist as part of a new age of humanity. There are few who are old enough to remember, for we, too, return to the cycle, as all things must.

"As all things must." Benjamin and Melody repeated; he had never before thought of the shadow creatures as mortal beings. They all seemed so timeless, they reminded him of Nimmawni. Though he supposed that one day, long after he was gone, she too would return to the cycle.

The old humans were among The People; they told our stories and carried our traditions. When they began to change their stories, casting themselves above The People, a new breed of human was born. Deaf to the world around them, they speak without thought and act without an understanding of consequence. What they do not speak of in this part of the world is that the Old Humans are not entirely gone.

This revelation startled both of the Windles, who had been given to believe that all humans had lost the knack of speaking to The People.

"There are others then? Others who can speak to The People?"

The giant shadow reached out to touch Benjamin's shoulder, which completely disappeared into a cool darkness that felt similar to the heavy air at the bottom of the root cellar. While the feel of its touch called to mind the musty smell of damp earth and vegetation, it was almost as though the shadow were trying to mimic a behavior of human reassurance.

I cannot be certain.

"Then what do you mean by 'not entirely gone'?" Melody

asked quietly.

There are those who still tell the old stories, who understand the value of the time outside of mind. They value the earth, and they speak with intention, they give honor where they kill, and they teach their young to do the same. Still, I have seen no indication that they retain the ability to hear or to speak. They appear to be of neither world, in truth.

Mother and son exchanged a glance, confirming their mutual curiosity.

"Why have we never heard of this before?"

You are blessed by one of the Sea-Folk; their interactions with The People are limited by the land and waters that touch the Sea. You live among The People, but their territories are small. Overlapping territories carry many stories around the world, immortalizing them among The People, but their numbers are limited. Additionally, if these humans are not of the People, their stories may not travel.

It was a strange thing to hear that their stories might be shared among other humans. Remembering the provenance of his necklace, he found himself grateful that the stories were still shared among another human culture but saddened that they might be cut off from the wealth of stories still told only among The People.

You are an empathetic clan.

The shadow remarked, responding to a comment that Benjamin hadn't even realized he spoke aloud. The shadow bobbed its head, coming to some sort of conclusion.

I give you my blessing as I move through this night.

The farewell felt formal and final. Before they could respond, the shadow dissipated, the stars peeking through its form and growing brighter as their visitor disappeared without a trace.

Mother and son returned to the house and were greeted by Aaron who, after realizing that he could only hear one half of the conversation, settled for retreating to the kitchen with a drowsy Mimsy and boiling water for four midnight cups of lavender tea.

CHAPTER 22

"Sometimes, bad things happen. One can rationalize this fact however they please, but the simple truth remains - sometimes bad things happen. At times, it could, perhaps, be said that it is someone else's stars which are aligned for good fortune - at cross purposes with one's own goals and intentions. Is it then true that a person may be destined for sorrow? It certainly seems that, no matter how fervently one wishes for balance and peace, there are times when it simply is not meant to be. Or perhaps, though it has long been accepted that the movements of the Sea Above are in concert with the world below, the stars themselves have been gifted the misfortune of greater blame than they deserve.

It seems to me that sometimes the voice of human avarice and lust speaks with such clarity that it appears with the power and resonance of the voice of a righteous god. Such a voice would clearly appeal to those who crave control and a future of their own design, with little regard for the cost. How better to create a zealot? Though the human gods have many times sent their children in search of glory in battle, the task they set is in accordance with their nature. Contrariwise, the insidious cruelty of men is rarely the will of the divine. Despite this, it is cruelty that spreads like a sickness among the ostensibly devout, infecting those who wish to believe themselves superior.

Upon reflection, though very little is required, it is hard to deny that across the many generations of human history, one finds that the arrogant belief in one's superiority is a frequent expression of the language of cruelty. This idea was not an unfamiliar one; we have known it to be true for quite some time. Still, knowing a thing is far removed from experiencing it in truth. It seems that this was a lesson that we, as a family, were meant to learn firsthand. So I leave this message for you, my beloved descendants. Though we live immersed in the world of The People, I implore you, keep a weather eye on the human world. I wish you safety, but more than that, I wish you Joy.

Melody Windle"

As time carried on, the world carried on with it. The port and the town continued to grow and expand, technology advanced, and the Temple thrived. While the Windles continued to attend the Temple of the Sun, it was largely a gesture that affirmed their part in the community, a way to reassure their neighbors, and an easy way to stay in contact with their family as a whole. The goings on within the Temple rarely concerned them in the slightest, as the Temple rarely changed in fundamentals. However, when a new young cleric found himself a position at the town's Temple of the Sun, that was destined to change.

The new cleric was far more extreme in his beliefs, praising the Sun God with a sort of ecstatic fervor and infectious zeal that drew a very clear line between the morally superior devotees of the Sun and those who, intentionally or otherwise, were following the dark path laid out by the Adversary of the Abyss. Where the previous clergymen had recognized this corrupting force, their concern was minimal in the face of the Sun God's glory. The Adversary was obviously an inferior, if not minor, entity. A being that challenged one's faith on occasion and was to be symbolically overcome once a year with the winter battle between darkness and light. Not so, this new man. Instead, each speech was designed to inspire each temple-goer to call into question the neighbor who sat beside them, casting judgment and laying blame. Each week, Benjamin felt the growing hypocrisy of the young cleric's teachings. As, within the man's vitriol, Benjamin saw the very attributes that had been assigned to this supposed "darkness." The spirit of the cleric's messages flourished among the townsfolk; embraced and, at times, even celebrated as it manifested itself in actions among those who claimed to champion the path of light. It was unnerving to see how readily the townsfolk internalized and justified the practice of casual cruelty, even as they espoused a doctrine of virtue. In light of this, Benjamin kept a wary eye on the treatment of his mother and his sister, becoming more vigilant as the young cleric began to rage against the *occult*. He was particularly concerned as the cleric went so far as to depict simple things, such as infusions and tinctures for the purpose of healing, as temptations to follow the shadowed path into the Abyss. What he did not think to do was watch after himself.

The problem started, as many do, as a matter of flirtation. Miss Annabelle Varrows went to Temple every Sun's-Day, and every Sun's-Day she was the picture of poised femininity. Every Sun's-Day she smiled sweetly at Gerald Ortney, every Sun's-Day she smiled even more sweetly at Benjamin Windle, and every Sun's-Day the young Mister Ortney saw her smiling sweetly at the young Mister Windle. Though Benjamin was never more than civil to Miss Varrows, the involved parties proceeded as though his interest were a given. Had Young Mister Windle expressed an interest in another time and another place, in another year, or with another environment, it may have simply been a matter of rivalry. The two might have engaged in a civil competition of charm with some degree of familial interference. In a less than ideal case, a punch might have been thrown, but this was neither of those cases. In an environment of growing suspicion, it was a simple thing for young Mister Ortney to attribute Miss Varrows' infuriating attentions toward his perceived rival to a manifestation of the occult, citing the works of the Mistresses Windle as proof of the entire family's unrepentant corruption.

When the morning's routine of ceremony and ritual came to a close, Benjamin gathered with his mother and sister, his uncle and cousin, his great aunts and their children and their children's children, in the square outside the temple. They came equipped with picnic baskets, satchels, and blankets that they would carry either to the shore or to the park to share their luncheon and enjoy one another's company. There was a time when such gatherings would have taken place far from town in the company of his great-grandmother's family, but as the immediate Windle family grew in number, their gatherings became closer to home. It was at these gatherings that potential spouses were introduced, upcoming births were announced, and life achievements were celebrated. The nature of their gatherings was so apparent that, as the Windles and their extended family gathered their things, Miss Varrows looked on with a vague sort of longing.

From where Gerald Ortney stood among a group of other young men, he could see Miss Varrows and her parents. He could see her parents chatting with other townsfolk, and he could see exactly where Miss Varrows had focused her attentions, the sight of which left him seething. It was short work to enlist his companions when he decided to follow the Windle family. That family had always been strange and raised enough curiosity among his fellows to make their spying feel like quite the lark. Between the three of them, Gerald Ortney was certain he could find some way to turn Miss Varrows against the Windles and guide her affections toward himself.

The family rounded the side of the temple and proceeded a short way down the road to their destination. The ten acres of parkland was all that remained of the great forest that once stood a short distance from the very center of town. The forest stood tall, back when the town was a small village; when the port was frequented only by small fishing vessels; before the northern homesteads expanded into expanses of farmland; when the houses to the south were just being built and, along with them, a solitary dock was erected that extended out into the waves. In that time, there bobbed a small boat that knocked gently against the pillars with the passing waves; the forests of the south extended west and north where they teemed with verdant life, interrupted only by the winding dirt road that connected the small fishing village to the rest of human civilization. Over time, the road widened, displacing the rabbit warrens and their predator's dens and replacing them with the human houses that rose in their stead. Little by little, construction ate away at the wilderness, and even that remaining slice of the wild became more civilized, home to manicured lawns and charming gazebos. It was in one of these clearings that picnic blankets were spread and food was shared, all manner of stories passed between them as they enjoyed one another's company. At the edge of the clearing, from a shady area, sheltered by a copse of nearby trees, the three young men watched the Mistresses Windle assess a cousin's clammy face and motion for young Benjamin to check among her things for a strange concoction, which he delivered to her hand. From that simple motion, a plan emerged. A plan that would result in absolutely no good for anyone involved.

It takes only one malicious voice to start a rumor, and young Mister Ortney had three. They began small, commenting on the Mistresses Windle and their potions with concern. Some of the townsfolk adopted their worry, but in a town where most everyone had a loved one treated by the Mistresses Windle, they were loath to do much more than grumble and cast suspicious looks. When they cast their net to include Benjamin, they hit pay dirt. The Mistresses were strange but well known. Benjamin spent his days on the water as a relative unknown to all but the fishermen and dock workers, who were not always known for their sound judgment. He was strange as his ancestors and quiet, but what more could be said for him? And *if* he were following the path to the Abyss, what did that say of his family? The requests for the Mistresses Windle decreased; few people wanted to be seen receiving their services. Though, in the duplicitous manner that much prejudice presents itself, the tea shop made steady sales in the prepared Windle remedies they kept readily in stock. It was when Gerald tried to escalate that he could not find traction. Unfortunately, the issue was not that the townsfolk he influenced disapproved of action against the Windle family; they just didn't want to take it themselves. It was with this feeling of tacit approval that Gerald Ortney, his compatriots, and their small troop of believers took the punishment of Benjamin Windle into their own hands.

In the stillness of the night, Benjamin woke to an unnatural silence. In the absence of cricket song, the cry of a solitary owl in the darkness was jarring, and his sleeping mind had trouble interpreting what it had to say, right up until the smell of smoke wafted into his room. He rolled out of bed, disoriented and uncertain, only to find that the roiling smoke had increased, becoming thicker and harder to see through. As he ran down the stairs, he heard the growl of hungry flames cracking the dry wood and rumbling like an oncoming storm, as flames climbed the walls to lick the ceiling of the great room. Benjamin froze in his descent and ran back up the stairs, pounding on doors to wake his parents and sister, the wood beneath his feet heating as the fire spread and crackled beneath them. His father pushed his mother out of the bedroom first, urging her to run down the stairs still wrapped tightly in their blanket, the two men following closely behind. Aaron ran out the kitchen door, bypassing the hand pump, to the old well and began hauling up bucket after bucket in an attempt to put out the fire. Benjamin did his best to push his mother out of the house, but she had stopped near the door to the kitchen, untangled herself from her blanket, and was pulling all of the family journals off their shelf,

"Benjamin!" she called breathlessly over her shoulder, barely audible above the din "Where is Mimsy?"

Benjamin looked around frantically. Had his sister not followed them down from her room? He ran back up the stairs, just in time to catch Mimsy as she barreled through her door and onto the landing followed by a rolling cloud of smoke, coughing and hacking, they practically tumbled down the stairs as the sound of the fire swelled to what felt like a deafening roar. Singeing their feet as the treads superheated and swelled, sounds of cracking and popping filled the air as the structure splintered and caught the spreading flames. Melody had already managed to save the family journals, dragging them out the kitchen door on her blanket; she was trying to save baskets full of dried herbs and remedies from the spreading fire when both of her children grabbed her and dragged her out into the garden.

Aaron finally gave up on trying to douse the fire, instead moving what he could away from the side of the house and the flying cinders cast off by the flames, doing his level best not to be burned in the process. He made only one mad dash into the house, retrieving the money pouch hidden in the wall just beyond the kitchen, and was forced to roll frantically in the dirt to put out the embers on his clothes. The fire, which began at the front wall of the house, spread as though driven by some sinister purpose, punctuated by the sound of exploding oil lamps, and it was not long before almost the entire house went up in flames. When the raging fire reached the kitchen, it marked the edge of the slate floors with smudges like blackened fingerprints that crept along the tiles as the conflagration fought to grow. For a moment, it seemed that many of the kitchen's contents might be spared, until the embers landed among the grain storage and the sack of flour exploded.

It seemed like the house would never stop burning; the leaping flames and threatening embers continued their intended work for hours that felt like years as the family watched in horror. The light stood out against the darkness and attracted neighbors like moths; some who grumbled their discontent to be sure, but others who tried to help Aaron and Benjamin douse the flames, who wrapped Melody and Mimsy in warm blankets, who promised experienced hands to help them rebuild when the fires finally stopped.

Amidst the chaos, one voice caught Benjamin's attention above the raging growl of the flames and the murmurs of concerned neighbors. It was the voice of the owl who had called to him through his window. Glancing around, concerned that his behavior might raise suspicion, he followed the voice of the owl away from the crowd.

"Wing Brother! I give you my thanks. Tonight is a night of sorrow for my family, but our sorrow could have been made manifold had you not woken me from my slumber."

The owl bobbed his head in acceptance.

"Human child of The People, predators have taken your nest. They conspire to lay waste in the night, as sneakily and stealthily as the rat. I have seen them, I have seen where they travel, and I will take you. It is good to know the direction from which danger flies."

His mind numbed by shock, Benjamin had barely had a moment to consider how the fire had started, though the question had niggled at him from the corner of his mind. He supposed it would be easy to assume that a lamp had been left open or an ember had escaped the fireplace. It would also be a simple thing to set a fire in the dead of night, to blame catastrophe on unfortunate circumstance, and rest assured that none would be the wiser. The flames that flickered against the night sky seemed to mirror themselves in his heart and mind, his family had been put in danger, and for what?

"It seems I owe you all the more, Wing Brother. Please, take me to them."

The owl launched himself into the darkness, and it took Benjamin every ounce of self-control to walk calmly past his house and through the crowd. He scanned the sky for the silhouette of his guide as his feet flew down the road. He slowed briefly as he saw another crowd hurrying in his direction, this time made up of family who had heard the news and had come to their aid. He tapped his mother's cousin Leo on the shoulder, nodding in the direction of town. Uncomprehending but wishing to be of service, the man grabbed a few more of his male relatives, and they followed him swiftly back the way they had come.

Their mission complete, the rest of the small crowd of arsonists had dispersed. The ringleaders sat on the pier, sharing a few bottles of wine and celebrating their genius, when an owl landed on a barrel a scant few feet away. It was Gerald Ortney who threw an empty bottle at the bird on its perch, proclaiming it a winged rat and a demon. Perhaps he would soon feel that statement vindicated as it was only moments later that Gerald Ortney was dragged to his feet with a muscular arm wrapped firmly around his neck, as Benjamin Windle descended upon his family's attackers as though driven by the Adversary himself. Before Ortney's intoxicated companions could get to their feet, Leo and four other relatives of the Windle family joined them on the pier. Each one got in their licks as they pummeled their prey into submission. It was Benjamin's cousin Hadish who pulled a length of rope from the dock and began to hobble the men, ankles and wrists, linking one to another so they could march their prisoners back to the house they had so recently put to the flame.

The group of young men were driven before the Windle cousins, not unlike a herd of sheep driven by dogs who nipped at their heels and bullied them towards their intended destination.

Upon reaching the ruin of his home, Benjamin threw Gerald forward with enough force that their attached bindings sent all three captives to their knees.

"Look at what you've done." Benjamin gestured to the flames. "Do you dare to deny that this evil is of your doing?"

The interaction drew the attention of the assembled neighbors and townsfolk, who steadily drew closer to hear what was said.

"I *don't* deny it." Ortney sneered, causing an assortment of gasps, growls, and hisses from the crowd. "And why should I? As a matter of fact, I am proud of my actions, but where you say evil, I see justice. After all, is this not how we are meant to deal with Witches of the Abyss?"

Benjamin watched as the statement split the crowd, some pulling back as though to distance themselves from the accusation, others looming forward with anger at the smug assertion.

"Witches of the Abyss?" Benjamin asked in disbelief, "What perversion has taken hold of you, Ortney, that you would say such a thing?"

Gerald struggled but ultimately drew himself to his feet. He and Benjamin were of a height, allowing him to glare directly into the other man's eyes.

"You call it perversion to follow the evidence of my own eyes, Windle? Would that I could simply ignore the strange behaviors, the wicked concoctions, or the fact that wherever sickness is bred, you *find a Windle*."

Taken aback, Benjamin stammered his response. "Medicinal

remedies, Ortney, and for them to help they must go where the illness lies."

"So you would like us to think, I'm sure, but not all of us are willing to be taken in by your wiles. Illness and discord, potions that twist the mind and the heart. Who can believe a single word out of your cursed mouth?"

The crowd split further as the argument continued, ruled by indecision and mounting fear, and, in the very center, Gerald Ortney smiled triumphantly. The altercation might have continued along this vein were it not for a heavy hand that dropped on the self-righteous young man's shoulder and the firm grip that turned him from his rival to face a father wracked with anger and grief. The light that emanated from the conflagration flickered across Aaron's face, highlighting his scars and wind-worn skin, casting shadows across features twisted by rage, and it was all Gerald could do not to cower with intimidation. Aaron's other hand grabbed hold of Gerald's shirt collar and, squeezing it tightly, he shook the young man like a rag doll before pulling him close to speak directly into his ear.

"You pustulent worm." He spoke the insult quietly before raising his voice for the assembled townsfolk to hear.

"Do you see this? This is the house I raised my children in. This is the first place I truly called home after a lifetime of having none. This house saw generations of my wife's family from birth until death, and its walls held a million stories that made each and every one of them so incredibly kind that they sacrificed the health and well-being of their own family members to take care of *your town*. That made a family so accepting that when I came to this town, a man with empty pockets, a man with no family name, they embraced me nonetheless and offered me their own." He shook Ortney again for emphasis.

"Look at this house, and understand what you chose to destroy with your disgusting pettiness. And pray tell, what other word does it deserve but pettiness? Because what reason could you give me that could possibly compare to the stories that this home could tell, much less the lives of the people who could have *died* in that inferno of your devising? Our only home has been destroyed, every fiber of my being cries out for answers to make *sense* of this tragedy, and yet what do I see before me but *children* who have allowed their petty tantrum to make of themselves monsters? You *infants*, who play with fire and call yourselves men. Whatever the cause of your displeasure, I can promise you that you have not even begun to know suffering."

Aaron dragged the young man forward, forcing his accomplices to stumble behind, until they could both feel the heat blistering their skin. The townsfolk cried out in shock, but not a one moved to intervene.

"I could throw you into that blaze you created, and who do you think could stop me? For what you have done, who would even try? I would have you understand, in this moment, that your continued good health is the result of your undeserved good fortune, that the person you see before you would never do such a thing. Because, unlike you, I refuse to let the lesser aspects of my character turn me into a monster."

Aaron threw his captive to the ground, away from the fire, and Gerald scuttled backwards on hands and feet, fear evident on his face. Aaron was done with him. He threw Ortney and his accomplices a final look of disgust before seeking out Melody and Mimsy to assure himself of their safety, their embrace finally calming some of the rage inside him that mirrored the state of their home. As their supporters gathered round the Windle family, offering their aid, other townsfolk disappeared into the night. The cousins gathered up their prisoners once again and marched them back to the town, directly to the constabulary.

It was a harrowing two days before Benjamin and Aaron began to pick through the wreckage. The slate of the kitchen floor remained but little else had gone unscathed, the second floor had completely collapsed, the table and chairs that had been built and repaired by generations of Windles were little more than charcoal and ash; the decorative touches, the carved detailing, all of the pieces that made up a story that crossed generations were gone. Yet, standing tall and almost untouched among the blackened and disintegrating scene, coated in little more than a layer of ash, stood the House Guardian.

Benjamin's uncles found him there in the burnt skeleton of their family home, as though he were standing guard himself over the Guardian's visage. In the manner of their mother, his grandmother Denila, they each touched their first two fingers to their forehead, to their lips, and then to the Guardian who stood through the raging fire. Both having grown into rather stoic men, they held their sister as she cried for their family home and did not question it when Benjamin told them that they would rebuild on the same plot, custom and superstition be hanged. The house would be rebuilt around its guardian, each new post and beam adding its spirit and its strength to the steadfast old man. The protective spirit who would continue to peer at them from the selfsame wood where he had expressed himself through the language of the dancing blade in Toddy's hand. As soon as possible, the family erected a small structure near the edge of the woods, where the family could store what remained of their belongings. It was only then that the work of clearing and rebuilding began.

Benjamin and Aaron were both fishermen by trade, but Aaron's hands had first been accustomed to the varied rigors of the life of a farm hand, and Benjamin's hands were Windle hands. Windle hands had shaped wood for generations: building, carving, and embellishing; creating from the lives of the Rooted People the places and art from which still more life thrived. That being said, for all of their potential talent and enthusiasm, they were still fishermen with only rudimentary knowledge about the building of a sturdy house. It was Melody's brothers and *their* Windle hands that provided the necessary expertise, correcting Benjamin and Aaron's plans and giving instruction where needed. More than that, they knew the stories, and they valued The People's knowledge. So when Benjamin drew unorthodox nooks and oddly placed windows to incorporate The Light and The Shadow, they smiled their quiet smiles and took it in stride.

It turned out that these quiet men, who often seemed to their nephew and niece to be duskier imitations of their grandfather, were quite jovial at work and opinionated in their craft; attitudes that seemed to have dispelled some of the concerns about Windle weirdness from their own names. It was a notable difference, as they worked closely with other men from the town who offered to lend a hand. They laughed and joked among the men as they expertly wielded the tools of their trade. They had learned to foster an air of camaraderie, much like their Uncle Balian at the tea shop, and used the skill to bring the able-bodied townsfolk to their family's aid. It seemed that, at one point or another, almost every able-bodied adult made their presence known at the site of the old Windle home, citing old adages they proved correct, as many hands made light work of raising the new house.

It truly was in record time that the house came together, encasing the guardian, who had been cleaned and polished to a shine. They built on a more spacious footprint than the house had occupied before. The bedrooms were more sizable, the kitchen several slate tiles larger, the roof pitched to easily host a stargazer or two. The small hut that housed them during construction was reinforced with stone and converted into a separate still room, Aaron remembering a little too clearly the vision of his wife diving back into a raging fire in search of dried herbs and remedies. Among the belongings that survived the blaze were some of the glass shards from Benjamin's mobiles; others were shattered or melted by the heat and now incorporated dark streaks. Naturally, all of his shadow sculptures had been destroyed. He gathered and cleaned what remained, incorporating as much as he could into the new structures he was building into the very walls of the new construction, and began seeking out materials to make more. Slowly but surely, they reconstructed their lives, choosing to treat every new decision as an opportunity to improve upon and reinforce their sanctuary.

CHAPTER 23

It was during the chaos, while Benjamin juggled working on the fishing boat with the requirements involved in a house being rebuilt, that Mimsy met Evan. He worked the fishing boats side by side with her brother and had helped to raise more than one barn in his lifetime. When he heard that they had begun to raise the new walls, he offered his assistance. When the first wall went up, their eyes met across the yard, and they shared a shy smile. After the second wall was in place, Mimsy approached him and offered a cup of water. The two spent a short while in conversation while the rest of the construction crew took a moment to rest.

As the house came together, and Benjamin and Evan continued to man the same fishing boat, he and Mimsy were thrown in each other's way repeatedly. The two continued to dance around each other for a time before finding their footing and finally deciding to marry.

After the ceremony, Mimsy moved herself and her few belongings into his small house on the other side of town, though she still made the daily trip to her family's house to work beside her mother in the garden and still room. In this way, she made a life for herself - one with which she was genuinely content, as she fell into a rhythm during her days and into loving arms that returned each evening and held her through the night.

The day the storm moved up the coast, Mimsy was already in the still room with Melody. Midday, the harbormaster marked the barometer and the roiling darkness that appeared to be racing the wind down the coast, from the North. Reluctant to leave his wife and daughter alone to worry and wait, Aaron hurried home from the docks to the sound of the warning bell as the clouds rolled heavily across the skies and the rain began to fall. The winds were too high, the rain driving across the waves from the North, and the mild swell off their normally protected shore had been whipped into a frenzy. The vessels that remained near to the shoreline had seen the oncoming storm and made for safe harbor. Some managed to make their way by reefing their sails, while others were forced to drop sails altogether and take to oars. The few steel-hulled boats did their best to avoid getting tossed up against the rocks of the jetty as the waves rose and crashed over their decks. The small boats that ferried the crews from the larger ships to the pier began to take on water as the furious wind came whipping down the coast. From those ships, already safe from the storm, the crew members tumbled over each other into the tavern for a warming drink, in no time at all, launching into exaggerated tales of their battle against wind and sea - making clear their concern that it might be a ship killer.

The words "Ship Killer" hung in the air of the Windle's still room, and for a moment, it was as though time had stopped to hold its breath along with them. Silence thickened the space between them with unseen tension, a pressure that built in a matter of excruciating seconds, then popped, like a bubble bursting, when they all launched in motion.

Aaron was back out the door, hurrying for the docks, while Melody and Mimsy grabbed their shawls and leaned into the wind, doing their best to run in the direction of town. By the time they reached the tavern, both women were soaked to the bone. The building was packed with bodies and a horrible tension that wove itself tightly through the families and loved ones of the men still battling the elements out among the waves. Some sat eerily still and heavy with silence, some could not seem to stop their bodies in motion - each inevitably finding their way out the door to stare toward a horizon rendered invisible by torrential rain.

The tavern mistress shoved mugs of mulled wine into their cold fingers and stared, hollow-eyed, out the window, waiting for her brother to come home. Hours later, when a single ship limped back to the dock, Aaron and the rest of the dock workers rushed to meet them. The mast was reduced to a mere stump crowned by a shattered mass of splintered wood, the rails were broken to pieces, and the single remaining sail was shredded and just barely able to catch the wind that brought them home. It was five of the ten fishermen who had set out that morning who took turns monitoring the injured as they slowly limped back to the pier. The tavern mistress burst into tears as her brother pushed through the doors and practically fell into an open chair, his face gray with prolonged shock; his expression was that of one who had seen a horrific beast and was still unsure he had escaped with his life. The knowledge that someone had managed to weather the storm circulated the room with an almost audible sigh of relief. This may not have been the ship they were waiting for, but its arrival breathed hope into the assembled townsfolk. Every moment the ships remained away from shore, it was less likely that they would ever return, and yet, in that moment, it felt to the collected parties as though it were somehow more believable that their loved ones would make it home.

It was strange how often stillness seemed to be the predictor for oncoming disaster. Benjamin knew in retrospect that he should have respected the stillness of that morning that reminded him so much of the awful stillness he experienced on the night of the fire. The birds that would normally be stirring were silent - as though there were no sun to greet - and he had rarely known the birds of the town to hold their peace. Another reason he should have known better than to set foot on that boat.

In the horrible stillness, the wind barely rippled across the water, and yet the air felt full and heavy - so much so that he would have sworn that the boat sat low in the water, too full by far with the invisible weight of anticipation. The men knew, even if they didn't know they knew. Most spoke quietly as though they couldn't stand to disturb the stillness. The exception being those who spoke too loud, whose characters were the sort determined to whistle in the dark. When they shoved off, they needed all oars out just to clear the anchorage. They watched in silence as one of the newer steam-powered boats passed them by, an occurrence that would normally be met with jeers and yelled obscenities. Before long, the wind began to pick up, and the men let out a muffled cheer. Tucking their fears in their back pockets, Benjamin and Evan stashed their oars and exchanged an optimistic grin before manning the sheets.

The initial gusts of wind came and went. When the wind finally rose, it was sudden but also not unexpected. All morning, the wind had traveled in bursts over the horizon, often leaving them in irons and dependent on oars, before the bursts began to sustain themselves, growing and swelling like ghostly riders drawing forward the oncoming storm. When the clouds rolled in, they were dark and angry, so gray as to be black, and purple, and blue, hanging heavy and low in the sky. Benjamin felt like he could reach up and touch them if he were so inclined, like the air was charged with energy, and the sky was ready to open up and unleash its torrential rage upon them all. The captain ordered some of the crew below; the rest he tossed lines to secure themselves to the rail. The storm would be upon them soon, and they had ventured too far from shore to beat a hasty retreat; there was no avoiding its wrath. It seemed mere moments before the waves began growing, some reaching heights taller than a man, each one causing the ship to pitch and roll. The deck was awash as the squall and the swell battered the hull relentlessly, its crew quickly losing all sense of time and direction. Some of the men had been ordered to furl the sails, protecting them from the worst of the gale, but the order was too late, and the task too time consuming; the ties were ripped from calloused fingers, dragged off by the storm to parts unknown, and the sails whipped open, catching the wind and drawing them further into the control of the unrelenting skies. It was this unsustainable force that caused the mast to break with an audible crack, dropping the ripping sails into the water and inviting the current to take part in the destruction. Benjamin could barely see more than a few feet before his face, but he could feel the hull of the boat tremble, its groan resonating through his feet in a manner he could have sworn was audible, even as he struggled to hear his brother-in-law yelling scarce inches from his face. Positioned as they were, Benjamin saw what Evan could not, as the giant open maw of the sea rose up from the water as if to swallow their entire vessel whole. He listened to the storm that sang with an intensity and percussive energy that rattled his bones, to the hollow whistling of the wind unleashed and unencumbered and, beneath it, the eternal song of the Great Mama of the Deep.

When Benjamin came to, he was adrift, supported by a chunk of the ship's hull, along with his brother-in-law and an old sailor he only knew as Bean. Bean held Evan in place as they crested another gigantic wave, and his body began to slide. They exchanged frantic looks over the unconscious man; Bean tried to yell over the rumble of the storm and the sea, but the wind tore his words away unheard. Beneath the waves, Benjamin felt a fin rub against his feet and began to panic. He'd never spoken to a shark and wasn't sure he would have a chance to appeal to one before things took a turn for the worst. Thankfully, before he could get too panicked about planning for a potentially toothy encounter, a hand grabbed his arm. He looked over his shoulder and found a familiar face breaking through the violent waves. He was certain he had never been happier to see anyone in his life. If anyone could get them through the storm, it would be Nimmawni.

"How did you find us?" he yelled.

"I was following the storm up the coast!" She responded, "I thought I recognized you, Winken!" She stared with wide eyes into the roiling mass that still ruled the skies.

"Can you help us?"

She considered the state of the three men and the sky above, submerging with a passing wave that choked him and threatened to knock him from the plank.

"The storm is not half done, Winken! I will do my best, but I can not be sure that I can get all three of you to shore."

Bean had finally caught on to a fourth head bobbing above the water, he stared at Nimmawni as though certain that he was either hallucinating or already dead.

"The shore is that way," Nimmawni pointed across the very teeth of the storm as yet another wave pushed them down the shore and out to sea. "I will do my best, Winken, but it may not be within my power; I can not fight the storm."

Benjamin nodded. Even if she could make no promises, his odds had improved. Aside from what guidance she could give them, there was at least one concern he could let go of, he need no longer worry about the large predators of the sea.

As exhaustion overtook him, he couldn't help but wonder at the pattern of his life. He could not escape the nagging thought that, perhaps, he was never meant to escape his burning house. In the course of his life, he had never aspired to anything more than to spend his days at sea and ensure his family was safe and sound. He had never fallen in love, he had sired no children; it was as though he had always known how it was meant to end. Perhaps he had come to the end of the thread of his life that horrible night among the flames and, having been saved by The People, had been living on borrowed time until he had the chance to rebuild what had been lost. The flare of lightning mingled with the vision of rising flames as his eyes closed, and he slipped into unconsciousness.

The piece of hull made it to the shallows, and when Bean's feet touched the sand, he was certain it was on the forgotten shores of some ancient god's kingdom. There was no way that he could have made it through the night. There was no way that what he had seen was real. The raging swells of the storm had opened up like some sort of monstrous sky creature and swallowed them whole. He dragged the wood to shore, the dead weight of two unconscious sailors more than his own weakened and dehydrated body could manage. He collapsed onto the sand with a groan before losing consciousness again himself.

As the sun burned off the remaining clouds and the town began to come back to life in the wake of the Ship Killer, the call went out along the shore that bodies had been found on the beach. The tavern emptied onto the street as the families of the sailors who crewed the three remaining ships raced to the water's edge for any word of their loved ones. The three bodies on the beach were caked in sand and salt; their ripped clothes and battered bodies were not immediately identifiable. When one of the poor bastards groaned and tried his best to roll over, the cry went out for good clean water. A canteen was soon provided by one of the townspeople, allowing him to drink and rinse his face.

"Bean! It's Bean! They must be from Greyson's ship!" The announcement was met with a combination of relief and tears. The other two bodies were dragged up the beach before they were checked for breath and pulse, only to find that there was none.

"Dead, both dead, it's the Windle boys." The cry carried through the crowd.

"Windle boys?"

"Windle and his brother-in-law."

Mimsy and Melody had just gained the sand when they heard the news being carried from voice to voice through the crowd. Mimsy's knees went out from under her and they collapsed together on the shoreline as Aaron ran to check the bodies, double checking their pulses, and cradling the waterlogged body of his son. Mimsy crawled through the sand to her brother and husband, finally collapsing over Evan's body like a puppet without strings.

When Bean had fully regained consciousness, he began ranting about mermaids. All but three people were certain he was mad with dehydration. Those three people listened very closely to absolutely every insane thing that Bean had to say.

CHAPTER 24

Mimsy sat at the end of the dock, her brother's necklace dangling from her fingertips. Part of her wanted to throw it into the waves; without Benjamin, it seemed so pointless.

"Is he alright?" a small, sad voice asked from beneath the dock.

"Nimmawni?" Mimsy hung her head over the edge of the dock and stared deep into the shadows. The mermaid had wrapped herself around one of the pilings and clung to it as though it was the last solid thing in the world.

"Is he alright?" The voice was laden so heavily with desperate hope Mimsy felt the tears begin to stream down, or in this case up, her face all over again; streaming over her forehead to drop into the water.

"No. No, my friend, he's gone."

The mermaid gripped her tail to cover her face, hiding her big dark eyes away. Mimsy wondered if the mermaid could cry. It was obvious that she was doing something to the same effect, and much like Mimsy's mother's and father's, her grief was palpable.

"I tried! I tried. I held him and the other man above water through the storm. I brought them home. I brought them as close to the shore as I could."

Mimsy saw her body shaking, and realized it was not just emotion but exertion. The mermaid had watched over the men through the storm, a ship killer; she had fought the waves and the current, and she had brought the men home. Just like that, the tension around her brother's necklace drifted away. She sat up and secured it around her neck with a deep breath and a sigh.

She had always heard more than other humans; she spoke with her Grandad's crows, and they could mostly communicate. When her brother rebuilt the house, she saw the spaces where the wee folk walked in the shadow and the light. The beginnings were there, and she could only imagine how much more Benjamin had seen and heard, wearing the necklace as he had from the time that he was eight. The beginnings were there, and when she placed the necklace around her neck, it was as though those beginnings bloomed and opened around her. The sky and the sea whispered, and she heard the resonating song of the deep as it swept her up in its embrace. She had heard about the song so very many times, and in experiencing it for herself, she couldn't help but feel closer to Benjamin, more secure in the knowledge that he had returned to the cycle of creation. She moved closer to the piling where the mermaid clung and draped herself over the edge of the dock, extending her hand in friendship to the being that had tried so hard to save her brother's life. Human fingers touched mermaid fingers, with softer skin than she had imagined, the slick wetness sliding over her hand as the base of her thumb met the webbing by Nimmawni's. They stayed there, hand in hand, looking into each other's eyes as heartbeats ticked by.

"Thank you."

The mermaid bit her lip and nodded.

"Thank you for trying your best to save Benjamin and to save my husband."

Nimmawni's eyes widened with sudden understanding, she must not have known why Benjamin wanted that particular sailor to survive, and how could she? It had been seven long years since she had last returned. The mermaid unwrapped her arm from the piling, her body shaking with effort spent, and wrapped Mimsy's hand in both of her own.

"My deepest sorrow for the loss of your loved ones, dearest Winken. They have returned to the cycle."

Mimsy nodded, responding almost reflexively.

"As we all must."

Nimmawni nodded in return.

"As we all must. Is there anything more that I can do for you?" Her voice and her hands shook as she made the offer born of misguided guilt.

"No, my dear friend, you have done enough. You need to rest."

"I wish I could do more." The mermaid slowly returned her hands to the piling, where she leaned her head. Mimsy worried she would cut herself on the rough barnacles that made it their home.

"I know."

"Perhaps, if I rest here, I can tell you a story. Your brother liked stories, as did your mother, and your grandfather, and his father before him."

Mimsy was tempted to refuse, but looking at the expression on her friend's exhausted face gave her a sense of understanding. The comfort offered was not just for Mimsy's sake, it was also to satisfy Nimmawni's very real need to honor those who had passed. Mimsy accepted with tears in her eyes and they both found themselves comfortably lying on their backs, one rocking with the gentle waves, the other with solid wood beneath her back, as the mermaid's voice spilled from her lips and across the water.

CHAPTER 25

A long time ago, in the space that is now and always, the Great Mama of the Deep floated among her creations in the deepest depths of the Sea Below, where the clay of creation continued to roll along the ocean floor. In the depths of the night, she reached out to mold a new creation, combining the clay of the Sea Below and stardust still scattered throughout the Sea Above. She formed the shapes of many of her previous creations, mixing and matching their features. Combining the fins and scales of The People of the Sea Below with the bodies and arms of apes, she molded them with infinite care, that they could thrive anywhere within the Eternal Sea. She breathed into them a graft of her own creation, one that refined their features and blessed them with insight, then released them into the Sea Above to dance among heavenly bodies. They lived happily among the stars of the Sea Above, getting lost in its depths and cavorting with the Gods. The Light grafted the glow of the comb jelly's shimmering rainbow, and The Shadow grafted the ability to see in the darkest of places. Pan'chan gifted them curiosity and a mischievous spirit, and these boons were followed by the playful gifts of many other gods.

The more blessed they became by the multitude of deities, the more curious they became about the Sea Below. The more they learned of the goings on in and around the Sea Below, the more they wished to share their knowledge with the creatures they had seen developing on the earth and in the waters to be found there.

Humans were still very much among The People at this time; they flocked to the water's edge for fish, for fresh water to drink and to water the fields; they flocked to the great rivers, the lakes, and ponds. They flocked to the sea, for all it provided no water to drink. It has always been understood that, in the presence of water, there exists the essence of life. Although at this time we knew the mysteries of walking on land, it is where there is water that my people truly thrive. So they swam from the expanse of the Sea Above to make new homes in the many waters of the Sea Below. We spoke to The People of the many waters, The People of the shore, and The People of the air, and we showed ourselves to the humans who struggled to eke out their survival. We emerged from ponds and rivers, often in the time of rains, and began to share with them the mysteries of the gods and the gifts of Pan'chan. In time, we taught the humans how to swim, to fish, and how to make a boat that could ride the waves. It was told among the human folk that one of Pan'chan's first tricks was the fishing net, but it was the Sea-Folk who taught humans the art.

We taught the earthbound People of the paths of the stars, describing their positions as they spun through the sky, charting the fates as they sang into being the shifting shape of the Eternal

Sea. It is the misfortune of man that the more they knew and the more they learned, the more convinced of their own importance they became. I suppose it was our enthusiasm that led to so many of the humans distancing themselves from The People. For belief in one's superiority does not breed understanding, and it is the humans who have ceased to share the ancient stories, who lord their grasping thumbs over The People, who have lost the ability to listen, to hear, and to understand.

"Nimmawni, can you tell me of your parents? Where did you come from?" For a moment Mimsy thought the mermaid would ignore her question; by all accounts she had rarely been forthcoming when it concerned information about herself.

"It was a long time and many cycles ago, the last time I saw them. I do not remember where I came from, but I remember that he had the kindest smile you ever saw and the tail of a striped sailing fish. She was pale as the roundest moon, and her hands held me so gently as she darted through the water, but I never slipped. They both told wonderful stories."

CHAPTER 26

Mimsy returned to the home of her parents, she had no interest in living in her small house across town without Evan to keep her company in the evenings. Melody welcomed her home with tears and open arms, happy to have one of her children returned to the home they had all built together. For Mimsy, Benjamin was everywhere; his mark on every wall and step. The tiny places built into the structure to carry light into the building, and the intricately shaped shadows in which to hide from light as well. He was absolutely everywhere, and being home was like being wrapped in her brother's embrace. She packed all of Evan's belongings along with her own, and her room was transformed in such a way as to hold her close to him as well. His sheep skins lay over the bed, trapping her body heat on cold nights and lying beneath her as a source of soft support when it was warm. His small collection of books sat on his night table, across the bed from her own, untouched but for the nights when she missed him too much to sleep.

So lost in the loving embrace of the departed she was, that it was truly no wonder that it took her two month's time to realize that she was missing her courses. In the third month after the ship killer, she presented her suspicions to her mother. Her mild morning sickness had disguised itself within the inappetence of her mourning, and sure enough, it was soon thereafter that she began to grow in size. She spent her pregnancy torn between joy that some part of her Evan would live on and sadness that he would never have the opportunity to meet his child. Seven months after the ship killer took her husband and brother, Andromeda was born; named for her husband's love of the stars and their ability to guide a sailor home at sea.

Despite local superstitions about wee folk harming children or stealing away with them in the night, the evening after her beautiful daughter was born, Mimsy laid out milk sweetened with honey for the wee folk with a whispered prayer that they watch over the child. In a short matter of days, the milk was gone without a trace. Two days later, she repeated the process, laying out the pleas of a loving mother, feeling the lack of the hands and presence of her child's father. Once again, the milk and honey disappeared without a trace.

Andromeda was a happy child, she rarely woke her mother or grandparents in the night. Andromeda smiled and laughed as her mother carried her, wrapped close to her body, while she worked in the garden of her foremothers. She waved to The People and basked in the breezes that stirred the plants. Andromeda was such an easy baby that her mother and grandparents wondered at her natural good temper, until one night Mimsy woke and snuck away to relieve herself. Upon returning, she saw that the baby was not asleep as she had thought. Andromeda lay on her back, smiling up at tiny lights that danced and swayed above her bedding. When the little girl laughed with delight, Mimsy could have sworn she heard a shushing noise and perhaps saw a shadow move near the bed. She nodded gratefully in the direction of whatever it was that she had seen. Then Mimsy returned to her bed to feign sleep, watching in silence until her child was once more dreaming peacefully and the little floating lights had been laid to rest. Mimsy continued to regularly lay out milk and honey, though now the act was carried out with gratitude rather than prayer.

The little girl was a joy to behold as she grew, with her wildly curly black hair and stormy gray eyes, smiling happily from wherever she was laid to rest or tied tightly to her mother's back. Even Aaron, who never recovered from the hefty price of the storm, would crack a smile as the baby waved her tiny fists or smiled at the passing of a butterfly. The loss of Benjamin laid heavily on Aaron, and shortly after Andromeda's first birthday, he succumbed to its weight. His absence was felt keenly, leaving the Mistresses Windle to persevere, holding one another up and bearing each other's weight as they carried on.

CHAPTER 27

When the seabird next called for a child of the Windle line, Mimsy was in the still room with Andromeda at her skirts. She was showing the girl how to grind poppy seed into powder to make a sleeping draught. The seabird waddled in through the open door with cries that would have sounded imperious even *without* the benefit of the mermaid's gift. Both wearing the necklaces, they came to hear, via lengthy explanation, what had long been clear: That the birds had passed on the information from nestling to nestling, apparently becoming progressively more certain of their entitlement to enter a human home in search of the Windle family and the sea urchin recompense they would receive for their troubles.

Mimsy and Andromeda walked with bare feet, hand in hand, down to the end of the dock where their old friend waited. Mimsy, of course, introduced her daughter, knowing full well that she would be called nothing but Winken, just as every child of Toddy Windle had been called before them. Andromeda was uncertain of this new person; stories were all well and good, but it was not at all the same as meeting the subject of that story in real life. Being that she was an inquisitive little thing, it did not take long for her to overcome her reservations. Realistically, it took exactly as long as it took for Nimmawni to lay on her back at the water's surface, asking after the health of Mimsy and Melody, Winken and Old Winken.

"Why do you have a belly button?" the girl interjected "Belly buttons are where the baby's cord is attached to their body, fish don't have belly buttons, birds don't have belly buttons because they don't have cords, they have eggs, the same with snakes, they don't have cords." She glanced from the mermaid to her toes, which she wiggled against the grains of the dock.

"I heard that you were born from a giant deep sea oyster, but then you wouldn't have a cord, which means you wouldn't have a belly button." She looked pointedly at the offending body part, which challenged the stories she had been told from infancy.

"I heard once that humans are told that their babies are brought by a large white stork. Why, Little Winken, do you have a belly button?"

"I've heard that too, but it's a story that isn't so. I saw a lady give birth once because the midwife wanted my Mama to come with herbs for the bleeding. You don't need herbs for bleeding if you just need to grab a baby in a blanket from a nice old stork. Sure enough, there wasn't no stork. That baby came out of her private bits, and it had a cord. Nobody will tell me properly how the baby got in there, though."

Mimsy's eyes closed as though silently praying for help or patience.

Nimmawni stifled laughter.

"Well, perhaps once you figure out how human babies come to be, you'll come one step closer to understanding why I have a belly button."

The little girl sighed dramatically.

"Will no one ever answer my questions?"

"In time my darling," Mimsy murmured, "When you older."

"I'm older than I was when I asked the question the first time." Andromeda offered helpfully.

Mimsy sighed in frustration.

"Andromeda. Now is definitely not the time."

The little girl sat on the dock and sulked as her mother turned her focus to the mermaid bobbing with the waves at the end of the dock.

"Where have you been these eight years?"

"It is a strange story, I'm not sure you'll believe me."

Mimsy stifled a laugh, knowing full well that her stories about her time away were always difficult to believe. She motioned for the mermaid to carry on.

"I was stuck, you see, in the empty sea with no boundaries."

"Nimmawni, I cannot begin to tell you whether I believe you or not; I'm not even sure what that means."

"Out at sea, far from here, there is a strange place. A place where ships do not leave, but disappear, where strange lights fill the sky, where the song of the Great Mother does not penetrate, and direction has no meaning."

It sounded strange but not unheard of. Like a story she might have heard in town or from a sailor home from sea. It was that thought that unlocked her memory: it was Evan - Evan had told her a story that had been told among the merchant sailors. Stories of a place where the compasses spin as though there was no north, and ships were lost, rarely to be seen again. She conveyed the story to the mermaid, who nodded vigorously.

"I was turning round and round, and the night sky lit with aurora and fire. The People swam round in circles, but not like a school of fish who spiral together, instead we all moved in different directions, oftentimes barely knowing the direction to the surface from the direction to the sea floor."

"How did you escape?" Andromeda asked, drawn from her sulk by the sense of mystery.

"I'm not precisely sure." Nimmawni said thoughtfully, "I think I may have found my way to the sea floor, that maybe I could hear her there. The Great Mama of the Deep, her song is meant to be heard everywhere."

"Did any of The People escape with you? Did they, maybe, follow you? Are they all still just swimming round and round and round?" The accusation of abandonment was clear in the little girl's voice.

"There were two little remora who stuck themselves to my fin who I know escaped with me. Unfortunately, it was so hard to know anything that all of the other People probably needed to find their own way." There was a moment of silence, the mermaid caught in memory as the younger Miss Windle mulled over the strange combination of details.

"Sometimes, when we look up at the night sky, we see the stars falling through the darkness. They look like they might be bright, like fire, close up. Do you think that the fire in the sky was falling stars?"

"No, I don't believe so. They didn't feel like falling stars, and there were certainly enough of The People wishing they could leave that a falling star would have done something."

The little girl's gray eyes popped open wide at the comment about wishes.

"I heard that if you wish on falling stars, your wish is bound to come true, but no one I know ever had that happen."

The mermaid paused in contemplation before addressing the child's words.

"Star Bodies are filled with the magic of creation. They pulse with the energy of the Great Mama of the Deep, each one beating in time with her very own heartbeat. Sometimes they pulse so hard that they snuff themselves out; others knock themselves into the astral tide and fly through the Sea Above, allowing pieces to fly off in their wake. Those are the ones we see showering through the night sky. Tumbling and rocketing through the heavens and falling to find a new resting place in the Sea Above or the star-body of our home. Each one, the seed of new life and a million possibilities. I had heard that humans still wish on falling stars, casting their hopes and dreams into the night sky in the hopes that it might inspire the seed of creation within. Humans are not alone in this. The People have long done the same, and that magic has saved and created and nurtured The People all over this world."

"Really?" Andromeda's little face screwed up in skepticism.

"Of course! When the Branch Stalkers of the deepest woods were thought to be extinct, it was a wish that brought them together once more to flourish and grow in number.

When the lonely black bird wished so sweetly for her children, Pan'chan found her, and thus her children who populate the whole world came to be. The People of the shore have caught their wishing stars, planting them in drought and flood, breathing new life into the Rooted People and rejuvenating the cycle of life."

At that, all thoughts about the silent sea and the lost People were cast aside, Andromeda's mind was now filled with thoughts about wishing stars. Some nights, she and her Mama would climb out onto the roof and look at the stars that spun through the deep nighttime skies. Every so often, a star would fly through the Sea Above, and her Mama would lean in to kiss her cheek and then tell her to make a wish. How many wishes had she cast into the night sky? How many wishes had met their mark? And, when they didn't, what wishes had been chosen instead? Could they still be out there, waiting, full of the seeds of creation?

"How do you catch a wishing star?"

CHAPTER 28

It was a long walk to the grove of apple trees. Andromeda had started her journey with energetic enthusiasm, but it was only a matter of time before her feet had begun to drag, kicking up small clouds of dust as she traversed the road into the countryside. After slipping from the schoolhouse, she had run home and done some of her best sneaking yet to get into her room and change into her favorite disguise. She changed into pants and a simple shirt with a belt and stuffed her braided hair under a cap. On her way out the door, she grabbed a large satchel before running off down the road to the orchard. Certainly, she was not meant to be there, and certainly, she was not meant to climb the trees, and even more certainly, she was not meant to cut the small branches of the trees, though the Rooted People gave her their blessing. It mattered not at all that the harvest had passed and new growth would take its place; humans got so tetchy about what they considered theirs. Never mind that, in reality, The People mostly just belonged to themselves.

When her satchel was nice and full, she made her way,

ducking branches and climbing over low stone walls, back to the road homeward. Andromeda's mission had taken far longer than the length of a day's study at school, and her arrival garnered more attention than she had intended. Having anticipated the fallout from her unsanctioned adventure, the young girl cut through the woods toward the beach. If the boy's clothing weren't bound to give away her extracurricular activities, the satchel full of twigs was a clear sign of her absence from the schoolhouse. Once her Mama and Grandma realized what she'd done, they were bound to be cross, and who knew what would happen to her haul of materials then. The only remaining choice was to hide her hard earned treasure and take her lumps for skipping out on school as she must.

The next day, Andromeda donned a dress that was deemed a proper uniform and went to school as was expected of her. She sat through her lessons, even math, with as much patience as she could muster, barely even fidgeting at all. When she got home from the house of boredom, she tore off the offending article of clothing almost as soon as she walked through the door. She traipsed through the house in her undergarments as she unbound her wildly curling black hair, returning to her room in search of an old gingham day dress. Her boy's duds had been confiscated for the foreseeable future, but she might as well be as comfortable as she could be. Once she had changed, she went out to the garden and filled a pail with water from the hand pump and retrieved her bag of sticks from the head of the path to the beach. The act of splitting her twigs into strips was almost meditative. Each strip was soaked in the bucket of water to make sure it was moist and flexible. As the next few days progressed, she began weaving her materials into baskets. She had thought through her process many times since her meeting with Nimmawni because she intended to catch those falling stars, so she would fill her basket with symbolism. She bent five of her longest strips of wood, intertwining them to make the beginning spokes of her basket's base. The apple tree grew delicious apples, and every apple housed a five pointed star inside its juicy flesh. It only stood to reason that if branches could breed stars, they would be perfect for weaving baskets to catch wishing stars. The basket widened, and she added more spokes; there was no telling how large a wishing star would be, in truth. She made her basket wide enough to sit in before bending the spokes upward and building the sides.

Over the course of the next few weeks, Andromeda spent every stolen moment she could find building not one, not two, but three baskets. When they were finally completed, her fingers were sore and scraped from her work, but she proudly placed all three in their intended locations nonetheless. The first, she took down to the seashore. She dug a hole at the base of the furthermost tree and placed the basket inside, filling the edges of the hole to keep it in place. The second, she similarly secured at the base of an old yew tree that edged the plot where her family buried their dead. The third, she set among the creatures of darkness, wedging it between the rocks where the bats streamed forth at night. One for where life began, one where it laid to rest, one that rested among The People living in darkness.

When the shooting stars next flew through the sky, the

three baskets were laid out in waiting. Andromeda watched the lights streak across the sky and flutter toward the earth. The next morning, she found that her waiting baskets had gathered glittering dust. When she touched it, she felt her fingertips brimming with potential, like it was a material from which she could build absolutely anything. She gently collected the tiny grains into a pouch which she hid in the back of the root cellar, as far away from the wishes of her family and The People as she could, to ensure it would be there when the time was right.

Though the sun continued to rise and fall, and the moon continued to wax and wane, though Andromeda often thought wishing thoughts and paused to consider whether they were important enough to use her precious stardust, the hidden stash remained untouched. Rather than dwindling, with every shooting star, it continued to grow. Her baskets remained ready to receive, and many of the shooting stars that passed through their small corner of the night sky released into them the sparks of creation. The growing cache continued to lay in wait for something worthy of their magic.

The seasons passed and turned, the flowers bloomed and wilted, the fruit ripened and fell to rot. It was after five more cycles of the seasons that Melody's body began to give way, no longer full of its customary vitality and strength. Once again, the Mistresses Windle called upon the gifts of the Moon Tree to assuage the impact of time. Still, it is a universal truth that all things must be subject to time and tide, and over the next two years, Melody continued to decline. It was seeing her Grandma in such a state that Andromeda finally took some of the dust from her precious stash and made a wish. The fifteen-year-old wished dearly for her grandmother to pass from her state of discomfort, to move on to whatever was meant to come next. Though in her heart of hearts she hoped that Melody would recover, she couldn't bring herself to make a wish to stall her death; after all, it was an accepted knowledge among The People and her kin that we all must return to the cycle.

It was not long afterward that the older woman passed away, peacefully, in her sleep. That night, she sipped quietly at her soothing tea, surrounded by her nest of blankets and pillows, wished her daughter and granddaughter goodnight, lay her head to rest, and passed swiftly into the night. In this way, Andromeda was content with her wish, lovingly recognizing the end of Melody's suffering. The peace with which she passed would have been confirmation enough of the stardust's power, but the realization of the wish was far from over. When the time came to move Melody's body, they found the task far more difficult than anticipated. It had begun to grow roots, and in the time that she lay resting, the tendrils began protruding through her mattress and nearly wrapped themselves around her bed frame. Not only had Andromeda's wish released her grandmother from her suffering, it had progressed through her passing into the next stage of the cycle. The literal seeds of new life were not only forming but growing swiftly within her. By the time they buried her body in the family plot, a shoot had begun to sprout from her chest. When the soil was set into place above her, anchoring the joined symbols of life and death to the earth, it took only a few days before the tiny tree began to emerge into the light. Its growth continued unabated; it did not slow until the sapling yew had grown two branches sturdy enough for the birds to perch and just enough foliage to shelter Andromeda in its shade. Melody would have wished for nothing less.

CHAPTER 29

Andromeda thrived in the house her uncle imagined into being, though surely in his imagination, he would have lived to see it completed. The house Andromeda knew was run primarily by women, two strong women who taught their daughter and granddaughter to be strong in her own right. So Andromeda grew to be wild and independent, often slipping from the schoolhouse when the schoolmaster was distracted. Keeping this singular young girl anywhere that she did not wish to be was a full-time job in and of itself. She sewed, as most felt a young woman should, but unlike other young women, she used the skill to make for herself short pants like the boys wore. With her boy's kit, she could tuck her long braid under a cap and run rampant without the weight of judging eyes. She often disappeared into the woods, running wild for hours at a stretch, and came back with stories told by the most reclusive denizens of the forest. At night, it was not uncommon to find that she had climbed up to the rooftop to stare at the spinning constellations overhead. At a time when most young ladies her age were taken with finding a suitable husband, Andromeda was far more interested in mapping out the stars in the sky and seeing just how far from shore she could swim before being seized by the conviction that great tentacles would reach up to grab her from the deep.

It was no surprise to anyone when her twentieth birthday passed, and Andromeda could still be found at play with her cousins outside the tea shop. It could hardly be said that the men of the town lacked interest; in point of fact, men of various ages had expressed their interest, genuine and greed-driven alike, in both of the Windle ladies, to no avail. Unfortunately for them, it was equally true that very few of those men could comprehend how to court a woman such as Andromeda Holt Windle, who had adopted the name of her foremothers without a single raised eyebrow. When she passed twenty-five without showing a lick of interest, the local menfolk gave up hope. Now considered a confirmed spinster, even the few neighbors who had cared about her lack of womanly graces could no longer be bothered to pay her much mind. In that indifference, Andromeda found a renewed sense of her own freedom.

Shortly before her twenty-sixth birthday, a ship arrived from the south, from further abroad than most of the townsfolk had seen before. The captain himself was a burly man who hailed from a main port of call and was of relatively little note. However, in his travels, he had gathered an odd assortment of men to crew his ship, some with skin darker than the tavern's malt ale, others with broad faces and jet black hair. They worked together with an easy familiarity and were all brusque efficiency as soon as the hull met the dock and the hold was open. When the ship unloaded, it was one man in particular who caught Andromeda's eye, with skin like burnished copper and heavy lidded eyes, pin straight black hair, and a lithe form that danced through the rigging as easily as breathing. He was stoic at first and stood out among the raucous crowd that gathered around the pub. Surrounded by locals who would happily exchange rounds of ale for a good yarn, he kept his stories to himself and let his gaze drift. Glancing across the shipyard, he saw two of Andromeda's young cousins kicking a ball, watched over by the young lady herself, seated in a casual dress and pinafore, sipping tea. The man, who his shipmates inexplicably called Blue, sauntered across the yard and intercepted the ball, kicking it to the younger child with the hint of a smile playing about his lips. The cousins laughed and cheered, accepting the stranger's presence without question, happy to include more players in their game. Andromeda smiled at the scene before her over the rim of her teacup. The game continued, but as he ran around enjoying the company of her young cousins, his dark brown eyes rarely left her stormy grays.

The ship stayed at port, bobbing patiently in the harbor, waiting for the northern winter storms to pass. The ship's crew laid low, renting nearly every room to let in town, while Blue and Andromeda allowed themselves to fall into one another with abandon. Both knew that the romance that blossomed in the interim was destined to end with the coming of the spring. Still, when one smiled, the other was sure to follow. He did not frown when she played with her cousins like a child, but joined in on the fun in his own quiet but joyful way. He sat in the great room with both of the Windle women, exchanging stories late into the night. He followed her into the forest and barely batted an eye when she spoke to The People; he had, after all, traveled a great distance and seen many a fantastical thing at sea. Despite that, when the fairy lights bobbed around them with curiosity for the first time, his dark eyes widened in shock. He momentarily reached out as though to touch the elusive beings before letting his hand drop to his side as they giggled and danced away, always just out of reach. He climbed trees as easily as a ships' rigging, retrieving sprigs of mistletoe to charm Andromeda for a kiss. Charmed, indeed, she responded with genuine enthusiasm, pressing lips to lips and skin to skin with little restraint. It was that night, in the depths of the woods, on the moss beneath an old oak tree, that she gave herself to him completely; their breaths visible as they mingled in the cool air before the coming of dawn.

When Blue boarded the ship, Andromeda was left with a simple ring: a small band that could be easily misunderstood, and a promise to return, should the wind will it and the fates be on their side. In truth, she was left with one thing more, a secret that she kept to herself, knowing better than most that a wild thing must be allowed its freedom - and, like herself, Blue was indeed a wild thing. Near six months after the ship's dock lines were thrown from the pier, a tiny bundle was brought into the world with black hair and deep brown eyes, and his wild mother wept at the sight of him. Mimsy was well aware that her daughter was unwed, there were few secrets between the two in that house by themselves, but Blue had sat at her table and listened to their stories on the long winter nights. In the manner of most of their family, it was as though his heart knew Andromeda's long before their eyes met; if that were not being handfast by the very stars, Mimsy didn't know what could be. So she let the simple band he left behind be a symbol of whatever the nosier neighbors wished it to be. When pressed, she said they went abroad for their joining, which was technically not a falsehood, and she doted on Kerish with all of the love a grandmother could give.

Where Andromeda had been a wild adventurer from the moment she could walk, Kerish was a careful child, prone to worry, and forever in his mother and grandmother's shadows. The crows startled him with their loud voices, the fairy lights made him wary when they ventured from the forest. When he and his mother went to town, they were often looked at with eyes full of unanswered questions. Questions he didn't understand and had no answers for, and he hugged her all the more tightly for it. On the first day of compulsory education, his mother brought him to the elementary school and marveled at the changes enacted on the property since her time in the old one room schoolhouse. The building had grown substantially, with rooms separated by age groups. The thick brush that had once so capably covered her escape had been cleared away to make a proper yard for the children to play. A few older children spun recklessly on a merry-go-round, their laughter splitting the air with abandon. Kerish steeled himself, not wanting to attract undue attention for clinging to his single point of safe harbor. He straightened his shirt and his vest, let his mother brush aside his wavy black hair, and followed his teacher into the room already dedicated to the education of six and seven-year-olds.

Surveying the orderly rows of desks and chairs, the shelves of books, and the small writing slates stacked neatly by a basket of chalk, he felt that the experience might be manageable after all. This was, of course, until a loud bell was rung and the room filled with other, noisier, children. He soon came to the conclusion that he was fine so long as his teacher was present but that the hour they spent in the yard at midday was worthy of dread. Kerish did his best not to draw attention, but it seemed that everything about him already did that on his behalf. His father was known only as Blue, though he was certain that his mother knew his proper name and had left him no surname. The name Windle drew attention because everyone knew that the Windles were strange. "Weird Windle," they called him, "Witchy Windle," "Windle the Warlock." They asked him questions about his Mom and his Grandma: did they dance around naked? Did the Adversary come for tea? Were there frog chunks in their potions? And Kerish did his best to ignore them. In the manner of bullies determined to find or create fault, they picked apart his appearance. They looked at his cheeks, sprinkled with his mother's freckles, and the slightest tilt of his father's eyes; they noted his differences and made faces in cruel imitation, pulling their eyes into exaggerated squints with their fingertips and threatening to paint his freckles with mud. They pulled at his tidy shirts, mussed his tidy hair, and took every opportunity to bump into Kerish, knocking his tidy knees into the dirt.

It was only a matter of time before it occurred to someone in Kerish's class that carrying on his mother's last name was often the mark of a child born out of wedlock. Soon after, the word "bastard" was whispered in corners and muttered under breath in passing, though some held out in favor of the idea that he had been fathered by the Adversary himself. In a class of twenty children, four were the architects of his perpetual discomfort; six followed their lead without thought or question; eight might join a crowd or avoid it altogether depending on day or disposition; one was Kerish, and one was a little girl who cared not at all about the rest, having decided on the second day of school that she and Kerish were destined to be friends.

Miranda Gleason was small for her age, with a mop of curly strawberry blond hair that resisted all efforts at confinement. She had a pertly upturned nose with not a freckle in sight and a twinkle in her light brown eyes. She had decided, at the ripe old age of seven, that what she wanted most in life was to be a witch. Not a witch like those cranky old folk at the Temple of the Sun talked about, but a real witch who made poultices and magical remedies, who spoke to spirits, and rode upon a flying broom to be closer to the stars. By her approximation, being a real witch sounded like the most splendid thing in the whole wide world.

It might seem like an odd life's ambition; there certainly weren't many who seemed to share her opinion, but Miranda had her reasons. Her great aunt had once taken horribly ill from a gaping wound in her thigh that refused to heal proper; then one day Mistress Windle just appeared, with her satchel full of magical remedies. The fact that it happened the very same day that the physician was banging on their door seemed like more than a coincidence to Miranda, and having the both of them arrive for the same job was hardly a peaceful encounter. Particularly as the two had quite a few differences of opinion on treatment. To be sure, Mistress Windle and the doctor had both wanted to fill the wound with nasty squirming maggots. The difference was that the old blowhard doctor seemed to think that just him saying so was enough to make a person happy about maggots in their leg. Meanwhile, the lovely Mistress Windle explained that the maggots would *debride* the wound, eating away the dead and fevered tissue. Elsewise, flesh would need to be cut away with a knife before the wound would heal. Beyond that point, there was no reconciling the two. The doctor recommended a salt of arsenic, iodine, and bloodletting, with which Mistress Windle took obvious issue, stating that, with very little effort, his prescription could become toxic and that Great Aunt Adelaide hadn't the blood to spare.

In the end, the physician had left in a huff, and Mistress Windle administered the horrible squirming creatures to the angry wound, then prescribed a regimen of teas and broth. Over the next several days, she returned to check on her patient; some days, she applied a strange smelling poultice, another she sewed the wound as though the edges were made of cloth and slathered it with honey. Despite her Mam's disapproval, Miranda did her best to spy on the goings on around the sick room, particularly when Mistress Windle was witching about.

On the first day of school, Miranda had been too put out with the necessity of attending to bother much with the other students. On the second day, however, she heard some of her classmates in the yard being inexcusably rude to a small child with the tidiest clothing she had ever seen on a boy her age who wasn't bound for private academics. The boy didn't look like a toff, nowhere near self-important enough, as he flinched in response to the jeering of his fellows but did nothing to defend himself. This prickled Miranda's sense of justice. She was already making her way toward the crowd when the words Wicked Windle and Weird Windle began to become distinguishable from the noise. Could this be *Mistress Windle's son?* Her personal heroine's son? If that was the case, then this *definitely* would not do. She rushed to his side, using elbows and knees as necessary. Miranda soon burst through the crowd, hair flying from its braid in several unruly directions, to stand with arms akimbo between the boy and the current instigator of this mess of juvenile humanity.

"Does your Mam know you've got such a mouth on you, Harris Ortney? Think shame on you all, picking on a single young boy like a pack of wild dogs."

The resistance from an unexpected quarter took some of the children aback, undermining the mentality of the miniature mob, while the six-year-old Harris Ortney doubled down instead.

"No use bringing my mother into it Miranda, that boy you're so keen on defendin' comes from a family of wicked witches and we all know it." He sneered.

"That is *Miss* Miranda to you. I'm a young lady now, and

you'll address me as such." Harris gaped at her for a moment as though he couldn't have been more surprised by her assertion if a fish sprouted legs and did a bit of a jig. Setting aside the unflattering thought, Miranda took advantage of the moment of silence and pressed on.

"It's no matter what you think of the Mistresses Windle, it don't give you the right to judge; that's what they say at Temple after all. No judging. Seems to me, if them's ones that are going about healing people and you're the one going about judging people, that makes you the wicked one, Harris Ortney." The group of assembled children pulled back in shock, while the boy she was defending looked very much like he would prefer to be anywhere else.

"I am not wicked, no more than you'd be a lady. You might want to fix your hair 'afore you go about putting on airs, *your ladyship*. Might want to think twice before you go about defending a Windle too." Not for the first time in her life, Miranda wondered if Harris practiced sticking his lip out that far in the mirror. It might have been impressive if it weren't attached to his bothersome self.

"Look to your own troubles, Harris Ortney, before you go nosing about creatin' mine. Have you managed to learn your letters yet?" The boy screwed up his face, making it surely obvious to anyone among the crowd that letters were a sore point.

"Shows what you know, we're here to learn our letters, it's no matter whether I know mine yet or not. And *that* boy is trouble, you mark it."

Harris Ortney scuffed his feet in the dirt before turning and leading his small remaining group of cronies across the yard where they prepared to play red rover, pretending as though they had intended to from the start. After confirming that the threat had passed, Miranda turned to the boy behind her who still had not uttered a word.

"Hello there, my name is Miss Miranda Gleason, and you are?" she extended her hand in what she felt was an obvious offer of friendship. The boy in question, however, stared at it like it was a snake preparing to strike.

"Why did you do that?" he mumbled quietly. "They'll come after you now, too."

Miranda shrugged.

"Harris doesn't worry me none; he's the idiot son of me Grandam's cousin, thank the stars we aren't more closely related. Bad enough we have to live on the same lane, without claiming any sort of closer relation." She rubbed at her cheek absentmindedly. "He won't do nothin' to me, I know his Mam."

He stared at her with wide eyes that almost managed to make her feel a touch self-conscious. She felt about her braid and tried to tuck the loose ends back into its weave.

"What are you staring at? You seem a rude boy, you know. First, you'll not introduce yourself, and now you go about starin'."

The boy straightened his shirt, which was about as unnecessary as teats on a bull, so far as actions went.

"My name is Kerish Windle, and you talk kind of strangely."

She didn't bother to stifle the amused but unladylike snort that escaped her.

"What I do, Kerish Windle," she enunciated like her Mam, "Is talk like my father. He traveled down the coast from the Northern Isles." She accepted his nod as the acknowledgment it was and continued in her normal bantering cant. "As for why I'd be stepping in, my Da would never stand for that sort of bullyin', and I have decided, Kerish Windle, that we're bound to be friends."

After this pronouncement, there followed an uncomfortable silence and an intimidated-looking gulping of air, which was far from promising. In fact, he looked like he might be sick all over his tidy shoes.

"How are you at your letters?" She pressed on, "You seem bookish; are you bookish Kerish Windle?" He nodded, continuing to resemble nothing more than a deer in the face of an oncoming train. Still, Miranda was sure that she was right: they were going to be friends - because once she set her mind to a thing, she would surely make it happen.

Kerish found Miranda terribly intimidating; in fact, he spent weeks doing his very best to avoid her notice, with very little success. Everywhere he went, she seemed sure to follow, right up until it was time to leave school. Even then, it seemed that she would find a reason to walk in the same direction or that he'd find her waiting at the center of town. Despite her rather assertive approach to making friends, her perpetual presence did have its good points; when the children in class followed Harris'

lead to gang up on the *witch boy*, it was Miranda that stepped in with enough energy and occasional venom to keep all but the most persistent at bay. Though it was only a matter of time before the ringleaders of his torment began planning strategically, distracting her first so that the rest could get at Kerish unhindered. If he was honest, those were the moments he dreaded the most.

In the manner of most familial feuding, neither boy actually knew where the vitriol came from or that the pattern of behavior started with a snubbed grandfather, vengeful arson, and the prison sentence that haunted him. Kerish only knew that no Ortney would call on a Windle for healing, and that his Grandma Mimsy avoided the Ortneys as though they carried a pox, though not a word of clarification had been said about it. So it was that Miranda Gleason wormed her way into Kerish's reluctant affections, even if it was rare that he could bring himself to show it. Ortney and his closest friends continued to find new and interesting ways to express their loathing, their group of followers shifting in size and enthusiasm as time passed.

In year two, when Miranda had just turned nine and Kerish was still only eight years old, Kerish finally asked his one and only human friend if she would like to come to his house during the market day. They were sitting in the schoolyard, waiting for the bell that would call them back to class. It took Kerish the entirety of the mid-day recess to work up the nerve to ask this pushy creature who had invaded his life to invade his home as well. His friend squealed, a sound he had not been aware that humans could make prior to meeting Miranda, and one he was still uncertain wasn't limited to Miranda alone. She accepted with an unfortunate degree of enthusiasm. He trudged home, second guessing himself the entire way, to tell his Mom that they would have company.

When Miranda arrived the following day (everyone knew how to find the Windle house), it was in her second best dress with her wild hair braided as tight and as neat as her Mam could manage. Upon knocking, she was greeted at the door by her heroine, who looked just as happy to see her as Miranda was to see Mistress Andromeda Windle. She was shuffled, with smiles and a great deal of welcome, into the house and over to a table set for three, complete with freshly baked biscuits. The door swung firmly shut, and the sound of footsteps stomping down the stairs followed shortly thereafter. Part way down, the footsteps paused. Peering up to where the staircase met the ceiling, she saw her friend crouched on the stairs, his brown eyes peeking from beneath the railing. She heard him sigh heavily before he continued to stomp down the last of the stairs, his hair flopping as though to emphasize his discomfort.

"You're here." The statement was all blandness.

"I am most certainly here, how could I not be!"

Andromeda bustled back into the room from the kitchen, carrying cups for both children.

"Kerish, don't be rude to your guest."

Kerish sighed and went to sit at the table beside one of the cups of juice. As it became obvious that her friend would not be making an effort at polite conversation, Miranda felt compelled to pick up the slack.

"You have a lovely home, Mistress Windle." She did her best to sound ladylike as she gazed around at what had, at first, seemed like a simple structure. The more she looked, the more she saw light drifting in from unexpected angles, beautifully tasteful carvings that adorned the walls, and all of the touches that marked it a home well loved.

"Why, thank you, Miranda. The whole structure has been a labor of love by our family. To this day, my cousins sometimes still show up just to install another touch of filigree."

"That's lovely!" Miranda replied enthusiastically, tracing the leaves that bordered the table with her fingertips.

Kerish snorted into his juice but continued to say nothing. His mother rolled her eyes and smirked at the child who glared at her over the top of his cup.

"Kerish has a limited tolerance for people. From what he has said, I do believe that the two of us represent far too much exuberant disregard for propriety in one enclosed place for the dear boy. Would you like to come have a look at the garden while Kerish assembles his faculties? Hopefully, followed by some basic hospitality and manners."

Miranda stifled a laugh and nodded, exiting the room to the sound of shoes sulkily scuffing against wood and fingernails tapping without rhythm against glass.

The yard was lovely and verdant, the air filled with the fragrance of herbs and flowers, and the sounds of crickets chirping, birds singing, and bees buzzing happily among the multicolored blossoms. The garden itself was divided into distinct areas; Miranda was sure there was a witchy sort of logic to it, lined with rocks the size of an adult fist. At one end of the yard stood a tall platform; atop it perched a crow that looked her over with a beady black eye. In the far corner was a huge willow tree with long, thin leaves and branches laden with unopened buds. It was the weirdest damn tree she had ever seen and she loved it on sight. Not far from the tree was a small stone shack with a drying rack outside. She supposed this must be the still room for making magical remedies for the ill. Miranda had just walked into paradise.

Mistress Windle, who quickly tired of being referred to formally and told her to call her Andy or Andromeda "if you must," took her on a tour of the garden, introducing her to plants as though they were old friends. She spoke to them, almost as though they could understand, and then smiled as though they had responded. Andy waved to the crows and touched the strange tree with a reverence Miranda had only ever seen in temple.

"My mother planted that tree." A friendly voice carried across the garden from the open kitchen door. The elder Mistress Windle stood there, holding Kerish's hand as he looked at the garden spread out before him with a degree of reluctance that Miranda couldn't understand. She saw him fiddle with the shell he wore on a chain around his neck as he eyed a beetle that marched on spindled legs down the garden path.

"It looks like the wee folk ought live in it." Miranda scratched her head nervously, loosing several strands of hair. Andromeda laughed and shot her mother an unreadable look as

Kerish seemed to shrink further against his grandam's side.

"Perhaps they do. Tell me, Miranda, what do you know of the Wee Folk?"

"Not much; my Da tells me tales from the Northern Isles at times. Me Mam doesn't care for it."

The elder Mistress Windle petted the top of Kerish's head, not unlike a skittish pup, and smiled,

"I would love to hear your stories some time, young lady."

Miranda swelled up at that, not just with pride for herself but for her Da. He loved the stories of his country, and he loved that she loved them, and she loved that she would get to pass on those stories to someone who would maybe love them a bit too.

Eventually, Kerish joined them in the garden. He spoke, though not much more than he did at school, and there, in the presence of his mam and grandam, he even smiled a bit. It was a small, shy smile, but it was a smile, and Miranda had learned to take even the smallest steps that Kerish made as a personal win. It seemed that his family was of a similar mind, and she was soon invited back.

In very little time, her visits became a matter of habit, one that no longer required second best dresses and neat hair. Instead, Miranda would escape her house in play clothes and make her way to the Windle home on the day of the Great Market, often arriving before breakfast was on the table. Over time, Kerish learned to relax just a little, no longer requiring time to adjust on her arrival, and Miranda learned the rudiments of working in their garden. After three months of market days, she finally summoned the courage to ask Andy to teach her how to be a witch. She would have been insulted by the laughter which followed, but it was so joyful and free that, after the initial moment of shock, she could hardly take offense. What followed was a frank discussion about witches, Andromeda insisting she was no such thing, which did absolutely nothing to convince the girl that it wasn't so. Instead, Miranda took note of her mentor's issue with the topic and let it inform the method of her next approach.

Once the winter months had passed, having given the earth time to rest and renew in fertility, the autumn sown seeds began quickening beneath the soil's surface, and the Mistresses Windle began to prepare the garden for the growth to come. Miranda approached Andy and Mimsy and asked to be taught the arts of medicinal plants.

"You wouldn't even have to pay me none, I just wish to learn!"

The two women exchanged knowing glances, then slowly nodded.

"I'll speak to your mother after temple," Mimsy said, always the more cautious of the two about what Miranda saw and heard. It baffled Miranda how the two women, so unlike anyone else, would still find moments to treat her like all of the other adults. Adults, as a rule, did not credit children with the ability to see and hear and come to their own conclusions. Miranda knew there were secrets in the Windle house; anyone with half a mind could rub two thoughts together and come to that conclusion, but it had never been her aim to expose them to anyone; she only ever wanted to learn what she could and perhaps put it to good use one day.

"Might be best to approach my Da." Was all she said, and

Mimsy nodded in understanding.

CHAPTER 30

On the day that Nimmawni returned, the sea bird came just after the sun had breached the horizon. She wheeled above the house for long moments before diving to dart through the heavy shadows in the yard to beat strong wings against the windows on the second floor.

Mimsy's bed was empty. As she had done on many of the occasions where she slept poorly, Mimsy had risen before the sun and strolled along the shore to sit on the great stones by the pier; the same stones where her father once stood in search of employment. She sat through the early morning stillness, listening to the song of the Great Mother of the Deep rising and falling with every wave. She listened to the animals rising beneath the dock and taking to the air, she watched the first fishing boats leave the harbor, and she watched the men assembling to stand on the stones as her father had, and as her brother had done until he moved from the pier to the open water. She watched until the nostalgia seemed to drift away on the open sea, and then she rose and took tea in the shop that was now run by her cousin.

Andromeda's bed was also empty. The morning song of birds outside her window and the urgent press of her bladder woke her and sent her stumbling wearily toward the outhouse to relieve herself. Kerish's bed, however, still contained his sleeping form. He sprawled out on the sheepskins that had once belonged to his grandfather, wrapped in a heavy quilt made by his great-great-great-aunt Bella and her daughters after the fire. The rattling of the window in its frame woke him with a jolt, the beating of wings and the sound of avian feet pounding the glass confused and scared him. When he identified the source of the sound, he stomped over to the window and smacked the glass ineffectually with his pillow.

"Downstairs!" He yelled, not wanting the seabird to come in through his window. "Downstairs!" He wrapped his quilt around his shoulders, doubling the fabric over so as not to drag too much on the ground, and stomped down the stairs in search of his mother. The bird had found a more receptive target as Andromeda made her way back to the kitchen door. The two were arguing in the garden, Andromeda insisting that she needed to retrieve her son while the seabird remained focused on her reward, when Kerish made it to the kitchen door.

"Well, that makes things simpler," Andromeda snatched up his hand with a tired smile, "time to go to the dock sweetheart." It was obvious that, despite her fatigue, his mother was genuinely happy; not wanting to ruin it, Kerish simply nodded and wrapped his quilt tighter around his shoulders before making his way toward the path to the beach. He knew what the arrival of the seabird meant; every story that started this way was told with a measure of joy that Kerish envied. Of course, now that it was his turn, he found that he was more anxious than excited. What if he messed it up? What if he did something and the mermaid never came back? What if she was disappointed with him? Grandmama had given him her shell necklace when he was seven, and in the last three years, he had mostly done his best to ignore all of the ways in which it made him even more different than he had been to begin with. His feet slowed as he neared the point where the trees met the dunes, his mother's strides carrying her across the short expanse to the sand beyond without any sign of hesitation. The further she got from him, the more anxious he felt, the more he felt he would call attention to himself when he arrived after her. So he ran, kicking up sand with his bare heels as he sprinted after her, finally catching up as both of their feet found the wooden planks.

The Windles' front door still felt like a gateway to a magical world, even if it no longer barred Miranda's way as she barreled into the living area with a greeting on her lips. When her Da had agreed to let her learn from the Mistresses Windle, he had taken her aside to talk to her about responsibility. His Da had tilled the land of the Northern Isles and knew full well that, while growing things needed little more than water and sunlight to grow, the work of ensuring that they did so unimpeded was ongoing. Despite her Mam's obvious displeasure at the entire situation, she had promised most sincerely that she would maintain a schedule, stopping by to lend a hand on the first, third, and fifth days before and after school. She continued to visit on market days, though this was less consistent, as her Mam complained of her perpetual absence. It did not escape Miranda's notice that the absence had not been so troublesome until she was taken under the wing of another child's Mother.

Still, when she arrived this particular morning, it seemed that there was no one there to greet. She called through the house, even going so far as to take the stairs two at a time and peek into the empty bedrooms. Having confirmed that the Windles were all absent, she returned to the first floor and continued out into the garden, grabbing her pinafore on the way, to spend a bit of time pulling weeds. She had adopted the habit of speaking to the plants as she worked, having listened to Andy and Mimsy more times than she could count, and what started as a poor imitation had grown into something larger with just a touch of imagination. The other townsfolk would probably think her as mad as could be, but she swore the roots came free easier for it.

Having worked up a sweat, she helped herself to some water and an apple and rinsed her face. Judging it not quite late enough to head to school, she took a closer look at the contents of their bookshelves. She had been offered a few of their old printed books one cold rainy day, when they all huddled up inside with hot tea and Mimsy made stew and fresh baked bread; but it seemed that many of the books were old and worn but had no print on the binding. Having certainly not given up on her witchy dream, the suspicion that they might be books on herbs or witchcraft filled her with excitement. With one last glance about her to ensure that she wouldn't be caught, she pulled the oldest of the bunch from the shelf. It was worn and a touch singed around the edges, with no title on the cover at all, and when she opened it, she found that the entire thing was written by hand. There were no pictures, no diagrams, no sketches, just line after line of neat script that rivaled her teacher's for precision, and every page was filled with stories. The writer of the first book had clearly devoted herself to meticulously transcribing stories they had been told, and when she returned to the very first page she found, in the same hand, an inscription.

> "*I have found myself a part of a fantastical world,*
> *One in which all that I had once thought to know is*
> *Called into question. Being presented with the choice,*
> *To either believe myself and my loved ones to be taken with*
> *A shared madness, or to believe the proof of my senses*
> *And embrace a new, more vibrant reality; I choose*
> *To immerse myself in limitless wonder.*
> *What follows within these inadequate pages is the faithful*
> *Retelling of the stories of those Windles, blessed beyond*
> *Measure with the knowledge of The People and the*
> *stories which they impart. I put pen to paper, saving*
> *these stories that I might tell them to my children and*
> *my children's children, and so that future additions to*
> *our family might learn the stories which shape us.*
> *With all of my love,*
> *Mira Windle*"

This was not what Miranda had expected, but even as she read the first page, she found herself drawn in. Devouring page after page, it was long past time for school when she reverently turned the rear cover to close only the first of Mira's many journals. Reverently staring at the shelf full of unnamed books, it was easy to justify not running to class; she could learn far more interesting and important things by staying put. She slid the book back into its vacant spot, used the tips of her fingers to tilt forward the next, and returned to her favorite chair with it hugged to her chest. After the first story, a story told by a barnyard cat, it occurred to her that the only thing that could possibly improve on this moment was a cup of tea and some biscuits. The Windles still hadn't returned. Being quite familiar with the layout of their kitchen, she set about making some tea of peppermint. As she waited for the water to boil, she climbed up on a stool to reach a large ceramic container, humming to herself in satisfaction when she found it full to the top with ginger biscuits. Only after placing a plate with four tantalizing pastries and a mug full of steaming hot tea, liberally sweetened with honey, on the table beside her chair, did she return to her seat to continue reading.

As though she somehow knew that Kerish would need a moment to acclimate himself, it wasn't until both mother and son were settled comfortably at the end of the dock that the mermaid made herself known. She did not grab his dangling feet, nor did she speak to him from beneath the dock like some invisible specter; instead, her head emerged slowly from the gentle waves where the ladder entered the water. She smiled sweetly without showing her teeth, the corners of her eyes crinkling to show that the smile was genuine. Everything about her behavior was designed to make the anxious child feel more at ease, and he felt some of the tension drain from his shoulders.

"Good morning Winken, Little Winken." She nodded.

"Good morning, Nimmawni. It's wonderful to see you again." Andromeda smiled as Nimmawni looked at Kerish with curiosity. In order to spare her son the discomfort of ongoing attentions, Andromeda endeavored to move the conversation along.

"Where have you been for the last seventeen years, Nimmawni? I do believe that is the longest we have gone without seeing your face."

Surely, there was a truth to this because the face that looked up at them was one of a young woman grown. She had lost the last of the roundness to her face, revealing a sculpted jawline and slender neck that bobbed above the waves. She had pulled back her hair from her face, fixing it in place with a long fish bone that allowed the rest of the tentacle-like mass to float free in the water. As she considered the question, the mermaid appeared all at once tired.

"I apologize, Winken, it *has* been quite some time."

"Where have you been?"

"A long ways from here, a journey that marks the moon's passing many times. Far across an expanse of the Sea Below, there is a stretch of open waters where the many Shark People dance. It lies at the midpoint of three reefs much beloved by The People, though travel between them is made treacherous by the sharp teeth that await the unwary who make the journey.

Did you know, Little Winken, that sharks are some of the oldest of all of The People?"

Kerish shook his head, still quietly in awe of the family legend come to life before him.

"They have existed since a time before the sun made its journey across the sky, before the great star of the north was drawn into position, before time as we know it. In many ways, they are not much changed from how they were formed to begin with. In others, they are as different as can be. They vary so much in shape, color, and temperament. Some have no care for who or what they eat, while others are as large and as peaceful as the Great Filter Feeding Whales."

"There are sharks as big as whales?" Kerish breathed the question, barely above a whisper, but Nimmawni heard it all the same.

"Yes, Little Winken, huge sharks that eat nothing but the tiniest among The People. They are the color of deep water with a speckling of white dots like the sun reflecting on the surface of the Sea Below. They migrate in the warm coastal waters of lands far from here; though in this case, it was unfortunately not them who I traveled to see. I went in search of the oldest shark I could find, so I went to where so very many sharks congregate to begin my search.

"One shark sent me to another and another, and each time I listened and I learned new stories, but none had the answers I seek and none could claim to be the oldest. Indeed, most were younger than myself. Until one day, I spoke to one of these supposed elders, and they told me of a shark they had only heard of, one who lives far to the north in the coldest of waters and dives deep beyond the realm of the sharks that dance in sunlight. So I journeyed up the far coast of what you humans call the ocean, and I made my way to the cold waters of the north to search among The People there. There are sharks in the north with dark skin and tiny eyes; their bodies are long and almost as round as the barrels that fall from your ships, and they live for hundreds and hundreds of cycles."

"Weren't you cold? What did you want to know so badly?" Kerish asked, engaged despite himself.

"I suppose there was a bit of a chill, I don't find that I get cold the same way that humans seem to. I followed one of these strange sharks for a few days before I asked where I could find the oldest of his People. He said I could find their elder in the deep, down where the fish set out their lures made of light in the darkness. So I dove. I dove deeper and deeper, and I searched the midnight waters until I found another of these small eyed sharks. She let me catch hold of her fin as she took me to where the oldest, most solitary of their People preferred to spend his days. It was there that we found him, and twice he tried to scoop me up in his mouth to make me his meal before he would even take the time to listen as I spoke. It is my misfortune that when I was finally able to ask him my questions, he had no answers. If his People ever knew, the knowledge was long gone. He did ask me why I searched, and while some of my query he disregarded as folly, he did remember a single story of the Sea-Folk walking on dry land, and he could not fathom why I would wish to know how."

"Is that not why you went to the pink dolphins?" Andromeda asked, remembering the stories of her childhood.

"Of course. Though they either could not or would not give me that knowledge." The mermaid's voice was tired, almost dejected, as though she might be losing hope.

"Did the old shark tell you the story?" Kerish wondered.

"Yes, he did. *His* People say that humans were once Sea-Folk, only they could not return, in truth, to shore."

Kerish eyed the water nervously. He knew how to swim, but only because his mother said he must, and he took no joy in it. He couldn't say that he was keen on the idea of having somehow emerged from that mysterious place, one that seemed perpetually full of hidden dangers.

CHAPTER 31

The ancient shark told me that he had heard a story once, long ago, told by an elder among the Sea-Folk. It was a story of The People, a story of the Sea-Folk, and a story of Humans.

When it came to pass that the exposed parts of the star-body became the earth and The People of the Sea began to change and shift to crawl on the land, it became necessary that the Sea-Folk learn the magic of feet and legs, that they could walk the earth and learn the stories to be found there as well. Having come to understand the nature of legs and land, the Sea-Folk would pass down this magic from generation to generation for many, many cycles, until it was eventually lost, though I know not why. When the Sea-Folk walked upon the land, trading their fins for legs, it was always true that the sea would call them home.

They said it was akin to a whisper that existed just out of hearing range or a tether from the heart to the depths of the deep waters. From the moment their fin became foot, from the moment that foot touched the shore, the call was felt deeply, and it was omnipresent. Furthermore, the longer they went and the greater the distance that they strayed from the water, the more intense the sensation became. The inaudible whisper rising to a silent rushing roar, the gentle reminder of a home beyond the waves becoming a crushing pressure on the Sea-Folk heart.

Yet, somehow, there were some who went to shore and, even as the sea called them home, they did not listen. The longer they ignored their nature, ignoring the call and living through its pain, the more distant it became; the more they settled in their new skin and long legs. They took to living among The People of the land, building shelter and forming villages a distance from the shore. It was not until the day came that one young person decided, of his own volition, that he wished to return and frolic in the sea, that these Folk began to understand the consequences of what they had done.

As he submerged himself, his body tried to return to its natural state, but he could not find his fins; his body had settled, and his legs would not merge. He called to his companions in alarm, alerting both the Once-Sea-Folk who walked the land and the Sea-Folk swimming along the shoreline. Their finned families looked on in alarm as their cousins cried aloud at the horrible loss, panicking when their fins would not return and make themselves known. Some attempted to swim, awkwardly paddling further out to sea, crying out for their family's help and guidance. The further from shore they swam, the rougher their skin became, filling them with hope that would be washed away with the tides. For as soon as the rough and scaled portions grew to cover their arms and legs, these signs they mistook for a mark of the change began to slough off and fall away, leaving raw, soft skin behind.

Their Sea-Folk families turned away, some in horror, others in disgust, but not before one such Folk grabbed hold of that first newly made human and dragged him beneath the waves; not out of malice, but in one last attempt to return him to his truest form. This attempt was not successful. As you know, humans cannot breathe beneath the surface of the Sea Below. Instead, the water fills their bodies, and without gills, they find no nourishment. When the young human's body floated to the surface, having already returned to the cycle, his land bound fellows retreated to the shore in shock. After all, it was only natural that they found themselves suddenly afraid of the wild expanse they had once called home.

Though they continued to speak for some time, Nimmawni's mood barely lifted, and Kerish found himself haunted by the shark's tale. The idea of something so familiar being the source of one's demise gave him chills as he sat on the dock and as they picked their way through the undergrowth on their way home. When Kerish and Andromeda returned to their house in the early hours of the evening, they found Miranda and five family journals sprawled across the floor of the great room. The girl was asleep, the books were open and very obviously in different stages of being read. Kerish sighed dramatically and yelled his friend's name, startling her awake. Seeing that she was no longer alone, she scrambled into a seated position, clutching the nearest book to her chest and blinking her eyes in an attempt to focus.

"Hello, Miranda," Andromeda spoke with a touch of concern in her voice.

"Hello, Andy, Kerish." She glanced around at the books surrounding her on the floor, wincing a little at the mess and perhaps contemplating the distinct possibility that she wasn't meant to be reading these journals to begin with. "I think I might have some explainin' to do. Though, to be fair, it seems you've things to explain yourself."

CHAPTER 32

The Windle household was full of stories, stories with many sources that paid little to no attention to time. The town had many stories of its own; some were the natural result of the constant flow of sailors making ports, many were to do with the Temple of the Sun, but some had stood the test of time and held over from a time before. At times, a story returns as though the telling is remembered somewhere deep within the blood, an ancestral joy or fear that retells itself and makes itself known once more.

In a time before the gilded spires were built, when the temple grounds held a small stone structure dedicated to a god whose name would be scrubbed from history, a story was told of a spirit that rode the wind, foretelling death and carrying the souls of the departed from their bodies. Though it had been many years since the story had seen the light of day, it was only natural - when the baying of the Night Hound was heard once more on the hillside - that its tale was resurrected. The story told and retold: the tale of a family member who heard the baying in the night and died the next day; a townsperson who swore they saw a great beast hulking above a neighbor's body just before they passed.

The stories were traded among adults in hushed tones, lowered by fear and superstition more than out of care for who might overhear, often in the presence of children. Children, loving a good scary story, circulated the tale amongst themselves, whispering tales of the Night Hound in the schoolyard and under the nose of their distracted teacher. For most, it was a wild tale, one to raise goosebumps in the dark and perhaps keep one awake at night. Guessing who might be next became a childish game of morbid anticipation. Where other children relished or rejected the creepiness, they could always dismiss the Night Hound as a fantasy, but Kerish had grown up steeped in the power of stories.

It was shortly after his grandmother passed that Kerish first heard the stories of the Night Hound, and he was immediately overwhelmed with fear for his mother. Mimsy was no longer with them, and only Andromeda remained. So he contrived a way to stall the beast based on all of the knowledge he didn't want to have but was raised with just the same. He double and triple checked his plans, then he planted a long row of white lilies along the fence line, hoping to appease the beast so that it would pay no attention to his home and his dear mother. He planted every lily bulb he could find, thirty-three in all, and considered it a job well done.

Unfortunately, fear is rarely known for inspiring critical thinking. So, while the boy had given a great deal of thought to finding the right plant, choosing flowers that often signified death, he forgot that there had been no sign that the beast stalked his mother at all. And while he contemplated the right place, going so far as to measure out distances by foot length, close enough to make his plea, but not so close that he endangered his mother as she slept, he forgot that appeasement required attention and that the offering itself invited a presence. Beyond that, he forgot that it is best to extend invitations only to what one is prepared for.

When his lilies began to bloom, Kerish vigilantly patrolled the edges of the garden before he retired for the night, hoping to make his offering clear and keep his mother safe. He grabbed his necklace in fear rather than wonder, in trepidation rather than understanding, and he called to himself a fearsome incarnation of its ability. The hulking creature loomed in the darkness with burning eyes full of hunger and starlight. Its face was a swirling mass of shadows that crudely imitated muscle, sinew, and teeth longer than Kerish's fingers. Its breath stank of rotten meat as it exhaled heat along his face and neck. His voice died in his throat as he gestured vaguely to his offering. Its monstrous claws dug at the earth as it ate a lily from bulb to bud before snorting in Kerish's face and disappearing into the night, leaving Kerish shivering with fear.

The next morning, Kerish buried his necklace beneath the slate at the base of the step down to the garden in front of the kitchen door, never wishing to see it again. To see and to hear, to speak and understand, it was all meant to be a blessing, but this world was too big and too overwhelming, and that creature last night was no blessing at all. He watched his lilies and waited, having become somehow certain that he had decided the length of his mother's life. He wilted on the inside, agonizing over the uncertainty of his results, wondering how much time his mother had left. Would it be thirty-three days? Would it be thirty-three weeks? Thirty-three months? Or Thirty-three years? Had his desperate wish shortened her life? Or had she now been promised a life that would see its seventy-first year? Regardless of the answer, it was all simply too much responsibility.

Every action Kerish took from there on out was with a singular goal in mind: moving away from home and into the city. His dream was to live in a place he was sure was so completely removed from the world of his family that he could live as other humans lived, with little thought for what existed beyond his personal wants and desires. He worked toward leaving this world behind, and he watched the fences, only breathing a sigh of relief as the second lily was unearthed the night after the lilies bloomed the following year. His mother would live to see her seventy-first year. For all of his doubts and misgivings about the world into which he had been born, he had little doubt of that. He might, at times, feel a twinge of guilt for intending to leave Andromeda in the family house alone, but at least he could leave and know that his mother would live a long life without him.

The morning after the third bulb was unearthed, Andromeda went out into her garden and found a large black dog sitting patiently by the well. He had a long, narrow body and a long, narrow face, his fur a mixture of shaggy and short, his eyes a deep dark brown that seemed to sparkle with hidden warmth. When he stood, he came full to Andromeda's waist, and when he jumped up on his hind legs, he licked her face with ease.

"Well, we'll have none of that now, sire," she scolded him gently. He huffed a bit in amusement.

"You may address me as Augur," he told her with a sort of clarity she rarely heard from the village dogs.

"Augur, then. I prefer to clean my face without spittle, Augur. In exchange, might I interest you in some breakfast?" he leaned against her legs in obvious approval and loped into the house ahead of her.

Kerish was never a fan of Augur, he always felt as though the dog was eyeing him as though taking his measure. Kerish was quite sure he was perpetually found wanting by the large dog. When he tried to convince his mother that the big dog could eat him alive, the argument got him nowhere. It was an irrational, fear based argument, and Andromeda was not prone to taking irrational, fear based arguments seriously. Particularly when the dog in question was well mannered and huffed in amusement as he promised not to eat Kerish alive. The fact that he could keep his promise by simply killing Kerish first seemed to escape his mother's notice.

Augur was a strange dog; some nights, he would rest at the foot of Andromeda's bed, others he would simply disappear from behind closed doors and locked gates, and they would find him happily resting by the well in the morning. Some days, he followed Andromeda wherever she went; others, he loped off down the road, and no one but Kerish ever seemed to notice. No one ever seemed to notice a giant dog that could easily belong in a traveling circus as it just wandered off toward town or the nearby countryside, and Kerish didn't trust it in the least.

Sometimes, Augur would look at him, and Kerish felt as though a night breeze was tickling the back of his neck in a manner that brought to mind the smell of flowers at dawn.

The day the black dog followed him to school, Kerish thought he would die of fright, his growing anxiety slowly suffocating him as he went through the day. Its hulking form sat outside the building, clearly visible from the classroom window, as it appeared to wait. When the midday bell rang, the children ran out to play in the yard, a group of them laughing and joking with Davis, whose father owned the market. Davis swore he had heard the Night Hound baying outside his window just before dawn. He made light of the sound and bragged of his bravery as he told the tale, but Kerish saw the way Davis chewed his lip while the other boys were consumed with mirth; he saw the spooked looks Davis darted towards the shadows and knew he was just whistling in the dark. Auger watched the boys play, and when the school day came to a close, he did not follow Kerish home, only returning to the front yard later that evening. The next morning, Davis wasn't at school. An accident, they said.

When the spring winds began to blow on Kerish's nineteenth year, he lifted the slate tile by the kitchen door, gathered up the bundled collection of treasure he had hidden beneath it, and buried it inside a bag filled with his possessions. He checked and rechecked his wallet and the stash of money he had saved up, tucked beneath his cot, for exactly this occasion. Bowing more out of habit than any real sense of connection to the House

Guardian and hugging his mother tightly in farewell, he avoided Augur as he left the house for the final time. It was a sunny day, but the journey was far too far to walk, regardless of the weather. He hitchhiked to the closest rail station and bought a one-way ticket to the city. Nervous in nature, Kerish expected to spend the entire ride at sixes and sevens but soon found that the swaying rumble of the car and consistent noise lulled him so that it was only the loud clanging as they entered the station that roused him.

Disembarking the train was like entering an entirely new world. The station teemed with People, both human and otherwise. Rock doves and humans alike congregated in numbers Kerish had never seen before as he moved through the columned expanse of the terminal. Their movement flowed, only diverting around the men in uniform who stood in pairs at regular intervals around the main terminal, conspicuously ignored by the shifting crowd. When he emerged from the building out onto the street, it seemed that he saw more automobiles in five minutes than he had in his entire life. He dodged a bicycle as he stepped from the curb, referencing a small notebook for his meticulously recorded directions. Surrounded by unfamiliar sights, sounds, and smells, he went in search of a boarding house from which he could take the lay of the land and find employment.

Life far from the shore was the future he had been working towards, but now that he was there, he found himself a little at a loss for how to proceed. Despite all of his preparation and the many hours lost to inane conversation with vacationers on the coast, he was suddenly daunted by the magnitude of the tasks before him. He had known that the city was big, but the town where he was raised had given him little sense of proportion. Each time he stopped to ask for directions, he became more uneasy, worrying that it might be one thing to dream of the city, but quite another to actually be there.

Despite his concerns, it didn't take Kerish very long to acclimate. After a few nights at an inn, he found himself an establishment that offered half-board, with shared washroom and laundry. Owned and run by a widow with three sons, the eldest being the same age as Kerish, it was a comfortable establishment that prioritized a homey atmosphere and privacy. His room was small but tidy, with more than enough space for the small collection of possessions he carried. His fellow lodgers appeared to be mostly the quiet sort; a literary scholar inhabited the room beside his, and across the hall, two spinsterly sisters shared a room of their own. Two empty rooms awaited lodgers, and some sort of businessman resided on the ground floor. It was a week before Kerish chanced upon the final resident. She sat at the dining table early one morning, nursing a hangover with a steaming cup of black coffee. Beryl was a dancer at a cabaret. Having never personally encountered coffee or cabaret dancers in his past, he was torn between the urge to leave the dining room and the tempting aromas wafting from the kitchen where breakfast was being prepared. Beryl stared at him over her mug with red eyes and heavy lids before pouring another cup full of the suspicious looking black liquid. She pushed it to the place setting across the table and gestured to him to take a seat. Good manners finally breaking his indecision, he joined her at the table and brought the warm cup to his lips. His first taste of coffee left him spluttering. His early morning companion let loose a dry laugh and pushed first a small carafe of milk and then a small bowl of sugar in his direction. Eyeing the cup suspiciously, he added both to his concoction. He continued until the color could almost fool him into thinking it was a nice cup of tea, though his nose would not be so easily tricked. His second sip was far more pleasurable, if still alien, and the two sat in silence sipping their coffee until breakfast was served and the other residents sleepily trickled into the room to take their seats and break their fast.

It was not long after he settled into his room that he found a job as a bookkeeper at an accounting firm. With his new sense of security, he found a discarded cigar box in which to store his valuables and pried a section of baseboard loose next to his bed. Inside the newly created hidey hole, he stored the box with his remaining funds and his shell necklace. He could not bring himself to discard or destroy the mermaid's gift completely, and he could not be sure that doing so would have negated one fundamental truth. Because even hiding the shell behind the baseboard did not negate the fact that he was still, fundamentally, a Windle. Steeped in the stories of The People, and awake to the knowledge of a wider, wilder, world. The side effect of being a Windle was that, even without the necklace, the pigeons flocked to him, the household cat perpetually snuck into his room, and he could hear the trees outside his window whispering at night. This was as it had always been, and he was largely adept at ignoring them; the moments where he slipped, often easily dismissed. After all, who didn't tell pigeons to shoo when they milled about one's feet? And he was hardly the first human to speak severely to a cat.

Being a creature of habit, he soon fell into a regular rhythm: rising in the morning early enough to be first to the washroom; a mug of his newly discovered coffee in hand as he waited for breakfast in the dining room; a stroll to work as weather permitted, a dash to a streetcar when it didn't; hours making sense of sequences of figures; lunch at the cafe down the street before returning to work; strolling home, and spending time in quiet recreation until the evening meal was set at the dining room table. His life moved like clockwork, breaking only on the Sun's Day, with one exception: Beryl, the cabaret dancer in room two. Over time, he had developed an easy sort of acquaintance with the majority of his neighbors. They were all private sorts of people, game to help solve a puzzle should their presence coincide in the lounge, but unlikely to pry. Beryl was something different. He didn't see her often, and when he did, she was just as likely to be silent and hungover as anything else, but when they caught each other in passing, Beryl reminded him of nothing so much as his mother and Miranda. There was little physical resemblance, Beryl was a petite woman with black hair she styled into large curls, large dark eyes and pale skin, the combination of which gave an impression not dissimilar to a life sized doll late in the day, or a hungover ghost hovering in the steam above her coffee cup in the early hours of the morning. It was her character that was somehow both comforting and highly disconcerting. Much like the two most important women in his life, Beryl cared little for propriety or the opinions of others. She was nosy and carefree in a fashion that sometimes made her careless of others. However, where Miranda and his mother had known when to push and when to leave him alone, Beryl had no such sense of boundaries.

On occasion, she would sit across from him in the lounge with a glass in hand and a deck of cards or a chess board; she would sip her cordial and ask him about his day, and then she would ask about his life. She would joke and laugh, and he would engage as little as possible as he fought the quirk of a smile on his lips and the anxious racing of his pulse. The woman seemed to take an odd sort of enjoyment out of his company, though he could hardly pinpoint why. She had a knack for disrupting his solitude, serving some ambiguous but not entirely unwelcome function he lacked on his own, and reading him like a book. Two days after he met Alice, it was Beryl who drew it out of him. She laughed, and she teased him mercilessly and then, just as his mother would, just as Miranda would, she smiled and gave him advice that was far too bold for his character.

Among the rows of women on the factory floor, Alice moved as just another cog in the human machine that was the production line. The heat made her hair stick to her scalp with sweat, and every joint in her arms and hands ached from repetitive motion. Glancing at the clock, she counted down the minutes until the whistle would blow and their lunch hour would begin. When the shriek split the air, hundreds of hands lay their work to rest. Alice twisted her body from side to side, taking pleasure in the series of pops that moved along her spine. She ripped her scarf from her head in order to dab at her brow and run her fingers through her hair. The air filled with the sound of tired women's voices, and the yard filled with women carrying lunch pails. Most days, she would have been among them, but today, she had petitioned to leave early in preparation for a weekend in the country visiting her aunt. The streetcar let her off a few short blocks from the women's boarding house she called home, and, having gone to work without her lunch pail, she decided to treat herself and stop at a nearby cafe along the way. She chose her seat among a row of small tables, all vacant except for one, where a young man sat with tidy clothes, wavy black hair, and smart wire-rimmed glasses. He read a book while sipping coffee. The server brought him a pastry before turning to Alice with a painted-on smile and asking to take her order.

The tea was perfection, she breathed in the calming aroma as she stared out the window and watched the world pass by. The quiet ambiance of the cafe and the warm sunlight through the windows, soothing after the rigors of the morning. She calmly ripped apart chunks of croissant with her fingers, savoring the light, buttery layers of puff pastry. A quiet voice drew her from her thoughts, catching her attention.

"Excuse me, miss?" the man beside her repeated. "Your scarf."

And there, in his hand, not far from his tidy cuff, was her dingy scrap of a scarf that surely smelled of sweat and machine oil. She snatched it away, her grayed and worn nails in stark contrast with his clean cuticles that were as tidy as everything else about the young man. She mumbled her thanks as she shoved the material back into her pocket. She had scrubbed her face before leaving the factory, and her clothes had been quite clean before she left the boarding house for work that day, but a machinist's job was hardly easy on one's clothes, and she was suddenly self-conscious.

"So sorry for distracting you from your book."

"No. You didn't. That is... I was gathering myself to leave, and I happened to notice your fallen scarf; it was no bother. Really." The man fumbled with his words in a manner that made him appear almost as embarrassed as she was. The two smiled shyly at one another.

"My name is Kerish, Kerish Windle." He extended his hand, this time empty and open with expectation.

"Alice. Alice Bernard," she tentatively placed her discolored fingers in his and was reassured by his gentle squeeze.

"I haven't seen you here before. That is - I take lunch here almost every day." He paused. "Am I likely to see you here again?"

It was strange, but Alice almost wished she could say yes. The handsome young man adjusted his glasses. His face was not terribly expressive, so perhaps it was her wishful thinking that made him appear hopeful.

"No, I was just passing by."

"Ah, well... I'll wish you a good day, then." He said quietly, before turning and gathering his jacket from the back of his chair. As he walked to the door, Alice had the impulse to stop him. To somehow make him stay. Or perhaps the wish was that she could turn back time and spend the last however many minutes in conversation rather than staring out windows.

"I do live in the area, Mister Windle." She daringly offered, "Is it possible that you do as well?"

"In some ways, I might as well," he spoke with a smile that filled his voice rather than his face. "I'm here most days, I work less than two blocks away." Another momentary pause. "Might I convince you to have dinner with me one of these evenings?"

She savored the fluttering feeling his invitation inspired for only a moment before replying

"I'm away for the next few days, but I might be free next week."

The two spoke for another few minutes, and not once did Kerish check his watch. When he returned to the office, the secretary looked at the clock in shock. Punctual Mister Windle was nearly seven minutes late coming back from lunch.

When Alice left the cafe, it was with a small smile on her face, a smile that lasted all the way through packing her bag for the weekend, only disappearing among the mass of humanity at the train station. She had a lovely weekend to look forward to and a date with a charming stranger on the horizon. The smile slowly returned as she stared out of her window while the train rattled along its tracks.

CHAPTER 33

The sun rose and fell to find its rest in the sea; it did so repeatedly. The birds tracked its course across the daytime sky, its journey becoming shorter and lengthening again. The moon waxed and waned, the tides rose and fell, and with it, time passed. Miranda continued to spend her days with Andy, tending the garden and working in the still room. Eventually, she began to visit the ill with her mentor, and one day, she was even brought to the tea shop, now run by Andy's cousin Ambrose. There she met his children Marcia and Denis, the next generation of Aydin purveyors of exotic herbs and spices. Miranda and Denis hit it off almost immediately, and, in the manner of a meddling aunt, Andy took to sending Miranda on her errands to the tea shop. The two were soon inseparable, laughing heartily at the drop of a hat, taking great pleasure in her brash nature and his generous smiles. While Miranda flourished, she was hardly blind to Andromeda's lingering sadness. Kerish's departure weighed on the woman, and the letters the taciturn little bugger sent home were hardly full of significant information. Andy's letters, in contrast, were full of

338

the comings and goings of humans and People alike. Nothing of significance was left unwritten. When Miranda and Denis set a date for their union, the invitation was slipped in with one of Andromeda's letters; Kerish's response was short and hardly sweet.

"So happy for Miranda and Denis. Unfortunately, I cannot take the time away.
Please express my congratulations."

If it hadn't been obvious before, his response made it clear as could be that Kerish would be happy to never again return to the sea.

Two years after Kerish left home, Andromeda shook off some of her depression, just enough to be taken with the impulse to install modern indoor plumbing. Although she had never expressed much interest in technological advancements, and certainly not to running water beyond her old reliable hand pump in the kitchen, the workmen seemed to be at the house constantly. In addition to installing new pipes that carried water to the kitchen, they knocked a hole in the side wall of the great room to build a new bathing chamber.

When the seabird arrived, it was to a confusing array of humanity. It landed on the walking path and strutted toward the house, squawking loudly to see who responded with any semblance of intelligence. Unfortunately for him, Andromeda was not among the mass of humans milling about outdoors. Fortunately for Miranda, she was. In all of her time working with Andy, she had never seen a seabird among the avian life that flocked to the Windle house. She knew this without a doubt because she was still very much the little girl who read all of the Windle family journals. As such, she knew exactly what the arrival of the seabird entailed. Despite having no magical connection to The People, she did have a knack with plants, and she had grown up with her father's stories weaving their way through her dreams. So when she saw the seabird, she addressed it in a fashion that she hoped it understood.

"Pardon me, I know who you are looking for. I'll get her for you. It will be just a moment." Then she turned and sprinted into the house with Andy's name on her lips.

The seabird soared back to the dock as Andromeda navigated the path to the beach. It had surprised her that Miranda had not lobbied to accompany her; the sweet girl was enthusiastic about everything to do with the Windle family's stories and knowledge. So enthusiastic that she still occasionally slipped and made it sound a whole lot like witchcraft. After suddenly appearing to grab her by the arm and bring her attention to the presence of the bird, Miranda had taken up her dishcloth, pushed her out of the way, and set herself to washing dishes.

"You do go on and see your friend, Andy, and be sure an' tell me all about it when you get back. After all, someone has to keep an eye on this lot." She had nodded out the window at one of the men in the yard who leaned against the edge of the old well with a cigarette drooping from his lower lip.

When she arrived at the beach, Andromeda didn't step out onto the dock, instead, she stripped down to her underthings and walked out into the water until it was just above waist deep. The Mermaid found her quickly and, using her tail for balance, mimicked Andromeda's position in the water to the best of her ability.

"Greetings Winken. Where is Little Winken?"

Andromeda could feel her face tighten against its instinctual fall, though her attempt at neutrality definitely failed to deceive her friend. Nimmawni's contrite expression just highlighted the guilt that Andy had felt for quite some time. Guilt for not knowing how to help Kerish more, guilt for how she carried her sorrow at his absence. She never meant for her depression to make anyone else feel bad, and here she had done it again. Soft hands grabbed hers and drew her down until she half floated, half crouched, in the water; strong arms encircled her, drawing her chest to chest with the mermaid who guided Andromeda's head to her shoulder. Held in the arms of sea and Sea-Folk alike, she felt her muscles relax as her body swayed, and she allowed herself to finally let go.

The day dawned clear and cool, a touch of frost in the air made the light seem crisper, and the steps to the temple were patterned with an intricate lace of hoarfrost the day that Kerish married Alice. It was a small service, with only two guests in attendance. Alice's aunt, as her only living relative, and Beryl, who couldn't be stopped even if Kerish had bothered to try. The cleric invoked the blessings of the Sun, and they spoke their vows, binding their lives together. When the pronouncement was made, Alice's aunt wiped a tear from her eye, and Beryl, uncontainable Beryl, let loose a whoop that echoed through the empty sanctum, earning a glare from the cleric. When the ceremony was over, the tiny wedding party sat at the very cafe where they met, sharing pastries and memories. In the evening, they bid their guests farewell and continued with their simple plan to spend their first night together in their new apartment.

Kerish accompanied Alice to the door of the boarding house where she lived. The owner stood with him at the familiar wooden door, not inclined to break her rules about men in the building simply because they were newlyweds. Kerish's boarding house was far more flexible about guests and, much to his chagrin, in the time it took for them to collect Alice's belongings, Beryl had enlisted all of their fellow residents in celebrating their nuptials. Kerish was anxious to leave, but, despite being surrounded by relative strangers, Alice thought it a treat, so they stayed until the first of the other residents wandered off to bed. They circled the lounge for a final time, making their goodbyes before grabbing their combined luggage. Kerish hailed a metered cab, and the couple loaded it with their worldly belongings. Thankfully, it was only a short way home, and that was a nice word indeed: home.

Home was a two bedroom apartment on the third floor of a recently constructed building. The narrow stairways were difficult to maneuver with their suitcases in tow, but as soon as they slid the key into the lock and the door swung open wide, they knew that this was where they were going to make their life together.

When Zophi was born, The People took note. Her nursery window was often visited by birds and squirrels, stray cats would try to sneak into the house; it was as though the news of her arrival had been spread among The People. The People were not the only ones who felt she was something special, as she seamlessly became the light around which Kerish and Alice organized their world. As Zophi grew, Kerish told her the only stories he truly knew, the stories his mother had told him, the stories of The People. Though he avoided all references to Nimmawni or his family, his wife raised her eyebrows at the stories he told, having never heard the like before. Zophi and her love of her father's stories gave her mother a window into her father's past. The past was a place Kerish had previously been reluctant to share, and she loved them both all the more for it.

Being a father woke something in Kerish, though he would never be carefree or wild; the three could often be found picnicking in parks where the two adults would indulge in playing tag with their little girl. Her wavy hair flew about her face as she raced around on chubby legs, secure in the knowledge that she would soon be caught up in loving arms. Arms that would cuddle her close and, every so often, throw her up into the sky so that, for just a moment, she could feel what it was like to be a bird. Zophi reminded Kerish of his mother and his grandmother in the best possible ways, a tiny bundle of creative energy that seemed to call out to The People, even though it meant calming Alice when abnormal things occurred. He also saw in her Alice, in the calm way that Zophi took information and made it into something actionable. She was Alice in the way she floated into a room or stuck out her tongue just a little when she was writing. What he didn't see was that she was him as well, in the methodical way she formed a plan and the precision with which she brought her schemes to fruition. What he saw most of all was Alice, and he couldn't bear to see it when Alice was gone.

When someone falls ill on a production line, it can have grave consequences. A sniffle or a mild cough may be easily overlooked, and yet the most horrible diseases begin in exactly that way. Alice left her job when Zophi was born, but when the time came for Zophi to begin her education, Alice decided to go back to work. It was not difficult to find a job; they always needed machinists on the production line. The sniffle and the cough came with the cold winds and spread with unfortunate ease. In time, the majority of the women on the floor were expectorating into handkerchiefs and breathing with discomfort. Accidents became more common on the line, and one by one, the women stopped coming to work, until the factory shut down as a preventative measure; whether it was a concern for the workers or their continued pay was open to speculation.

Alice's symptoms steadily increased in severity. At first, she sent Kerish to stay in the nursery, worrying she would infect them both. It was only a matter of days before she was confined to a hospital bed, too weak to walk, surrounded by others who lay ill and dying. Kerish and Zophi were discouraged from visiting, uncertain as the doctors were about the spread of the virus. When Alice died, they burned her body as a matter of course and presented it to Kerish in a surprisingly compact box with little ceremony. How a whole life could fit into such a small box was beyond his understanding; he stood in the lobby, lost in thought until Zophi began to squirm. Holding the hand of an uncomprehending seven-year-old in one hand and the ashes of his wife in the other, he exited the hospital with his world falling to pieces.

There was no consoling Kerish, in part because he never properly broke down or fell apart; he would not be consoled. The world shattered around him, and he emptied himself to keep the evidence from showing. Work became Kerish's world, though some small part of him remembered that Zophi needed him. His routine was redesigned to keep the child alive and himself inundated in numbers and calculable answers. He woke to make breakfast, setting food before the child with barely a word, only participating as necessary to make sure she was prepared for school. He went to work with a packed lunch so he would barely need to leave his desk and returned home to make a simple dinner, eaten largely in silence. Zophi was ferried to and from school by a neighbor in the course of delivering two children of her own. When Zophi wasn't at school or haunted by the living ghost of her father, she was alone by human standards. She read her books and spoke to the birds and squirrels, and she surveyed her mother's things in search of memories.

It was on one of these occasions where Zophi carefully picked her way through her mother's all but untouched vanity that she saw that a floorboard had been removed and improperly replaced. Curious and home alone, she lifted the edge of the wood and found beneath it a lock box, a stack of papers, and a small wood cigar box she had never seen before. The lock box would require a key, so she set that aside. The papers were full of numbers and other things she didn't understand. The cigar box held her mother's wedding ring, a small bundle of paper money, and a shell strung on a chain. She passed over the money to admire the wedding ring, but when her fingers closed around the shell, she knew the treasure she wanted most. She took the necklace from the box, returned everything else to her father's hiding place, and replaced the piece of wood to cover the hole. When she returned to her room, she perched in the deep frame of her window, and the birds who liked to visit the window began to chatter away about the day. She had always loved to listen to their little voices; they told stories like her father had done before Mama passed away, but today, she heard them with a clarity she had never imagined. Shocked, she put down her father's necklace, and she heard everything as normal. She picked it up again, and the clarity returned. She sat and listened in fascination, hearing more than she ever had before. When one of the little sparrows asked her why she was so quiet, she responded, and the birds went wild. They asked her how she had spoken so very clearly. They wondered what could have changed; the birds had always understood her but never so well as they understood The People. When she heard her father's key in the lock, Zophi panicked and hid the necklace under her mattress. She missed it the moment she let go.

For weeks, she waited for her father to find out that the shell was missing, wearing the necklace whenever he wasn't around. She wondered why he didn't wear it, why he didn't talk to The People the way she could, though that hardly compared to why he barely talked to her either. The worst of the isolation came when school was on vacation, and she was left largely to her own devices. It was halfway through a lonely summer when Aunt Beryl finally realized that there might be an issue, taking time away from her busy life to take Zophi on trips around the city. She took her to museums, the ballet, and the circus. Aunt Beryl even took her shopping for new clothes to replace what she outgrew before school began again in the fall. There were times when Aunt Beryl took her father aside, in another room just out of earshot, for conversations when Zophi was left alone for far too long. Zophi was almost certain that it was Aunt Beryl who convinced him, after two summers without Alice, to reach out to Zophi's grandmother for a place to spend the vacation from school.

CHAPTER 34

The ten-year-old jumped from her grandmother's truck almost before it could be put into park. Her feet hit the ground with a bounce, and she ran around the car to hurry the older woman from behind the wheel, absolutely buzzing with excitement. Andromeda laughed as she was pulled by the hand toward her own front door.

"Sweet child, the door is unlocked. You can go on ahead as you please." With a quick squeeze, her hand was dropped, and the child sprinted toward the entrance. With a sharp turn of the knob the door opened into a room that was old and timeless and perfect. She could feel the pleasure of the house guardian, her grandmother had told her about him - all hung with sprigs of fresh flowers and herbs. It was like an invisible embrace that hugged every inch of her body from head to toe. The girl giggled and raced through the kitchen, out into the garden that burst with all of the vibrant life that summer had to offer. She stood in the center of the walking path and closed her eyes, her hand grasping her father's shell, and listened.

These were not the voices of the city. Rats, pigeons, dogs,

and cats, they could all be lovely companions, but the Rooted People had little space to grow, and The People's voices were often drowned out by the humans traveling to and fro. Here, in her grandmother's garden, she could hear the Rooted People, the insects, the birds, the slithering snakes, and the four legged folk. She could hear the singing of the Moon Tree, the constant rush of the waves on the shore, and beneath it, the song that her father rarely spoke of in his old stories that must be the eternal song of the Great Mama of the Deep. She stood in the center of her grandmother's garden, feeling as though she were exactly where she was meant to be, listening to the world dancing around her, and she felt a trail of warm tears trace themselves down her cheeks to drip from her chin to the soil below. She didn't hear her grandmother enter the house or pass through the kitchen into the garden. Zophi wasn't aware of the new presence until just before her grandmother's arms wrapped around her shoulders and a kiss was placed on the crown of her head.

"Welcome home, my love. I do believe it has been waiting for you."

They stood this way for a time until Zophi's hand was lifted by the damp nose of a massive hound. The great beast pushed forward so that her hand rose to the level of her chest, and her fingers rested in dark fur that was as soft as if it had emerged from a dream. She looked down to meet two strange but intelligent eyes that blinked at her slowly, as though allowing her time to adjust to the dog's presence.

"Hello, child of The People," it spoke as clearly as any human, "Be welcome."

"Hello, my name is Zophi." The girl said shyly.

"You may call me Augur, as your family has done for the last twenty-three cycles."

"Twenty-three years!" That was quite a lifetime for a dog. Zophi inspected Augur further; he did not appear old, and the more she took him in, the less dog-like he felt. He was like something stranger and far more ancient that had chosen to be a dog for a while.

"Come," he said, snagging the hem of her shirt gently with his teeth, "settle yourself before it is time to dine."

He tugged lightly on her clothes before releasing it and proceeding into the house, obviously expecting that she would follow. She paused at the door, glancing back to check with her grandmother.

"Go on ahead, Sweet Child, Augur will show you to your room."

Zophi supposed that she should find all of this odd, but everything about this place seemed so completely natural that she shrugged off the moment of uncertainty and followed the great dog-who-was-not into the house, retrieved her bags, and followed him up the stairs.

The garden had rejoiced when the little girl had arrived. Andromeda realized that her sadness had changed its daily rhythm and song, and she felt that recognition deeply. Once the child returned to the house, she took the time to acknowledge that, despite all of her progress, she had never fully recovered after Kerish's departure. The woman who had rejoiced so long in the freedom of her youth and receded so intensely in her sorrow took a moment to apologize for her distance. There was a tentative feeling of acceptance among The People, most of whom were not prone to holding a grudge. Still, Andy knew it was done without comprehension - because the reality remained that chicks grew and flew the nest. This was a fact of life. The young found their own burrow and rarely returned, and very few of The People of wing or paw were old enough to remember Kerish.

It was the Rooted People who understood, who remembered that Kerish's absence was not simply the act of a seed carried away on the wind, but a rejection of all that connected him to The People. A chick who flew the nest did not reject the song or all that allowed it flight. Andromeda stood silently, listening, and thanked the trees for their kindness before returning to the kitchen. She wasn't quite sure what to feed a ten-year-old, but she supposed that they would figure each other out as the summer proceeded. For tonight, she would prepare food as she always did, and tomorrow, they could walk into town for groceries. As she washed a bowl full of lettuce, the sound of her granddaughter's laughter carried down the stairs, and Andromeda felt some of the tension in her body ease. It was good to have a child in the house again, and they would have every chance to finally get to know one another now that she was here.

At the top of the stairs, there were three doors. The first door opened to a large room with two beds; one was empty and had another cot tucked beneath it, and the other was covered in sheepskins and had a beautiful old quilt folded at the end. The walls were lined with shelves and books and small, meticulously made models.

"This was where Kerish slept before he left," Augur huffed.

Zophi took it all in one more time, noticing the telltale marks of her father's fastidious personality, as well as the layer of dust that told her quite clearly that the room had been left just as it was since the day that he hopped a train for the city.

Augur bumped her side with his head and proceeded back into the hallway. The second door was closed and hung with a colorfully embroidered scene. Augur did not stop there for her to explore, and she assumed it was her grandmother's room. Instead, he came to a halt in front of the third door. The room revealed was freshly cleaned and larger than the first, with a huge bed made up with vibrant yellow-flower-patterned blankets. There were more shelves, one of which was lined with a collection of large shells, the likes of which she had never seen. Possibly the most wonderful part was above the bed, where a great big window looked out over many of the treetops and gave Zophi her very first view of the sea.

Kicking off her shoes and dropping her bags at the door, she scrambled up onto the bed to peer out the window, only to be knocked to the side by Augur as he jumped up on the mattress beside her to put his paws on the window's ledge. Giggling, she rolled back onto her feet and bumped playfully into the giant dog. The ancient creature bumped her back with equal playfulness, and the two bounced off of each other until their play devolved into rolling around on the bed, Zophi laughing so hard that tears streamed down her face while Augur's tongue hung from his mouth as he panted happily. Breathing deeply, Zophi finally got her laughter under control and retrieved her things from the hallway. She unpacked her clothes into the standing wardrobe, though it was already populated with old dresses, then organized the rest of her belongings on the shelves. She took one more look out the marvelous window before she padded down the stairs in stocking feet to the unexpected sound of women in conversation. One was easy to identify as her grandmother Andromeda, *Grandromeda? Androgramma?* The other was unfamiliar but very enthusiastic. The voices in the kitchen carried on, oblivious to her presence.

"I can't believe she's here! That little humbug should 'ave brought her here to meet you ages ago, you know. I should 'ave met her years ago. I should 'ave gone to that city and dragged him home by his ear."

"'Should' does no good to anyone, Miranda; all it does is breed guilt and resentment, neither of which I would wish upon you."

The sound of metal on metal, a pot being dropped in the kitchen sink perhaps, rang through the air.

"Andy, you've been better to me than my own Ma, you deserve every happiness in this life... Even if your son is a bit of a cantankerous twit, he ought to know as much."

The women jumped as Zophi knocked on the frame of the kitchen door. Her grandmother looked amused while her visitor looked a bit pink in the face. Ignoring the previous conversation, rather than getting defensive on her father's behalf with relative strangers, Zophi opted to involve them in her thought process:

"Do you prefer Grandromeda or Androgramma?"

The stranger made a startled squeaking sound that rapidly evolved into a rich laugh that shook her shoulders as well as her mass of wild red hair.

"You must be Zophi." The woman extended a hand in greeting. "You've a bit of the look of your father about you, though it seems you're not so much of a finicky bore as he was at your age."

"Miranda!" Andromeda scolded, then turned her attention to her granddaughter. "Miranda does love your father, truly; she means nothing by it."

The woman snorted.

"Speak for yourself, Andy. My dearest friend, who I stuck by t'rough thick and thin, couldn't be bothered to come to my wedding nor to invite me to his own; and it's only now, ten years past, that I finally meet his daughter. I can call him an old stick in the mud if I so choose, and I wouldn't be wrong saying it neither."

Andromeda rolled her eyes at the woman's theatrics.

"Would you mind helping to set the table, Zophi?"

She nodded, and her grandmother, *definitely Androgramma*, placed settings for three on the end of the kitchen table.

"You're staying for dinner?" Warily enthusiastic about the prospect of spending time with two people she'd only just met.

"Of course, I've got to stick around and get to know you.

After all, we might call you my niece and get away wi' it, though technically you'd be my children's fourth cousin. Is that right, Andy?"

"Sounds about right," Androgramma said, waving a hand dismissively as she bustled into the great room with a few covered dishes on a tray.

"I have cousins? I've always wanted cousins." Zophi spoke with barely contained excitement.

"Oh, you have cousins, alright. Not as closely related as some, but you certainly wouldn't know it by the way they've their nose in each other's business. The Windles are a close knit bunch, and the Aydin's are part o' that by marriage, which makes me a part of it as well. Of course, I always did want a big family, so that does me just fine."

The name Miranda had rung a bell; it took Zophi a little time to figure out why, because her father *was* a bit of a curmudgeon and he was very close lipped about his childhood. Miranda was a name on a letter and a few short stories told with the same brusquely fond frustration as any reference to his mother or Aunt Beryl. Zophi imagined that if they lived closer, Miranda might be the type to show up unannounced and barge into her father's life with the same self-assured attitude that Aunt Beryl did once in a blue moon. Aunt Beryl said that Father needed people in his life who shook things up, and that's why the universe gave him a fractious friend like her. If Miranda and Androgramma were like Aunt Beryl, it would seem to prove the theory. The two women seemed delighted when Zophi told them as much, Miranda going so far as to say she was glad he had someone in his life to act as a splash of cold water. Miranda lifted her glass and toasted fractious women. With a laugh, they joined in clinking glasses, and Zophi found that she was even more certain that her summer was destined to be wonderful.

Zophi had been at the house for just over a week when the seabird came to call. During that time, Miranda had come by most days. She worked in the garden and still room with Androgramma and was happy to help teach what she knew. It was on the fourth day that she spied Zophi's shell necklace and stopped dead in her tracks.

"You 'ave it." Miranda whispered, "I thought it was lost, but you 'ave it." The tone of voice was unreadable, and when the woman grabbed her shoulders and dropped to her knees, Zophi couldn't help flinching away from the intensity.

"Do you know what that is?"

Zophi nodded.

"Do you know where it came from?"

Zophi shook her head, her father had never mentioned the necklace, much less anything about where it could have come from. Miranda searched her face, as though looking for a lie or a hidden piece of information, then nodded and got to her feet.

"Come wit' me."

She led Zophi into the great room, to a wall lined with shelves, and ran her fingertips lovingly over the spines of a collection of what appeared to be old journals until she found the one she was looking for.

"Here it is. The story of how your great-great-great-grandfather Anders came into possession of that shell. And here," she grabbed the very first of the journals from the shelf, "is when *his* father, Toddy, was given the coral Andy wears."

Holding both books, Zophi was guided to a comfortable chair and directed to sit.

"I'll be about the only person not descended from or married to a Windle who's read those books. They're a treasure, and they are your birthright."

With that final remark, Miranda strode from the room, presumably to head back to the garden, leaving Zophi alone with the journals and at a loss for where to start. Eventually, she picked up the oldest book and began to read. The tales within were a mix of old familiar stories and others that were completely new and wondrous. Reading the first book alone, she found herself placing the aged book carefully on her chair and running to tell her Androgramma about a story she already knew. Nobody back home ever knew the stories her father told her, and to find them here was beyond exciting. More than anything, it seemed that, through these stories, he had told her more about the world she was a part of than she had ever imagined. She spent the next four days taking time to read her family's journals, even taking one up to her room to reread the stories of The People before she went to bed. She settled under the covers with Augur curled at her side and read the stories out loud, punctuated by his contented sighs.

On the morning that she read the story of Benjamin's passing, she sat in the garden contemplating the commentary about returning to the cycle when she heard a group of crows jeering at another bird that was circling the garden. Shielding her eyes against the sun with her hand, she saw the seabird dive toward the mint patch before banking and landing heavily by the door to the still room. A few moments later, Androgramma left the little stone hut, pausing only to grab Zophi's hand so they could race down the footpath to the beach. Zophi had seen the old wooden dock when she and Androgramma had walked to town for groceries and the few times she had snuck away to the shore for the thrill of putting her feet in the water. It was hundreds of years old by now, even the ladder Toddy added to the end had been in place for more than one hundred and twenty years. The planks that had been replaced were so weather-worn that they were indistinguishable from the rest, assuming any single piece still stood from the original construction.

The stories of this dock were all brand new to Zophi, she had not had the time to build Nimmawni into a figure of heroic stature. However, she had certainly been made aware that the being she was preparing to meet had shaped her world in indescribable ways, ways she was only beginning to understand. All of her life, she had been told that she was People on the inside, more so than any other human The People had encountered in all of their memory. She was the product of a lineage steeped in stories, absolutely, but it seemed that the missing ingredient bobbed merrily in the water at the end of a nondescript wooden structure held together by carpentry and dreams. In the moment, Zophi could not put these feelings into words, but she would reflect on it often, recreating in her mind the trance-like state in which she stood, with her toes on soft wood and her heels in the sand. The moment before she met the mermaid who would inhabit her dreams.

"Hello, Old Winken, Little Winken, it's good to see you." The creature who spoke to them was everything the books had said and more: she was beautiful. No one had written about her being beautiful. The girl stood shyly, in a fashion that seemed to baffle Androgramma, who had barely had a timid moment with her granddaughter, not even when her grandmother, the stranger, came to take her away from the city. Zophi was grateful for the moment Androgramma took to introduce her properly, though by all accounts, it would come to nothing.

"This is my granddaughter, Zophi."

"I see! You have a bit of your father's looks, Little Winkin. Though I feel you are more like Old Winken in spirit."

She leaned against her Androgramma with a smile on her face, and the older woman wrapped an arm about her waist in a one-sided hug.

"It is good to see your joy, Old Winken." Nimmawni smiled up at them kindly.

"It is good to see you again at all, dear friend."

Zophi stared at the mermaid with her own big, dark eyes, assessing the bigger, darker eyes of the beautiful creature that floated below. Nimmawni noticed her attention and swam about in circles and figure eights, showing off her fins, the flickering reds and whites, the long, fluttering tail of gray. Zophi's jaw hung slack in amazement, and when Nimmawni finally came to a stop, the three exchanged a grin.

"So," Androgramma began, winking at Zophi before she continued, "Where have you been these fourteen years?"

The mermaid slithered her tail across the surface of the water, the look on her face distant and introspective.

"It is a strange thing, how far humans have advanced into the sea with so little understanding of its nature. Your ships keep getting bigger, their materials harder and more strange, and their cargo more inexplicable. Those who once chose to make their lives at sea understood that they were subject to the whims of the elements. They made their peace with it, and they carried on with a thirst for adventure. Now, your ships are made of metal and carry pieces of your world within them as though to make the luxuries of land seaworthy. I was exploring the northern waters, once again, when I heard the strangest music floating through the deep waters. It was not the song of the Great Mama of the Deep, nor was it the song of any of the Sea People of my acquaintance, so I set off in search of its source. It was on the sea floor, caught up in the silt, that I found the wreckage of a great metal ship being reclaimed by the Sea. The eerie music filled its halls, reverberating around the spiral staircases and the great halls lined with pictures painted in colored glass. When I re-emerged from its halls, eaten by salt and worn by water, it was onto a large flat deck. The sides were hemmed in by railings and ornamented with tubes so huge I have rarely seen the like before, and in the center of the deck was the source of the melody. There had been corpses of the fallen in the rooms below, but it was only there, on the deck, that spirits remained. Dedicated spirits who still clung to their instruments, playing music in the face of disaster and destruction. They paid me no mind, so I curled up, and I waited, and I contemplated the nature of things. The nature of humans, the nature of The People, the bravery of gill-less musicians who played on as the water rose around them, changing the voices of their instruments and rendering every note haunting."

This was a far more serious response than Androgramma was expecting.

"Was it like the skeletons were playing instruments?" Zophi asked, enthralled.

The mermaid seemed uncertain about the question but, after a moment of thought, continued,

"There were many skeletons throughout the boat, their bones already picked clean by the carrion eaters of the water, but the spirits on shipwrecks tend to be echoes of the body more than they are connected to the body. The players' bodies lay out on the deck, but the instruments were held firmly by the echo of their musicians still intent on their ongoing melody. It seemed that they showed no sign of bringing their final performance to a close."

The girl sat with that response for a matter of seconds before opining,

"Well, what else are they going to do? It doesn't seem there would be much else *to* do."

"Most would choose to pass on in the manner of all spirits, becoming part of the all and part of the other. It is not generally considered a choice not to."

The three were silent for a moment, the two humans contemplating what they had heard, while the mermaid stared off into the distance.

"Is it that important?" The girl asked, "So important that we aren't given a choice?"

Dark eyes considered Zophi for a moment before she received a response.

"What is important is the continuation of the cycle; it is woven into every living being that inhabits the Star-body, and it takes something very strange, or very powerful, to interrupt it."

CHAPTER 35

A long time ago, in that space that borders the past, the future, now, and always, The Great Mama of the Deep and her children entertained themselves with the molding and forming of their many creations. They created the First People, the progenitors of all of The People who would come to be. In this space that was populated by gods, however, there was no concept of death. All beings lived indefinitely, unendingly, within the Eternal Sea. It was when the very first egg was laid among the great elders of The People that the gods looked upon their creations and saw with clarity what might come to pass.

It is an undeniable fact that a People with no limitations would come to overrun the Star-body. In this time, the fly might sit beside the spider without fear, the smaller fish had no cause to be wary of the shark. There was no true concept of predator and prey, only a sort of play acting in accordance with their natures. Each being existing as one of only two of their kind, who were destined to live forever. When the first among the shell people laid their eggs, it caused a great dispute. It is the nature of creation to create, the nature of life to breed further life, to curtail that for the sake of simplicity was anathema to the many deities who had participated in the great shaping. Still, the world would get very crowded should all of The People begin to breed and should that breeding go unchecked. It was in the midst of this conversation that one of the youngest of the sibling deities, one who had claimed or been given no domain of her own, decided to voice her opinion.

What if, said the deity, *each being was given a finite time for their body to walk among the living. What if, at the end of this time, their body would no longer take up space and thereby make room for more People and more children, souls who would have a brand new experience of all that the Eternal Sea laid before them.* The combined assembly of deities was silent. Some were shocked at the audacity of the idea, to end life? It seemed strange and cruel. Others were silent in contemplation, could this strange new idea truly work? Could they truly entertain the idea of a being living and then living no longer?

Would you truly wish to put an end to all that one of The People is and all that they might be? The Forest God, Fyi'thunn, put forward his question in shock.

Brother, we all of us know that there is more to a being than its body alone. Do you truly believe that I would wish to snuff out all that any being is, was, or could ever be? The young deity was impassioned but still spoke softly, its words ringing out clear and true.

What is it that you wish for then? Pan'chan asked his sibling.

I would wish that each being be given time, that they

might make their mark upon the Eternal Sea, but that their time be fleeting to give the span of their life value, and that they be limited so that the generations to follow might make their own marks as well. The Deity fell silent, waiting for its siblings' response.

We would need to strike a balance. The Light put forward, unsurprisingly The Shadow concurred.

Do we propose to just strike The People down at random? Surgani, the Goddess of the Molten Star, I believe you call magma, said skeptically.

"Perhaps," said the Great Dragon who encircles the Star-body, "I might gift them the passage of time. Let their bodies feel the passing of the moon and stars, that they might count their cycles thusly and feel the fleeting sensation of which the little god spoke."

Perhaps, said Orai, the God of lightning, whose touch forms glass from sand, we might make them more fragile than their forebears. Some great accident might shatter the body, releasing the soul therein.

Perhaps, said Pan'chan, I shall gift them with Hunger. For hunting and eating is a great pleasure. However, instead of the joy of the hunt and the empty flavor of a creature who will simply wink back into existence a stone's throw away, let the bodies of the no longer living truly nourish their captor, and let fortune favor the clever, the quick, the strong, and the wise.

Were this but a conversation among The People, it might have taken days or years to bring this plan to fruition, but this was a council of the Gods, and as they spoke of it, their words came into being. Little by little, The People all began to procreate, and each found that their children were hungry and fragile and subject to the passage of time as the First People had never been.

And what will become of their bodies once the soul no longer resides? The Light asked.

Those who are hunted will be eaten, of course, replied Pan'chan.

What of those who are casualties of time, brother? The Shadow inquired.

The collective sat in contemplation until one of the First People, so small they had not noticed its presence, decided to speak.

"My children and those like us can be of assistance. We are not large enough to hunt and kill, but our hunger is still great. We can be the carrion eaters and let our detritus serve to nourish the Rooted Folk. They shelter us often, and we would wish to repay their favor."

At that, The Light and The Shadow sat back in satisfaction, for they saw the greater pattern of the work of the divine and were at peace with it. The Tiny People and The People built better to graze than to hunt and tear flesh would feed from the Rooted People, and their Predators would find in them their prey. The chain would continue and when the predator died, it would be feasted upon by the carrion eaters who would return their bodies to the soil from which grew the Rooted Folk, who fed the Tiny Folk, and so on, and so on, and through this cycle, balance could be achieved and maintained.

It was at this time that Great Mama of the Deep turned her

gaze to the young goddess and asked:

What would you have us do with their Souls?

The Deity was silent in thought, basking in the moment and proud of being entrusted with such a question. When the Deity spoke again, it was to explain that it would split the soul into pieces,

I would return the majority of the soul to all that is. I would wrap them in the wonder of our Mother's song, that they might continue to shape the Eternal Sea. For the second part, I would maintain much of the essence of their being, that they might be reborn and continue to learn and grow in a new time and place, in a new body, all of which will bring experiences the likes of which they have never known before. The last, I would maintain something of their memory, a spirit or shade to act as a conduit between realms and to carry out their wishes, inasmuch as a disembodied spirit might. To watch over the loved ones who mourn their passing, to honor that which they honored in life, and to influence their reborn self, that they might be guided to live and thrive in accordance with the balance.

The assembled deities listened to her idea reverently without interruption, and when she fell silent, they too did not speak, knowing it was a moment to be honored and remembered, for death had been spoken into existence and its deity named. They looked upon their younger sibling and bestowed upon it the name Ghurnak, The Spinner of Life and Death. She was gifted a blade fine enough to be an instrument with which to cut the threads of many lives and sharp enough to split their souls, that they might return to the all exactly as Ghurnak had described.

"So, you see, Little Winken, when the soul does not carry on its journey, when it does not return to the all, its essence cannot be reborn, and its shade cannot console the living. This is why it is so very strange that the souls on the ship would dedicate themselves in such a way, in defiance of the cycle to which we all must return."

Throughout the summer, Zophi returned to the water often, hanging her feet off the dock or simply staring out at the sea as though she could will the mermaid back to shore. She learned the names and properties of at least twenty of the Rooted People, she harvested flowers from the Moon Tree, her Androgramma bought her a beautiful set of paints, and for the first time in her life, she met family. She had Aydin cousins, just as Miranda had said, and she met descendants of Melody's brothers and Toddy's sisters. Children who had grown up with many stories, including the stories of The People. She and her cousin Juniper, who traced her lineage back to Melody's brother Adem, got along famously. They ran through the fields racing birds in flight, played tiddlywinks on the stones of the breakwater, had sleepovers in Zophi's Great-Grandmother's big bed, and late at night, Juniper would ask Zophi in hushed tones what the fireflies were saying.

When the summer drew to a close, the two girls clung to each other as though the world would break in two should they be separated, right up until Andromeda tucked Zophi's bags in the back of her truck and climbed into the driver's seat. Zophi dragged her feet, holding her cousin's hand all the way to the open door of the vehicle. They shared one last hug, and Zophi made herself as comfortable as she could for the ride back to the city. Back to their lonely little apartment, surrounded by brick, cement, and iron bars. Where her father would feed and clothe her and make sure she went to school, but also avoid her in favor of long silences and burying himself in his work. She fell back easily into the familiar routine of her father's house, wrote letters to her Androgramma and Juniper, rejoicing whenever she got mail from any of her family on the coast.

The Sun rose and fell, and the moon waxed and waned, the seasons changed, Summer to Autumn, Autumn to Winter, Winter to Spring, and then it was Summer again. On the last day of school, a familiar truck pulled up in front of the apartment building. Every inch of her bursting with excitement, she ran down the stairs to open the door to the street for a huge hug seasoned with happy tears. Her things were loaded in the back of the truck in no time at all, and, in an eternity that was over before she knew it, she was pushing through the front door of the most wonderful house on earth, being wrapped in its warm embrace. This pattern would continue for years to come, Zophi in the city for the school year, maintaining herself on stolen moments among The People and the letters the postman delivered; returning joyfully to spend the length of the summer at her family's house where she ran free, surrounded by loving family, and taking every opportunity to stare out at the sea.

CHAPTER 36

It was during the fifth such year that she found herself, as she had many times before, sitting on the dock with a pad of watercolor paper and her pencil case, staring off into the waves as she attempted to sketch the perpetual rush of waves in motion. She was about to lift her pencil again when she spied a long shadow moving through the water. It was not shaped like any of the big fish that sometimes ventured close to shore, and, on impulse, Zophi set aside her art supplies, slipped from the dock into the water, and swam out to meet it. To her absolute delight, she came face to face with the beautiful maid of the sea. In the time since their last meeting, Nimmawni had not changed much, but Zophi had sprouted up significantly. Her body had long begun shifting shape, the curves of imminent womanhood clearly visible as her wet clothes clung and drifted in the water. Her rich brown hair had grown long and wavy, and as she treaded water, it spread in a fan around her; her tan skin sprinkled with freckles, glowing in the reflective light. Long legs churned to keep her head above water while the mermaid, with barely a flutter of her tail, continued to make it look easy.

"You swim well, Winken." The compliment made her blush, and she found herself tongue tied. Face burning, she realized all at once that she had seen this happen to her schoolmates, and when Juniper wrote to tell Zophi about her crush on a boy, she described this moment. This exact moment.

"Thank you." She finally croaked, "Though I suppose I will never swim as well as you."

The mermaid gave it a moment of thought before responding,

"It is unlikely that you will ever swim as I swim, but with enough practice, I suppose you could swim as well with the tools that you have. Shall we swim back to shore?"

Zophi shook her head. "I'm alright, I've been taking swimming classes in the city. They say I'm doing swell."

"I have heard of cities before. When your father left, Old Winken spoke of a place that was full to the brim with humans, a place where few of The People make their homes, a place of stone that is far from the water. How does one swim in a city, Winken?"

It was, she realized, a reasonable question, though not one she had expected to address.

"Well, some cities have grown right next to the water, but in those that lie further inland, we must make our alternatives to the rivers and seas ourselves. We swim in things we call pools - though they aren't much like the tide pools that form naturally along the shore. Except, I suppose, that they are water contained all the way around. A hole is dug deep in the ground, shaped, and then lined with material to keep the water from escaping into the earth. Sometimes it's outside, but other times it's inside a building so that humans can swim no matter the weather."

"This sounds unnecessarily complicated." Nimmawni's head tipped to the side adorably; Zophi was enchanted

"You would think so, of course, but then you can duck below a storm or swim off to the warm waters when the frost comes in."

The mermaid did not respond to her teasing tone but rather asked:

"Aren't you going to ask where I've been?"

"Do you want me to ask where you've been?"

"It seems like tradition at this point."

Zophi giggled at that assessment, and the mermaid looked almost charmed.

"Where have you been these last five years, Nimmawni?"

Nimmawni's smile was soft and sort of wistful.

"I heard a rumor that another of the Sea-Folk had been spotted out among the islands near where the sea stars congregate. I went to see if it was true."

Zophi swallowed around a great knot that had settled in her throat; so many thoughts crowded her head that it was hard to make sense of them all.

"When's the last time you saw another of the Sea-Folk?"

Melody had written a note in one of the journals, pondering the feeling that Nimmawni might be all alone out there. It was a thought that had caused her some concern, but, whether on the page or in person, there were few exceptions to the impression that she was content with her life.

"Before I met Winken. The first Winken." She clarified.

"That's a really long time to be alone."

"Silly Winken, I was rarely alone for long. What a *human* thought to entertain. When it is just you and the birds, are you alone? When you sit beside a tree, are you alone? When you are here beside me, are you alone? Am I alone because you are not Sea-Folk? You are People enough to know better."

"That's not what I meant, Nimmawni. I meant without your family."

The mermaid stilled at this.

"It is the nature of the Sea-Folk to travel, to wander the Sea Below and gather its many stories. It is part of our role in the great cycle to hear and to tell, to keep stories alive. There were places we used to congregate, or so the stories say, but that was a long time ago." The mermaid stared out towards the horizon, not meeting Zophi's gaze. Zophi felt certain that Nimmawni was picturing a time or a place where she might once have been surrounded by family.

"Did you find who you were looking for?"

"Hmmm? Oh, yes. He spends his days among the starfish, they tell strange stories within themselves and among each other, passing stories from the tip of one leg to another and on to their neighbor. There are many other People there as well. It is a beautiful place full of color and light, a place that the humans call the bank of stars."

Zophi was happy that Nimmawni found another of her Folk, but the happiness was bittersweet, and the knot in her throat seemed to grow and tug on her heart when her friend said the Sea-Folk she found was male. Without knowing much about romantic relationships among the Sea-Folk, it was silly to jump to conclusions. She didn't even know if their meeting had meant anything.

"Did you get along?"

"What's not to get along with? He's interesting Folk, with interesting stories, but very few of the answers I seek." Nimmawni's search for answers had been the source of much speculation, scribbled into the margins of various journals or theorized on outright when recounting her visits. It had become clear that she wished to know how to walk on land, but the general consensus was that there was something more that she wished to find.

"What are you looking for, Nimmawni?"

"Old knowledge, I have found hints within stories and the vaguest of clues among The People, but nothing certain. The knowledge itself seems to be lost, and Sea-Folk are few and far between. Who is to say what knowledge is to be found in the stories they carry with them."

Zophi set aside her discomfort and the vague sense of jealousy she found herself entertaining at the thought of Nimmawni with another of the Sea-Folk. She focused instead on the question at hand. Focused on the answers that might help her understand the personal history of the mermaid. Casting light on just who had blessed her family with her presence and her gifts. More to the point, she worried for Nimmawni, and the answer to her question might soothe or justify her concerns:

"Why Nimmawni? Why are there so few of you? Why has it been so long since you've come across your People?"

"It's a sad story, Winken." The mermaid sighed, leaning her arms on a half-submerged ladder's rung.

"I would suspect that the dwindling of a People would be a very sad story." Zophi held onto the piling beside her. "Even so, sad stories still deserve to be told."

CHAPTER 37

After the fall of the sunken city, humans did their best to forget about us. We became stories, but becoming a story is by far the most effective way to become immortal. The stories were often a mix of older tales and the fictions of human imagination - but so long as the ships continued to leave port, there were bound to be those who saw the truth, and there were still humans who gave their lives to the sea. With enough time and dedication to a life on the waves, one is bound to cross paths with one of the Sea-Folk, and it was they who breathed life into the human stories as the sailors returned to shore with words like "mermaid" and "siren" tumbling from their lips.

Sea-Folk who crossed paths with human ships soon became targets, meant to be captured, as though their magic would imbue their captor with luck or protection. Where the figureheads of their forebears were shaped in the image of dragons and rams, swans and lions, meant to imbue them with strength and curry favor with their gods; the bowsprits were often now adorned with stylized Sea-Folk, whether to fool us or to receive our blessings in the open waters was hard to say, as any of the Sea-Folk spotted from the deck by human eyes thusly became a human objective. Some sailors dove from their ships, wishing to swim among us; others endeavored to capture us, and it was not altogether uncommon to see a man with a harpoon hanging over the rails in search of us as prey.

It should come as no surprise that the Sea-Folk, as a people, became wary of humans: creatures no longer of The People, who wore the skins and scales of our fins like trophies, for reasons that were, for so long, beyond comprehension. For every bit of reasoning that I have just presented was a mixture of conjecture and knowledge that would come much later. As it happened, we had no explanations for the actions which caused the silhouettes of ships to inspire fear. In time, there were stories that spread among the humans, stories of Sea-Folks who dragged sailors beneath the waves, drowning them in the deep, or feeding them to monsters of legend. It was indeed our actions that inspired these stories, though, to the best of my knowledge, the humans rarely died in truth. We needed to understand. We needed to understand why our people were hunted. We needed to know the story of our danger. Although it is true that we all must return to the cycle, the methods of that transition, taken into human hands, were barbaric and incomprehensible to us.

A predator eats its prey to survive, as the prey feeds on that which is yet smaller, and so on, until you reach the beings who feed on the decay of all that has passed before them, the tiniest of beings who feed upon sunlight itself, and the Rooted People who feed upon both. The cycle is complete, it is all encompassing, it contains moments of both great joy and great sadness, but it is not cruel. So it was out of concern and curiosity that men who jumped from their ships were dragged through the waves, taken to the rocks that broke the surface of the ocean and asked the questions of those who had no words for their sadness, the questions of those who had found an unknown that was truly worthy of fear. It is said that the humans were often left on shores foreign to them. Occasionally, they were abandoned on the rocks where they stood, and perhaps we could have done better, but our actions were tainted by sadness.

As is the nature of the sea, the stories were told in passing, passing from Sea-Folk to Finned People and Shell People and finding their way back again. So, it was in this way that we came to know a range of human motivations. Some of the human folk believed that we were a magnificent oddity, that keeping us alive and captured would bring them riches and fame. Others believed us masters of the sea, in control of the great squalls that wrecked ships with their fury. Some believed that our scales and skins were imbued with magics that would keep them safe. Yet others believed us a temptation that lured men into the water with our beauty for physical pleasure, food, sadistic joy, or some combination of the three. What threatening creatures we had become by virtue of your stories, Winken. We, the keepers of knowledge and tales, children of the primordial deep who value little more than understanding, were now cast as the very embodiment of man's fraught relationship with the ocean. So it was that, with our numbers much depleted, we did our best to disappear, and in doing so, we lost much of each other.

"So you see, Zophi, it is a sad story, but you need not feel bad for me.

I have a knack for finding the most wonderful company," and on that note, she submerged herself completely and was gone. It was only after floating for a time out in the water by herself that Zophi realized that the mermaid had called her by name, and it was then that her heart skipped a beat.

The door to Androgramma's room had long since lost its mystery. Her grandmother rested in bed with a book, a cup of tea, and a soothing record playing in the background. Zophi flopped down beside her with a heavy sigh and waited for the lace bookmark to find its place and the book to be placed on the bedside table.

"Androgramma, I think I am very much in love. I also think I am very much destined to be hurt by it." She picked at a loose thread on the colorful quilt while she worried at her lip with her teeth. Her grandmother's voice was quiet and soothing.

"Why would you think so, sweetheart?"

"Firstly, I think it is quite possible that I'm a homosexual," her jumble of nerves flip-flopped in her stomach.

"I feel like that's probably the sort of thing that will make itself clear in time." Androgramma's response was calm and accepting. It was just as Zophi had hoped as she walked up the stairs, but, as poorly as some might take that piece of information, the first bit wasn't nearly so problematic as what came next.

"Yes, well, does it count as homosexual if the woman in

question is not so much a woman as she is a mermaid?" At this, there was a longer pause; she glanced in her grandmother's direction and caught her worrying at her lip in an expression that made her wonder who mimicked whom.

"Ah..."

Zophi could see that her grandmother was not going to reprimand her for her feelings, but she also understood all of the factors left unsaid when one found one's self in love with a mermaid. A mermaid who appeared to age at least fifteen times slower than the humans of her acquaintance and who had the tendency to disappear for decades at a time. Reading the reflection of her own misgivings on Androgramma's face, the hopeless feeling that she had felt when the mermaid swam away returned, unavoidable and intense, taking root deep in her chest.

"Do you know," Andromeda said thoughtfully, "That your many times Great-Grandma Audry was quite convinced that her Toddy was in love with Nimmawni? They used to say that none of the other women in town could catch his eye, though many tried at one time or another. They said that if you tried to talk to him about his future wife, he would just stare absentmindedly out at the sea. That was right up until the day that he met his Mira. That was the same day Nimmawni returned, and she could see it as clear as day that Toddy and Mira's hearts were already meant to be together."

Zophi wondered what it must have been like for Toddy, he would not have known that the mermaid didn't age; he would have carried a torch for a little girl who grew with him in his imagination and then been faced with a little mer-girl's body in truth.

"As for your concerns about homosexuality, I'm not sure it's worth worrying about in this situation. My Mom told me once that Nimmawni had not understood why the desire for love necessitated a man, so I would say that's neither here nor there."

Zophi could think of no response to that piece of information. She was confused, confused with herself and her feelings, confused with what should be done about them and uncertain that anything *could* be done at all. Lacking anything productive to say, she chose to stay silent, face down, kicking her legs against her grandmother's bed.

"My Uncle was quite taken with her as well, I believe. She cared for him quite a bit, it seemed; he told my Mom that she blushed when he took off his shirt. Regardless, she has always looked on her Winkens with fondness, and it seems that we have always loved her to whatever degree made sense to us. She has always looked after us, in her own way, but it's difficult to say whether it makes sense to hope for anything more than that, My Love." Her grandmother pulled her close to lay a kiss on Zophi's forehead. "I would never presume to tell you what to feel, Zophi, but I would hate to see you miss out on love for want of someone who may not be able to be what you need."

They lay curled up together for long moments before Zophi revealed what was possibly the strangest thing of all:

"She called me Zophi, Androgramma."

"What's that?" It was clear from the look on her face that Androgramma thought she'd misheard, and Zophi didn't blame her; for over a hundred years, her family had shared one single name, anything else was unheard of.

"Right before she left, she called me by name. Not Winken

at all; she called me Zophi."

To that, it seemed, her grandmother had no answers at all. After a period of contemplative silence, Androgramma clapped her hands together, disturbing the stillness, and rolled her feet. She linked her fingers with Zophi's, pulling her from the bed, and with her other hand, she snatched up the handle to her record player. They skipped down the stairs to the great room, where she set the machine on the dining table, bringing it to life and placing the needle on the vinyl. The air filled with upbeat retro rock 'n' roll, and Zophi watched as her grandmother began to dance around the great room with the abandon of a child. Moments later, Androgramma grabbed her hand again, pulling her into the dance. Zophi felt her distress slowly melt away as they twirled around the house - eventually emerging into the yard to soak in the light of the moon.

The sun continued to rise and to set, the moon to wax and wane, and time moved on. For the next three years, Zophi continued to quietly carry a torch for an absent love who carried on with her search for answers among the dancing waves.

CHAPTER 38

There was a single lily left by the garden fence, its stem emerging slowly from the softening earth. It grew, all unobserved, at the edge of the yard, reaching steadily toward the sun. On the morning that the bud began to open, a flurry of black butterflies flitted through the garden before disappearing on a midmorning breeze. During the heat of the day, the chorus of the ticking beetles among the woodpile rose and fell. That evening, Andromeda and Miranda were finishing up work together in the still room when Andromeda collapsed. The woman swayed heavily on her feet for just a moment before pitching sideways in a faint. Catching the motion out of the corner of her eye, Miranda grabbed her dearest friend and mentor before she could hit her head on the still room table. Miranda sank slowly to the ground, bearing Andy's weight and cradling the older woman in her lap. Thankfully, it seemed her loss of balance was a momentary issue, and Andy soon regained awareness. Blinking her eyes blearily, she shot Miranda a wobbly smile before dragging herself into a seated position. Despite her quick recovery, she remained unsteady, slowly rolling over onto her hands and knees. Miranda helped her to her feet, slinging Andy's arm across her shoulders. The two old friends slowly hobbled into the house and then up the stairs, Augur stabilizing them from the other side. After Miranda laid Andy down in her bed and pulled up the covers to keep her warm, Augur curled up beside her, laying his head on her abdomen as Miranda went back to the kitchen to fetch some water.

"Andy," she called as she returned and pushed open the bedroom door, "can I get you anything? Do you know what's wrong?" but Andy did not respond, having already fallen asleep. Augur lifted his head to stare at Miranda as she checked over her sleeping mentor's worryingly pale complexion and thready heartbeat.

"I'll be right back," she said, whether to the sleeping woman or the dog she was not sure. Another trip down the stairs to assemble a warm compress took far longer than she would have liked, and by the time she returned, Andy was gone. Her still body imitating sleep, her fingers still peeking over the top of her blanket where she had held it to her chest, and yet the room felt profoundly empty with her passing. The indent on the bed beside the body was the only sign that the dog had ever been present. It seemed that Andy's final breath had escaped, and Augur had disappeared with it into the ether. Overwhelmed with the sudden sense of loss, Miranda ran back down the stairs and into the garden, unable to face the somehow vacant body of the woman who had been as much a second mother as a close companion. A huge white moth whipped past her face and landed beside the hole that was all that remained where the final white lily had been unearthed. The moth did not take flight when she approached, it sat beside the hole with its wings slowly opening and closing. As Miranda stared at the creature, watching the slow oscillation of the fuzzy white wings, a greater pattern began to take form in her mind. With her fingers to the disturbed earth, Miranda took a deep breath and released it with an audible sigh. Her dearest friend might be gone, but she had had seventy-one beautiful years on this earth that deserved to be honored. Knowing Andy, she wouldn't want her to stand about weeping; she would want her life to be celebrated and for her family to see her off.

With a renewed sense of purpose, Miranda dried her eyes on her smudged pinafore, then returned inside to make a phone call, her fingers shaking so severely that she missed the numbers on the rotary dial more than once. First, she called her husband; then, a few local cousins; and finally, she called Zophi.

"Hello?" The tired voice at the other end of the line had Miranda's heart in her throat, she hated to be the bearer of bad news.

"Hey, Honey, it's Miranda."

"Miranda!" the voice perked up immediately. "How have you been? How are the kids? I'm all set to head out that way in a month or so, and I can't wait to see you all." Miranda massaged the tension building at the center of her brow.

"Oh, Zophi, hush! It's not time for all of that." She began to choke up again and stumbled over the rest of her words. "I have news that can't wait, for all that I wish it could." There was a long pause from the other end of the line.

"What's wrong, Miranda? Is everyone okay?"

"She's gone, Zophi, just now. Andy's passed on." There was a sharp inhale on the end of the line.

"No. That can't be right." The ache in Zophi's voice was damn near heartbreaking.

"It is Honey, and I'm going to need you to head this way early." Miranda searched for the right words, the ones she'd always found a little creepy but the entire damn family had a weird reflexive response to:

"Andy has returned to the cycle."

"As we all must."

"Yes, as we all must. I'm going to need you to come out this way and bring all of your things with you. Everythin' has been drawn up and settled. She told me a while back that she was leavin' you the house, Honey."

"Miranda, I love you." Zophi responded shakily, "That's more than I can deal with right now."

Despite that assessment, it was only a matter of days before Zophi had everything of value packed. She kissed her father on the cheek before she left, suppressing her anger at his absence from his own mother's funeral. For her part, she would be saying goodbye to the city and her Androgramma all at once. She had the sense that the house and the garden needed her, and she felt the intense need to look out across the ocean.

It was a beautiful ceremony, if you liked that sort of thing. There were flowers and family and little pastries to snack on once all of the talking had come to a close. The clergyman at the temple liked the sound of his own voice far more than was warranted as he droned on and on about servicing the community and the rewards of the afterlife. Andromeda's body was to be returned to the earth beside her mother and father, in the shadow of Melody's yew tree, which is precisely what she would have wanted.

Zophi had come home and made the room with the beautiful picture window more completely her own, lining the shelves with all of the collected pieces of a life in progress. Opening the wardrobe, she found that her clothes and her great-grandmother's dresses were of similar size, and she slipped on a worn day dress before wandering the house in search of something she couldn't place. The rooms were all the same as they had been when she'd last visited, but the house seemed empty without Androgramma and Augur. Even the shadows and lights seemed subdued, feeling the absence in Andromeda's passing. It was not long before she decided that, rather than remaining in the house, surrounded by the deafening absence of daily life, she would remove herself to the dock. There she sat quietly, sketching the faces of people she loved, wishing with every fiber of her being that they had had just one more summer. That she could have packed all of her things and moved into her room beside her grandmother, and the three of them - Androgramma, Augur, and herself - could have lived that way into the fall and winter, drinking cocoa and sitting by the fire, something they had never had the chance to do.

She had just begun to feel the evening chill when damp fingers touched her leg tentatively, as though expecting rejection. The two were silent for a long while, content in each other's company, even if Zophi didn't understand how Nimmawni knew that she needed her. They existed together as the sun set and the sky filled with starlight. When warm tears began to run down Zophi's cheeks, she lay down on the cool wood of the dock, and Nimmawni reached up to grab her hand. They stayed there like that until dawn. There was no one waiting for Zophi back at the house, no one to take issue with her absence or worry that she didn't have a coat, but here she sat in the presence of someone she loved, even if she wasn't certain that she was loved in return.

"Zophi," the mermaid finally broke their silence as the sun broke over the horizon. "I'm so sorry about Winken."

Zophi nodded, the flow of tears resuming.

In an obvious attempt to lift the mood, Nimmawni asked,

"Aren't you going to ask where I've been?"

"No. I know where you've been." The mermaid looked startled, but Zophi continued, "You've been gone."

The two fell back into silence, now weighed down with heavy emotions. When the mermaid slid her hand from Zophi's grasp, moving as though she meant to leave, Zophi couldn't just let her go.

"Nimmawni!"

The mermaid paused, her lips just above water, and stared intently back at Zophi with some unnamable emotion in her eyes.

"Thank you. Thank you for coming. Thank you for sitting with me."

"It was my pleasure, Zophi." She began to sink into the

waves once again, but Zophi called out once more.

"Do you have to go?" She felt so lost. She had so much to say, but the words would not form, and she knew it wasn't the time. Nimmawni always left, that was her way, but this time her absence seemed unbearable.

"The sea is calling, and I have answers yet to find."

"When will I see you again?" She whispered, shattered. The mermaid smiled sadly,

"When the time comes to return."

That night, Zophi curled up, bundled in blankets and rocked by the swaying motion of her grandmother's hanging bench, lulled by the creak of the chain and the rushing sound of the ebb and flow of the distant waves. She fiddled with her Androgramma's necklace where it now lay against her chest, side by side with her father's. She stared out at the twinkling of the stars and listened to the singing of the crickets, the stories of the fireflies, and the gentle melody of plants finally at rest after the heat of the day.

As she closed her eyes, she was overtaken by the feeling of weightlessness, as though her body slowly spun end over end and side to side, over, around, under, and through, and when she finally redeveloped some sense of gravity, she stood in an open field before an enormous tree. Every surface appeared to be dusted with starlight, the sky so dark it whispered colors in waves and spirals from horizon to horizon. She stood and listened as she had done every day of her life since she found her father's necklace, and it was not long before she realized that the song was different. The oldest song, the song her four times great grandfather heard that very first day on the beach, the song she had heard so often for so long that she didn't hear it any longer. The song she felt deep inside, like she knew the spaces between her own heartbeats. The song was different somehow. Not bad, not wrong, but perhaps a little less lonely. Perhaps a song that had seen less, heard less, and hoped more. The song that always held within it notes of possibility and creation now somehow overflowed with it. She soaked up the song into her pores and her lungs, into her very bones.

Wherever she was, it was just her

And the open field

And the tree

All shimmering with starlight,

Or so she believed.

Though she could not remember moving, she found herself under the lowest boughs looking up through its branches, watching the wavering of leaves, iridescent in the moonlight. It was then that she saw a small bird hopping from branch to branch. What sort of bird she could not say, too small to be a crow, but sharp of beak and claw, not quite so focused as a magpie, but still, she had a cleverness about her. When she took notice of Zophi, the look the little bird gave her was full of understanding. The little bird had the darkest, blackest feathers Zophi had ever seen in her life, so dark as to almost absorb the light around her. The little bird swooped down and perched on the branch near Zophi's upturned face, tilting her tiny head back and forth to better see her visitor.

Zophi continued to take in her surroundings. "Where am I?"

"You are here, with me, beneath the branches of the Old Evergreen."

"Am I really here?"

The little bird cocked her head at the question, assessing, then ruffled her feathers before responding,

"Of course, in all the ways that anyone is anywhere."

Finding very little useful information in the bird's response, she tried again.

"What is this place?"

"This is a place that is Long Ago, Now, and Always. This is a place of waiting and a place where waiting comes to fruition."

It was a curious description; everything about this place looked and felt so ancient as to have existed since before time was time, and it occurred to Zophi that there probably was no better place to wait than a place that was always.

"My name is Zophi. Who are you?"

"I am Little Darkness." The bird preened and did not appear to notice Zophi's spark of recognition, though in that moment, she couldn't quite place the name.

"What are we doing here?"

"Waiting. He will come for me soon." Little Darkness' gaze was drawn with absolute certainty to a single point just above the horizon. "What is it that you are waiting for, Zophi? What is it that you desire so greatly that you would find yourself here?"

Zophi's vision filled with a pair of big, dark eyes that saw the world with such great clarity. With the quirk of lips that revealed small, sharp teeth. With hair like glowing tendrils of moonlight and a slim body that shone with veins of shimmering rainbows. She sighed over the point where smooth skin met rough fins and the skin of a tail coarse like sand and salt and tiny pebbles of starlight that shimmered in the water as they moved. Her mind was filled with charming laughter and the voice that spoke beneath the human tongue almost beyond hearing. She was caught in generations of stories that shaped an entire family and the strange tales that did almost nothing to explain an ongoing pattern of absence. Her mind was filled with Nimmawni. Her fingers wrapped themselves around her necklaces so tightly that her knuckles showed against the stretch of her skin.

"Little Darkness, wing sister, I am waiting for someone who will never be mine. I am waiting for a mermaid."

"What is this thought of owning?" the little bird hopped a little closer on the branch, with an inquisitive tilt to her head. "One cannot own another."

"I do not wish to own, Little Darkness, I wish to dwell in her heart as she dwells in mine. I wish for her to feel that our futures belong side by side. In this sense, I am already hers." It had been a long time since she had expressed her emotions aloud; the last time, all she had had were inadequate words like "crush" and an early adolescent understanding of "love." A dramatic love which, judging by her peers, might just as easily have disappeared in time; but instead her feelings had only deepened. The words that now spilled from her mouth unbidden rang with a deeper truth that struck her so deeply she almost swallowed her last words.

"Belonging? Do you feel that you belong together?"

"Absolutely. I feel it with a certainty I find hard to describe."

"If your hearts are meant to be entwined, then they will be, for whatever time your stars allow. It can be a matter of waiting for those stars to align," she ruffled her feathers in a fashion that almost appeared excited, "but sometimes it is the stars that wait for us. It is your time. If you are called to action, do what it is that calls to you and your love will follow."

"What do you mean?"

"What do you love, Zophi, who is human and People as well? I love to sing. I love to sing, and I will sing from that branch so close to the highest branch of the Old Evergreen, and *He* will come in the space between now and always, and we will make our children who will sing in all of the corners of the earth. What do you love, Zophi?"

"What do I love?" She thought of how she spent her days and what brought her joy. "I paint." She said shyly.

"Then you paint. Paint her into your story and paint yourself into hers, paint with all of the colors of affection intertwined, paint the songs of hearts in love and the cradle of its creation."

The little bird fluttered her wings and then launched herself joyously to the branch so close to the top of the gigantic tree and trilled her song. She sang, and as she sang, Zophi saw the imposing shape of a great dark bird dusted with the light of a million stars and every color of the Seas, Above and Below. That great bird with the sharpest of beaks and claws and the scales of a serpent from his legs to his toes swooped low; she took a moment to admire him before he careened joyfully back up into the sky and landed beside the little bird with a nuzzle of his head.

Zophi gasped in recognition:

"Pan'chan..."

He swiveled his head to look at her with a single shiny black eye, and he winked - at her. Little Darkness - she suddenly remembered where she had heard the name before. Little Darkness would birth the ravens, crows, and all of the other corvid children of Pan'chan. She would be a great mother among The People, and it was not *just* because he chose her; she sang to him. *She* sang to *Him*, their stars aligned, and he came. She felt her face split into a smile and blinked against the brilliance of the fated divine.

Zophi blinked in the morning sun, blinking away tears and a strange sense of relief that flooded her body. If such a little bird could take part in changing the stars and fates of so many, perhaps she could at least change her own.

CHAPTER 39

The idea of the call of the sea hung about Zophi's shoulders, never far from her thoughts. It had sounded like the deep called to Nimmawni, and no matter how intensely she wished to stay, the mermaid couldn't help but heed it and go. Yet the journals spoke of her returning in a time of great sadness, and when Androgramma passed, she was back within days. There was something that spoke to her, something she was listening for, and there had to be a way to catch her attention and call her back. Remembering the words of Little Darkness, Zophi spent every moment that she could on her art. She painted the intimacy of fingers intertwined, the imagined feeling of being breast to breast, sharing each other's heartbeats. She painted Nimmawni with all of the accuracy and detail Toddy poured into his carvings; some were even renditions of the hair pin Zophi found in Androgramma's dresser. She knew it as soon as she saw it, running her fingers over the worn surface of the mermaid child's face before tucking it into her tresses to hold both her beloved and her grandmother close. She painted Nimmawni on two legs, she painted herself with fluttering white fins. Wherever she painted them together, there always existed at least one point of contact, as if to affirm that their destinies were inseparable.

After a few months of living on her own, she asked Juniper to come and stay for good. Her cousin had been in and out of the house frequently, their friendship just as strong and close as it had ever been, and the best times Zophi had had since Androgramma's passing were in her company. It seemed only right that she make herself at home, so the two emptied Kerish's old bedroom, and Juniper's brothers dragged the old furniture away, swearing all the while that they were happy to be rid of her. Zophi kept some of her father's things as reminders of the little boy he had once been, but the room itself lay empty - right up until Juniper showed up three days later with the "perfect" paint color and the furniture from her old bedroom. The two set to work immediately, and in only a matter of hours, the dreary old room was no more. For a time, this new life was enough; she helped her cousin to make the old room her own and set herself to the task of teaching her cousin all about the garden. The two giggled over Juniper's most recent crush as they worked with Miranda in the still room, pulled weeds in the garden, supplied the tea shop with remedies to stock their shelves, and carried on their family's traditions; and it was enough, for a time. Though Zophi would still stop at random moments to stare out to sea, and the question of how to call a mermaid haunted her like a specter dancing in her peripheral vision.

"... the weirdest thing, you know, they've recorded the sounds of whales talking under water. They call it song, but it's

like this weird, mournful call that floats through the water."
Juniper's babbling finally broke through Zophi's trance.

"Wait, what?"

Juniper sighed dramatically before flashing her cousin a
knowing smile.

"I was down by the record shop talking to Ricky, mostly to
give him the opportunity to *finally* ask me on a date, you know?
Anyway, I was talking to Ricky and he started telling me about
how these scientists have gone out to sea with this crazy
recording gear, and they recorded the sound of whale song.
That's what they call it, 'whale song.' Ricky put the record on
for me because he was so intrigued by the idea, and it sounded
like nothing you've ever heard before. On second thought, who
knows what *you* lot have heard. It sounded like nothing *I've* ever
heard before."

Zophi let her trowel drop to the ground and began stripping
off her gardening gloves. It felt like a piece of a puzzle was
falling into place, and she needed to run with it.

"Juniper, take me?"

Her cousin excelled at shrugging off any and all strange
behavior, so she hooked her arm through Zophi's without
comment.

"An excuse to go flirt with Ricky some more? Yes, please!"
she announced with a laugh. Zophi pretended not to notice the
curious glances Juniper shot her way as they walked into the
town, a boundary that had grown progressively closer as the
population had continued to expand over time.

Ricky was more than happy to have someone else to introduce

the whale song to, he launched into an explanation that Zophi only half listened to once the 33 hit the turntable and the soft scratching of needle on vinyl began. The sound was haunting, but she could barely interpret what the whale was saying - like listening to someone speak from a long ways away or in a tunnel where echoes bounced too freely. Regardless, the sound was compelling, and she could have easily sat there for hours.

"Do you have a copy for sale?" Ricky nodded enthusiastically and disappeared into the back of the shop.

"Really, Zophi? Am I going to come home and hear moaning whales about the house now?" Juniper paused. "Do we even have a record player?"

"Maybe, and yes, Androgramma had one. It is most likely still in her room."

Juniper's long suffering sigh told Zophi everything she needed to know about her cousin's thoughts on the topic.

"Ricky?" Zophi called as she drifted toward the entrance to the back room. "Do you have any flute music?"

The young man's head popped out from behind a curtain, followed by the rest of his body. "Of course. Are you looking for something in particular?"

"I'm not sure."

"Well, you're welcome to listen to anything you like," he told her as he guided her around the isles of tables laid out with wooden milk crates full of 33s. Ricky led her past bins marked classical and showed her the area where she might find what she wanted. "There are some headphones you can plug in right there - if you don't want to play it out loud." He gestured to a record player on the center table and the headset that lay beside it with a stack of 45 rp adaptors.

"Thank you," she responded absentmindedly as she began to collect a stack of records depicting a variety of people playing flutes on the jackets. Ricky returned to the front desk where Juniper had positioned herself, completely prepared to monopolize his attention for as long as she could call necessary.

After sampling several records, searching for a quality she couldn't put into words, Zophi returned to the front counter with the one she wanted. Still inspecting the words on the muted colors on the jacket, Zophi interrupted a conversation about Juniper's brother, who Ricky had attended school with.

"Ricky, if I wanted to make one record with the sounds of whale song playing over the sound of this flute, could you do that?"

He scratched his head as he answered,

"Unfortunately, no, I would need special equipment for that. I don't make records, I just sell the ones other people release."

"But there are people who could do it?"

"Yeah, absolutely."

Zophi slapped her payment for the two records down on the front desk, kissed Ricky on the cheek, and sped out the door with her newly acquired treasure.

"See you later, Ricky!" Juniper yelled as she sprinted after her cousin, headed back home. Sliding her arm through her cousin's, she confided with a conspiratorial wink,

"Well, that was a wonderfully productive visit for us both, I think. You found your records and a new way to make my life stranger, and Ricky and I are going to meet up when he gets off work tomorrow."

Even though it had only been a few months, it was strange to return to the city. Zophi had become accustomed to the pace and sounds of her town by the sea. She stepped from the train onto the platform, barely looking at the station that had hardly changed in the time since her father arrived, and spent a moment dealing with the overwhelming nature of the sights, sounds, and smells of the city. She carried her backpack and a large shoulder bag with her two records nestled inside. They were the primary reason for her trip: she was in search of a shop that would create the record she was looking for. Her backpack, stuffed with enough clothes to last a week, spoke to her commitment on the subject.

When she showed up at her father's door, he barely responded, as though he was completely unsurprised by her sudden appearance. The man was still as prim and proper as ever, though he had lost something fundamental when Alice passed, something which had never returned. Zophi, on the other hand, was a bundle of energy and creative chaos, attributes she had never understood until she met the rest of her family. Zophi burst back into Kerish's life like a whirlwind, and Kerish took it in stride, with only minor external displays of annoyance. He remained unsurprised and unflappable with only one exception: when he realized that she had not, in fact, fled *back* to the city, as he had done around her age. While his response was hardly what one could call expressive, Zopi could barely remember receiving so much focused intensity from her father. The look was heavy with incomprehension and obvious disapproval, though she thought she caught a moment where he searched her face before he stalked out of the room. Apparently, having an obvious opinion didn't mean Kerish was willing to engage with Zophi about her plans to return to his mother's old house just as soon as she found what she was looking for. The search began almost the moment she walked through the door. After dropping her bags in her old bedroom, her first order of business was to go about locating a business directory with which to narrow her search.

She stayed in the city for eleven days. It did not take long to find someone to create the record that she wanted, combining the two she carried with her from place to place like infinitely precious cargo. It took longer than anticipated to convince the business owner that it was, despite their skepticism, what she wanted, and significantly longer before the finished product would be ready for her to come collect it. In the meantime, she wandered the city, connected with old acquaintances from school, and sat in the window of her old bedroom, conversing with the birds. Kerish himself made almost no adjustments for her presence. He left early in the morning for work, returning late in the evening to cook himself and his offspring a small, quiet meal before he retired to his favorite chair to listen to the radio and read, barely taking notice of his daughter at all. In her father's home, Zophi felt as though she moved through his life like a ghost, a role she had been placed in almost as soon as her mother was gone. By the fifth day, she was practically itching to hop on a train and return to the world she loved, the world where she existed.

On the evening of the sixth day, not long after the two had dined, a sharp knock shook the door, and a familiar voice called from the hallway.

"Yoohoo! Kerish, you wretched man, open the blasted door so I can see my niece!"

Zophi hopped from the window sill and was at the door before her father could even rise from his chair. Flinging the door open, she threw her arms around the petite, yet larger than life, woman she found on the other side. No one else would dare to brave Kerish's den with such volume and bravado. Thin arms wrapped around her waist and gave her a tight squeeze before the two released each other. Small hands grabbed Zophi's face, tilting it back and forth in search of any sign of distress.

"You look good, kid." The older woman said with her signature smirk.

"It's good to see you, Aunt Beryl." Doing her best to keep the relief from her voice.

"Do you know that that *man* didn't even bother to tell me you were here? If I didn't have your neighbor to spy on him, I'd never know anything." She shrugged out of her chic coat and hung it up by the door.

"I'd love to say I was surprised, but I'm not."

The two moved slowly into the living room, where Kerish had settled back into his chair with the obvious intention of ignoring their conversation in favor of his book. Beryl, as a consequence, raised her voice further and inquired more energetically as to what had brought Zophi to their humble city, grabbing her by the forearms and guiding her to the love seat directly across from the inhabited chair. Zophi obliged by recounting, in great detail, her trip from the shore, her intended purpose, and her conversation with the shop's proprietor that resulted in her continued presence in her father's apartment.

"If we only have you for four more days, then I simply must steal you away. You won't mind that, will you, Kerish? Of course, he won't. You'll need to pack up some things, of course. We'll just give Katerina a nice big surprise."

When Zophi hesitated, Beryl practically shoved her in the direction of her bedroom. Once the door was closed, she could hear the murmuring of lowered voices but nothing of the content of their conversation. Beryl had been like that for years, swooping in to take her on wonderful shopping sprees and to shows at the theater, never letting her go ignored for too terribly long, as the father who had once adored her barely spoke a word in her presence. It didn't take her long to shove her belongings back into her backpack. The voices carried on, so she took some time to lean out the window and explain to her friends that she would be leaving. By the time she returned to the living room, Beryl was standing beside the door, ready to leave, and her father seemed somehow smaller than he had before, or perhaps as though he had sunken further into the dark leather cushions of his chair. She kissed him on the cheek in farewell, as she always did, but just as she turned to leave, he reached out and grabbed her fingers. It was more shock than the action itself that stopped her.

"Zophi..." he paused as though his words escaped him, cleared his throat, and tried again. "I know that I am not what I should have been. You deserved more. I just want you to know, Alice... Your mother... She would have been so proud."

That, in some ways, was the crux of the issue, Zophi thought. Kerish had let so much of himself follow Alice into her grave that it was only through the lens of her eyes that he could see the world around him, but Alice's eyes were long closed, and she was just as incapable of a parental embrace as Kerish had become. Zophi could be angered by it, could ask why he had done nothing to change it if he knew he should have been more, but she chose to take it for what it was. She looked down at the lost man who sat before her and simply replied,

"Thank you, father, I love you too," before completing her turn towards the door and leaving him behind, just as alone as he had made himself.

The metered cab came to a stop in a familiar, upscale neighborhood. Aunt Beryl lived in a lovely townhouse with her companion, Katerina. The former cabaret dancer had long been engaged in the sort of subterfuge that was often necessary for people of her inclination. She was a kept woman, her benefactor a wealthy gentleman who found it convenient to be seen in her presence publicly from time to time - for much the same reason. Ostensibly, Katerina, a musician with the philharmonic orchestra, had heard from a mutual acquaintance that Beryl had a room to let. She had enjoyed both the accommodations and the company and opted for a long-term rental. In actuality, they had known each other for many years, and her bedroom was more of a practice-lounge-cum-guest-room; a perfect hideaway for a teenage girl once she had been let in on the secret.

When Zophi was seventeen, Aunt Beryl had let her stay for a whole week, as opposed to her usual night or two, at which point the charade was dropped. Zophi no longer slept on a couch made up with sheets and blankets, and Beryl and Katerina allowed themselves the comfortable intimacies of their own home and shared bedroom. Having already suspected that she might be of a similar, if somewhat more complex, inclination, Zophi was enchanted by their easy affection. Eventually, they were all so comfortable that she was allowed to stay even when Charles came to visit his "mistress" for an evening meal. Occasionally, his *"friend"* Desmond would join them, the four adults making an effort to keep up appearances. More than once on their excursions, Zophi had caught other women looking at Aunt Beryl with envy; now the two were finally able to share a secretive smirk, not letting it bother them in the least.

"I'm home!" Beryl sang out as they entered the foyer, "and I've brought home a little dove, rescued from the grips of terminal boredom!"

The sound of slippered feet raced down the stairs, and Beryl's taller, blonder counterpart wrapped her arms around Zophi with so much affection she thought she might just break down and cry. Thankfully, Beryl's playful grumbling about being second in Katerina's affections distracted them both, resulting in the loving embrace of two of her favorite people and a moment unobserved for Zophi to pull herself together.

As always, time with the pair was like a wondrous vacation from life. They rose at their leisure, ate in lovely cafes, went to the theater, and stayed up late into the night talking and sipping wine. It was one such night, seated by the fire in their living room with a wine glass in hand, that Zophi told them a story about a woman who loved a mermaid. It was her story, but she framed it as a tale she was developing in writing, the truth being so far from the ordinary that she worried they would think her insane. When her story caught up with her present, and she was at a loss as to how to proceed, Katerina sighed wistfully,

"Does it work? Does the young woman find a song that will tempt her mermaid to shore?"

"I'm not sure." Zophi blinked back tears at the thought of the alternative, certain the wine was getting to her.

"That can't be the end of it." Beryl chimed in. "They absolutely must end up together, otherwise it's a pretty shit story if you ask me,"

"Beryl!" Katerina scolded, then turned back to the topic at hand. "I certainly hope it works. It would be so very sad if the mermaid didn't return until the woman was old and gray. Or would she have children to carry on the story?"

"I don't think so," Zophi responded, shaking her head. She had never thought much about having children, had never met someone that she was interested in having children with. *Except...* her mind went back to Androgramma's assertion that Nimmawni had not understood why a male was necessary. Was the mermaid just too young to be considering children? Or was there some quirk of their anatomy that made it irrelevant? Could the old story about the giant oysters be true? The line of thought soon became overwhelming, so she set it aside in favor of conversation with her aunts.

"I certainly want the mermaid to return."

"It's your story, Dove; you can write it however you wish," Katerina said, reminding her that she had presented her story as a matter of fiction.

"But even if she did return, the mermaid is a creature of the water, and the woman lives on land."

The three women sat in silence for a moment, contemplating her supposed narrative conundrum.

"It seems to me," Beryl said, finally breaking the silence, "that it is an issue of transformation. You have several stories that could argue the possibility of transforming from mermaid to human and back again; so could your mermaid not find her legs, so to speak?"

"I suppose, if she ever found the secret as to how, that would certainly be an answer."

"Well then," Beryl seemed quite satisfied with the response, "it seems you have your answer. It also seems to me that it is time for bed. Join me, my love?" she asked as she rose to her feet.

"In just a moment, dear. I'll be right behind you." Katerina smiled, following the woman with her eyes as she wove her way tiredly toward the stairs, then turned to Zophi with a look that said she suspected something more was afoot. "My Dove, do you know of the Rusalka?" Zophi shook her head.

"It is a tale from the far north, and far enough east to almost border the lands your grandfather might have been born to." Zophi was startled at Katerina's reference to Blue; mostly, no one spoke of him. The willowy blonde continued her story. "The Rusalka are sprites of the wood or of water. This story is of a water sprite who could not walk on land. She fell in love with a human prince who hunted in the woods near her lake. She went to her father in search of the magic to make her human, but he would not approve of her desires. She found a witch with the ability to give her what she desired; the witch said she would turn the Rusalka human, but take her voice and her immortality, and if the Rusalka and her prince did not find love together, he would die and she would be cursed."

Katerina paused, adding another measure of wine to the bottom of her glass.

"Did it work? Did they fall in love?" Zophi asked with rapt attention.

"Mmm..." Katerina took a moment as she sipped and then resumed her story. "At first, but the actions of others interfere. Some believe their love to be a result of witchcraft, a jealous woman curses their love, and the Rusalka is rejected and sent back to her lake where she is cursed. When the prince finally remembers his love, it is their kiss which kills him."

The two sat in silence for a long moment.

"Why are you telling me this, Katerina?" Zophi asked warily.

"It seems to me, my Dove, that there is more to your story than you wish to admit. That perhaps you may have a decision to make. I would remind you to consider that every decision has unforeseen consequences, most especially in stories. You have reached an age where you can truly follow your happiness, and you deserve that happiness. You deserve happiness, and joy, and love, in all of their many forms; and should the thoughts of others ever hold you back, I would remind you that no matter what choice you make, we will love you." At that, she rose, kissed Zophi gently on the forehead, and began to follow the path Beryl had taken up the stairs.

"Sleep soon, little Dove. Dreams have a great knack for unraveling our thoughts and uncovering our truths."

The house was waiting for her when Zophi returned. As always, it seemed that it was happy to keep her close. Juniper was also enthusiastic in greeting her cousin before rushing off to meet up with Ricky once again. Zophi greeted the guardian and paid her respects to the shadows and lights currently in residence. Then she walked out into the garden to hug the Moon Tree and wave to the crows among the branches. In the evening, she cracked open the door to Androgramma's room in search of the record player, the echoes of their joyous dance parties playing in her mind. The small, brightly colored briefcase was surprisingly easy to overlook, tucked as it was between the far wall and the vanity. When she found it, the machine had built up a year's worth of dust, and the needle was worse for wear, but otherwise, it seemed like a perfectly serviceable little machine. It was short work to clean it off and make a quick run to the record store for a new needle. Ricky took this as an excuse to follow her home, almost certainly to see where Juniper lived, but ostensibly to switch out the needle. The enthusiastic suitor very clearly took advantage of Zophi's lack of knowledge about record players, as the process was so simple that the pretense was essentially laughable.

From that point on, Zophi took the portable record player, along with her pads, pencils, and paint, down to the shore. Day after day, whenever her work was done or she could find an excuse to get away, she sat on the dock with her picnic basket listening to her record calling across the waves and following Little Darkness' advice.

CHAPTER 40

Results were slow in coming, and it was difficult to determine whether her efforts were doing anything at all. In between visits, it seemed that Nimmawni traveled all over the world, limited only by the oceans and waterways. Without any knowledge of where the mermaid had gone, it wasn't as though Zophi could speculate on distance and reasonable travel time. Particularly because, in the wake of tragedy, Nimmawni seemed to show her face in a matter of days. The thought was intrusive, but Zophi wasn't inclined to become destructive and didn't know how else to expedite the process. She often found herself wondering whether she would take advantage of such a method if she found one; it seemed to her that she ran the risk of causing the mermaid distress. So she continued to spend any time she could painting, listening, hoping, breathing life into a dream.

After a month, the experiment finally yielded results. Zophi was on her way back from the shore, laden with all of her supplies, when the seabird she had just finished disturbing with her presence landed ahead of her along the path. The bird squawked angrily at her to turn around, obviously unhappy with the idea of the human and her record player returning to his nest. Not bothering to set aside her things, Zophi jogged back to the dock in excitement. She wondered whether the visit was the result of her efforts or if Nimmawni had simply returned on her own. Zophi only put everything down once her feet met the smooth wood of the dock. She moved slowly to the end of the platform with her heart in her throat, choking on anticipation and nerves alike. When she finally saw the mermaid, floating near the end of the dock with a confused expression on her face, she knew she needed to take a chance. She had to use this opportunity to tell Nimmawni the things that she regretted leaving unsaid when they last spoke. To open herself up and bare her heart, the idea was terrifying.

"Nimmawni!"

The mermaid turned to her slowly, as though distracted by something beyond Zophi's range of hearing.

"Zophi? There was a call. I-I thought I heard something... but now it's gone, a-and only the echoes remain. It was so very strange."

There was the answer to one question.

"Oh, I did that." The mermaid's gaze snapped upward, unerringly finding Zophi's face so that the two stared into one another's eyes for a long moment before Nimmawni asked,

"How did you do this thing?"

Zophi motioned for her to wait, jogged to where she had dropped her things, and retrieved the record player.

"I didn't know if it would work," she said awkwardly as she placed the record player gently on the end of the dock and lifted its cover, "but I wanted to find a way to communicate."

Rubbing the back of her neck self consciously, she freed some of the shorter wisps of hair from her mess of a bun. The strands fluttered in the breeze as she searched for the right words - for any words for her fluttering heart.

"I wanted to let you know I missed you... and maybe you would want to come see me."

As the needle began to trace its path across the vinyl grooves and the air filled with the chorus of flute and whale in concert, the mermaid stared, open mouthed, the tips of her canines just visible between her open lips, dumbstruck. Zophi wasn't sure, but it almost looked as though the mermaid might cry. This raised the question of whether mermaids had tear ducts, but it didn't seem like the appropriate time to ask.

"You wanted to see me?" Nimmawni said quietly and waited for Zophi's nod in response.

"So you found a way to..." she fumbled for the right words, probably not having a context for record players, "make this music, to call across the waves?" Zophi nodded again, self-consciously.

"To see me." Nimmawni pulled the fish bone that pinned her hair back from her face and fiddled with the sharp end as though it were very important. "Why?"

The word sank into the uncomfortable quiet that sat between them like an awkward accomplice in their conversation. Zophi tried to speak past it, tried to sneak around it, but ultimately, the only way that they could continue the conversation was to push it out of the way. She swung her legs off the end of the dock, finally asking the question that had played on her mind since she was fifteen years old.

"Why do you call me Zophi? Everyone else in my family has been Winken to you - though they've all told you their names. What makes me different?"

That was how the penny dropped.

Nimmawni continued to fiddle with her makeshift hair pin, her long hair spreading like a serpentine cloud around her body, but the bemused expression on her face was gone. With a sharp inhale that bordered nervousness and shock, she appeared to fight the urge to sink back beneath the surface. Her brow crinkled, obviously contemplating the information at hand; her eyes flicked back and forth from Zophi's feet to her nervously fidgeting fingers, never rising to meet eyes, and then her already large eyes widened further with comprehension and then... fear.

It was the fear that got to Zophi; the last thing she wanted to see on Nimmawni's face was fear. Well, the last thing she wanted to see was probably disgust, but fear was a close second, and she wasn't about to let that fear grow and make an already complicated situation impossible. She slipped from the dock into the water, catching Nimmawni's fidgeting fingers in her hand as she used the other to hold on to the weather-worn ladder. Dark brown eyes stared into deep black ones with a depth of emotion that, Zophi had to admit, was actually kind of frightening.

She'd kissed a boy once, on a dare. She'd gone along with it out of curiosity but found the experience highly underwhelming. There was a scratchiness, and a sloppiness, and unfortunate body odors - the sort her cousin seemed to have no problem with. The boy in question had not had the same poor opinion of the encounter, as had been made extremely obvious when he pressed his body against hers, and she found yet another reason to find her situation objectionable. Pushing aside the memory, Zophi shifted her hand from the mermaid's hands to cup the side of her face. She gave herself and Nimmawni only a moment to pull away or second guess before drawing her closer. Pushing aside her bottled up nerves, she bridged the gap to allow their lips to gently meet. The feel of soft skin and a smell like salt air, sunshine, seaweed, and beach roses filled Zophi's senses. The kiss lasted for only a couple of precious moments before Nimmawni gasped, pulling away to touch her fingertips to her lips in wonder.

"I've wished for you for most of my life," Zophi whispered, filling the statement with as much hope as she could muster.

"So have I," the mermaid whispered back, her fingertips still touching her lips as though the kiss might have changed them somehow. "But... I am Sea-Folk, and you are human. I cannot walk on land, and the sea is not your home." She drew further away, breathing heavily, as though the distance was a strain. The next words to leave her lips clearly pained her; they pained them both: "It's impossible."

"But, couldn't you stay?" Zophi asked quietly, "nearby, at least. We could see each other all the time. It wouldn't be a bad way to live, would it?"

The mermaid shook her head, drawing further away.

"I *can't*." She said with a finality that felt like Zophi's chest might crack in two. "There are answers I need, there are stories..." she gasped, and there was no doubt in Zophi's mind that she was crying, though no tears fell.

Another question answered, Zophi thought morosely.

Nimmawni raised her hands as though she could defend herself from their mutual sadness.

"Isn't there something we could do?" Zophi's mind raced. "There has to be a way…"

Still, Nimmawni kept drawing herself further and further from the dock where Zophi felt herself frozen. Nimmawni continued to shake her head, whether for her own benefit or Zophi's was anyone's guess, as she began to sink beneath the waves.

"Zophi, I am what I am. The sea calls, and I must follow."

The shimmering shadow of the mermaid's form beneath the waves was visible for only moments before she was gone completely, and a sob ripped itself from Zophi's chest. A mermaid's eyes might not be built to cry, but enough tears streamed down her face for the both of them as she continued to hang from the ladder, waiting, even though she knew that Nimmawni wasn't coming back. Not now. The salt of her tears mixed effortlessly with the salt of the sea. When her eyes finally dried, there was no evidence of the sorrow that had spilled with such abandon mere moments before, swept away into the endless progression of waves.

CHAPTER 41

The envelope was nothing special. Inconspicuous in its simplicity, it had no decorations one might note, just postage and a perfectly legible address written with a blue pen in simple handwriting, nothing ornate about it.

The woman who wrote it was unaware of how special she was. She lived a life on the edge of the fantastical and, despite many hours and days spent disconnected from the world that was meant to love her, she was filled with an exuberant joy for living. Over the course of several days, she sat before a blank piece of paper, smoothing her fingers along the edges in agitation, knowing that the words she chose might become the most important thing she ever wrote. When she finally put pen to paper, the words flowed out of her in a torrent, leaving smudges and crossed out sentences in their wake. Then she sealed it up in a simple white envelope to contain its sentiment and render it innocuous, dull, and nondescript.

The envelope was nothing special. It arrived on a beautiful day when the postman dropped off a bundle of mail at a lovely townhouse in a fashionable part of town. There was absolutely nothing special about the envelope, up until fingertips reshaped by the rough vibrations of strings slipped between the body of the envelope and its sealed flap, to free the writing within. It was then that two women, sitting together at a small table, held hands as they read the following:

My Dearest Aunts,

I am writing this letter, with my heart in my throat, to tell you the end of the story. The woman found her song, a song that she played for days and weeks along the seashore as she painted herself and her love into one another's stories. Her fingers smudged in rainbows of unspoken affection; every time the record came to its hissing end, she lifted the needle and began it all over again, until one day the mermaid returned. She returned, and their longing was mutual, but the mermaid still had not found the answers to her questions. She didn't know how to walk the earth as a human does, and believing their desires to be doomed by time, tide, and stories lost, she swam away. Not even willing to hold out hope. Still, I cannot believe that hope is lost; I cannot let her go.

You see, my wonderful Aunts, the story I told you (aside from some small details) is absolutely true. Understanding that, it is also true that I am consumed with an impossible love - but, then again, I certainly seem to be living an impossible life. After all, who would believe that my family has been blessed with association with a mermaid, much less that I have been blessed with her affection.

I write this because it is possible that what I intend to do may not be undone, and if that is the case, these will be my final words to you.

How do you choose the last thing you'll ever say to someone? Is it even worth trying to articulate everything that a person, or in this case two people, can mean to another? I don't know, but I know that I would feel like a horrible niece if I didn't at least try. I do not know that I have ever thanked you for saving me when it seemed I was destined to be lost, like a shadow that lurked only in the darkened corners of memory. Every time I began to lose myself, there you were, like sunshine and fresh air and every wonderful thing about freshly baked cookies all rolled into one. I grew up in the momentous shadow of one woman, but it was in your light that I thrived. I can never thank you enough for that.

When I last saw you, Katerina told me to follow my happiness. That I deserved all of the joy that love could bring. I know that what I'm about to do is probably not what you meant, but I see no other way forward but to follow her. To believe in the stories. To set my future into the hands of the fates and let the chips fall as they may. I can only hope that you will understand and that you will find it in your hearts to forgive me for my absence.

With all of the love my poor besotted heart can spare,

Your Dove,
    Zophi

They stared at each other with wide eyes over the letter. A letter which now sat, like a ticking bomb, in the center of the table. When Beryl moved as though to make a call, Katerina stalled her, squeezing her hand tightly,

"She's going where she belongs, Dear Heart."

The confirmation of returned affections and the efficacy of her record lit a fire in Zophi. For a short while, she stopped visiting the shore. She knew full well that the seabird would find her if Nimmawni returned. Instead, she read through her family journals like a woman possessed. With a spiral bound notebook and a mug in constant need of refill, she double checked her memory of her family's stories, taking notes and drawing webs of information that occupied page after page with little regard for their fine, orderly lines. Then she began to quietly set her affairs in order. She added Juniper's name to everything she owned and searched the house from top to bottom for her Androgramma's bag of stardust. Or perhaps it would be better to say she searched from bottom to top, starting with its last known location in the root cellar.

The stardust was no longer there, but the Tiny People who inhabited the dark shelves still told stories of what had happened when their ancestors came across the bag. Zophi wondered how it had escaped her notice how very human the behavior of The People of the cellar had become. She had a nice long chat with their alderman, who may have once descended from a daddy longlegs. She made a mental note to mention the burgeoning civilization behind the fermenting jars to Juniper before pressing on. When she finally found it, hidden among her grandmother's stockings in her mostly untouched bedroom, Zophi was relieved to find that it still hummed with potential energy. She and Juniper had found, shortly after Andromeda's death, that the baskets she had so lovingly woven had fallen to pieces with her passing; the contents of the bag in her hand were all that remained. Zophi felt the small mass, little more than a couple of tablespoons, through the supple leather of the bag and felt wishes dancing on the tip of her tongue with an indescribable sort of urgency. Having identified its hiding place, she shoved it back where Androgramma had left it, and she titled a fresh page in her notebook "Wishes."

When Zophi returned to the shore a few months later, it was to swim, long laps that alternated strokes, sometimes following the shoreline and other times venturing away from the water's edge until her muscles ached and she labored to breathe. In those moments, she laid out on her back, staring at the dance of the spinning sky, the drifting clouds, and the wheeling of the Winged People. She let herself drift, melting into the energy of the open waves, before slowly paddling her way back to the dock. After her morning swims, she took herself home, readied herself for the day, and made a deliberate point of valuing every moment spent with her family. She visited with Windles and Aydins, she had Miranda and her cousins over for tea, she called her Aunts weekly to catch up, but at no point did she tell anyone about her plans; plans that, the clearer they became, seemed less and less likely to lead her back to them.

In time, she began to paint again, her wishes taking form on page after page and canvas after canvas as the record played over and over again. She didn't expect a response, not yet. Though she held no proof and no guarantees, she felt it with a bone deep certainty she could hardly explain, she could feel it plainly: she knew that their stars had not come together yet. She was reminded of the absolute confidence of Little Darkness, the little bird who knew that Pan'chan would come, who knew where he would be, and who waited, even as she changed her stars with her song, for the time to be right.

One morning, after returning from her date with the rolling waves, Zophi finally ran out of patience with untangling her sea-worn locks. She grabbed Juniper by the arm and dragged her into the washroom. With a pair of old scissors and a speed razor - more well-suited to legs than to scalps - the two joked and giggled as they removed all of her waist length wavy tresses. Once she was completely shorn, and Juniper pretended to shine the finished product, she gave Zophi a considering look before disappearing up the stairs, singing out:

"Be right back!"

Alone, the washroom tiles scattered with clumps of hair and wayward strands, she allowed herself a moment to mourn the loss. For a moment, she thought she might cry, but the urge was a confusing mixture of distress and freedom. Despite the feeling of being overwhelmed with mixed emotions, she got the sense that a puzzle piece had just clicked into place. One more star was finding its place in her fate, as she let go of a long-ago vision of herself and faced the future bare. Zophi glided her hand across the smooth skin of her scalp, contemplating this release. Examining the impulsive step she would never have guessed she needed to take, that brought her that much closer to her goals. Juniper barreled back into the room and held up her hands triumphantly, her fingers dripping with hoops and long earrings - treasures scavenged from both of their rooms and Androgramma's vanity. Juniper assessed her options before holding up a pair of big, bright blue and white acrylic hoops.

"Trust me, Cuz, you are going to look gorgeous!"

Zophi laughed and obligingly took the ridiculously large earrings. After threading the posts through her earlobes and clicking them into place, she took a look in the mirror. She had to admit the effect was kind of spectacular, accentuating the length of her neck and offsetting the gold tones in her skin and the darkness of her eyes.

"And the best part," Juniper said, shaking her jewelry laden fingers in the reflection as though reading Zophi's mind, "is you have options for days!"

Laughing, Zophi turned to give her cousin a hug, filling it with every moment of love and gratitude she could, as though she could stock up on affection.

It was two full years before Nimmawni returned. Two birthdays passed, and Zophi marked a quarter of a century of life. Twenty months of mornings spent swimming from the shore; ninety-six weeks of family gatherings and affectionate phone calls; one hundred and seven paintings, sketches, and line drawings created; over four thousand seven hundred repetitions of the custom made record; four hundred and ninety two days without hair on her head; seventy sessions with a razor, only twelve involving blood; two spiral bound notebooks, one letter, and a sticky note; and there she was.

Almost two years to the day after Nimmawni fled their last encounter, Zophi woke up and knew that it was time. She retrieved the precious letter to her aunts from beneath a stack of sketchbooks and walked it to the post office in town. The day was bright and beautiful, and she savored every moment of The People's song on the morning breeze. Upon returning to the house, Zophi took the leather bag of stardust from her grandmother's room and her first spiral bound notebook out into the backyard to sit beneath the Moon Tree. She flipped through the worn pages to the one marked "Wishes" and looked over the list which had been added to, subtracted from, edited, and re-edited until much of it was an unintelligible mess. She dipped into the bag, removing the grains one pinch at a time, which she held to herself as though in prayer. The wishes that she ultimately made were not for herself.

"I wish," she intoned aloud, "for the happiness of my family, let them live lives full of love, peace, and prosperity." She gently rubbed her fingers together, feeling the soft grains as they fell, leaving a tingling sensation in the pads of her thumb and middle finger. Zophi dipped her fingers back into the dust.

"I wish," she began again, "for the magic to carry on in this place and among my kindred and People. Let the stories carry them forward and open their eyes to the interconnected greater world around them." This time, the tingles felt like tiny shocks that traveled along her extremities, and she almost thought she saw the grains glow as they dropped to the earth by her feet.

"I wish," she said finally, "for Nimmawni's happiness. Let her stars bring her a fate full of joy and wonder." Releasing these last grains left her with a buzzing feeling in her skin that did not dissipate with time. On the contrary, it seemed to grow, as though the sound of bees in flight was a living vibration beneath her skin.

Zophi peered into the bag, there was still a small amount left, perhaps enough for one or two wishes down the line. She cinched the drawstring to protect its precious contents. Then returned it to its hiding place, among the undergarments of the departed, before returning to the shore with her paints and her record - now worn and distorted with use towards the end of the tracks. Though the actions remained the same, something was different. Perhaps it was the aftermath of the wishes, perhaps she accidentally rubbed some stray grains of stardust into her paintbrush as she spun the fine hairs absentmindedly between her fingers. Whatever the case, she was struck by the feeling that something was coming.

The next morning, it began to rain. It rained so hard that it was inconceivable to go for her morning swim among the wind and the waves. It rained so hard that, after setting out tarps above the more delicate plants, the two cousins spent the day inside by the fire, sharing tea and memories. The storm carried on for three more days, dropping buckets of rain, sheets of rain, torrents of rain, howling through the branches and painting the sky with persistent bruising among the gray. Tremendous gusts of wind ripped around the coast before finally dissipating in the night. And then, the morning dawned bright and cheerful. As though making up for its absence, the sunlight danced with exuberance through its refractions and sculptures, filling the house with cheer.

The People were out in full force, searching for sustenance after the storm, and the crows cackled happily when Juniper emptied a bowl full of treats onto their platform. She startled a bit, spun on her heel, and jumpily returned to the kitchen, glancing back over her shoulder repeatedly the entire way. Juniper was mumbling to herself quietly, and Zophi watched with interest as her cousin moved through stages of denial. The tiny light being that often danced around the windows in the kitchen caught Juniper unawares, confronting her directly. Juniper shrieked in surprise, scaring the little one, before she fell over herself with muddled apologies. It was a good start, Zophi thought, listening to the small melodic voice that chimed like tiny bells and her cousin's awe-filled response. It was a very good start. Catching Zophi's amused expression, Juniper excused herself and stomped over to where her cousin sat so quietly, nervously wringing a dish towel in her hands.

"What," Juniper asked, poking her cousin in the sternum as she spoke, "did *you* do?"

Zophi shrugged in a way she knew Juniper would find infuriating and gave a reply that was neither helpful nor incorrect:

"I made a wish on a star."

Juniper threw up her hands in frustration and swept out of the room, tossing the dish towel on the countertop and narrowly missing a small shadow that bent to observe their interactions, reshaping the darkness with its curiosity.

At noon, the seabird landed heavily among the fiddlehead ferns, squawking at Zophi to hurry and shocking Juniper for what must be at least the hundredth time that day. Zophi wiped her hands on her jeans and told the obnoxious bird that she would be down at the dock shortly.

"Don't dawdle!" The seabird clearly felt it ought to be in command of the situation. "I will be most put out if I don't get the promised urchin because you move so slowly."

"You'll get your reward. Don't worry. Now let me be so I can do what needs doing. Or will *you* be the one who makes me so slow?" Zophi asked with a raised eyebrow and a smile. The seabird made a sound of disgust and launched itself into the air, leaving crumpled ferns behind. Zophi clicked her tongue at the thoughtlessness and resisted the urge to stop and tend to the poor Rooted People. Instead, she ducked back into the house, grabbed a sticky note from near the telephone, and ran up to her bedroom. She changed into a mid-length skirt for mobility's sake; if her plan worked, the pants would be problematic. Grabbing her spiral notebooks, she put the sticky note on top and scrawled:

> *Juny -*
> *Everything you may need to know*
> *can be found in these pages and the*
> *Journals.*
> *I love you forever*
> *- Zophi*

She placed the books on the dining table before rushing out into the yard, grabbing her cousin up in a fierce hug, and sprinting off down the overgrown path to the sea shore for what might well be the last time.

Hours later, after the sun had begun to set and the dinner that she had somehow managed to prepare, despite a *multitude* of distractions, was ready. Juniper stood at the door to the garden, debating. There had been no sign of Zophi since that back-breaking hug before she raced down to the dock. Everyone in the family knew the deal with those birds, and anyone with eyes who had seen Zophi's paintings would know that this was meant to be a private encounter. At the same time, the food was done - cooked to perfection, if she did say so herself, and she was not a fan of eating alone. As though intending to call her thought into question, her ear caught the sound of two bats arguing as they soared past the house, and it occurred to her that she might never feel alone again. The thought was both comforting and disturbing. Juniper had always been curious about what it would be like to hear The People properly; like most of her family, she had a sense of The People that seemed different from other humans. Now, after just one day, she wondered how Toddy, Zophi, and the rest ever got any-damn-thing done.

After a few more minutes of debating the interruption of her cousin's private interlude, she turned away from the doorway with a sigh. Her eyes panned across the empty house that lay before her, momentarily pausing on the spiral bound notebooks Zophi had forgotten on the table before eventually landing on the phone. There was no reason why she had to eat by herself and no rule that said only one of them could indulge in a touch of romance at a time. She picked up the phone and dialed Ricky's number from memory.

When she hung up, she took stock of the room and decided to take a moment to tidy up a bit, humming to herself all the while. The notebooks were placed on the bottom step, where they would inevitably find their way upstairs at some point. She vaguely registered a note addressed to herself on the cover, but she would get around to that later. Juniper put the notebooks out of her mind and glanced at her watch. She estimated she had about ten minutes until Ricky knocked on the door, less if he pedaled fast. In the meantime, she scanned the shelf where the player lived when her cousin wasn't carting it around, pulled out an old favorite, and smiled as the house filled with the bluesy sound of a lone trumpet before being joined by the rest of the ensemble. She had to hand it to Andromeda, her music collection was pretty groovy.

Juniper slunk her way back into the kitchen, keeping time with the music, and pulled two bowls and two plates from the shelves. She took the time to plate the soup, bread and touch of salad greens nicely. She may not be an artist like her cousin, but Juniper Windle's meals were nothing to scoff at. The thought of her cousin drew her back to the sticky note on the notebooks. If Zophi had wanted something, why hadn't she told Juniper herself? The thought was interrupted by a swift rap at the door. Juniper eagerly sprinted across the great room to greet her man, who was met with the full power of her undivided attention. That was the last time she considered the note until the wee hours before dawn, when, with kiss-swollen lips, she said goodbye to Ricky as he mounted his bicycle. She didn't bother to watch after he wheeled onto the road to stealthily make his way back into town.

When the door swung back into place with its reassuring weight, she got to wondering whether she had been too distracted to notice her cousin's return or if Zophi had not returned that night at all. She rode her endorphins up the stairs, past her room and Andromeda's room, and opened the door to Zophi's bedroom to find... nothing. The bed was untouched, her room was suspiciously organized. Zophi hadn't been there. The next place to check was the hanging bench outside. Zophi had fallen asleep there on more than one occasion. She told herself it wasn't worth worrying until she'd checked there at least, but she was no longer riding her post-Ricky high. That rush had come crashing back to earth as soon as she opened her cousin's door.

Zophi was not outside.

Juniper considered walking down to the beach but, in a sudden moment of clarity, remembered the sticky note addressed to her that she'd moved from the dining table. The spiral-bound books were still on the bottom step, and the closer she got, the more they seemed to be staring back at her.

The sensation only increased, though whether the feeling was a warning about their contents or an accusation for not exploring them sooner remained to be seen. She pondered the sticky note as she brought the notebooks back to the table, then turned the cover of the first notebook over to expose a page crammed with information. After a moment of consideration, she decided that she required caffeine to deal with the contents of what, at first glance, looked like the ramblings of a crazy person. In the time that it took to boil water, steep a delicious smelling black tea, and add a touch of milk and honey, she told herself to take deep, calming breaths. As though anything would be enough to calm her nerves and to prepare herself for the idea that her cousin had somehow quietly *gone insane* without her knowledge.

When she finally sat down and began to read, she found pages full of references to the old books that lined the shelves, full of The People's stories. One by one, she began to pull them out to check their contents against her cousin's notes. Little by little, she began to reconstruct the details of Zophi's plan. It was utterly, bat-shit crazy. It was kind of genius in its simplicity - but so very dangerous.

She cursed quietly to herself as she flipped the back cover of the second spiral bound notebook closed. The sun had begun to peak over the horizon, and she couldn't help but worry that she was already too late. It was that thought that vaulted her from her seat, hurrying around the room to gather her wrap and her shoes. Just before she could bustle out the back through the kitchen, she heard the sound of people outside the front door. One voice shushed the other, and the following quiet was interrupted by the staccato rap of knuckles against wood.

CHAPTER 42

It was clear to Zophi the moment that she arrived that Nimmawni was uncomfortable. The mermaid appeared uncertain in a way that Zophi hadn't seen before; she held herself painfully distant, and yet those large, dark eyes kept flicking in Zophi's direction. It was like the moment before Nimmawni left two years ago, but somehow worse; only this time, Zophi was prepared to make sure that she wasn't left behind. This time, it was Nimmawni who broke the silence.

"Zophi..." she worried at her bottom lip with daintily pointy teeth, "I heard your call, I heard it so many times, but I couldn't..." she sighed, her eyes rolling skyward and then closing as though praying for help. "I didn't know how to come back and face you, knowing that nothing can come of this. Knowing how disappointed you must be... with me."

Zophi stood silently on the dock, clutching the paired necklaces with white knuckled fingers, not knowing how to respond to her beautiful mermaid's assessment of their situation.

"Nimmawni," she finally said, "Where have you been these two long years?"

It seemed to be ritual, after all. The mermaid blinked at her in confusion before slowly responding,

"I have been in the deepest and darkest of crevasses I could find. In truth, I have been wallowing."

Zophi was shocked by her candor, and it took a moment for her to find the words she had scripted for herself on the walk to the beach.

"And have you come any closer to the answers you seek?"

Nimmawni dropped her face into her hands for a long moment before facing Zophi once more,

"Oddly, I did come across an enormous crab who made its home by the burning vents of a deep crevasse. The crab told a tale of a great bridge that carried The People between the Sea Below and the Sea Above, though where it lies is unclear, and I did not pay as much attention as I might."

Zophi began to lower herself onto the ladder but paused when Nimmawni said sharply,

"Please, don't."

Turning on the top rung, Zophi's expression asked so many questions; it was more than enough to receive the response:

"I can't... we can't... and if you come in the water, if we are close, it will be harder... and it's difficult enough as it is."

Zophi couldn't help but smile at the response, filled with a previously unknown sense of confidence. She held Nimmawni's eyes with her own as she slowly and deliberately took the step to the next rung. She held the mermaid's gaze and saw the indecision there, her body moving as if to retreat, even as some part of her wished to stay. She proceeded to the next rung, the cool water slipping over her toes. Nimmawni's teeth worried through the skin of her lip, and a single droplet of blood swelled before the pink tip of her tongue swept it away. Zophi moved to the next rung. The water now embraced her legs, just below her knees, flirting with the hem of her skirt. A passing wave cooled her thighs and pooled the fabric of her skirt at the surface; Nimmawni's eyes slid over her exposed legs, and she let her face submerge until only her eyes were visible, giving off an air of embarrassment. Zophi held onto the ladder, stepped backward into the water, and let her body slip into the waves. The skirt fluttered around her as the rush of the ocean enveloped the bare skin beneath, and her shirt clung almost obscenely to her torso. Nimmawni backed further from the dock, and Zophi was almost certain she only had a matter of moments before her actions pushed her love to once again flee.

"It is difficult," Zophi admitted, "but does it have to be?" Before an argument could be made, Zophi continued,

"There has to be a way. I have to believe that there's a way. After all, what is the use of stories if our beliefs about the world are meant to remain so limited? If we were meant to live without possibilities?"

The plan would have been seriously flawed if it hadn't anticipated Nimmawni attempting to argue with her logic. So far as Zophi was concerned, any attempt at talking sense was ultimately senseless, so the woman pushed herself away from the dock before a word was spoken. All of those mornings spent in the water came in handy as she swam as fast and as hard as she could out into the waiting arms of the sea. She vaguely heard the sound of shouting behind her, and soon she could feel it in her bones that the Sea-Folk was gaining on her. After all,

Nimmawni had the upper hand, where Zophi had simply employed the element of surprise. The skirt was snagged by what she assumed was a hand, and she shimmied out of the garment. What did she care if the wheeling Winged People saw her bare backside? She pushed herself further, summoning more speed, free of the soaked fabric that impeded her kicks. The brush of Nimmawni's hair and tail was a momentary distraction as she passed Zophi from below, and when the Sea-Folk surfaced, it was directly in the human's path as they both breathed heavily from exertion.

"Go back!" The demand was so intense with emotion that Zophi could hear the language of the Sea-Folk bleeding through, the high whistling of the wind, the rustling of sand, and the rushing of the tide. "Go back now!"

Fingertips prodded Zophi's shoulders roughly, attempting to turn her in the direction of the shore.

"No," Zophi said calmly, not even sparing a glance for the safety she left behind. Instead, she tried to swim around the living obstruction Nimmawni had made of herself. All arms and fins and as quick as could be; it was beyond Zophi's ability, but that wasn't the point. The point was to be so tired, and out so deep, that when the water claimed her, she couldn't fight back. She would make of herself a child that the ocean could embrace, and so she continued to struggle until finally Nimmawni grabbed her by the shoulders and yelled in a voice like a storm at sea:

"What do you think you're doing, Zophi!?" and at that, the woman, tired from her exertions, could not help but smile.

For the second time, she gently cupped the cheek of one of

the Sea-Folk, but instead of leaning in for a kiss, she let their foreheads meet, bringing her ear close enough to hear as she replied,

"Dearest, don't you see? If you cannot come to me, then it is up to me to follow you."

Forehead to forehead, eye to eye, breath mingling in the space between their lips, Zophi chanced a swift hug before backing away, taking advantage of the unexpected space to roll her body forward and dive. She dove as deep as she could, pulling herself arm over arm away from the watching sky, and when her lungs began to burn, and her heart began to race, she turned and saw the glittering lights that darted beneath Nimmawni's skin before the air vacated her lungs.

In her blurred and dimming vision, Nimmawni glowed like a thing divine. Despite that, Zophi had just enough wherewithal to struggle when loving hands began to tow her in the same direction as the escaping bubbles. The hands stilled, and soft lips pressed themselves firmly to her own, exhaling sweet air into her mouth and willing her to breathe. And breathe she did. She breathed through the body of the Sea-Folk, and in the absence of their struggle, she was inundated with the song of the ocean, the omnipresent voice of the Great Mama of the Deep. She let the song fill her as surely as the breath of her beloved filled her lungs. It filled her until her bones seemed to vibrate, and her skin tingled and sparked with a feeling not unlike making wishes on stardust. Muscles pulsed and clenched, bone ground against bone, and she gasped in pain as her lungs collapsed completely before reforming and expanding again.

The moment seemed to go on forever, dark and frightening,

her body returning instinctively to the fetal position, as though waiting to be reborn. She closed her eyes, and, rather than darkness, she somehow saw the concerned face that pressed to hers more clearly. It was only when, inexplicably, she seemed to close her eyes *more* that she slipped from consciousness in the loving arms of Nimmawni and the Goddess of the Deep.

CHAPTER 43

The darkness breathed, the long respiration flowing across minutes and brushing on eternity. It was the breath of the moss on the tree, the breath of the jellyfish's slow expansion and contraction, the breath that suffused the spinal cord from top to base, the breath of the wave rolling between ocean floor and water's surface. The darkness breathed, and Zophi found herself breathing with it. Soft lips touching her lips and intertwined fingers were the only touch points anchoring her to any sense of her body, though it hardly felt like her body any longer. There was a newness there, as though she had been rebirthed through the burning pain of her lungs' contractions, emerging on the other side, immersed in the unequivocal knowledge of being loved. It felt like the warm afterglow of too much champagne and the dark sweetness of raspberry cordial combined, merging in a kiss so perfect that she barely noticed the alterations wrought through her palingenesis. Until, that is, she was struck by her utter inability to wiggle her toes in the flow of the current.

Opening her eyes to the dim light of deep water, she took in the sight of her stunning mermaid whose hair billowed around them both like a cloud. Zophi marveled at being there, simply breathing, before glancing down to where her long legs had been replaced by the fluttering of a flowing white tail. Nimmawni's eyes were wide with surprise as she surveyed the changes - because there were certainly more than one. The mermaid, *her* mermaid, circled her and ran a finger gently along the newly formed row of barbs that extended up her spine. The curious sensation made Zophi shiver in a manner that made her feel as though she ought to be covered in goosebumps and raised hairs. Instead, the feeling sparked little zaps of electricity that pulsed through the water and licked across her skin. She raised newly webbed fingers, examining the feel of them scooping through the current, and brought them to her neck to find a petite set of gills. The shimmering rainbow that shone through Nimmawni's skin now traveled beneath the skin of her own arms and torso, catching her eye as she examined what she had become.

As she explored her new form, the stories of the Sea-Folk who turned human and the baby saved by dolphins came to mind. The stories of her childhood: pieces to a puzzle that had made her believe that maybe, just maybe, a dream could come true. Words floated differently through water, her speech muted, spread thin, and garbled. Nimmawni shook her head and spoke in an unfamiliar fashion that barely moved her lips,

"Let go of the human words, think of how you speak to The People, listen, and breathe," she ran her finger along the surprisingly sensitive edge of one of Zophi's gills. In that moment, she would have liked to say that her breath caught in her throat, but that no longer felt correct. Perhaps her gills snapped shut, or maybe it was some completely different function of her new and unfamiliar aquatic biology. Whatever it was, it was far from unpleasant, and while she was still confused by all of the new sensations, it seemed that Nimmawni knew exactly what she had done. Particularly if one judged by the coy smile that graced her lips. Webbed fingers reached out, and like an echo of Zophi's previous action, Nimmawni cupped Zophi's cheek in her hand.

"Let the words flow from a place of truth; the question of how is unimportant."

The newly made mermaid leaned into Nimmawni's palm and let herself simply breathe. The water rushed through Zophi's gills, unobstructed and almost audible, giving her all of the air she required. She set loose her words as though they were breath, and they came out in sounds she had never before created but understood nonetheless,

"I love you, Nimmawni."

The centuries-old being held her close, allowing the familiar sinuous tail to curl around the opalescent scales of Zophi's tail. They floated in their embrace, wrapped in the arms of the sea, and for what felt like the very first time, Zophi knew peace.

The feel of comforting arms and hearts pounding in tandem had lulled her to sleep. They drifted with the tide, completely unaware of where it dragged their entwined bodies at rest. It was

a sort of abandon she had thought long forgotten, along with a kind smile and a mother's lullaby. She woke with a jolt. In the manner of dreams, the answer had untangled itself in her unconscious mind, and it was Zophi, dear, wonderful, Zophi who had handed her the key. There *was* no single place where the Great Seas met; that would be impractical. The bridge moved; it was constantly in motion, just as much as the stars, which moved steadily across the night sky. The stories told of the place where the bridge of stars met the water, as though it were a single destination that could be found, or perhaps that was what she had chosen to believe. She had chosen to believe a great many things in her three hundred and one cycles at sea, and Zophi had called them all into question when she followed Nimmawni into the depths of the Sea Below. Zophi had come with no secret knowledge; she was armed with nothing but love, faith, The People's stories, and two small shards of an ancient magic. The same ancient magic that lay, in far greater abundance, resting firmly about her very own neck. Perhaps, if there was no great secret to mysteries of Land and the Sea Below, the path to the Sea Above was similarly obscured by her search for an enigmatic absolute.

She woke Zophi from her well deserved rest, eager for confirmation of her theory. She swam hand in hand with the newly made Sea-Folk, the human woman of her dreams who still tried to breathe as though on land and had not yet grasped the full use of her fins. She returned them to the surface in search of a sign, the added benefit being that, at the surface, Zophi could speak as she normally would, could tell her the story that led her to that harrowing act of abandon.

While they rested their fins to float on the surface hand in hand and stared at the spinning mandala of the midnight sky, the sound of Zophi's voice floated across the water - comforting in its familiarity, familiar in its wonder at what had come to pass. While Nimmawni's eyes searched the waves and the skies for a sign that her suspicions were correct, she listened absentmindedly as the human who was People and now Sea-Folk mused on something she called nictitating membranes. Eventually recognizing that Zophi spoke of the protective inner eyelid, Nimmawni blinked those lids at the precious woman with a smile, barely stifling a laugh as Zophi attempted to do the same. The woman thought too much, scrunching up her nose and dropping one inner lid before closing her eyes completely. Moments later, when a wave swept over their faces, they snapped over her rich brown eyes automatically, just as they should. In time, Zophi fell silent. Nimmawni was just beginning to doubt her newfound thread of hope when she saw it - off in the distance, an arch that spanned a great expanse of the heavens that was entirely composed of starlight. As with many beautiful things in the Sea Above, it was reflected in the Sea that was its mirror Below. If her guess was correct, that was exactly where they needed to be. Where she wanted to be. What she had been looking for for as long as she could remember. She could only hope that Zophi would wish to join her. This trip was far further from the shore than the Sea Below could ever be.

It was with that thought and in that moment that she knew a whole new kind of fear and uncertainty. Only hours from the terror that she might lose Zophi to the deep, convinced that Zophi was stupidly returning her human body to the cycle, and already Nimmawni feared that she might be demanding too much. That, despite her obvious resolve, Zophi might not choose to stay. After all, if she could become Sea-Folk, it seemed likely that she could also return to human form. For years, it was the certainty that there was no way forward, no way that this feeling of spirit calling to spirit could be acted upon, that allowed Nimmawni to keep her distance. Yet she returned. She returned more often than she had ever done before, more aware of the passing of the cycles, in the hope that she would not return and find Zophi suddenly old and gray or gone. Unwilling to miss so much of a lifetime, as she had done with Andromeda and Melody and the rest of her Winkens, all the way back to sweet little Toddy; the names she never spoke, but that were indelibly etched in the story of her soul. She had been a wanderer all of her life; that was her way, but some time between dawn and the dark of the night, she had become discontent with the idea that she might continue to wander alone.

"Come with me?" she asked meekly.

"Always," Zophi replied without hesitation.

With a great sigh of relief and a small shared smile, Nimmawni squeezed Zophi's hand tightly before diving through the waves. They swam with a purpose, Nimmawni all but dragging Zophi with her in search of the reflection of the celestial bridge. When they were nearly there, Nimmawni stopped for a moment to check on her love, who was pale with exertion but determined to keep up.

"Are you ready?" Black eyes searched brown for traces of uncertainty.

"I haven't the slightest clue - but I've come this far and, as I said, I'll go with you anywhere."

After that response, there was nothing for it but to kiss the poor woman who had no way of knowing what she was getting into. She had discovered on that day two cycles ago that she enjoyed the frightening intimacy of lips pressed to lips. Many times, she had seen humans on ships and along the shore engaged in the practice and thought it odd. She could not remember if her parents had ever done it themselves, but when she breathed to keep her human alive, she had to admit - if only to herself - that she had lingered. She had stolen a heartbeat here and there to savor the feel of Zophi's soft lips pressed to her own. Shivered at the intimacy of shared breath, tiny bubbles escaping to trace the space between their cheeks. Cherished the breath when their bodies shifted, causing the feathery edges of Zophi's eyelids to tickle her cheek, and Nimmawni struggled to breathe herself. Each moment was hidden beneath the overriding sense of urgency, each a moment to be secretly treasured. Now there was no such pretense; she kissed Zophi frantically, on her lips and cheeks and both of her hands, grabbing them tightly before diving deep into the reflection of the celestial bridge.

They dove until up and down had no meaning, until the tiny points of light that had spilled haphazardly across the water's surface began to expand and grow closer and clearer to the eye. The pattern of the heavens came into clearer focus, each star finding its place in the cosmic dance. The water thinned and became not water at all, fizzing and drying the gills as they adjusted to their new medium. Then, for an instant beyond time, the seas themselves seemed to hold their breath as the sky above them shifted on its axis - sliding outward, downward, and away -

to be replaced by a vision of the sleeping world below.

As they swam further, climbing to greater depths of the night sky and the Sea Above, a great body passed over their heads, and they felt themselves get caught up in the wake of an enormous whale shark. The spectacular beast was larger than any Nimmawni had seen before, its body glittering and scattered with starlight that reflected the patterns of passing constellations. Caught in a swell just as palpable as those of the Sea Below, they tumbled through the night sky hand in hand. Rolling end over end, they clung to their single point of contact and rode the shimmering waves. When the grip on her fingers tightened in a reassuring squeeze, it drew Nimmawni's attention to Zophi and the radiant smile she wore as she let out a whoop of joy. Something loosened deep inside Nimmawni's chest at the glorious sound, embracing it as it ricocheted through her bones, along with the shining realization that they had made it. They had found their way to the Sea Above, and they were not alone. Nimmawni caught glimpses of creatures of the Eternal Sea, peering curiously from behind celestial bodies, traversing the great expanses, and in various states of rest. An entire smack of jellyfish undulated in the void, an unexpected sight. Nimmawni wondered how they had managed to find the bridge and if they even knew they were in the Sea Above. One could never tell with Jellyfish. She was pulled from her thoughts by Zophi's sharp intake of breath as a pair of large sea turtles circled them, inspecting the newcomers, their shells glistening like sunlight off rolling waves. In a voice barely above a whisper, Zophi tried to ask her,

"Could that be..."

"Long Tide and Deep Wave, first among the Migrating Shell People." One of the turtles completed her sentence with a nod, bringing its dark eye level with the woman's face in a manner that made Nimmawni feel strangely protective. "In time you must tell us how a human was made Sea-Folk and brought to the Sea Above, it has been cycles beyond number since your kind last ventured among the stars."

The turtle assessed them one last time, its penetrating gaze seeming to gather far more than could possibly meet the eye, before banking to follow its mate away and continuing on their journey. Nimmawni wrapped her arms securely around her beloved, as Zophi was left gaping and awestruck.

It must be certain that time carried on - though in the expanse of their new surroundings, they had not yet learned to measure its passage. The tides did not rise and fall, though the energy around them ebbed and flowed in a peculiar fashion. The sun did not rise above them, though it held a place of honor in the celestial dance - its illumination reflecting and refracting among the cosmic bodies. The ubiquitous song of the Great Mama of the Deep emanated from the Sea Below, but it was no longer the same familiar song; it changed among the vast expanse of the celestial bodies. It grew and shifted, as though to define an even greater pattern of the divine dance, swelling with mysterious harmonies that defied comprehension. The two held one another close, much as they had as they drifted in sleep following the excitement of Zophi's transformation. Entwined and reassured by each other's presence, they observed their surroundings, occasionally drawing one another's attention to something unfamiliar and spectacular.

It was during one of these moments that they watched in awe as the body of a great serpent, originally camouflaged within a shimmering cloud-like expanse of colors, uncoiled itself from where it rested and approached them. Nimmawni was briefly reminded of the dragon who encircled the star-body, its serpentine body looping itself lazily about them at what might be considered a respectful distance. Before their eyes, the form began to shimmer and shift, reasserting itself in the shape of a great crow-like bird.

"Greetings, Pan'chan." Zophi's quiet voice carried strangely in the expanse, meeting her ear at about the same time as her shocked realization of their present company.

"Greetings, Pan'chan." Nimmawni echoed, almost choking on the words. Speaking to the First People, revered almost as gods among their descendants, was an honor, but to speak to Pan'chan was to speak to one of the very first among the Gods.

Greetings children. The words resonated with warmth that suffused their bodies and brought a flush to their cheeks. *You have, at long last, arrived.*

The statement filled their mouths with so many questions that the words struggled to emerge, and their minds with the pieces of a puzzle so vast they could hardly begin to comprehend it. The Great God humored them, but his replies were so vague as to resist being answers at all, and the growing sense that they were a source of amusement was hardly complementary. When, at long last, the well of their words had run dry, and they felt no more knowledgeable than they had to begin with, the great god ruffled his feathers. He shot them a glance that commanded their attention before his voice, warm and soft, surrounded them in a manner that shook them to the bones as he began to tell them a story.

Once, among the stars, in a space that is now and always - in a moment defying the sense of chronology that places one step before another, yet so fundamental as to be beyond the act of forgetting - my Great Mother sang herself into being.

The great god paused

As such, the soul of the Great Mother is fundamentally complete, she exists as she was always meant to be, ebbing and flowing much like her tides, shifting and malleable, strong and indomitable. It is the nature of her song to take part in the eternal cycle of creation and destruction, it is her nature to create and birth new life. Being birthed of her womb, it should come as no surprise that her first creations were likewise complete and shaped to their own purpose. Though some of their natures were more hidden than others, thus were the Gods born. It is her nature to create and birth new life, and so my Mother, with the help of myself and my siblings, breathed many new beings into existence; but each was imbued with a soul complete, and their nature was often solitary. There is a place for this, a place for utter self-sufficiency - for such is the lot of dragons, who were molded into being and left to find purpose and thrive or dissipate and fall before the impartial hands of my sister, she who weaves the tapestry of the departed. In time, we began to experiment, first splitting the soul in two. This, too, had its place; it was fundamentally sound that it inhabit the paired forms of the First People who, being the only two of their kind, reveled so deeply in one another's company. They were shaped by the gods to exist in tandem, to balance and support, and to never be truly alone.

As the First People took form, pair by pair, this practice continued, and for what you might perceive as quite some time, this was satisfactory. It is, perhaps, true that my Mother also foresaw that creation is progressive and that offspring were inevitable, and that the pair combined, dictated the soul and natures of their descendants. However, as The People began to procreate, it became apparent that the practice was flawed. As The People became more prolific, there were many who struggled to find the other half of their souls, who buckled under the weight of futility, becoming shadows of themselves and thus could not, in truth, take their part in the eternal song. The despair of these creations saddened those deities who were given to care, my Mother among them. Thus, it began to be understood among the Gods how a soul might perceive itself to be cursed when split in two. When not created and birthed in tandem, as the First People had been, destined to live with your other half eternally by your side. To be merely half of a whole was to live with a gaping wound that might never be healed.

It was the sisters closest to Ghurnak who proposed a new way. Upon receiving the apportioned souls of the departed, they deftly began splitting, spinning, warping, and weaving the souls in their care. The youngest, who would be called Triskera, gently seated this soul in the soon to be born, casting it as one does fibers onto the instrument of its design; a soul separated not unlike the threads of a rope, but mostly complete; a soul which sheltered within it the splintered pieces of loved ones yet to come; a soul imbued with the seeds of new life. It then fell upon the sister who would be called Wayafi to interweave the souls to their fates, to one another, and to the stars. Wayafi, who had looked on in awe and endeavored to understand the repercussions when I rearranged the stars of the Sea Above. Wayafi, who looked upon the warp and weft of life's tapestry and saw its most infinitesimal patterns. It was Wayafi who intertwined your fates, children, and it is Wayafi whose spirit you swayed with the ferocity of your heart's desire, thus realigning your fates with the stars. It is a powerful thing, I think, to take hold of one's fate in this way. Then again, I always knew you could do it.

The great bird winked at them conspiratorially, in a manner that left them both utterly flummoxed.

So I say to you, children, Welcome Home.

At that, the great blackbird, beloved of Little Darkness, melted away into a cloud of stardust that whipped past them into the depths of the

Sea Above, leaving them both shimmering with the residue of the deity's departure.

Once again, Zophi and Nimmawni floated intertwined in the darkness of the Eternal Sea. It seemed that this comforting coil that their bodies created was one that her love enjoyed, and Zophi rejoiced in their closeness. The Sea-Folk dozed, finally drained of energy after their improbable adventure, but Zophi found herself alert. She examined the curves of her beloved's face, each feature and small imperfection another blessing she felt deeply, like raindrops that saturated and revitalized something essential within her. She ran the pad of her thumb over Nimmawni's brow, relishing in her contented sighs, before allowing her eyes to drift outward once more to the vastness of her surroundings. She sank into the unfamiliar feel of her fins billowing and rippling in slow motion, soaking up the shifting colors beyond color, blues deeper than the deepest blue, and black so full that it spilled over with vibrant starlight. Multicolored auroras wisped and surged across the expanse, highlighting yet more of this marvelous space to be discovered and explored.

It could be the adventure of a lifetime, or ten. It was there that she found her mind wandering back to the very first among the journals that populated the wooden shelf of her Androgramma's great room. In that moment, she could almost smell the warm vanilla scent of the old book in her hands, feel the rough cover beneath her fingertips, as she read the delicate scrolling handwriting of her Great-Great-Great-Great-Grandmother:

> "I have found myself a part of a fantastical world,
> One in which all that I had once thought to know is
> Called into question. Being presented with the choice,
> To either believe myself and my loved ones to be taken with
> A shared madness, or to believe the proof of my senses
> And embrace a new, more vibrant reality; I choose
> To immerse myself in limitless wonder."

POSTSCRIPT: THE DOCK

The waves lapped gently against the weather-worn wood of a small dock that reached, without pretension, into the great blue-green expanse of the Ocean. It was not large enough nor long enough for the great vessels that rode the winds up and down the coast, making port along the way. The crews of the massive ships that circumnavigated the globe would barely take notice of it in passing. This dock was just the right size for a small skiff, not unlike the one that limped to shore on the rising tide, appearing to have lost both its captain and its way for a good long time. It came to rest beside the aged structure, the sound of wood bumping against wood carrying through the silence that prevailed in the space just before dawn. When the sun rose and the tide began to recede, it was three women who found the little boat where it remained, mysteriously in place, without even a line securing it. The two older women, one small and dark, the other so blond her hair shimmered gold in the early morning light, stared off at the horizon as though looking for a sign. It was the young woman whose eye caught on the single item that rested inside the boat, as though gently placed on the seat beside the tiller. Eying the vessel with suspicion, she climbed from the dock to retrieve the small treasure, tying the skiff up to the nearest pylon for good measure before calling her companions' attention to what she found. Resting in her open hand was the familiar sight of the wooden hairpin, lovingly crafted by hands that knew how to make their medium sing. The hairpin with two long tines to balance and hold in place the figure of the mermaid child, her body and tail twisting to form a symbol of infinity. However, where her hand had previously been empty, it now held a small heart formed of the richest, reddest coral.

The dark haired woman began to cry, though whether the tears were for sorrow or joy was difficult to determine. Her companion held her close and used the marvelous pin to sweep her lover's hair from her face, affixing it with the pin in a simple chignon. The young woman stared out at the waves for long moments before a smile split her face and a low chuckle burbled up from her chest and through her open lips, building on itself until tears streamed down her face as she laughed. She laughed because she needed to laugh or be lost to sadness. She laughed because all signs pointed toward something so crazy and ridiculous and impossible; there was nothing for it *but* to laugh. She laughed because the laughter filled the silence with an almost tangible warmth that her cousin would approve of. She laughed for so many reasons, but most of all, she laughed for joy - because the story was beautiful and timeless, and now and then and always, just as a story ought to be. She laughed because, somewhere out there, Zophi had followed her heart and, in doing so, found her way home.

That very evening, all three would return to the end of the little dock, as though the sea might be more forthcoming with its story, answering all of their questions about what had taken place less than a stone's throw from where they stood. When they arrived, however, the dock lay empty. The mysterious ship, ancient and hardly seaworthy, had disappeared without a trace; even the seabird's nest was empty. The breeze whistled along the coast, whispering its secrets among the dunes and rustling loose strands of hair in passing. Though there was not one among them who could understand its message with real clarity, the youngest woman found herself comforted by its passage. In the silence which followed, the three women held each other close, two of them supporting the third as they made their way along the fifteen widths of weathered planks to where the dock met the sand, back across the beach to where the sand melted into the dunes, along the winding path to where the mullein and lavender grew, into the loving embrace of a sanctuary built and maintained by generations of devoted hands. They sat through the night, reading stories and sharing memories, only taking to their beds as the birds began to sing in anticipation of the dawn.

POSTSCRIPT: THE BOAT

The messenger had served its purpose. It's ancient wood, pulled from the memories of man and resurrected from the depths with a singular mission. Having delivered the spirited wood, shaped by human hands and imbued with an enduring love of its unique family, there was no reason to abide.

In the later hours of the morning, the small creatures of the shore swarmed the old wooden dock, working as one to let loose the line that secured the strange old skiff in place. Claws and pincers, beaks and teeth, made short work of its tether. The seabird sat proudly upon the prow, like an unconventional bowsprit, as the gentle waves brought the little ship about and drew it steadily away from shore. The small vessel made its way out past the promontory that sheltered the ancient dock, and the further it proceeded out into the wide expanse of the sea, the stranger its passenger became.

The familiar shape of the seabird grew and shifted, twisting and morphing until it took the form of an old fisherman with a wicked glint in his eye and a generous smile. With the dexterity of a spider, he clambered toward the tiller, took the helm with practiced ease, and directed the small craft on its long journey past the horizon. There, where the light shimmered and swayed in such a way that an onlooker might think themselves audience to a trick or an apparition, the tiny sailboat glided smoothly into the depths of the Eternal Sea.

Cosmology

Deities

The Great Mama of the Deep - *Creatrix*

The Shadow

The Light

Pan'chan - *Trickster*

Ghurnak - *The Spinner of Souls (Death)*

Wayafi - *The Weaver of Souls*

Triskera - *The Caster of Souls*

Andromeia - *Goddess of Fertility and Growth*

Fyi'Thunn - *Guardian of the Forest*

Inyastrom - *God of the Water's Currents*

Areiapali - *Spirit of the Shifting Sands*

Amu'ya - *Goddess of the Rain/Sky*

Cercha - *Goddess of the Rolling Plains*

Surgani - *Goddess of the Molten Star*

Orai - *God of Lightning*

First People

Long Tide & Deep Wave

First among the Great Migrating Shell People (Sea Turtles)

Other People of Note

Little Darkness

Corvid Mother

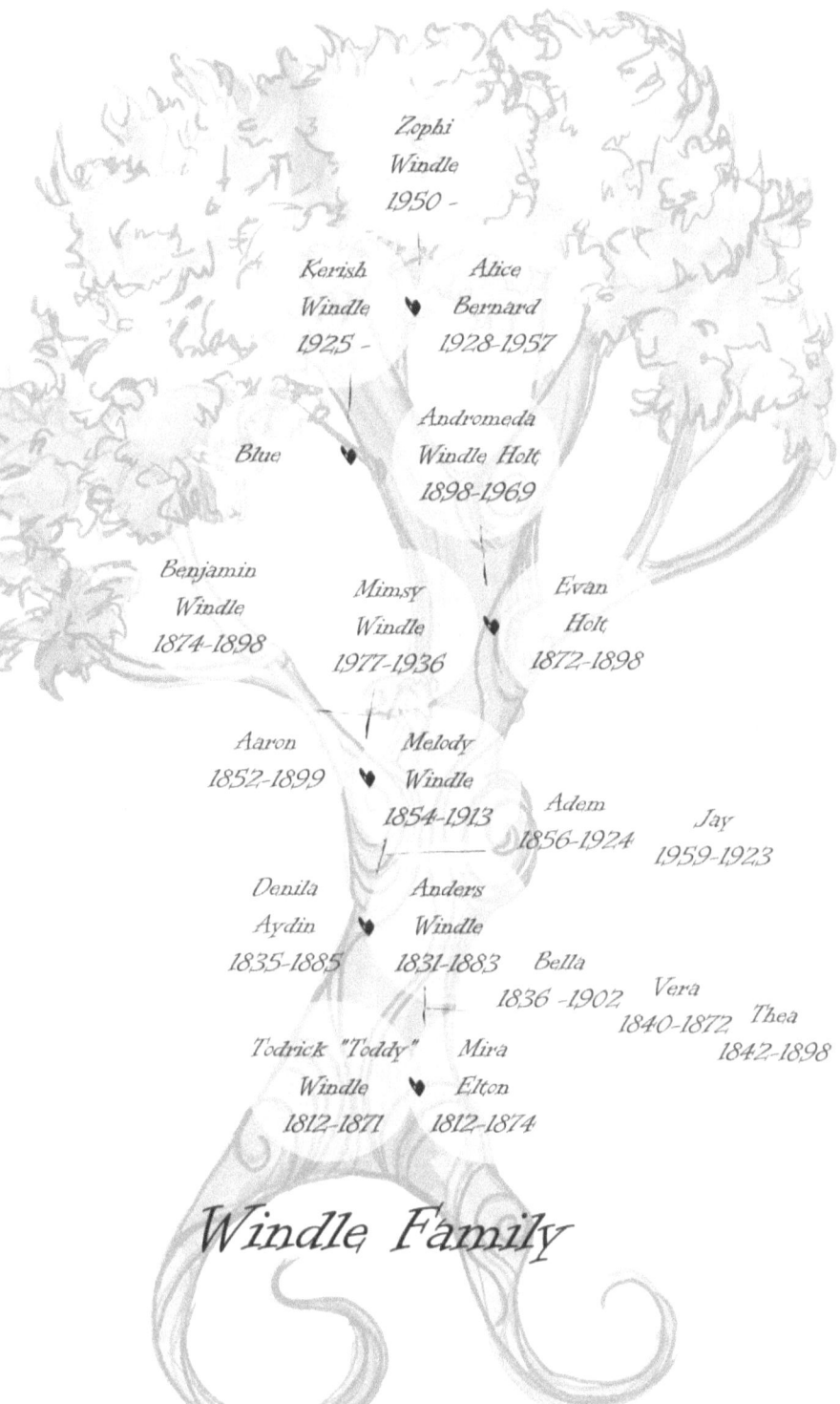

Zophi
Windle
1950 -

Kerish
Windle ♥ Alice
1925 - Bernard
1928-1957

Andromeda
Blue ♥ Windle Holt
1898-1969

Benjamin
Windle Mimsy Evan
1874-1898 Windle ♥ Holt
1977-1936 1872-1898

Aaron Melody
1852-1899 ♥ Windle
1854-1913 Adem Jay
1856-1924 1959-1923

Denila Anders
Aydin ♥ Windle
1835-1885 1831-1883 Bella
1836 -1902 Vera
1840-1872 Thea
1842-1898

Todrick "Toddy" Mira
Windle ♥ Elton
1812-1871 1812-1874

Windle Family

Author's Sketch
Nimmawni

Well, here we are...

I'm not sure I thought I'd ever finish a story once I started; they've always been more about the journey than the destination, and the graveyard of my abandoned stories is stacked notebooks high. Nevertheless, what started off as a cute little idea for my first ever NaNoWriMo has certainly grown into something far beyond anything I'd initially imagined. I've sat awake a number of nights (because insomnia is evil, not because my thoughts were plaguing me), thinking about how this all came together, and this is where I landed.

This particular journey may have started as a cute little "what if?" What if a mermaid got caught in a fishing net? What if it wasn't anything malicious, but dumb luck? What if the fisherman wasn't quite so fisherman-like? But, in time, chance became an act of fate, and Swimming in Starlight, more than anything else, became a love letter to stories.

It seems that there have been any number of people who've opined on the transformative power of giving a child a book, and isn't that the truth. It would not be inaccurate to say that the seeds of this abiding love of tales were planted in early childhood, with every story my parents read to me; from The People Could Fly and Peter Rabbit & Friends to A Wrinkle in Time and The BFG. Each story, a dearly loved companion that contributed something special to the way I view the world.

If books were seeds, then nothing could water them quite so well as the stories of my family, and there are an abundance of those, I assure you. My family is sometimes big and always quirky and rich with laughter and the gift of gab. More to the point, it's full of people who appear exceptionally dedicated to keeping their memories alive through stories full of mischief and mysticism, laughter and introspection. If you've never sat among multiple generations of family who appear to have gathered with the primary intention of retelling old stories and collecting a few new ones, I highly recommend it. You may just learn something interesting - or weird, weird is a definite possibility.

A love of stories met natural curiosity, and the resulting love of myth and legend woven through the world around us met the aforementioned genetics for loquacity, and now here we are! Over 400 pages, 2+ years of almost perpetual second guessing, innumerable hijacked conversations, and an actual earthquake or two later, and Swimming in Starlight has become... Real!

I can only hope that these pages have been a good companion, and that the real life inspirations for some of The People's stories spark a similar curiosity in someone else.

So, for all of the NaNoWriMo sprinters

For my parents and the hundreds upon hundreds of nights listening to the bedtime stories that shaped me

For my family of storytellers, who made their "then" stories a constant in my life

For Avina, who was an awesome alpha reader and the post-earthquake cheerleader I didn't know I needed.

For my Mother, who spent countless hours reading, editing, and providing constructive critique and support.

For my beloved son and other impromptu sounding boards (willing and otherwise)

Writing, in the moment, is often a solitary pursuit, but a story truly comes to life when it is shared... To all of you wonderful people, without whom Swimming in Starlight might never have taken form, Thank You!

www.ingramcontent.com/pod-product-compliance
Lightning Source LLC
Chambersburg PA
CBHW022018110726
47901CB00006B/1573